Also available from ROBYN CARR and MIRA Books

**Look for Robyn Carr's next novel
in the Sullivan's Crossing series,
THE BEST OF US
available soon from MIRA Books.**

ROBYN CARR

The Family Gathering

mira

mira

Recycling programs for this product may not exist in your area.

ISBN-13: 978-0-7783-0795-2

The Family Gathering

Copyright © 2018 by Robyn Carr

All rights reserved. Except for use in any review, the reproduction or utilization of this work in whole or in part in any form by any electronic, mechanical or other means, now known or hereafter invented, including xerography, photocopying and recording, or in any information storage or retrieval system, is forbidden without the written permission of the publisher, MIRA Books, 22 Adelaide St. West, 40th Floor, Toronto, Ontario M5H 4E3, Canada.

This is a work of fiction. Names, characters, places and incidents are either the product of the author's imagination or are used fictitiously, and any resemblance to actual persons, living or dead, business establishments, events or locales is entirely coincidental.

® and TM are trademarks of Harlequin Enterprises Limited or its corporate affiliates. Trademarks indicated with ® are registered in the United States Patent and Trademark Office, the Canadian Intellectual Property Office and in other countries.

For questions and comments about the quality of this book, please contact us at CustomerService@Harlequin.com.

www.Harlequin.com

Printed in U.S.A.

For Dr. Kochy Tang with grateful thanks
for the tender loving care and special friendship.

The Family
Gathering

In our family, we don't hide crazy...we put it

on the porch and give it a cocktail.

—Anonymous

1

Dakota Jones pulled right up to the barn that was now a house, and parked beside his brother's truck. He left his duffel in the Jeep SUV and went to the door. He stood in indecision for a moment—they had a six-month-old baby. He knocked rather than ring the bell, just in case the child was sleeping. A few moments later, he knocked again. And a third time. Finally the door opened.

"Dakota!" Cal said with a grin. "What are you doing here?"

"I came by way of Australia. It's a long story—"

"I can't wait to hear what that's about," Cal said. "Want to come in or stand out there awhile longer?"

"I don't want to wake the baby," Dakota said.

"The baby is in Denver with Maggie. They'll be back tonight."

"That sounds like an interesting arrangement," Dakota said.

"Like a tug-of-war, my friend. Something to drink?" Cal offered. "Food?"

"A cold beer would be nice." He looked around. The place was beautiful, but that came as no surprise. Cal's house with his first wife had been a showplace. Given the way the Jones siblings had grown up, something like a good, solid house that a person was proud to come home to would fill a need that had been neglected when they were kids. Cal put a beer in Dakota's hand. "The place looks great," Dakota said.

But Cal didn't respond to that. Instead, he said, "What were you doing in Australia?"

"I'd never been there," he said. "I wanted to walkabout. That's when—"

Cal cut him off with a laugh. "I know what a walkabout is." He tilted his beer toward Dakota in a toast. "I've never seen you with that much hair. On your face and everything."

Dakota stroked his beard. "I could probably use a trim."

"Why don't you tell me what's going on before Maggie and Elizabeth get home."

"Well, in Australia I visited one of the Rangers I served with years ago and together we checked in on another one. Then, with some input from them, I hit out on the trail for about a month, seeing some of the country, camping, fishing, practicing the identification and avoidance of snakes and crocodiles—"

"I meant, the Army! You're out? I knew you weren't happy there anymore. You said we'd talk about it someday."

"I wasn't sure where I'd end up but I was sure I'd get out here for a visit. With you and Sierra here and a new baby—I wanted to at least drop by."

Cal sighed. "Dakota. The Army."

"Well, I'm a little surprised I was in as long as I was. I never intended to make it a career. I wanted their offer of free travel and education."

Cal just lifted one brow. *Free travel? To a variety of war zones?*

Dakota grinned. "I had a small disagreement with a colonel. We didn't see things the same way. Apparently I was insubordinate. It was time to think about doing something new."

"Were you honorably discharged?" Cal asked, pushing him.

Dakota shook his head. "But I wasn't dishonorably discharged."

He was simply discharged, but that said something. You had to screw up pretty bad to not get an honorable discharge.

"What'd you do?" Cal asked.

"I disagreed with his forward action and told him it would get people killed. Rangers—it could get Rangers killed. I had ten or a hundred times the experience he had but he was in competition with me or something because he was hell-bent to drive five of our best Rangers right into the known hotbed of ISIS training and it was going to get people dead. I think they plucked that idiot out of the motor pool and put him in charge of a unit. I overrode his orders and he threatened me with jail. I thought that it was probably time for a career change."

"They sent you home?" Cal asked. "You must have done something even worse than disagree for them to send you home!"

Dakota squirmed. "I was acting in the best interest of my men."

"What'd you do?" Dakota didn't answer. "You hit him or something?"

"No, my guys wouldn't let me do that," he said. Then he hung his head briefly. "I let the air out of the tires until I could get in touch with another colonel I know who could try to intercede with the orders that would put us directly in harm's way."

"Jeeps?" Cal asked.

"No. MRAPs."

"MRAPs?"

"Mine resistant assault protective vehicles. The big ones."

"Those big mammoth desert beasts with tires taller than I am?" Cal asked. "How the hell do you let the air out of those?"

"With a .45," he said softly. "Or M16."

"You *shot* out the tires? How is it you're not in jail?"

"I was. Good behavior," he said. "And it was determined the colonel was incompetent and had done even worse things before. Cal, he was crazy. Homicidal. He had no idea what he was doing. He wasn't a Ranger—he had very little combat experience. He was a joke. I wasn't going to let him get any more people killed."

They sat in heavy silence for a little while, each tilting their beer bottle a couple of times. Finally Dakota broke the silence.

"Listen, it happens in the military sometimes. They take a guy who just made rank and give him a unit to command and sometimes the fit is bad. A buddy of mine, a doctor, his boss had no experience in the medical corps. He was a pilot. And he was making decisions for a bunch of doctors and a hospital that were dangerous to the patients, but he wouldn't compromise, he wouldn't listen to reason, he wouldn't ask for advice. According to my friend, people were left untreated, in pain, mishandled. A whole fleet of doctors mutinied and the colonel retaliated. That kind of thing doesn't happen all that often—usually there's at least one clear head in the game…" He took a breath. "They got my guy from the knitting battalion, I think. Jesus, I've worked for a few dipshits, but this one was exceptional."

"But you got out. With three years to retirement."

"Yeah, I have plenty of time for my next career move," he said. Then he grinned. "I'm still a kid."

"So you went walkabout," Cal said with a laugh. "Proving you're just like the rest of us?"

"You did it after Lynne's death. And it worked. But why? That's my question. Why do we wander? It was the wandering while we were growing up that I hated the most."

Dakota's parents thought of themselves as wanderers. Or hippies. Or new age thinkers, whatever. What they really were was a father who was schizophrenic, often delusional and paranoid, and a mother who was his keeper and protector. They took their four children with them as they roamed the country in a van and then later a school bus converted into an RV. They made regular stops at their grandparents' farm in Iowa and finally lived there full-time when Dakota was twelve, Cal, the oldest, was sixteen and their two sisters, Sedona and Sierra, were fourteen and ten.

Cal was still patient and understanding with their parents, with the father who wouldn't consider medication that would make him functional, or at least more functional. He was even tender with them. Sedona acted responsibly toward them in a kind but businesslike way, visiting regularly and making sure they weren't in need or in trouble. Sierra, the baby of the family, was mostly confused by how they chose to live. But Dakota? He'd spent much of his childhood not going to school, taking his lessons in a bus from his mother. The whole family worked when there was work, mostly harvesting vegetables with other migrant workers. When they did settle in Iowa on his grandparents' farm, he went to school full-time. He'd taken a lot of bullying in junior high and high school because his parents, Jed and Marissa, were so weird. Dakota was ashamed of them. They made no sense to him. Dakota was decisive and action-oriented and would have gotten old Jed on meds or kicked him out, but instead his mother coddled him, shielded him, let him have his way even though his way was crazy. So Dakota had been a loner. He'd had very few friends.

Dakota left the second he could, right after high school graduation when he was seventeen. He enlisted in the Army and had visited his parents about four times since. Each time he went back to that farm in Iowa they seemed more weird than the time before. He rarely called. They had apparently hardly noticed.

He also protected himself against anyone getting too close while he waited to see if he was going to become mentally ill, as well. At thirty-five, he was now pretty sure he was safe from that. And, after all this time, his independent and aloof behavior was accepted by his brother and sisters.

It was easy to remain unattached in the military. He had friends whose company he enjoyed but there were very few with whom he had really bonded and their bond was one of military brothers. He would join the guys for a few beers, as he was regularly included in social events—parties, outings to the lake, ski trips, whatever his group was doing—and he was called, *You know, Dakota, the bachelor.*

There were women, of course. Dakota loved women. He just wasn't the type to make long-term commitments to anyone, especially girlfriends. Even if he was with a certain woman for a while, he wasn't exactly coupled. Well, there was one, but it had been so brief, and had ended so tragically, it reminded him that it was better not to get too involved. He wasn't the marrying kind. He was better off on his own. He was never lonely, never bored. The way he played it he didn't have to explain where he came from, how he grew up, how bizarre his family was. In seventeen years in the Army he had never met a guy who grew up like him—essentially homeless, raised in a bus by a couple of wackos.

But recently, something had changed for him. It was slow. Subtle. Cal lost his wife and then, two years later, remarried. Maggie, a neurosurgeon of all things, was awesome. Now they had a baby, were a family. Cal had never shied from commitment, as if very confident he'd be a better family man than his father was. Their little sister had joined Cal in Timberlake and was also settling down. Sierra had hooked up with a firefighter, a fantastic guy. Connie, short for Conrad, was smart, physical, loyal, the kind of guy he admired. Dakota knew in five minutes that Connie had integrity. And watching the way Sierra was with him almost made Dakota long for something like that. Sedona had been married since right after college, had a couple of kids, was by all accounts living a normal life. So far none of them had decided to live in a bus like their parents had. Little by little it had begun to tease his mind that possibly he could have a normal adult life. Maybe he could actually have friends and family and not have to protect himself from being himself.

But he was damn sure taking it slow.

Cal called everyone. Sierra and Connie came straight over with their golden retriever, Molly. Maggie's father, Sully, came after he had closed up the general store at his campground, Sullivan's Crossing. Maggie arrived with the baby and walked into a party atmosphere.

Since Dakota's arrival was unannounced and Cal wasn't

prepared, everyone brought something to the table. Sierra had a platter of chicken breasts swimming in barbecue sauce and a big seven-layer salad, Connie brought beer and some of the cold green tea Sierra favored. Sully brought some broccoli sealed in a foil with garlic, olive oil, onions, mushrooms and pepperoncinis. They put it on the grill with the chicken. Cal supplied baked potatoes.

"How long are you staying?" Sierra wanted to know.

"I don't know," Dakota said. "I've been using the last few months to explore."

"Unfortunately, ain't nothin' to explore around here," Sully said.

"Oh, Cody," Sierra said, using his nickname from when they were kids. "Don't listen to Sully! I think I got my brain back hiking around here. Cal did the CDT for a month."

Dakota raised his eyebrows. "Did I know that?" he asked.

"I can't remember. But yes, I took the Continental Divide Trail north from Sully's place. I walked and camped for about two and a half weeks, then turned around and came back."

"Because I was here," Maggie said with a smile and lift of her chin. "And he wanted me. Bad."

"I wish I could do that," Connie said. "Longest I've been out there is four days. Sierra, we gotta do that. Go out there for a couple of months."

"I don't know," she said. "I'm so addicted to daily showers..."

"I have to decide where I'm going to stop exploring," Dakota said.

"As in, settle down?" Cal asked.

"I don't know if that's possible," he said. "After the

Army? I might not have the temperament for staying in one place."

"Are you going to hang around at least awhile?" Sierra asked hopefully.

"You bet," he said. "I'll be around awhile. Maybe I can help out."

"You can babysit," Cal said.

"Now, that's one thing I'm pretty sure I can't do," Dakota said. "I'm good with kids, but it's best if they're college graduates."

There was a round of moans and laughter.

By nine o'clock Sully had gone back to the Crossing, Maggie and Elizabeth had gone to bed and it was only Sierra, Connie, Cal and Dakota. The men were having one more beer. Sierra, in recovery, a year and a half sober, was drinking her green tea.

"I'll have to go to two meetings tomorrow after spending the night with you big drinkers," she said.

Cal laughed at her. "Three of us had eight beers in six hours. As celebrations go, it was pretty tame."

"If it bothers you…" Dakota began.

"It doesn't," she said. "But I'm going to feel a lot better than you tomorrow morning."

"Since you're going to feel so good tomorrow, want to take me out on the trail?" Dakota asked. Molly rose from her sleeping spot, shook herself awake and leaned against Dakota's thigh. Waiting. "Does this one go hiking?"

"Sometimes I take Molly and Beau, Sully's lab. But I can only stay out there a couple of hours at most if they're with me." She stood. "I'll come for you at 8:20. Come on, Connie. Time to put the baby to bed."

Dakota and Cal snapped to attention.

"Molly," she said. "I meant Molly."

"Shew," Dakota said. "If there was another one, I was going to run for my life!"

"There's just Elizabeth," Sierra said. "And they won't commit to whether they'll add to the family. And I'm definitely not in the game."

"Oh? And why is that?"

"Duh. Our crazy father and his genetic code, for one thing. Come on, Connie. It's past our bedtime."

Dakota looked at his watch. "This is a real lively crowd," he said, standing to say good-night. He kissed his sister's cheek. "See you in the morning. By the way, you're looking good."

"Thanks," she said, beaming. "So are you. A little shaggy, but good."

Dakota flashed her a grin. Behind his dark beard, it was dazzling.

Sierra combed her fingers along his cheeks, through his beard. "Little gray coming in here, Cody."

"I earned it," he said. He kissed her forehead. "See you in the morning."

In the seventeen years since Dakota left his family behind for the Army, the time he spent with them was infrequent and brief. Cal and Sedona tried to keep up with him. He visited them for important events—Cal's wedding to Lynne, then his wedding to Maggie. When Sedona's children were born, he checked in. He never stayed long. Sierra, who was so special to him, had been a wild card until she found sobriety. He had visited for a couple of days at a time, that's all. He didn't want to get too attached to them.

This time was different. The second, third and fourth days came and went. He hiked with Sierra, then Cal, then just the dogs. He dug out Sully's garden for spring planting. They repaired the grills and picnic tables and talked all the while. Sully was very cool for an old guy. He admitted he came home from Vietnam with some PTSD and asked how Dakota had fared in that regard. "Oh, I've got PTSD all right," Dakota said. "Probably more from my personal life than my military experience."

"Then aren't you one of the lucky ones," Sully said.

Dakota cleaned out the gutters around Sully's house and store and threw the balls for the dogs. Then he had to bathe the dogs because it had rained and they got into the freshly turned soil and compost in the garden. While hanging out at the Crossing he met Tom Canaday, the guy who helped Cal renovate the barn that was now his stunning house. Tom was Sully's good friend and part-time handyman, a single dad with two kids in college and two still in high school. When Tom told him all the jobs he'd had while raising his kids, Dakota was inspired.

Maybe it wasn't necessary for him to make big, permanent decisions about what to do for work or where to settle. Maybe he could coast for a little while. "Think a guy like me could work on a road crew?" he asked Tom. "Or haul trash?"

Tom laughed. "A vet who served? Who has ties to the town? Hell, Dakota, anyone would hire you. I'll give you a recommendation. You just have to decide what you want to do. I've been working for the county for almost twenty years."

"I should probably pick up trash," he said. "Penance for all my misdeeds."

"Misdeeds?" Tom asked with a laugh. "Cal said you were a decorated soldier."

"I just about undecorated myself before it was all over," he said. He scratched his beard. "I guess I should get a haircut. Do I need to lose the beard?"

Tom laughed. "This is Colorado, man. You look home-grown."

"Good. I've grown kind of attached." He grinned. "So to speak."

"I'll find out what they're hiring for and get you an application."

When he went home from Sully's after a productive day, he found Cal in his home office, just hanging up the phone.

"So, you're still here," Cal said. "It's been five days. I think that's a record."

"Am I getting underfoot?" Dakota asked.

"I've hardly noticed you," he said. "You feeling underfoot?"

Dakota shook his head, leaning against the door frame.

"Baby bothering you?" Cal asked.

"The baby is kind of awesome," Dakota said. "I'm not babysitting, however."

Cal laughed. "We managed before you arrived, we'll continue to manage."

"So, what if I hung around?" he asked.

"What if?" Cal returned.

"Would that be weird for you?"

"Nah. I actually like you. Sort of." Then he sobered. "You're welcome here, Dakota. And thanks for helping Sully. It's appreciated."

"Everyone was helping him get the grounds ready, but I think now it's going to rain. For days."

"That's what I hear," Cal said. "Every March the rain comes, every March Sully gets the campground ready for summer. Well, spring and summer. We all help out. It wasn't expected of you, so thanks. Now what?"

"Well," he said, scratching his chin. "I'm going to get a haircut, trim the beard a little, get a job, look for a place to live…"

"I'm not throwing you out," Cal said. "If you can live with Elizabeth, you can stay here. The rent's cheap."

"Elizabeth is a hoot," he said. "I thought I'd rent something because it's what I do. That doesn't mean I won't hang out with you sometimes."

"This sounds kind of long-term," Cal said.

"For me," Dakota clarified. "A few months, anyway. I like the Crossing, the trails, the lake, the people. Seems like a good place to collect my thoughts."

"We'd love it if you were close," Cal said. "Listen, you okay here by yourself for a few days? It's time for Maggie to go to Denver again. Three to four days a week she operates and sees patients. She has a babysitter there but I don't have any clients or court appearances so I'm going along this time. I won't be back unless someone calls and needs me."

Dakota laughed and ran a hand over his head. "All this flexibility is giving me a rash. I'm used to a strict routine."

"Fine," Cal said. "Have a strict routine, that won't bother anyone. But Maggie and I have Elizabeth and two careers. Not to mention Sully and a campground. Just let me know if you're going to be around for a meal, that's all I need from you. Well, that and if you're going to stumble in at 3:00 a.m. and make me get out the rifle because I think someone's breaking in. That would involve communication, Dakota. You haven't exactly excelled in that."

"So I've been told," he said. "You have my cell number, right?"

"You have enough money to rent your own place? Because I—"

"I got it," Dakota said. "And I'll be sure to call so you can throw another potato in the soup."

Cal was quiet for a moment. "It's been good. Having you around," he finally said.

"I'll do my best not to screw that up," Dakota said.

Cal, Maggie and Elizabeth left very early in the morning for Denver. If Dakota understood things correctly, Maggie would go straight to work, seeing patients all morning, then operating all afternoon, then repeating that cycle again and again. One week it would be three long days, the next week it would be four days. Once a month she would be on call to the emergency room, adding a fifth day to her cycle. And Cal, a criminal defense attorney, was seeing clients in his home office or other meeting places—the diner, the Crossing on Sully's porch, the bookstore—and for anything from wills to real estate deals. Once in a while he actually got someone out of jail. Dakota filed that information away in case he needed it.

That left Dakota on his own for a few days. And as Sully had predicted, it rained. And rained.

He dropped into a real estate office and picked up a flyer of local rental properties, then headed for a haircut. He looked up and down the street and found that the barbershop was closed so he dropped in to the beauty shop. Fancy Cuts. He stepped inside the door and spied six chairs and three clients with hair stylists. He flashed that million-watt smile of his and said, "I'm not looking for anything real fancy, but can you handle a head and a beard left unattended awhile?"

Less than a moment passed. A beautiful young woman took a step toward him. "I've got this," she said confidently to the other stylists, both older women. "Give me five minutes. Have a seat."

She went back to her client, an elderly woman whose hair seemed to be a mass of pink sausages. "You can't be done in five minutes," the client said a bit more loudly than necessary.

"Oh, yes, I will," said the beauty. "And you'll love it."

"Well, it better not be—"

The stylist applied a brush and went to town. She fluffed out the woman's hair, did a little backcombing and shaping, sprayed some spray.

Dakota picked up a magazine and idly paged through it. Good oral hygiene had never served him better. In five minutes he was in the chair with the beautiful Alyssa running a comb casually through his dark hair. "What are we doing with you today?"

Dakota was suddenly conscious of how long it had been since he'd had sex. "Nothing special," he said. *Up against the wall work for you?* "Just trim it up, and can you trim the beard? Not Hollywood, just not *Duck Dynasty.*"

"I've got it," she said, showing him a brilliant smile of her own. "Let's start with a good shampoo. Right this way."

He didn't mention he'd already done that in his morning shower but instead let her lead him to the back. While she massaged his scalp and quizzed him, he just let his eyes close gently. He had a brother not so far from here, he said. He was just out of the Army and planned on exploring the country a little, starting here. He liked to fish and hike. He wasn't making any plans for a while. He was deliberately vague. This was a small town. He didn't want to do or say anything that might reflect badly on Cal or Sierra and all those attached. Until he got the lay of the land, he'd be a little mysterious.

But her fingers in his hair felt amazing. "You married, Alyssa?" he asked in a soft, smoky voice.

"Still waiting for the right guy, Dakota," she whispered back. "Do you have a lot of friends around here?" she asked, smothering his head with a towel and leading him back to her station.

"My brother's friends," he said with a shrug. "A few nice people."

"No girlfriend?"

He met her eyes in the mirror. "No girlfriend."

"I take that to mean there's no wife or fiancée, either?" she asked.

He shook his head, feeling like great sex could be minutes away. It was a feeling, not something he'd act on. This was Cal and Sierra's town. Hit-and-run wouldn't work. The repercussions could make life difficult for people he cared about and he wouldn't risk it. But this Alyssa, long-legged, beautiful, friendly, ready—this held great promise. He might have found himself a woman to pass the time with. It was worth considering. And it was worth slowing down and using caution.

"You know your way around a pair of scissors," he said, looking in the mirror. The haircut was excellent; the beard was looking good.

"You okay with the gray?" she asked. "Because if you're not…"

"I think it's fine," he said. "I earned every one."

"That's good, because I like it. It's very attractive."

"Are you buttering me up for a good tip?" he teased.

"You're kidding, right? Since you're new to the area, could you use someone to show you around?"

"That might come in handy," he said. "Right now I have somewhere I have to be. Maybe you'd trust me with your phone number?"

"Sure," she said. She waited for him to get out his phone, then rattled off the digits. "I'd be more than happy to. This is a great little town. Full of possibilities."

"I can see that," he said. "Well, Alyssa, thanks for a good job. I'm sure we'll see each other soon."

He paid in cash; the tip was excellent. He put on his

jacket, turned the collar up and walked out into the rain. He went down the block and across the street to the diner. Sierra was working today. He'd have lunch and show her his flyer of rental properties.

Dakota took a booth at the diner and let Sierra wait on him. He ordered a bowl of soup, half a sandwich and a coffee. It wasn't long before Sierra slid into the booth with a slice of blueberry pie.

"Is that for me?" he asked.

She looked at it for a second. "Yes," she said. Then she went back behind the counter and got another slice of pie, making him laugh at her.

"You're so thoughtful," he said.

"I am," she said. "In the early summer we have rhubarb pie and rhubarb cobbler. I think this year I'm going to learn to bake."

"When are you going to learn to get married?" he asked. "Seems like six months ago Connie asked us all if we would give consent and I guess I thought..."

"Well, you old fogy, you." She grinned at him. "We keep meaning to plan something. Hey, Cal's gone, right? Connie's off tonight. It's going to be cold and rainy. We're having a fire and soup. Wanna come over?"

"I don't know. Is there any nightlife around here?" he asked.

"Yeah—at our house. Fire and soup. Connie's cooking. It's amazing. Firemen are excellent cooks. Maybe if you're very good, we'll put on a movie. Or play a board game."

He gave her a steady look. "I don't think it's going to take me long to get really bored."

"You coming?"

"Sure," he said with a shrug.

Blood is thicker than water.

—GERMAN PROVERB

2

Dakota had looked at three potential rental properties after lunch. They were adequate but a little large for just one guy and none of them felt right. He made an appointment with a property manager for the next morning and he looked at four more rentals. The last one was in the country, about ten miles from town. The cabin had a nice big porch. It was on a hillside and a creek ran past. There was a small bridge crossing the creek. "The creek swells in spring and early summer," the agent said. "It was built as a vacation cabin. The owner liked to fish. He claimed the fishing was good in that creek."

Dakota asked if they could go inside. It was a decent size, probably nine hundred square feet. There were two bedrooms, one medium-size bath, a galley kitchen and a nice big table, sofa and chair all in the great room. There was no TV but there was a desk. "Does it come furnished?" he asked.

"It can," the agent said. "The owner is deceased and the

heirs are letting it go. Our office is managing the property for now. We're prepared to remove what you don't want, leave what you can use. There's no washer or dryer."

"I hate doing laundry," he said, smiling at her. In fact, he had both a brother and a sister with machines he could borrow. And there was always commercial laundry. "How much?"

"It's pricey," she said. And indeed, it was more than the larger houses he'd looked at. It was quaint. Rustic. There was a stone fireplace. The appliances looked fairly new, maybe a couple of years old. "It's kind of isolated," she said. "The water heater is new, the roof is in good repair, everything in the kitchen is functional. Even the ice maker."

He didn't say anything. He just walked around, touching the leather sofa, opening the kitchen cabinets. He lay down on the bed. He wasn't sure about the mattress yet—it might need to be upgraded. He'd brought only clothes and vital papers with him to Colorado. It looked pretty well stocked. Based on what he saw, he could fry an egg, microwave a meal, dry off after a shower. He could get himself a small grill. He might trade out the linens for new but it was in good shape. Better than some Army quarters he'd stayed in.

Then he stepped back outside onto the porch. There, on the other side of the creek, he saw deer. A buck, a couple of does and a very new fawn. One doe looked ready to give birth. He looked around the porch. "It needs a good chair."

"There isn't one but you could pick one up pretty cheap."

"I'll take it," he said.

There was a rental agreement to sign and the property manager had to run him through a credit check. Fortunately, he knew his credit was excellent, and even though he'd been in the brig and stood a court-martial, he learned when he purchased the Jeep that his military incarceration didn't show up in civilian records. "You just tell me when you're ready for me to sign papers. You have my cell number."

He was oddly euphoric about this cabin in the woods. A man could sit quietly on that porch and watch nature, watch wildlife. He imagined that in the dark of night he would hear wildlife and in the morning, birds. He would be busy because he liked being busy, but he would thoroughly enjoy relaxing in a small, isolated cabin. He'd like sleeping there. He'd like listening to the rain there.

He hadn't really imagined this scenario—that he'd come to Colorado and get his own place and be within a short drive of family. Actual family. He thought he'd visit, check them out, maybe stay a little longer than was typical for him, then press on. But then, maybe he shouldn't be so surprised. He'd left his Army family. Where else would he turn? Even though Dakota was independent, he liked having people in his life. There had always been soldiers. He took good care of them, they took good care of him.

And something had changed with his siblings. Or with him. For the first time he considered them friends, not just family he was stuck with. He'd never been good about keeping in touch and the Army had always provided him with plenty of excuses. If he didn't feel like checking in with them, then the Army, he could say, had other plans for him and he couldn't get away. At the moment, for whatever reason, he wanted to be around them. Could it be they'd finally all grown up?

He went to the bar and grill in town for lunch. It looked like the bartender was just coming on duty. She was tying on her apron and talking to another employee, nodding vigorously and smiling. The man put a hand on her shoulder as she tied the last knot in the apron. Then she washed her hands and went behind the bar. "How can I help you?" she asked pleasantly.

"How about a hamburger, fries and Coke."

She flipped the menu around for him. "I have seven burgers for you to choose from. We're famous for them."

"What's your favorite?" he asked.

She pointed to one of the burgers. "The Juicy Lucy with bacon and pickles, hold the onion. The cheese is on the inside. That's my meal."

"Thanks," he said, squinting at her nametag. "Sid?"

"Sid," she confirmed. "Short for Sidney. And how would you like that burger cooked?"

"Medium," he said.

"Excellent," she said. Then he watched her go to her pay station to punch his order into the computer.

This was his first visit to this pub. It was all dark wood with red leather bar stools and booths, red leather chair seats at the tables. It wasn't real big but he assumed they could pack 'em in at happy hour. He took the menu and looked through it. The bar was open from eleven to eleven, no breakfast menu. They probably rolled the sidewalks up around here at nine every night. There was nothing fancy on the menu—just burgers, flat bread pizzas, salads, ribs and miscellaneous bar food. They did have a kids' menu. And chili.

The bar was beautifully crafted, with an ornately carved back wall with a mirror so he could admire himself. He chuckled and took a drink of his Coke, but he was watching Sid. She greeted everyone. One older couple, probably in their seventies, came into the pub and she leaned across the bar to give them each a hug, laughing with them. Everyone knew her, it seemed. And she presided over the bar as her domain. He watched her laughing and talking while throwing together two tall Bloody Marys for her elderly friends. She put them on a tray and walked around the bar to serve them at their booth. She chatted with them for a moment.

Relatives? he wondered.

She brought him his lunch. "It's going to be hot," she said. "Enjoy."

He was immediately disappointed. She was gone so fast.

He took a bite of the hamburger, burned his mouth but wouldn't let on. He closed his eyes, chewed slowly and swallowed. When he opened his eyes Sid was standing there, smiling at him.

"Burned your mouth, didn't you?" she said.

He nodded clumsily. "How could you tell?"

"Your eyes. Tears. Slow down, buddy. I'm not going to take it away from you."

And then she whirled away again. She served up a couple of sodas, two beers and a glass of wine. But she came back.

"Well? How is it?"

"Outstanding," he said. "As you know. But I would have put a couple of jalapeños on it."

She tilted her head, thinking about that. "Not a bad idea. I skip the onions so I don't drive away business."

"This is a popular place," he commented, making conversation.

"It's almost the only game in town. We don't compete with the diner—they're better for breakfast, pie, soup, hot meals like roast beef, meat loaf, chicken pot pie. Home cookin'." She smiled.

"Well, you're right about the burger. Damn near burned my tongue off," he added with a laugh. "You seem to know everyone."

She gave the counter a wipe. "That takes about three days around here. And you're not from around here."

"I'm visiting," he said. "I have some family nearby but today was a good day to look around. Have you been here all your life?"

"Unlike most of the population, no. Not from around here. Born and raised in South Dakota, worked a few years in California and now I'm here for a while."

"We have that in common," he said. "What's 'a while' for you?"

She shook her head absently. "It's been a little over a year so far. I didn't plan that."

"What's holding you?"

"Besides the clean air, views, weather and people?" she asked with a lifted brow. "This is my brother's place. I intended to help out for a little while, but…" Another shrug. He understood that—his future plans were full of shrugs, too.

"Your brother has a nice little place," he said.

"So, where do you come from?" she asked.

He stopped himself from wincing. He'd have to remember to ask Sierra and Cal if everyone knew they all grew up in a bus. "I'm fresh out of the Army. I'm going to take a little time to decide what's next. I'm going to see if there's any work around here to keep me while I think it out. Like you said, lots to like around here."

"Army? That's a big commitment."

"I went in as a kid," he said. Then he picked up his burger to avoid explaining any more to this completely pleasant bartender.

"Well, if you like the outdoors, you'll enjoy your stay."

A woman sat down at the bar, leaving just a stool to separate them. "Can I get a chicken Caesar?" she asked Sid before Sid even had a chance to greet her.

"You bet. Anything to drink?"

"Water," she said. And then she was texting on her phone.

He didn't turn on his stool to look at her, but as he ate his hamburger he caught sight of her in the mirror behind the bar. She was very beautiful, her mahogany hair falling forward as she concentrated on her phone. He bit and chewed, and as his eyes moved just slightly left, he caught sight of Sid, but she shifted her gaze quickly. It made him smile. She was watching him and everyone else. She might have wanted to see how he reacted to the woman beside him.

He looked at Sid. She was in her thirties, he guessed. Her long hair was blond. Or reddish blond. She had that freckly pale skin of an Irish lass. She was quick, physically and verbally. And she didn't flirt, but she was friendly. Or maybe *neighborly* was a better word. She treated him like she treated everyone else in the bar.

He was almost finished with his burger by the time Sid placed the salad in front of the woman at the bar. She shook out her napkin, placed it on her lap and picked up her fork. Then she looked at him and smiled. "Hi," she said. "I'm sorry, I should have been more polite and said hello when I first sat down."

"Think nothing of it," he said, picking up a couple of fries. "You were busy. Texting, I assume. Our world's great new communication tool."

She laughed lightly. "Actually, checking social media. It's a convenient way to stay up-to-date on friends and events, et cetera."

He just nodded and chewed. He'd been able to avoid indulging in the big social media machine. He was guilty of communicating by texts and emails, however.

"I don't believe I've seen you around here before," she said. "I'm Neely."

"Dakota," he said, giving her a smile.

"Passing through?" she asked.

He tilted his head and gave that now-automatic shrug. "Visiting," he said. "I have a brother not far from here. You?"

"Me? I'm a new resident. I have a couple of business interests in town but I actually live in Aurora, not too far from here."

"Is Aurora a nice place to live?" he asked, shifting the discussion from him.

"It is," she said, dabbing her lips with her napkin, leaving red lipstick stains on the white cloth. He glanced at Sid and caught her again, watching. "I couldn't find anything around here I liked but there's more to choose from in Aurora. And there's more to do, more restaurants, more shopping, a little more culturally upmarket, more of everything. But then, Timberlake is more of a sportsmen and ranchers and tourists kind of place. Of course, the population is much larger in Aurora. So," she said, spearing some salad. "Married?"

He chuckled. That was direct. "No," he said. And he didn't volley the question back to her.

"And how do you make a living, Mr. ...?"

"Dakota is fine. I'm just out of the Army. I have an interview with the county. I'm thinking of maybe picking up trash. I hear the benefits are excellent."

There was a sound from down the bar but Neely didn't appear to have heard it. Dakota knew where that had come from. Sid was amused. He was sure she'd snickered.

"Sounds like dirty work," Neely said.

"I hear they give you gloves," he said. Then he asked himself why he was doing this. She was bold. Bolder even than Alyssa. He must be giving off some kind of scent—available man who is in dire need. "The pay is good," he added. "And that's why we have showers."

"And I'm sure it's temporary," she said.

"And how do you make a living?" he asked, and immediately regretted it.

"I'm into a lot of different things. I've been lucky. I'm invested in a few businesses and properties. And that, my friend, turns out to be a full-time job."

"I'm sure," he said.

"Isn't this the best little bar?" she asked, to which he agreed. And she commented on this being the best time of year. She asked him if he liked to hunt or fish and he said he hoped to do some of that. She told him, between bites of her salad, that she was reading the most wonderful book about fly-fishing in Montana and she couldn't believe how much it made her want to try it. He answered her superficial questions without giving away too much personal information. He did not offer to teach her fly-fishing. He didn't elaborate on his connections here. Until he knew what was going on all around him, he didn't throw out information.

But he noticed things. She wore very nice clothes—knee-high boots and a brushed-leather skirt. A red sweater that showed off a nice figure. A shawl rather than a jacket. Her watch was expensive looking but he was no expert on women's jewelry. She had model-quality makeup. And the nails...

If this woman had walked into the officer's club, he'd have beat everyone to the front of the line to buy her a drink. But here, he just didn't.

They had a pleasant, meaningless conversation. Sid took his plate, refilled his Coke and put his bill on the bar. Neely took a few more bites of salad and then blotted her lips, looked at her watch and said, "Well, I'm off. Late again." She fixed her black wrap around her shoulders and stood. "Hey, I have an idea. I have a reservation for one for dinner tonight. A very interesting and cozy little restaurant in Aurora—Henry's. I'd be pleased to make it for two. Let me take you to dinner as a welcome-to-Colorado gesture. And maybe we'll get to know each other better."

"That's very nice of you," he said, not standing. "I'm afraid I have plans tonight. But thank you."

She very confidently turned over the receipt for her lunch, popped out a pen and scribbled on the back. The name of the restaurant and her phone number. Also, 7:00 p.m. "Sometimes plans change," she said, and then she winked at him.

Really, she winked. This was a moral dilemma. She was sex waiting to happen. He wasn't above that.

Sid was suddenly standing in front of him. "Can I get you anything else?"

"You were right about the burger," he said. "Outstanding."

"You had a good lunch, then," she said. It wasn't a question.

"It was the most interesting one in Timberlake so far."

"Oh?" she said, raising her tawny eyebrows.

"You're not fooling me," he said. "You heard every word."

"Oh, of course I didn't," she said. "I never do!"

"You're full of shit, Sid," he said, grinning. He threw some bills on the bar and told her to keep the change. And he left Neely's receipt on the bar.

Dakota had a very productive afternoon. He checked on Sully, did a little restocking for him, had coffee with old Frank, who was like a fixture at the store, and saw Sierra when she came by the Crossing to see if she was needed for anything.

"Want to come to dinner tonight?" she asked him. "It's just me and Molly. I'm thinking grilled cheese and a chick flick."

"Oh God, that's so hard to pass up," he said. "I'm going to take my chances on Cal's big screen. There has to be something on. Or I could read…"

Sully snorted.

"Hey, I can read!"

"I'm sure you *can*," Sully said.

"I guess that was a no," Sierra said.

"If you want me to come over, I will," he said.

"As a matter of fact, I enjoy my nights alone with the dog," she said. "I'm just looking out for you."

"As a matter of fact, I do okay on my own, too," he said. But he kissed her forehead in a very sweet big-brotherly fashion.

At six thirty he entered the bar and grill in Timberlake and sat up at the bar. It was only moments before Sid saw him. She pleasured him with a sly half smile. She put down a napkin in front of him. "You're going to be late."

"For what?" he asked, showing her his megawatt smile.

"Dinner at the chichi restaurant, which isn't Henry's by the way. It's Hank's. And it's expensive. She was buying, you idiot."

"She *winked* at me," he said. "I was terrified."

She threw her head back, her strawberry blond ponytail rippling in time to her laughter. "I bet you were torn," she said when she stopped.

"Okay, truth, I thought about it for a second. But my experience is, that is not a good sign. If it's that bold, it's loaded. With trouble."

She shrugged. "I couldn't tell you. I don't know anything about her."

He grinned at Sid and it was completely genuine. "You are such a liar."

"And what can I get you?" she asked.

"A beer. Whatever is on tap."

"Are you having anything to eat with that?"

"No. I'll be thinking about food with my next beer. I bet you see and hear some stuff in here."

"Oh, no, you don't," she said. She served him up a beer. "I had to sign a confidentiality agreement to work here. Your priest isn't as safe as I am."

"Cocky," he said. "You hear a lot of jokes, don't you?"

"Yes," she said. "I'm even learning to tell a few. I have to practice in front of the mirror."

"I bet you don't," he said with a laugh. "I'm very experienced in talking to bartenders and you're not what you seem."

"I can assure you, I'm exactly what you see," she said.

"Okay, what did you do before bartending?" he asked.

"Don't you think that's a little personal?" she returned.

"No," he said, shaking his head. "Unless you were in the Secret Service or something."

"If I was, I wouldn't be able to tell you."

"If you were, you'd have a cover," he said. He disarmed her with his smile.

"I worked in computers," she said. "Very dull. In a room without windows. Figuring out programs and stuff. It's what everyone in California is doing these days. What did you do in the Army?"

He leaned back, almost satisfied. "I mostly trained to go to war and then went to war. My last shift was Afghanistan. And that's when I decided I'd rather pick up trash."

"Really? That sounds like a dramatic change."

"Maybe," he said. "Do you know a guy named Tom Canaday?"

"Sure. I know Tom. Everyone knows Tom."

"I met him. Hell of a nice person, Tom. He's had all kinds of jobs, being a single father and all. He said roadwork, refuse pickup and plowing in winter pay very well and have great benefits. He said he still works for the county part-time."

"You weren't kidding about picking up trash," she said. And then her cheeks turned a little pink.

"Aha! I knew it! You never miss a thing!" He laughed at her.

"How'd you meet Tom?" she asked.

"If I tell you, promise not to tell your other customers?" She put a hand on her hip and just glared at him. "He did some work for my brother. My brother had a remodeling job and Tom helped."

"Well, that makes sense," she said. "Tom has worked all over this valley. He even did some work in this bar."

Dakota looked around. "I don't know what he did but it's a good-looking bar. Now back to you. Why'd you trade computers for bartending?"

She sighed. "Rob, my brother, is also a single father. His wife died and their kids were very young. So, he changed his life, moved here with the boys, bought this bar and it worked for him. He has some good employees so his schedule is flexible—he can leave someone else in charge and be available for the boys. They're fourteen and sixteen now and active. But then his manager gave notice and quit and he needed help right about the same time I wanted a change. Who better than Aunt Sid? And, as it turns out, I like this." She flung an arm wide. "I now have windows and everything."

"Really different, though, isn't it?" he asked.

"About as different as picking up trash will be from going to war," she said.

He drank a little of his beer. "Got me there," he said. "In my case, that could be a refreshing change."

"Did you ever find yourself married?" she asked him.

He gave her a perplexed look. "As in, you wake up one

morning and find yourself married? No, that never happened to me. Did you ever find yourself married?"

"I'm divorced," she said. "Over a year now."

"I'm sorry," he said.

She looked at him with a slightly sad or sheepish smile. Then she gave a nod. "Incoming," she said, and turned away to wait on someone else.

"Well, what a coincidence," Alyssa said. He saw her reflection in the mirror and turned toward her. She put her hand on the chair beside him. "Are you waiting for someone?" she asked.

Dakota was amazed at how quickly Sid could sneak away. She was all the way down at the other end of the bar. "No," Dakota said.

"All right if I sit here?" she asked.

"Sure," he said. "Of course. Can I buy you a drink?"

"That would be so nice," she said, fluffing her hair. "What have you been doing with yourself?"

"Nothing much," he said. "Looking around. You?"

She laughed brightly and he knew. He was being stalked. There must be a real shortage of men around here. This wasn't something that happened to him with regularity—women coming on to him. It happened, but not often. What was more common was him coming on to them. He certainly couldn't complain about their looks, the two women who'd hit on him since he'd arrived in town. Alyssa was gorgeous. She was probably five-ten and her silky hair screamed for a man's hands. And those legs, so many possibilities there.

She began to describe her day of styling hair, laughing at her own stories.

"Hi, Alyssa," Sid said. "What can I get you?"

"A glass of merlot? Whatever label you like."

"Coming right up," she said, turning away.

Dakota was disappointed. He enjoyed a little good-natured bantering with a woman who was capable of giving it back. Alyssa was very sweet and polite, nothing about her put him off. He asked her what she did for fun. She liked to shop. Did she ski in winter? "Sure, everyone skis. Do you? Is that what brought you to Colorado?"

"As a matter of fact, I do, but I'm no expert. What else do you do for fun?"

She liked to get together with friends. Sometimes they went to Denver, clubbing. Three of them, single girls, went to Las Vegas for a long weekend; now, that was a blast. Talk about hangover city.

A couple of uniformed troopers came into the bar, sat at the end and Sid brought them coffee without being asked. They had her laughing her head off in no time. She put in their dinner order and went right back to them. She seemed to have a lot to say to them, laughing and gesturing with her hands. She refilled their coffee.

"Did you hear me?" Alyssa asked.

"I'm sorry," he said. "I was distracted by the cops."

"I said, maybe we should go out sometime. What do you like to do?"

Crap, he thought. "Let me get a little settled first. I'm new around here, remember."

"I could help with that," she said.

"And I appreciate that, Alyssa."

A man in a plaid shirt brought out a couple of plates from the kitchen and went behind the bar, taking them to the cops. He put a hand on Sid's shoulder and they all laughed together. The brother, Dakota thought. They reminded him a little bit of himself and Sierra; you could feel the bond between them.

"Are you wanted or something?" Alyssa asked him.

"Huh?"

"I said, are you wanted? Do you have warrants? Because you can't take your eyes off the cops."

"God, I'm sorry," he said, running a hand down his face, over his beard. "I was wondering what it would take to get on the police force. Highway patrol, maybe. A lot of military men end up in the police department or fire department. I might not be that smart but I'm definitely in shape."

"Oh, I bet you're very smart," she said.

"So, tell me how you chose your career," he said, then inwardly cringed. He really wanted to run for his life. He was a bad person. She was just being nice; he should be flattered. But he wanted her to go away so he could talk with Sid.

"Ready for another beer?" Sid asked.

"Thanks, but…" He looked at his watch. "I'm going to have to go."

"No dinner?" she asked with a devilish curve to her lips.

"Not tonight, I'm afraid." He stood to dig out his wallet. "You take good care of the police," he commented.

"Absolutely. They return the favor."

"Take care of me and Alyssa here. Keep the change. Alyssa, you staying?"

"No, I'll walk out with you," she said.

He put a hand on her elbow to escort her out and asked her where her car was. At the beauty shop, of course. He prayed: *please don't try anything.* Wasn't that upside down? Didn't normal men want beautiful women to try things? Anything? But this was a real small town and he had no follow-through here. He took her keys from her, beeped her doors unlocked and nearly pushed her into the car.

"There you go," he said with finality. "I'll see you real soon, okay?"

"Okay," she said, clearly disappointed in him.

"Drive carefully!"

He plunged his hands in his pockets and sauntered back toward the bar to get his vehicle. *Ah, that was how Alyssa knew!* She could see the bar and grill from the salon; she could see his Jeep. He got in and started the engine. Then he sat there a minute. He thought about driving around the block a couple of times, then going back. He thought about just sitting there for a while, waiting for when Sid got off work. To do what? Follow her home? "Argh," he growled, disgusted.

Then he asked himself two questions. One—what was it about Sid that was threatening to turn him into a creep? And two—did Cal have anything in the refrigerator he could eat?

The happiest moments of my life have been

the few which I have passed at home

in the bosom of my family.

—THOMAS JEFFERSON

3

Sid enjoyed walking home from the bar. It was nine, it was a brisk spring night and she'd put in a full, long day. She rarely stayed until closing; one of the other waitresses and Rob could manage behind the bar with the dwindling clientele. She left the weekends to the men and more energetic women. She typically worked Monday through Thursday but was willing to fill in here and there when needed. And, of course, her brother being the owner, she had good benefits.

The bar had saved her life. Well, Rob had saved her. And now she was schlepping drinks and meals and everyone was her friend. From introverted mathematician to gregarious barkeep. She didn't know she could be this happy.

The new guy, Dakota, was a cocky one. He knew he was good-looking; she'd seen his type before and stayed far away from them. He downplayed it even though he had women crawling all over him. What was he doing? Playing hard to get? Letting the women make fools of themselves while he enjoyed the attention? If she could trust any man she might take the time to understand him. But she would only get to know as much of Dakota as could be learned with a nice big bar separating them.

She trusted one man only—her brother. Rob was the strongest, most genuine man she knew. When she was about to die of a broken heart, he came for her.

It had been a dark, desolate time. Without warning, her husband left her for another woman. They'd been together seven years; she'd put him through medical school and supported him through his residency, and when he was done, he left her. He'd been with the other woman for two years, he'd said. She had never suspected.

That wasn't how it was supposed to be. They'd had plans. After residency he'd study for his boards, and right after passing the boards, they were going to have a baby. They hoped to have three. She thought they were in love, but while he was intimate with Sid, he was making promises to another woman. She knew they didn't have sex very often, but wasn't that how marriage and familiarity worked out? They talked about their future family. Was she remembering right? Was it just Sid who'd talked about their future? With her brain constantly riddled with equations, she often missed things happening right in front of her. Friends called her the absentminded professor. When David left, he had no lingering med school debt—no debt of any kind. That course of events had happened often enough that it was considered an old story—one spouse supports the other through a tough program like med school, then they divorce. It was such a cliché.

But Sid hadn't had a clue. She should have known he didn't love her. She should have felt it. But she herself was overworked, putting in long, long hours at the lab, drowning in data to be analyzed and sorted. She'd only been married seven years and was already grateful when David just left her alone so she could either work or rest.

She was in shock for a few months. Paralyzed with disbelief. Rob was her only family and he was struggling to raise two beautiful boys alone. They were getting by; she was so proud of them. As far as she knew, Rob didn't date at all. But Rob had the boys. Sid had no one.

She didn't tell anyone at work, but then her work friends weren't social friends. They'd go out for a late-night drink sometimes after putting in a particularly grueling week; sometimes they'd have a meeting over breakfast or lunch. There was no girlfriend to call and cry to. It was different for a bunch of brainiacs. They were mostly introverts. Sid was one of the few who had a slightly social side to her personality but she could be content focusing on her work, living inside her head. Her husband had been so busy with residency she hadn't expected much of a social life, anyway. Once he left her, she realized they rarely went out with friends, and when they did, they were usually doctors or hospital staff.

She moved through her days in a fog, going to work, writing papers, delivering lectures on quantum computing, managing a specially trained staff on UCLA's DNA computing analysis. It seemed they were always close to a breakthrough—no time to relax, no time to play around—a quantum computer that sorted and analyzed DNA in a split second and made chromosome projections could change the world, eliminate birth defects, cure diseases. They worked off several huge government grants and contributions from foundations and patrons. They worked on tight deadline after tight deadline.

She was pretty far up the chain, on the top rung of a notable research team with only two PhDs above her. People brought their problems to her. She could hardly go to Dr.

Faraday and have a breakdown and get personal advice. He was grooming his work for a Nobel Prize.

She had been very well compensated, of course. She made enough money to pay for their medium-size LA home, David's medical school, five years of residency, her own advanced education, living expenses and, in seven years, two vacations.

She didn't talk about her marriage, or rather her divorce. Throw a bunch of computer programmers and analysts in a room and they don't tend to talk about their feelings.

One of the interns, a woman, noticed Sid was losing weight and seemed tired. Dr. Faraday asked her if she was getting sick. "Because we can't afford to have you get sick." She told him she was having some personal issues with her marriage, but she wasn't specific and he dropped it like a hot potato.

Sidney began to suspect David had never loved her, had never been faithful, and she was too busy and too inexperienced in things like romance and relationships to see the signs. She remembered his opening line to her. *"I saw an article about you in the* LA Times—*young physicist making waves in quantum computing."* He probably thought cha-ching. Meal ticket.

David began the divorce proceedings immediately. After all she'd done to support him he wanted half of everything they had accrued—half the savings, half the house, half of her pension! He was going to take everything she had and she'd be forced to start over. She should have found her own attorney at once but Sidney couldn't move. She couldn't function. She couldn't get out of bed. Her students and coworkers emailed but she didn't open the computer. They called her but she didn't answer the phone. She didn't answer the door. It was her elderly neighbor who had watched the house once when she visited Rob who'd unearthed his phone number and called him.

"Is Sidney there with you?" she had asked.

"With me? No! I've left her a couple of messages and she hasn't returned my calls, but Sidney gets like that sometimes. If she gets really busy at the university, she just doesn't pay attention."

"Ever since David left her—"

"What?" Rob had shouted into the phone.

"You didn't know? She didn't want to talk about it but I'm so worried now. She's been getting so thin, looking so wounded. I haven't seen her in days and she won't answer the door. I'm afraid she's done something to herself. Her husband hasn't been around. And she didn't say she was going away."

"Good God, call the police! Break down the door. Please make sure she's in there, that she's all right. I'll be on the next plane."

By the time Rob arrived Sid had been taken to the hospital by ambulance. An IV replaced fluids so she wasn't dehydrated any longer, and she'd been medicated. But mentally and emotionally, she was ruined. Rob sat on the edge of her bed, took her hand in his and said, "Sid, what were you trying to do?"

It took her a very long time to speak. At long last, she said, "I don't know. I didn't know what to do."

She felt she had failed so monumentally she couldn't move. It wasn't just that her marriage didn't work; it was that she could be so successful in her field and not even notice her marriage didn't work.

He pulled her into his arms and they wept.

Her doctors wanted to keep her in the hospital—in the psych ward. But Rob worked with them to find a good facility in Colorado. She needed medication and therapy. Rob brought Sid into his home after a brief and healing stint in the hospital, got her set up with a therapist. He hired a lawyer to represent Sid and helped her work through her divorce. Day by day, hour by hour, she got back on her feet. It wasn't easy; it wasn't quick.

Sidney had never been very emotional and she certainly wasn't a romantic. She was a scientist, a pragmatist, living in a world of equations and computations. But now she knew how dangerous a broken heart could be. And she learned how awful having no family, no real emotional bonds, could be.

She had had an emotional meltdown and what she learned was so ridiculously simple she felt even more stupid. She had not been living a balanced life. She had been completely absorbed in difficult work, had been physically tired, had no love in her life, became isolated and her defenses were down.

She collapsed.

Rob brought her into the bar, at first to lend a hand or have a meal with the boys. Eventually she worked her way into the business, getting to know the patrons, becoming friends with the other employees, getting to know the people in the town. Now it was her lifeline.

She still lived with her brother and nephews. She and Rob worked together to make sure the boys had everything they needed and the full support of parental figures. Sean and Finn were smart, athletic and funny. College was on the horizon.

"We're going to turn into one of those odd brother and sister couples who no one understands and who live into old age together without changing anything," Sid joked.

The town didn't know all she'd been through. She was divorced, as were many people. They only knew a little of what Rob had been through, burying a young wife when his sons were only six and eight.

There was one thing that continued to plague her. How could her ex-husband treat her with that kind of selfish cruelty, use her as he had, abandon her the way he did and sleep at night? She tried not to think about that too much; it made her too sad. She was not known as a sad person. She was well liked and considered to be bright and funny and helpful.

There were plenty of attractive, personable men in Timberlake. She'd even been asked out. Could she ever be friends with a man again? She thought probably not.

But she took an oath. She was never going to let herself be that isolated and overworked again. She planned to surround herself with family and friends. Casual friends, not lovers.

By the time Cal got back from Denver, Dakota had signed his rental agreement, moved in his meager belongings and been hired by the county to haul trash part-time, starting in ten days. There would be a few days of training first, though how one trained in picking up garbage eluded him. He hoped they'd let him drive the big truck.

"Wow," Cal said. "This almost sounds like you really are staying awhile."

"Awhile," he said, noncommittal.

"Gonna show me your place?" Cal asked.

"Certainly. Whenever you're ready."

"Let's go!"

Cal jumped in the Jeep and they drove for about fifteen minutes to the little cabin in the woods. Dakota drove slowly over the bridge. "I hear this creek swells in spring. If it gets bad, I guess I'll have to pole-vault home."

"This is downright...cute," Cal said.

"Be careful there," he said. "It's manly."

"That, too," Cal said.

"I just bought two canvas deck chairs. We can sit on the porch and have a beer and watch the deer and bunnies."

They went inside and Cal admired the wood floors, the appliances, the big table, the stone fireplace. "This is not bad," he pronounced.

"I like it," Dakota said.

"Kind of all alone out here, isn't it?"

"That's the part I like best," Dakota said. "But it turns out I have Wi-Fi. I'm not sure how good it is but if it's terrible I'll just spend a lot of time at your place. Or Sully's. Or Sierra's. Hey, when is Sierra getting married?"

Cal looked at him in surprise. "Are you concerned?"

"Nah, but I want to make sure she's taken care of. You know?"

Cal put his hands on his hips. "No, I don't know. You've hardly communicated, now you're taking care of people?"

"To be honest, I never thought I'd be around family. I don't hate it," he added, smiling.

"Why didn't that occur to you before?" Cal asked.

"Seriously?" Dakota said. "Let's see. Not only was I in the Army, you were in Michigan! What's the matter, was the North Pole full? Dad was in the twilight zone. Mom was pretty much there with him, and Sierra was under the influence. Are you suggesting I should have gone to live near Sedona so she could run my life?"

"You have a point," Cal said.

"Who knew you and Sierra would settle in a cool place?"

"I never saw it coming, either," Cal said. "I was just hiking. It was time and I was looking for the right place to scatter Lynne's ashes..."

"And you end up at some old guy's campground and he

has a gorgeous daughter who just happens to be a neuro-surgeon? How does that happen?"

"I must be living right," Cal said. "You need anything? This stuff going to get you by?"

"I don't need anything, Cal."

"You don't start your job for a while. It's only part-time. If you need a little help, just say—"

Dakota put up his hand. "I left home seventeen years ago. I've gotten by without help, haven't I?"

"I guess I always took it for granted that the Army was taking care of you," Cal said. "We sure didn't grow up soft, did we? But if there's one thing we figured out early—there wasn't much help available. Talk about training in making your own way."

"That brings something to mind. Does everyone around here know how we grew up?"

"Everyone? I doubt everyone knows the details. The people we're close to know. I took Maggie to the farm to meet the folks before we got married, giving her one last chance to run for her life."

"And she didn't run?"

"Nah," he said. "Maggie's tolerance and compassion far outpaces anything I've encountered. That's one of the things I love about her."

Dakota didn't look at his brother but he could feel Cal's eyes on him.

"You're wasting a lot of energy still being mad at them," Cal said.

"They weren't exactly sterling parents," Dakota said. "And it's not because they were poor—there's something honorable about being poor and holding it together. They were negligent. Jed should've been on medication! Marissa should have insisted."

"Know what Maggie said about that? She said she's had

a lot of people refuse medical treatment for a variety of reasons. Sometimes they find the treatment worse than the disease, sometimes they're afraid, sometimes they've made peace with their dysfunction and know how to live with it. He might not have been the best father but Jed is still a gentle soul. Crazy, but sweet. Scared of his own shadow but kind. He was always so good in his heart."

"As he talked about his design of Apollo 13, or his Nobel nomination or some other delusion."

"My favorite was when he was getting ready for a security briefing," Cal said with a chuckle.

"I don't want to laugh about it yet," Dakota said.

"Let's check out your new porch chairs and see if we can talk about things you find more agreeable."

They sat and talked for a while about general things, the town, Sully's place. Cal explained that Sully had had a heart attack a couple of years ago and ever since then those people attached to him—Maggie, Sierra, Cal, Connie—had all been checking on him regularly and pitching in with the chores around the Crossing. Dakota had fallen right into step, often showing up at the Crossing to help out.

In the late afternoon Dakota took Cal home and then headed for town. He parked way down the street and walked to the bar. He sat up at the bar and was promptly waited on by Rob. They chatted briefly while Rob served him a beer but there was no sign of Sid. Dakota nursed his beer slowly and eventually heard another customer talking to Rob. "Sid's day off?"

"Not usually," Rob said. "The boys had baseball tryouts and one of us had to take them so Aunt Sid offered. I told her to take the day off. She was just going to leave early, anyway."

Then Dakota remembered: she left the weekends to the

other bartender and waitresses because it got busy. That was good to know because Dakota wasn't into crowded, noisy bars. But he would have to wait until the following Monday to see her again. He could take a chance on Sunday but he was pretty sure she had said Monday through Thursday was her usual schedule.

Through the weekend he enjoyed himself with his family and their families. Cal and Maggie hosted a big Saturday night dinner at their house because Connie wasn't working and everyone was available. It was the end of March; the campground general store was still closing early and there were only a couple of intrepid campers. Sully liked to be in bed before nine so he left early, but the rest of them played poker until midnight.

At last it was Monday. Dakota was very calculating. He showed up at the bar between lunch and happy hour. He sat in his usual spot. The place was deserted. He waited for Sid to come through the swinging door from the kitchen. He grinned at her. And it was unmistakable…she smiled back. She slapped down a napkin in front of him. "And how can I help you today?"

"I'll have a beer," he said. "How've you been?"

"Me? Fine." She craned her neck to look out the windows. "Are we expecting company today?"

"We are not. I parked behind the diner and walked down. I'm undercover."

That brought a laugh out of her and she filled a glass with beer for him. "I don't know why you're fighting it. Alyssa is perfectly nice. And that other one is certainly beautiful and willing to buy you dinner. And, I suppose, other things…"

"I explained that," he said. "Trouble. And Alyssa seems awfully young."

"She's not that young," Sid said. "Just something to think about. How about you? How have you been?"

"Good. I thought we'd celebrate my new job."

Her face lit up. "Congratulations! And what will you be doing?"

He lifted his beer and took a sip. "Picking up trash."

She laughed and it was a wonderful sound. "Just as you planned."

"It's good money. I have to go to a training program first. Apparently there are things to learn about garbage. I hope they let me drive that big truck."

She leaned on the bar. "That's probably a senior position."

"I'm experienced. I've driven great big MRAPs. You know—those enormous military vehicles that are resistant to mines and bullets and carry troops around the desert. I could probably parallel park a garbage truck."

She laughed again. He could make her laugh. That was a start. "I might end up their star trash hauler."

"*After* your training," she reminded him.

"I bet I'm at the head of the class," he said, grinning. "I doubt you have to be a Rhodes scholar to get through it."

She seemed to snap to attention. "Why would you say that?"

"Just a joke. That was a strange reaction."

"What exactly is a Rhodes scholar?" she asked.

"A recipient of the Rhodes Scholarship that includes a couple of years at Oxford," he said. He judged her expression and it was his turn to laugh. "Hey, just because I'm hauling trash…"

"Huh," she said. Then she wiped the bar. "The Army must have educated you very well."

"In a manner of speaking. They have this nifty little

thing called the GI Bill. When I was in the States, I took advantage."

She didn't say anything for a moment. "I guess you're a little overqualified for the county refuse pickup."

He raised one brow. "How about you? College?"

She grinned. "What for? I love this job," she said. "Seriously, it might be the best job I've ever had. Except once when I was a babysitter for this rich couple who took the family to France and brought me along to watch the kids. That was pretty sweet."

"When do you get off work?" he asked.

"Why?"

"Because, Sid, I'd like to buy you a drink or a cup of coffee or something. Because I'm really not interested in Alyssa or Neely with her dinner at Hank's or Henry's or whatever, but I think I'd like to get to know you better."

She looked around. "Well, while it's not crowded and I'm finishing my chores behind the bar, we'll get to know each other. I don't date. I especially don't date customers."

"We don't have to think of it as a date—"

"I like you, Dakota, but no. The answer is no. I'm not interested in dating. Not even just a coffee date."

"I could tell you about all the times I got in trouble in the Army. You could tell me all your babysitting stories. You could fill me in on the town and I could tell you all about their trash."

"Seriously," she said. "Do I have to get my big brother?"

He slammed a fist to his chest. "Oh God! Not the big brother!"

"Don't be cute," she said.

He chuckled. "All right," he said. "Can I have a Juicy Lucy? With jalapeños?"

"Medium?" she asked.

"Yes, please."

"That's better. Now, enjoy your beer and don't give me any trouble."

"I wouldn't dream of it. What did you do over the weekend?" he asked. "On your days off."

She ignored him while she keyed in his order. He could tell she was deciding whether it was a good idea to talk with him about personal things. Then she was back. "I did laundry, took the boys to the store for sporting gear, went for a hike, made their favorite Saturday night dinner, watched two movies and read a book."

"A *whole* book?" he asked.

She just made a face. "What did you do?"

"We had a family dinner," he said. "I have family here, did I mention that?"

"A brother, you said."

"A brother, a sister, a sister-in-law and her father, a potential brother-in-law, a six-month-old niece. We ate, and after Sully went home we played poker till midnight."

Her mouth fell open. *Bingo*, he thought. He was going to keep his private life from the town for now, but getting this woman's attention had been too problematic.

"You're related to Sully?" she asked.

"You know him?"

"Everybody knows Sully."

"Then you probably know Cal, Maggie, Sierra and Connie. My family."

"You didn't tell me," she said. "I consider them all friends. Not that we socialize or anything, but we see each other here and there. I see Sierra sometimes since we both work in town. Hmm."

He smiled. "Now can we have coffee?"

"No," she said.

"But you like my whole extended family!"

"Right," she said. "And you're a perfectly nice guy but you're looking for a woman. Not a friend."

"You can't be sure of that," he tried.

"I'm sure," she said.

"What if I gave you my word we could be friends?" he asked.

"I'm getting Rob," she said, turning as if to leave.

"Okay, I give up," he said. "So, where's a good place to hike around here?"

"You didn't get enough of that in the Army? Sully's place is sitting in the middle of some of the best trails. When you wear out those, head up to Boulder—awesome views."

"Your nephews hike?"

"I need handcuffs and leg irons to get them to stick to hiking. They want to run, climb, dangle from cliffs, work out. They're athletic and at their ages the hormones are just kicking in—lots of energy there."

"How are they doing in school? You know, academically."

"Fine," she said. "As long as they're doing well, we don't harangue them. They're kids. They both help out here and at home. They're very good boys."

"So the whole family works in the bar," he said.

"Well, the boys can't be in the bar—they're minors. But there's plenty to do around here. What about your family? I know what Sierra does. And Connie. I get firefighters and cops in here all the time."

"We all help out at Sully's, especially in spring. He's getting ready for summer when his campground is full all the time. And after a long winter there's plenty to do. Cal does a little lawyering here and there and Maggie works in Denver three to four days a week. And then there's Elizabeth, who is brilliant. They keep trying to shame me into babysitting just to watch me squirm."

"You don't like kids?"

"Kids are great but I don't do diapers. If they leave me alone with her I know something like that's going to come up."

"You might have children of your own someday. Then what?"

"Well, I'm not counting on that, but if it does happen, the baby's mother will have to train me. I have no experience in that."

"So, there are three kids in your family…"

"Four actually," he said. "Cal's the oldest. I have an older sister and Sierra's the baby."

"Older sister?"

"Wait for it," he said. "Sedona. Two years younger than Cal, two years older than me. Cal's name is actually California Jones."

"That's kind of…amazing," she said. "Was there some significance? Something special about those places?"

"I don't think so. I've never been to either North or South Dakota. We did spend some time in California. My parents were… What's a nice word? Freethinkers. Kind of hippies, for lack of a better description. It got us two states, one city and a mountain range."

"That's very cool," she said.

"I spent most of my childhood on a farm in Iowa," he said. "The kids in rural Iowa didn't really find it cool. They found it strange."

"They must have no imagination in Iowa," she said. "I think it's lovely. Interesting and lovely."

She was such a nice person, he thought. And she was killing those jeans. He was going to have to be very patient. She had something going on in her head.

"Let me ask you something," he said. "Why the big aversion to any sort of dating? Even the most innocent sort?"

"Are we going to start this again?"

"I'm not looking for an argument," he said. "But really, it's such a firm decision. Is there some specific reason? That might help me to get it and not take it personally."

She sighed. "Ugly divorce. Divorce scars. Now do you get it?"

He shrugged. "Well, of course. But I've never heard of a nice divorce. I haven't heard of anyone singing happy tunes after one, either."

"Lucky you. You haven't had the experience," she said.

"I haven't been divorced, no. I've had a couple of break-ups and I agree they're very tough. I spent a lot of time thinking about how I might've known that was going to end badly. Eventually I just moved on." He drank some beer. "I guess you're not there yet."

Rob came out of the kitchen carrying Dakota's lunch.

"Hey, Dakota. How's it going?"

"Excellent, Rob. How are you?"

Before he could answer, Sid interrupted. "Rob, did you know Dakota is one of *those* Joneses? Cal, Maggie, Sierra, and by association Sully, Connie and there may be more."

"Sure," Rob said. "You didn't know that?"

"Did you know the Joneses are named after states, cities and mountains?"

"I don't know if I realized that," Rob said. "Enjoy your burger. That's Sid's favorite." Then he turned and was gone.

Dakota took a big bite. He chewed and swallowed. "Your brother likes me," he said.

"It's not going to do you any good," she replied.

Dakota fell into a very uneventful, satisfying routine. He worked three long days a week and had Sunday through Wednesday off. He started at the crack of dawn, punching in at 5:00 a.m. and out at 3:00 p.m. They told him over the summer he might be able to pick up one more day and additional benefits, but he wasn't too worried. He had the VA and a sister-in-law who was a doctor. There was still plenty of time in that schedule for him to help Sully and he managed to have dinner at the bar and grill at least two nights a week. He saw Cal and Sierra now and then, hung out with Sully sometimes, and although Tom didn't have all that much time to spare, they managed to have a beer at Sully's twice.

April was bringing the first blooms and campers, and the blossoming of his new friendship with Sully. First Sierra and now Dakota found in him the sane, philosophical and comical father they hadn't had. For Dakota it started when he told Sully, "I guess you know we grew up picking vegetables with other migrant workers, living in a bus and getting no proper education."

"For the life of me, I can't figure out why that worked," Sully said, scratching his mostly bald head.

"It didn't work," Dakota said. "It was awful."

"And yet look at the lot of you," Sully said. "You all turned out good. You didn't just survive it, you aced it. But offering a manual on child raising that suggested that kind of upbringing as a way of creating a success..." He shook his head.

"It's well-known that some lucky bastard will always rise out of poverty and ignorance and, in spite of hard times, make something of himself..."

"I know this," Sully said. "A kid here, a kid there, escapes a poor, uneducated family and makes good. But the Jones clan? Near as I can tell—there were four of you and all four of you not only survived, but excelled."

"Dumb luck, I guess," Dakota said.

"There was some nurturing there," Sully said. "Your

mother, maybe your father on his better days, each other. Somehow it happened. I couldn't have done it."

Dakota laughed. "No, you couldn't. Your daughter is Maggie!"

"Oh, I don't take any credit for Maggie," Sully said. "Her mother and stepfather raised her. Maggie's mother left me when she was just small, took her away. I had failed them, see. Not that Phoebe, my ex-wife, was any treasure, mind you. We're cordial now on account of Maggie, but it's no secret we'd sooner live on different planets. She's a giant pain in the ass. Her husband, Walter, a gentleman to the bone, not only puts up with her, he puts up with her generously. He's a saint."

Dakota chuckled. He'd heard from both Maggie and Cal that this Phoebe was annoying. "And you didn't remarry?" he asked Sully.

"Why tempt fate?" Sully said. "Proved the first time I had no judgment where women were concerned. I met her and married her in less time than it takes paint to dry. That's a clue."

"But don't you sometimes get…a little…lonely?"

"Did I say I'd never crossed paths with a woman? Even this old man can tell you, sometimes just being around a woman makes certain things better. Don't go telling Maggie I said that. She'll try to picture it in her head and get all riled up. But I've been friendly with women over the years. It's a wise man who knows his limitations, son. Remember that."

"I will," Dakota said. But he couldn't help but laugh.

He vowed to remember that. But he continued to go to the bar for two or three dinners a week. When Sid saw him coming, she gave a half smile and shook her head. She realized he was relentless. He liked her. And he could tell one of the problems she was having right now was that she also liked him. Well, maybe he shouldn't go that far. She enjoyed him. Whatever the husband had done must have been so devious she was afraid that lurking beneath the surface of every good guy was a monster. Why else was the idea of even a cup of coffee such a terrible notion?

But Dakota was patient. He spent the month of April settling into the world of trash hauling. The first couple of weeks he hung on the side of the truck and picked up scattered refuse while a man named Lawrence drove and dumped the buckets. Lawrence was forty-seven but looked much older. His hair was going white; he had a wife and six kids. When he talked about his wife, everything came with an appreciative laugh and a headshake. "Ooh-wee, Benita made some of the best taco pie this man ever had!" Or, "Damn me, that woman got her fist on those boys o' mine and they don't dare talk back at their mama!" In short, Lawrence had a good, normal, happy life with all the usual problems. Dakota wanted to work with Lawrence forever. But he really wanted to drive. "You get to do that soon enough, boy," Lawrence said.

April was full of rain and flowers. Hauling trash in the rain was just the same but wetter. But as the days passed, Dakota thought Sid might be softening up toward him, just a little bit.

The most extraordinary thing in the world

is an ordinary man and an ordinary woman

and their ordinary children.

—GILBERT K. CHESTERTON

4

Tom Canaday was a happy man in general, always upbeat and positive even when times were challenging. It was his nature. His father was the same way and his mother might fret sometimes but she was both hopeful and helpful. Lately his happiness had been elevated a notch or two. He had a good woman in his life.

Tom had married his high school sweetheart when they were very young. They'd had four children, a handful for anyone. Zach, the youngest, was still in diapers when Becky left them and Tom became a single working father. Had his parents, brother and sister-in-law not helped from time to time, he never would have made it. Becky had moved out ten years ago now. Tom was the first to admit he'd had trouble moving on, but he was emotionally free now. There wasn't a sliver of attachment to Becky left.

About the time Tom cut the ties he noticed Lola. Really noticed her. He'd known her almost all their lives; they were both raised near Timberlake and attended the same schools. They'd both married and divorced while still young. They saw each other around town all the time. Lola worked full-time at Home Depot, where Tom bought a lot of building supplies, and she was also a part-time waitress at the diner, just part-time enough for him to stop in for the occasional cup of coffee.

Tom had been getting a lot more pie and coffee the past six months than ever before.

Tom had been courting her for over six months and for two single parents to find time for romance was beyond difficult. But every time he kissed her he wanted more. He found Lola to be the most beautiful of women. She was strong and independent, but her strength and independence had not made her bitter. She was kind and compassionate. When he was able to put his arms around her and smell her sweet skin, he became aroused. She filled his arms with softness and he loved holding her against him.

But their schedules were impossible. They had to get by on what little time they could find here and there, maybe going to a home show or open house. They were both really into remodeling. In fact, they found they had many things in common. But they wanted to get alone together and just hadn't found the opportunity.

It was 10:00 a.m. on a Thursday morning when Tom Canaday knocked on Lola's door. When she opened it, smiling broadly, he handed her a gift-wrapped box.

"What is this?" she asked, taking it from him.

"Open it," he said.

"Oh, Tom, you're always so thoughtful," she said, pulling the ribbon off. "Always thinking of others."

"Oh, yeah, that's me."

She pulled off the top of the box and frowned. "What's this?"

"You know what it is," he said.

She pulled the item out. "A dead bolt?" she asked in confusion.

"For your bedroom door," he said. "And I have a matching lock installed on my bedroom door."

"I don't think either of the boys will surprise us today," she said with a laugh. "They're both in school." Cole had college classes and Trace was in high school.

"We're not taking any chances."

"They never open my bedroom door, Tom," she said. "They're scared to death they might see me in my underwear!"

"This is going to be different," he said. "There will be no underwear. And they might hear noises and mistake it for you screaming in pain." He grinned. "It won't be pain."

She put down the box and put her hands on his cheeks, kissing him soundly. His arms went around her to pull her closer, moving over her mouth with precision. He parted her lips with his, going deep, groaning as their tongues began to play. His hand slid down over her butt and pressed her close against him. The kiss went on and on, too long, really. He had to force himself to pull away. "Lola, quick—get me your toolbox."

"You sure know how to woo a girl," she said. She couldn't help but giggle as she went to get the box. Having done a lot of her own repairs and renovating, she knew exactly what he'd need. By the time she got back he was already getting the lock out of the package. She immediately started handing him tools. First the screwdriver to remove the old doorknob, then the chisel and hammer to enlarge the opening in the jam. "I wish I'd gotten this done before the kissing," he grumbled. "I gotta say, this is my first lock repair with a hard-on."

"Just how long has it been?" she asked.

"Oh, about two minutes now," he said.

"Not that!" she said with a laugh.

"You mean since I've had sex with a woman?" He wanted to clarify.

"Oh, my. Maybe we should talk about who else you might be having it with…"

He looked at her over his shoulder, lifting one eyebrow. "My left hand," he said. "Believe me, you have nothing to be jealous of."

"Tom," she said in a scolding voice.

"It's been such a long time," he said, drilling in the screws.

She put down the toolbox where he could reach it and backed away from him. He grumbled a little bit at a stubborn screw but he made very fast work of the job. He closed the door, turned the lock and tested it, trying to open it. "Success!" he said.

But he turned and she wasn't there.

"Lola?" he said.

She stepped into the doorway of her master bath wearing a sleek and satiny black robe. It took his breath away. "Whoa," he said, running a hand over the top of his head.

Lola was so voluptuous. She wasn't skinny or tiny. She was five-nine or so and full-figured. When they first started seeing each other she admitted she was self-conscious about her shape and considered herself overweight. Tom convinced her he loved her figure, loved her softness, loved that he could fall into her, fill his arms with her. She was full and rosy and smelled divine. He wanted to gobble her up from her dark, curly hair to her toes. "Holy God," was all he could say. And he frantically began to tear off his clothes. At the last second, seeing her standing there in that lovely black robe, he left on his boxers. But before he'd gone to the hardware store to buy the privacy lock, he'd chosen them carefully. These were his best boxers.

"God, you're so beautiful," he said. He lifted her chin to kiss her while his other hand untied her robe and let it fall open. "Oh my God," he said.

She rolled her shoulders back and the robe slid easily from her shoulders. And there she was, all pale flesh.

They'd been together for six months, and while they hadn't been able to make love yet they'd done a lot of touching and talking. They were prepared in every way except one—they hadn't lain down together without clothes.

"Why do you have these?" she said, giving the elastic of his boxers a snap.

"Why bother taking them off?" he said, pulling her against him. "I'm going to blast right through them."

She pulled on his hand and they found the bed, lying down side by side, rolling together, holding on to each other, kissing like teenagers, their hands roving over each other's bodies. Lola sighed, Tom moaned, lips were moving. He kissed her shoulders, her breasts, her belly. She stroked his butt, his thighs, and she managed to get rid of those boxers. Then he was on top, spreading her legs with a knee, moving closer and closer. He pushed forward and smiled against her lips. "I could embarrass myself here," he said. "I'm wound a little tight."

She shook her head. "Let's not worry about making it perfect, okay? We've had to wait so long."

"I know people who waited longer," he said.

"But we're forty," she reminded him. "And we're getting older by the minute…"

"You're right," he whispered. Then he found his way home. "Good God, it feels like you were made for me."

She just hummed and covered his face with kisses.

Tom moved, they rocked, the bed squeaked, they clung

to each other and it happened so fast. Both of them, bursting. Gasping. Then falling slowly and softly back to earth. He could not take his lips from hers; he didn't even consider rolling away. He held his weight off her by bracing on his elbows.

"You have the softest lips in all creation," he whispered against her mouth. "You have the sweetest body, the most beautiful dark lashes."

"How do you do it?" she asked him. "How do you always make me feel so beautiful?"

"You are," he whispered. "You're the most beautiful woman I know. And I love you." He kissed her again. "I hope it was all right, because I'm in heaven."

She laughed softly. "It was all right. Wonderful, in fact."

"God, that was perfect." He moved a little. "I'm not leaving."

"That's okay. I'm feeling very safe right now. Safe and satisfied."

"That's so good to hear."

"That lock really turned you on," she said.

"It wasn't the lock," he said, snuggling closer. "Please don't let me fall asleep…"

"Tom, we should talk about something…"

"What?" he asked, lifting his head from her shoulder.

"The lock—it's probably a good idea. A better idea is telling the kids we're more than friends. They're old enough that they deserve to know."

"I don't know. You have boys. I still have a young girl. Brenda is sixteen…"

"It's no different with boys," she said. "The kids all have to know the facts of life, the dangers and responsibilities, the joys. We've both been left by our spouses and have made good families while unmarried, but we're entitled to be happy, too. Do you worry that your kids still hope you'll reconcile with Becky? Because my boys don't want that for me, for us. They've probably already guessed that we love each other."

He smiled and moved a little. He moved a little more.

"You can't be ready again," she said. "That's inhuman."

"It's just what you do to me."

She put her arms around his neck. "Fine. We'll talk when we have our clothes on."

"Probably a good idea," he said.

Dakota went to Rob's bar for dinner on a Thursday night. It had become his habit for several weeks now and it had not gone unnoticed. When Sid saw him she just shook her head slightly and gave him a half smile. She slapped a napkin down on the bar in front of him.

"Back again, I see," she said.

"Great seeing you, too, Sid," he said, treating her to his sparkling grin. "How have you been?"

"Excellent. The usual?"

"Beer, then I'll consider dinner."

"And if Alyssa shows up, you'll bolt?"

"I'm afraid I've been a big disappointment to Alyssa," he said. "She wants a boyfriend and I'm not him."

She put his beer in front of him. "Alyssa seems to be more tenacious than I gave her credit for."

"Then I'll be an even bigger disappointment. Because I'm tenacious, too."

"I'm getting that."

"So, what's on your agenda for this weekend?" he asked.

"I'm pretty good at relaxing," she said. "I have a couple of things scheduled. Nothing terribly exciting."

"I'm off on Sunday," he said. "Saturday night, too. What's it going to take to get on your schedule?"

"We've been over that…"

"I could get a background check," he suggested with a grin.

"Just give up, Dakota," she said.

And then he noticed a little movement beside him.

"Isn't this a nice surprise," a woman's voice said. And just as quickly, Sid was moving down the bar, asking people if they needed anything.

Neely. He hadn't seen her in weeks. "Hi," he said. "How are things?"

"Excellent. And you?"

"Good," he said, lifting his beer.

"I'm Neely," she reminded him.

"That's right," he said, as if he'd forgotten. "Dakota."

"Oh, I remember." She snapped her fingers, bringing Sid back. He frowned at that action. "Can I get a chicken Caesar and a club soda with lime?"

"Absolutely," Sid said. "Dakota?"

"Nothing for me," he said.

"So, you've been in Timberlake for over a month now," Neely said. "Does that mean this little town appeals to you?"

"It's a nice little town."

"And have you settled in for a long stay?" she asked just as Sid put down her drink.

Dakota didn't really feel like discussing his plans with her, but on the off chance that Sid might overhear, he told the truth. "I have a job here and I've rented a place, but *long* means different things to different people."

"So tell me what you've seen and done since we last saw each other," she said, sipping her drink.

"Nothing very interesting," he said. He told her about the job, secretly hoping to put her off with his career as a garbage collector.

Then she told him she'd gone to a concert in Denver

and she'd been shopping for things for her town house—area rugs, throw pillows, art. She suggested she'd have to show him sometime.

Dakota frowned. She would just invite him over? She didn't know him. They had no people in common as far as he knew. All she knew was his first name and that he was a trash collector. That kind of rush to intimacy always made him suspicious.

She talked on, asking very few questions of him and those few he answered with one word if he could. He was thinking he would have to skip dinner tonight if she was going to hang around, but when she finished her salad she put her money on the bar. "Well, I'm off," she said. "I hope we run into each other again soon."

He was so grateful to see her go that he said, "I'm sure we will." And when she cleared the door, he sighed.

"How does it feel to be a chick magnet?" Sid asked with laughter in her voice.

"Do not make fun of me," he said. "There's something about her that's a little scary."

"She seems perfectly nice," Sid said. "Are you ready for your dinner now?"

"Almost," he said. He picked up a menu and opened it. "Give me a couple of minutes. I think I might have to try something different tonight."

"I thought you were close to doing that…but she gave up," Sid said, walking away with a laugh.

Dakota looked through the menu while Sid waited on other patrons and mixed drinks for the waitstaff to take to tables. She paused for a moment to laugh with young Trace, the seventeen-year-old busboy. Dakota was thinking about wings and potato skins when Neely appeared out of nowhere. He jumped in surprise.

"I'm so sorry to bother you," she said. "I have a flat. I

could call AAA but I thought maybe you wouldn't mind helping me out. I could make it up to you one of these days by buying dinner or even cooking for us."

He thought about telling her to call AAA. But he couldn't. He'd always considered it a point of honor to be kind and helpful to women. He said, "No problem." Then he called out to Sid. "Hey, Sid! I'll be right back. I'm going to help with a car problem. Reserve my spot, please."

"Sure thing," she said.

He held the door for Neely. He tried to walk behind her but she looped her arm through his.

"It's down this way," she said as she led him past the diner and around back. "The BMW is mine," she said. Her flashy little BMW sat in the dark alley, just two spaces away from his Jeep SUV. He wondered immediately if that could possibly be a coincidence. He bent at the waist, looking at the tires.

"Which one?" he asked, straightening.

Neely pressed herself up against him and her lips were on his so fast he didn't see her coming. Dakota had had many interesting experiences with women but this kind of aggression was a first. He gripped her upper arms and tried to move her away from him but it was hard—she was determined. Finally he managed to get some space between them. "What the…? Flat tire?"

She smiled and shrugged. "I thought maybe we'd get to know each other a little. Away from the nosy barmaid."

He wasn't sure what made him more angry—being tricked into leaving the bar for a potential tryst or Sid being referred to as a nosy barmaid. "Don't ever do this again. It's a bad idea."

"Little uptight, aren't you, Dakota?" she said, rubbing a hand over his chest.

He stepped back, out of her reach. He was seething inside, but he kept his cool. "Here's a lesson in manners. If you want to get to know someone, you ask them. If they say no, you move on. You never trick them. This is creepy. Now go home."

"Come on, you're a big boy…"

"Good night," he said, taking long strides away from her. He walked around the diner and back to the bar. He tried to shake off the weirdness of what had just happened. He got back on his favorite bar stool and saw that Sid had put a glass of ice water there. Grateful, he took a drink.

And left lipstick on the glass.

"Shit," he muttered, grabbing a napkin and wiping off the rim of the glass and his mouth. She'd nailed him good.

"Beer?" Sid asked, slapping down a fresh napkin in front of him.

"Oh, yeah," he said. "And the Juicy Lucy with onion rings instead of fries."

She looked at his face and pointed to her upper lip. "Missed a little here," she said.

"I did not kiss her," he said, maybe a little too loudly.

"You were attacked by a runaway lipstick tube?"

"You have it almost right," he said.

"I thought you were going to try something different tonight."

"Changed my mind. I like what I eat here. I look forward to it. I enjoy it."

"Don't get all goosey. I'll take care of it."

He wiped off his lips again. He sighed. No wonder he wanted to get to know Sid better and not Neely. He liked Sid. She was remarkably sane. She was so obviously smart. Her instincts were sharp. He thought she was pretty. She made him laugh and she challenged him by playing hard to get, except he knew she wasn't playing. She *was* hard to get.

His hamburger arrived and he realized he was sulking as he ate. Every time he came to this bar when Sid was working he was hopeful she'd warm up to him, and every time Alyssa or Neely showed up, things got strange. So, Sid had been through something painful and was playing it cool. Well, so was he. He wasn't looking for a lot, just a nice woman to spend time with, not some crazy broad who was always on the attack.

"You okay?" Sid said to him.

"No."

"Look, she's just a girl trying to make a date with a guy and—"

"There was no flat tire," he said. "She lured me away from my beer and my meal to get me alone in the dark and threw herself on me. I had to peel her off me. It was terrible. I know guys who would have jumped at the opportunity but there's something seriously off about her. If a man had done that to a woman, he'd be arrested. I don't know how to make it any more clear—I'm not interested in getting to know Neely any better, or Alyssa for that matter. Both of them creep me out. And put me in a bad mood."

Sid stared at him, transfixed for a moment. "Whew," she finally said.

"It was awful," he said, picking up an onion ring. "I'd never do that to a person. There's this thing called manners. And personal space. You know?"

"I know," she said.

"Sorry," he said, chewing on an onion ring. "I got pissed off."

"I understand completely." She picked up his beer and dumped it. "That got a little warm while you were breathing fire," she said, getting him a new frosty mug and fresh beer. "Here you go."

"Thanks," he said.

He nursed it slowly, done flirting for the night. In fact, he might be done for all time. He was a little surprised by the turn of events. He'd been on the receiving end of some blatant come-ons in his day but he could usually discourage the idea without anyone being hurt or becoming angry.

He finished his beer and stood to get his wallet.

Sid was in front of him with his check. "Two beers and a burger," she said in her usual businesslike tone. "And here is where I'll be on Saturday night if you still feel like coffee," she said, handing him a second slip of paper. There was an address on it. He raised his eyes to hers. "You'll be perfectly safe. Besides, that shade of red does nothing for my coloring." Then she grinned.

"I don't want your pity," he said, but he said it with humor in his tone.

"Good. Seven o'clock."

He walked to his car thinking that yes, she felt sorry for him. He was clearly insulted and angry about being played as he was. But that was okay. Even though it hadn't been a strategy of his, he was willing to take advantage of the situation. And over coffee he would charm her and make her laugh. It was with this very hopeful and encouraged feeling that his SUV came into view.

All four tires were flat.

He looked around to see if anyone was there. Neely's car was gone and the small parking lot behind the diner was quiet. He looked at the other cars—tires all fine. Then he went back to the sidewalk, where it was well lit. He pulled out his phone and called Cal.

"Hey," Cal said.

"Hey. I've never done this before. Called my big brother when something happened."

"Hmm. What happened?"

"I'm in town. I was having a burger at the bar and

grill—Rob's place two doors down from the diner. A woman asked me to help her with a flat tire, and when I went with her, there was no flat, just a very eager woman. So I extricated myself, but it was awkward—I must have offended her. Now, I find my tires are all flat." He took a breath. "I guess I have to find a tow truck…"

"Sheesh," Cal said, sounding more alert. "You know this woman?"

"Just her first name. I thought she was a nice woman, but her come-on could use a little polish…"

"You think she did it?" Cal asked.

"Doesn't that seem a little extreme?"

"You have to call the police before you call the tow truck. And I'll come and pick you up."

"I can handle this myself…"

"You want the next guy who's not interested in her to get four flat tires?"

"We don't know for sure that she did it," Dakota said.

"Sounds like we do, we just can't prove who did it. Call the police, tell them what happened, ask them what towing service they recommend."

"Aww," Dakota groaned.

"This is Timberlake, Cody," Cal said. "We don't experience a lot of that sort of thing. If you don't say anything, another guy could be vandalized. Or maybe she'll try something bigger on you."

"I think I'd rather just handle this…"

"Now you sound like a woman," Cal said. "I want you to think about that. I'll be there in twenty minutes."

The notion that women don't report crimes because they're afraid or they just want to forget it happened and hope it won't happen ever again had briefly crossed his mind, but he'd pushed it away. There was also a certain amount of humiliation involved in being victimized. Victimized and then tattling.

He wouldn't have called Cal if he hadn't been looking for someone to cut through his bullshit. *Of course it was Neely.* Of course she shouldn't be pulling that shit. Then his mind wandered further. He didn't want Sid to know. He didn't want to seem less than strong.

The way a woman didn't want her boyfriend or husband to know she'd been assaulted because she wouldn't want him to think she was dirty? Or think she'd brought it on herself?

Cal arrived before the deputy. "Show me the damage," he said. Once he'd checked out the car, he said, "That took a lot of effort. Look out for this one—she's mean."

To Dakota's relief, only one tire on his SUV was slashed; the rest were merely deflated. Odd that he should have that in common with Neely—deflating tires to prove a point. And it gave him no peace of mind to know she was traveling around with some dangerous sharp object. He thought about the incident a great deal more than he wanted to. The vandalism would probably just be a misdemeanor. He tried to imagine her in her fancy clothes and boots crouching in the dark, manipulating the air out of the tires.

His insurance company covered the tow but he had to get Cal to drive him to work early in the morning. He was pretty angry about the whole thing.

But by Saturday he was looking forward to seeing Sid. After work he plugged the address Sid had given him into his GPS. He focused not on his unpleasant experience with Neely but rather on going to some coffee shop in Colorado Springs where he would concentrate on demonstrating how desirable he was. He would find out more about Sidney, entertain her with stories of his world travels and, if necessary, exploit his actions as a soldier and hero. He never did that first. He always saved that as a last resort.

He looked around but couldn't find the address she'd given him. The directions were clear but he had trouble believing they were correct. He hadn't been to Colorado Springs before but he had trouble envisioning Sid inviting him to a trashy side of town. *Please, God, don't let Sid be a whack job! One is enough.*

He drove around the block but no coffee shop turned up. There wasn't even a Denny's or truck stop. He finally bit the bullet and took the slip of paper she'd given him and, after locking his car, went into the only place on the block that appeared to be open. It was pretty run-down, had a big cross on the door and the sign, which could not be seen in the dark, said Free Dinner.

He thought it might be a storefront church of some kind and they would at least know the neighborhood. He walked inside and discovered it was a soup kitchen. He had to weave his way through people standing in some kind of line to find whoever was in charge to get better directions. Then he saw her.

Sid was standing behind a serving counter, smiling like she'd never been happier. She wore a green apron, a scarf covering her hair, and rubber gloves, and wielded a big spoon. He chuckled and shook his head. He cut the line to walk up to her.

"Coffee?" he said, giving her his best smile.

"Glad you made it," she said. "Clay? Give this man an apron and show him what to do!"

A man travels the world over in search of what he needs, and returns home to find it.

—George Moore

5

Dakota felt as though he'd been tricked again, but this time in a good way. It took him about five minutes to get into the idea of serving free food. The clientele was as varied as the human race. There were a few grizzled old men—or maybe they were only grizzled and not so much old as worn down. A pair of elderly women came in together and passed through the line with their trays. He served a family of six, the oldest child no more than ten. There were several families, not always with both parents. A young man was there with his toddler son, who sat on his lap the whole time. He spotted a young couple, maybe twenty years old, followed by a few kids being led by what could only have been a big sister. A couple of boys around twelve came in with no adult. Then a vet, wearing a purple heart on his denim vest. To him, Dakota said, "Greetings, brother. Thank you for your service." More old men and women arrived and he wondered which were street people and which were merely poor. A few people came in over the course of a couple of hours who Dakota realized were not in reality and he thought this was what his father would have become without the anchor of his wife and family.

While a few looked as though they could benefit from some drug or another there were also those who appeared to have benefited too much. They were of every race and ethnic group—black, white, Hispanic, Middle Eastern, even a man with a strong Australian accent who said, "Thank ya, mate."

They had only one obvious thing in common. They were hungry.

Once the food had all been served, the next step was the inevitable cleanup. That was when Dakota became acquainted with some of the volunteers. Sid introduced him to a sixty-eight-year-old woman in jeans and a flannel shirt. "Dakota, meet Sister Mary Jacob," she said.

"You're a nun?" he stupidly asked. Nuns used to be much easier to identify.

"You were expecting Mother Teresa?" she asked. "I might not look like you think I should but I'm a damn good nun."

Dakota met a retired man who called himself a professional volunteer and gave his time to many organizations from the antidefamation league to animal rights causes. There was an elementary schoolteacher and her husband who liked to help out at least twice a month. He learned that a retirement community sponsored the soup kitchen as well as an at-risk school and there was always someone from their group there. And there was a youth minister from a local Methodist church. "Sometimes I bring a few kids with me, when their social calendars allow," he said. This particular soup kitchen was run and managed by Sister Mary Jacob. She knew just about everyone who came for meals and she knew every resource in the area from rehab to where to get clothes and haircuts for job interviews.

He was just about finished mopping the floor when Sid handed him a cup of coffee. "Thanks," he said. "Is this my coffee date? Because I was really hoping for a little pie to go with this. Like from a coffee shop or diner or maybe we could go batshit crazy and hit a Denny's."

She laughed. "We could do that. Let's head back toward Timberlake and go to the Denny's on the highway."

He followed her all the way to the restaurant, a little afraid she might ditch him on the long drive, but she waited by the door while he parked. They had no trouble getting a table, late as it was. They sat across from each other in a booth, ordered coffee, and Dakota asked for a moment to look at the menu. But he didn't. Instead, he looked at Sid and asked, "Soup kitchen?"

"I guess you don't meet too many of your potential girl-friends at a soup kitchen?"

He lifted his eyebrows. "You've upgraded your status," he said. "I thought I was going to have to work much harder for that."

"I feel sorry for you," she said with a smile.

"Whatever ticks your clock. Just explain the soup kitchen. Is it some kind of a test? To see if I'm charitable?"

"It actually has nothing to do with you. After my divorce I needed counseling. I struggled with depression. I think that's not unusual or unexpected. After some months of talking about myself and my feelings, the counselor gently suggested I might want to take the focus off myself and see what I could do for the less fortunate. She gave me an intimidating list of places that needed help. I just couldn't bring myself to cuddle terminally ill toddlers, and if I'd worked at an animal shelter, I would have brought them all home. I went to the soup kitchen and Sister Mary

Jacob tried to feed me. She couldn't wrap her head around me as a server, that's how bad I must have looked."

"Must have been worse than just a bad divorce," he said.

She paused for a moment as if considering how much personal information she'd give him on this, their first date. It made him smile for two reasons. One, it wasn't much of a date, and two, she was very protective of her privacy. When she continued, he decided she must have at least branded him as a good guy.

"Actually, I've heard about worse. It was very sudden and I never saw it coming. It turned out I didn't have good coping skills. My brother and I have suffered some losses, significant losses. Our parents. First my mom when I was just little, then our dad later. Rob was married by the time we lost our dad and I was in school and pretty much on my own. I was focused on school. Then Rob's wife passed away. She was twenty-nine. They had two little kids. Sudden onset heart disease. An infection. She was on a transplant list but..." She shrugged helplessly. "It all sounds so horribly pathetic, doesn't it?"

"Sounds horrible, yeah," he said.

"I don't know what Rob has told people but I don't like to go through that whole sad story so I've only told a few people... Mary Jacob is relentless. She wormed it out of me. I have a couple of friends from the bar. But if you wouldn't mind..."

"I don't have that many people to talk to," he said.

"Just on the off chance you decide to talk to Alyssa or Neely..."

"I don't think so, Sid," he said.

"Can we talk about you now?" she asked.

"As soon as we order cake."

"I thought you wanted pie."

He flipped open the dessert menu and showed her a picture of a three-layer slice of chocolate cake served with ice cream and whipped cream.

"That looks evil," she said. "And perfect."

When the waitress came back to refill their coffee, he asked for the cake—two pieces.

"Are you afraid to let me dip my fork into your cake?" she asked.

"Absolutely not," he said. "I'm just afraid you'll dip it too much." Then he grinned.

"You had your teeth whitened, didn't you?" she asked.

"No. I brush and floss."

"Okay, what's your story?"

"I'm not that interesting."

"I'll be the judge," she said.

It was his turn to pause, trying to decide how honest he wanted to be. The whole story might be overwhelming but he could give it a start. She'd trusted him. He could return the favor.

"As you know, I grew up with Cal. I grew up with California, Sedona and Sierra—our parents considered themselves hippies. But we grew up humbly on a small farm in Iowa and there wasn't much to spare so each one of us had a plan to break out of that poor existence. My plan was the military and I enlisted the second I was out of high school. I liked the military. I liked the standardized routine. It worked for me and I gave it my full attention. But eventually I burned out, just like I should have known I would. So I discharged, but without a plan. I went to Australia to visit friends and see the country, then came here because I am now an uncle. Because Sierra and Cal are both here. God knows I didn't want to settle in a small Iowa town and my plan was just to visit and get my head together, but this place? This is a real good-looking place."

"And your parents?"

"Getting old and still back on the farm. They don't farm it, however. They lease the land."

"How many times has your heart been broken?" Sid asked.

"How far back should we go?" he asked. "Pam Bishop ripped my heart out when I was fourteen. I'm not sure I'm over it yet. There were others but then I broke a few hearts, too. I never meant to."

The cake arrived and Dakota picked up his fork. "Things don't always work out the way we want them to."

"No," she said. And she lifted her fork.

"You're beautiful," he said. "I'm sure you've left several broken hearts in your past and you probably disappointed more than a few eager young studs."

"If I did I was unaware of it." She took a big bite of cake with a dollop of ice cream. "I never dated much."

"How is that possible?"

"You're flattering me, that's all. I was shy, I guess."

"You've definitely overcome that," he said. He ate some more chocolate cake. "You're a smart-mouthed wiseass."

"Well, I work in a bar. We're supposed to act like we're having fun. Most of the time I am. Plus, I have overcome a lot of my shyness. It was necessary that I either get over it or spend the rest of my life in a dark closet. With the door closed."

He shook his head. "It's hard to imagine you as shy. Nobody gets the best of you."

"Not even you, Mr. Jones," she said, licking her fork.

"See?" he said with a laugh. "See? You're a hard case. So tell me, how often do we go to the soup kitchen?"

"You don't have to go back to the soup kitchen, Dakota. I'll have coffee with you again even if you don't."

"I want to. I like it. I've done similar things, usually as part of the job, rescuing and helping the disenfranchised.

That's something the military is pretty famous for. We might be in pursuit of the enemy but the war-torn civilian communities need our help. Fills the well," he added, scooping more cake into his mouth. "Now, wasn't this a good idea?"

"I love cake and ice cream. Did Rob tell you?"

He shook his head. "I have no insider knowledge. I'm just very intuitive."

"I don't want a boyfriend, Dakota," she said.

"I don't really want a girlfriend, either, but sometimes I just can't help myself. So—the soup kitchen. How often?"

"For the next month I'm on the schedule three Saturday nights. I'm taking one Saturday night off. I have plans."

He did not ask what kind of plans. "They keep a schedule?"

"Mary Jacob needs to know how many bodies she has for serving and cleaning up. If she runs short at the last minute she has to call emergency volunteers."

"Maybe I'll just go every Saturday night," he said. "Tell me about some of those people," he said.

"The volunteers?"

"Yeah, sure. And what do you know about the people who come to eat?"

"Oh, they're all so different and interesting," she said, lighting up a little. There were more than a few kids who lived on the street, some elderly people whose social security wouldn't cover their expenses, a family who had enjoyed prosperity when both parents had been employed, but then their company downsized, leaving them unemployed. There were a few vets who weren't adjusting to civilian life, some PTSD going on there, and she went on. She talked about how Sister Mary Jacob tried to funnel these people in the best direction to get all the help they needed from counseling to government assistance.

Dakota asked a lot of questions and they finished another cup of coffee while Sid ran the tines of her fork over the plate to mop up every bit of chocolate.

"If you lick the plate, I won't be embarrassed," he said.

She laughed at herself and pushed the plate aside.

After he paid the check, he walked her to her car. "I'll follow you until I make my turnoff," he said.

"Okay. I'll go slowly for you so you can keep up," she said.

He laughed and then she stood still and looked up at him. "So, if you don't mind me asking, just how did you get over all those broken hearts?"

He was quiet a moment. It was dark in the parking lot. He looked down at her pretty, upturned face and sighed. "Who says I got over them?" he said softly. "Maybe there were one or two that made me cry like a girl every night for a year."

A very small smile curved her lips. "Well, hell's bells, Dakota. I believe that was not a bullshit answer." She gave his cheek a pat. "Thank you for that."

"Don't let this get around but some of my family calls me Cody."

That made her smile broadly. "See you around. Cody."

Dakota had not lied to Sid, he just managed to tidy and abbreviate his autobiography. He might as well have said, *Ah, I had my ups and downs*. He might be coming to terms with the truth for a long time to come. He'd found his teenage years torturous and humiliating and the pain of those years was still festering somewhere deep inside him. He'd been razzed, pranked and tricked. Pam Bishop really had hurt him, but it had not been as benign as he described. He'd asked her to a school dance and she had accepted, but as a joke. And when he went to meet her at the dance, she was with some other guy, a guy who had buddies. They all laughed at him for being stupid enough to think some cool girl might want to be his girlfriend. Dakota had gone alone, not with friends, and he had left alone, walking home. Miles and miles. With hot tears burning his cheeks, he schooled himself on what was and was not cool. There were other tricks and jokes, endless battering he took because everyone knew his father had secret friends, the kind only Jed could see or hear. He found his locker lined with tin foil, the kind Jed sometimes wore on his head to keep the government from reading his mind.

He felt like his throat ached in want of tears for four straight years. He'd remained mostly friendless and ashamed. And he was so angry.

And then he found his escape. In the military he was able to have his new beginning, spending the power of his anger on his physical performance. He became the Army's shining star and he was opened to a whole new world of friends. He might've been the only soldier he knew with a schizophrenic father but there were plenty of men and women escaping painful childhoods of poverty, abuse, homelessness and unhappy and disjointed families. He had taken comfort in their existence, feeling for once he was not the only one, the only square peg in a round hole.

There were women. Finally, there were women. In fact, most of them seemed honored to be noticed by him. He wasn't sure how he had gone from being the local town fool to the resident McHottie. He kept looking in the mirror and seeing the same long face, large teeth, bushy brows, nose with a bump that he found slightly too big, and yet the girls were suddenly breathless and eager. He even met a few who lasted, who he thought he might one day settle down with, who wrote or Skyped with him every day while he was deployed. There were also a few military women he spent time with here and there. It wasn't unusual to have a girl back in the States and a girl on deployment. It was just the way of the world, he thought.

Until he fell in love. That brought the whole world into focus for him. Colors became brighter, music held special meaning, words of love were not silly but profound. He'd taken a short gig as a recruiter near a university because it would give him a chance to pick up some credits toward his master's degree without being interrupted by deployment. He heard a speaker at the university who knocked him out. She was lecturing on human rights, and the second he saw her, heard her, he went into a trance. She was stunningly beautiful and brilliant. After the class broke up he approached her, stupid with lust and cunning, and said, "I'm an Army Ranger and I've been to most of the places you were talking about. Would you like to get a drink sometime and talk?"

She smiled and said, "What about food? Italian?"

"That would be perfect," he said.

Their connection was instant; their chemistry was powerful. He was a goner. They even had a great deal in common, given he had spent a large amount of his time in the Middle East and that was her humanitarian focus. It was perfect and, on a university campus, just another romance. To the students and professors, there was nothing unusual about them. He could almost forget that in the world at large they might be misunderstood.

Hasnaa was a Sunni Muslim; her parents immigrated from Jordan before she was born. She was finishing her PhD in international human rights, had worked as an interpreter for the UN and been in the peace corps. She wanted to dedicate her life to alleviating human suffering and raising the stature of women wherever she could. She sometimes wore a hijab. When he met her, her head was uncovered or he wouldn't have offered to buy her a drink.

On their first date she wore her hair free. She rarely wore a black scarf when she covered up, as she favored colors, particularly pastels. She explained to him the way she grew up. Her mother taught her that the hijab symbolized modesty and respect for their religion. Hasnaa honored the religion of her family even if she didn't practice strictly. She covered her head when she visited her parents, who lived in Los Angeles, when she worked alongside a male colleague who was Muslim, when she went to the mosque. But Hasnaa had her own interpretation of Islam, much to her parents' dismay. She had obviously pursued her education, worked and earned money, which she kept, and she refused to have an arranged marriage. It set her at odds with her parents for years. Then she introduced them to Dakota. Her parents, remarkably, did not die on the spot, but they were less than thrilled.

The passion between them was quick and hot and Dakota was consumed by it. At first he had trouble reconciling her Western ways, especially when seeing her wear the hijab, but he soon learned Muslim women were as individual as any others. She was a brilliant feminist, of course. He warned her that her parents would not approve of him; they would naturally prefer she accept a Muslim husband. She laughed wildly at that, asking him where she was supposed to find a Muslim man who would accept her as she was, so independent and demanding.

He told her he was in love with her before two months had passed. They began to discuss the challenges they'd face as a couple and how they were willing to find a way to bridge their diverse cultures. "Will *your* parents accept *me*?" she asked him. He had laughed before telling her about his father. "He could as easily take you for Abraham Lincoln as a Muslim woman."

Her mother could not hide that she liked Dakota, but

there was no question her father did not. Nothing mattered. In his thirty years, Dakota had never felt that kind of completeness. After being together just a few months, he would have walked through fire for her.

Then there was an attack. An act of terror.

She'd been in London at a meeting and had gone to dinner with a few colleagues afterward. Their restaurant had been targeted by a lone-wolf terrorist who drove his bomb-laden vehicle over the sidewalk and into the restaurant. Eleven people died and many were injured. His beloved Hasnaa was lost.

And so was Dakota.

Hasnaa's mother called to tell him the terrible news but he'd already heard from one of her colleagues. She was buried by her family in a sacred place and the prayers were offered in the Islamic tradition, but because Hasnaa had so many friends and colleagues who were not Muslim, her mother opened her home to them so they could gather and comfort each other.

That was the end of everything. There was no ongoing relationship or friendship with her family or her friends. He felt like he lived in a black hole, but he was back in training, then deployed, then sucked back into a world where someone in a chronic angry or dark mood didn't stand out. He was lured back in time to his first experience in the Army, when the best thing he could do to leave the past behind was to be the best, to achieve. One day, sometimes one hour at a time, he moved on.

He'd never talked about it. There was never an opportunity to say, "I was in love with the most incredible woman and she died a violent death, and I will never be the same."

When Sidney got home, the house was quiet except for the rhythmic purr of her brother's snore. He sat on the end of the sofa, feet up on the ottoman, book in his lap. She smiled to herself. If she'd been paying closer attention, she would bet he hadn't read an entire chapter in a month. But he was diligent. He kept trying. He probably got home from the bar at about eleven, took off his shoes, propped up his feet and read. He worked such long days, he never lasted long.

She touched Rob's knee and his eyes popped open. He stared at her for a second, then he grunted and sat up straighter. "Time's it?" he asked.

"Almost twelve." She sat down in the chair at the end of the sofa, kicked her shoes off and put her feet up. They each had their own ottoman, like an old married couple. "Are you home early or late?"

"I came home at dinnertime for about a half hour, got the boys fed and went back to work. They went to a ball game with the Rogers boys. I knocked off at eleven to be here when they get home. Mitch is closing the bar. Trace is cleaning up."

"If you'd told me, I could have arranged to be home for them," she said.

"No one really has to be home for them. They know how to unlock a door and lock it up again. But I wanted to hear about the game. And...you know...be here. Late for you, isn't it? You have a big crowd tonight?"

She shook her head. "Pretty regular. But I tricked Dakota Jones into helping out, then I had coffee and cake with him."

Rob looked startled. "Is that so?"

"Don't get that look," she said. "It was just coffee. He's been pestering me for a while now. It couldn't hurt."

Rob put his feet on the floor. "Sid, you don't have to be alone forever."

"Neither do you," she said.

"I'm not trying to be," he said. "I've had dates…"

"I think you've had hookups, but I make no judgment," she said. "But dates?"

"I'm low-key about it, that's all. I don't want the boys to get all up in my business about lady friends. It's not like I have a lot of spare time."

"You've had dates? Actual dates?" she asked. "Like where you go out to do something, like dinner or something?"

He let his chin drop in a brief nod.

"Like who?" she asked.

He gave a helpless shrug. "That woman from the kitchen supply warehouse—Tricia. I took her out three or four times. But she made it pretty clear she was looking for something with a future. Then there's a friend in Aurora who is the opposite. She doesn't want a serious relationship. That's working out a little better. It's been ten years," he said, speaking of his wife's passing.

Sid's mouth stood open. "You never once said…"

"What? That I'm ordering kitchen supplies and going out to dinner? Here's what I say, Sid. I say where I'm headed, approximately when I'll be back and that I'll have my cell if anyone needs me. If it's you or the boys, I pick up if I can. If it's work, I might call back in ten minutes. After I listen to the message."

"You never said you were going to see a woman!"

"Was that important?" he asked. "You've lived here with us for a little over a year. You've come a long way from that dark period. Your divorce has only been final for about a year and that was a challenge—that bastard was going to wring every last dime out of you. You were adamant that you weren't looking for another relationship and I don't blame you, after all you went through, though at the end you came out of that joke of a marriage with your purse. Thank God for decent judges. But you didn't want to meet men and you refused those who showed any interest.

"My situation is completely different," he went on. "I have a hundred reasons to be discreet. I'm a busy guy and a business owner. I have kids and I don't particularly want someone else's kids, too. I hate fix-ups and that's the first thing that happens when you admit you're open to the idea of dating. I avoid complicated women… Should I go on?"

"All this time, you've had a sex life," she said.

"All this time, for the last six or eight years, I've had a *private* life that sometimes includes sex, and not nearly as often as I'd like. What does this have to do with you? Have you been avoiding the opposite sex for me?" he asked.

"Of course not," she said. "It's just that…the first time I accept a date for a cup of coffee, I come clean! All this time you've been completely normal!"

"Normal for my situation, maybe. Not optimal but all right. Tell me about Dakota? Is he a nice guy?"

"Sure," she said. "Yes. You know he is."

"He's new around here but he has good connections. What made you decide to take a chance on him?"

"It was coffee. I didn't take that much of a chance."

"I knew we'd have to have this talk eventually. Sidney, I think it makes sense for you to be cautious and go slowly after what David did to you, but if I believed the majority of men were like him, I'd lose faith in all mankind. Just take your time. But when I think you might close yourself off from life, I could cry."

"There's more to life than finding the next man," she said.

"Way more, especially in your case," he said. "You gave up so much. He cost you so much…"

"So now I'm finding the balance in life. And apparently you already found it. But hey—the next time you have a date or whatever it is you have, just tell me you're going to the library and I'll be sure to cover for you."

Rob looked amused. "*You* should go to the library sometime, Sid. And I could cover for you."

"I think it's going to be quite a while before I need you for that."

The family is one of nature's masterpieces.

—GEORGE SANTAYANA

6

Connie Boyle was on his twenty-four-hour shift but he took a little personal time to go home. He wanted to talk to Sierra right away. He didn't think he should wait until his shift ended the next morning, although he did suspect it might be better if they slept together after having their talk.

"Well, isn't this a nice surprise," she said when he walked into the house they shared. She'd just been emptying the dishwasher. "Are you home for dinner?"

"I have a couple of hours," he said. "And we have that leftover lasagna."

"Let me make a salad to go with that and warm it up." She stopped what she was doing and looked at him. "Is something wrong?"

He sat down across the breakfast bar from her. Molly immediately stuck her cold nose into his hand for a pet. "Yeah. It was a bad day. There was an accident. A fatal accident. But there was a survivor. A four-month-old baby boy. We don't even know his name."

"Oh, Connie," she said. She walked around the breakfast bar and put her arms around him. "Sometimes I don't know how you do what you do."

"Sometimes I don't, either."

"Is he going to be okay? The baby?"

"Looks like it but he's getting an extrathorough workup."

"When did it happen?" she asked.

"This morning. There were three cars, out on the highway, but only one fatality. Plenty of injuries, though. And one car caught on fire. Everyone got out—just some minor burns. But the baby... There was just him and the mother and she died at the scene." He shook his head. "They're going to be looking for the family, but in the meantime, he's in emergency foster care. Tonight Rafe will take him home."

"Rafe?"

"Rafe and Lisa are certified foster parents."

"Those two," Sierra said. "Aren't they just pure gold? Three kids of their own, living on a fireman's wages, and they take in foster kids, too."

"Well, it's because they have three of their own that they're only signed on for emergency foster care. That means just until permanent placement is found."

"He probably has family, Connie. A dad at least. Grandparents. Aunties and uncles and cousins. If anything happened to Cal and Maggie, God forbid, I would raise Elizabeth."

"You're probably right. The county will be looking. Meanwhile, he'll be safe with Rafe and Lisa. But it brought something to mind I want to talk to you about. I'm going to ask you a very hard question but you can take your time on the answer."

"You really know how to scare me," she said.

"Oh, honey, don't ever be scared. Your answer is final with me, you know that. But here's what I want to know. Would you consider being a foster parent?"

She was clearly flabbergasted. "Huh?"

"I understand your worries about having children with me—primarily your father's mental illness in the gene pool. I am not worried about it, but I leave that up to you. I don't want you to ever go against your best judgment to keep me happy. But foster care might be something we can do together. If you like being around kids, that is. I see you with Elizabeth and you're so good with her. See, I'm already certified. And since I was single and working, I did what Rafe did—I was available for short-term coverage."

"I didn't know that," she said. "How could you be? You're not even married! Do they let single men be foster parents?"

He nodded. "And domestic partners and young couples and older couples and all kinds of unique situations. There's a pretty serious evaluation process but things like gender or sexual orientation are not disqualifiers—there are much more important considerations. They want to be assured of home safety, dependability, knowledge, and there's a background check. Then there are those home visits…"

"But you never had any foster kids…"

"Not in a while, but before we moved in together I had a few temporary kids. The longest was two weeks until his relatives were located. The youngest was four—what a pistol he was. Lisa helped out while I worked. I had a teenager once. A girl. That was the most complicated. I was obviously the only resort—they don't usually place a teenage girl with a bachelor but she was out of options. It was me or juvenile detention. Lisa and Rafe went to bat for me and promised they'd be around daily, and they were.

It was only a few days. They found her a good permanent foster home almost right away. She's doing great."

"Oh my God, I'm totally stunned," she said.

"I'm sorry, I never thought of it. For no particular reason, the county hasn't called me or Rafe and Lisa in a year. Since we met, it hasn't come up."

"Oh God, did it come up today?"

He briefly hung his head. "I had this little regret seeing Rafe hanging around the hospital waiting to take the baby home. And I thought, *Why didn't I talk to Sierra about this?* Because you love taking care of Elizabeth and we both wish we could have kids around but you don't think we should have them. And he's so... He's in good hands with Lisa and Rafe and their brood..."

"He's so what?" she asked.

"He's so vulnerable," Connie said. "This makes no sense but I asked myself, what if that was me? What if I had no parents? What if I lost everything in one second and my whole future depended on if a conscientious, reliable family took me in?"

"Oh my goodness, you're reeling me in... We're not even married!"

"We should probably do that one of these days, Sierra."

"We will!"

"Okay," he said. Because he never pushed her. Too much. "Will you think about it?"

"Connie, why are you doing this?"

"Well, obviously I can't bring home a kid without you being on board—you live here. This is your home."

"I mean, why are you a foster parent?"

He sighed and raked his hands across his chest. "You know, every now and then there's a kid. Maybe he was pulled out of a bad home situation, maybe there was a fire or accident, maybe a kid was abandoned. About ten years ago a guy took his son into a diner and left him in the booth to go out to his car to get his wallet and never came back. A little kid. Who does something like that? Anyway, every once in a while, there's a kid who needs a place to stay. I just like to help out. Want me to put that lasagna in the microwave?"

"Let me do it," she said.

When Sierra first moved to Colorado a little over a year ago, she stayed in a little one-room cabin at Sullivan's Crossing. Sully had the coffee going by around five in the morning and Sierra would join him in the general store for her early-morning coffee. A few days a week she'd go on to work at the diner in town. That coffee wasn't all that gave her a good start on the day; she was also fortified by her conversations with Sully. He had a way of zeroing in on her issues and making her think. Because of that, she'd occasionally still get up extra early and drive out to the Crossing just to have coffee with him.

She could see the light was on in the back of the store so she parked back there and gave a couple of warning knocks before opening the unlocked door. "Morning," she said. "You ever think about locking that door? I mean, it's dark as pitch and you're here alone..."

"And didn't you just bring your best sunshine into the room," Sully said. Molly rushed to him, wagging her tail madly. "And I suppose this freeloader wants breakfast, too?" he said, bending to give her a robust rub.

"If you wouldn't mind," Sierra said. "I'm working today so I'll swing by the house and drop her off on my way."

He poured her a cup of coffee. "Connie working?" he asked.

"He gets off in a few hours. He was on all night. Sully,

did you know Connie was a foster parent? I mean, a certified one?"

"Hmm, I don't believe I did. I know he helps out with kids all the time. I knew he'd had a couple stay with him just because he was helping out. I didn't know he was any kind of official foster parent."

"Rafe and Lisa take in foster kids—short-term. They have a four-month-old baby at the moment—his mother died in a car accident."

"That big one? Over on the freeway?"

She nodded, sipping her coffee. "Connie wanted to bring him home but he didn't want to do that to me. He asked me to think about signing up for that—to be a foster parent. I don't feel particularly qualified."

"What would qualify you?" Sully asked.

"Experience, for one thing."

He laughed. "Not very many regular parents start out with experience. I certainly didn't. I imagine they have a program. And probably a test," he added with a chuckle. He waited for her to say something. "I suppose you're about to tell me why this bothers you."

"It's personal," she said. "I'd like it to be between us. I mean, I talked to Connie but no one else. Do you still want to know?"

"I ain't gonna beg, but I don't usually find the need to talk about personal things. It's up to you."

"Well, it's like this. I know Connie loves kids. He's always helping out with the kids when they come to tour the fire department. He takes them on hikes and helps some learn to rock climb. But I don't think it's a good idea for me to have kids because, well, you know. Because of my dad. He's mentally ill. I worry about that gene running loose inside me. What if I passed it on?"

"There's any number of things you can pass on," Sully

said. "Not to mention all the things you might just end up with on account of fate or accident. Speaking of accidents—those happen all the time. You might have a perfect child and then lightning could strike him. But if it worries you, it's your right to play it safe. Is Connie giving you a hard time about it?"

"Oh, not at all," she said. "He totally understands. And so he came up with a possible solution—foster kids. But what if I fall in love with one and they have to move away?"

Sully just looked at her. "You been up all night trying to figure out all the bad things that could happen?" he asked her.

"I did toss and turn a lot," she admitted. "It's just that there was something I didn't tell Connie."

"Aw, now, don't be telling me secrets between a man and woman…" he whined.

"I didn't tell him that I'd love to have kids more than anything. I've always wanted kids. I love Elizabeth so much sometimes it aches in me. And I don't think I could have a child and live through something awful happening to him. And I don't think I can take care of a child, especially a baby, and give it up. But wouldn't it be selfish and wrong of me to have a child if there's a chance it could inherit a disease?"

"Lord above, girl. I didn't know you even knew how to think that much! You must be exhausted!"

"I am a little tired…"

"If I thought that much I'd have to sleep for a month!"

"You must have had some thoughts about children when you were having Maggie!"

"The problem was it never once crossed my mind. One day, real early in my marriage, Phoebe said, 'Congratulations, genius—you got me pregnant!' From that moment on is when I thought about it. By the way, no one was a worse parent than I was. Ask Phoebe sometime. And look at Maggie now. I suspect there are special angels assigned to the children of terrible parents."

"Drunks and children," Sierra said.

"How's that?"

"As the saying goes, God takes care of drunks and children. Some would argue they're practically one and the same."

"Sierra, you better talk to an expert about this," Sully said.

"You mean like someone in genetic counseling?" she asked.

"I was thinking more along the lines of someone familiar with your alcohol disease. Because I think this might be a symptom, this thinking till you pass out."

She sighed. "Of course you're right," she said. "It's one of my character flaws. I tend to create these complex scenarios in which I'm the star. Not usually in a good way."

"I'd say talk to your sponsor, Moody, but if he ain't even more impatient than me…" Sully let Beau and Molly out the back door for a little run. "If you like kids, maybe you should try something that puts you in touch with them but you can't keep 'em even if you want to. Here's what I think—one week working in a day care should cure you of that notion."

"There's a thought."

"And here's another thought. You in this with Connie for real?" Sully asked.

"Oh, yes," she said. "We're going to get married. We just haven't planned anything yet. There's been so much going on with Elizabeth coming and everything."

"I doubt Elizabeth has been standing in your way, but if you're in this with Connie for the long haul, for the love of God talk to him! Not some old man with a heart condition!"

She smirked at him. "Your heart is fine," she said.

"But I am old," he argued.

"No, Frank is old. You're just ornery."

Sierra knew she could get like this sometimes, get obsessed about something and work it like a hangnail. This thing about kids was doing it to her. Or maybe she was doing it to the thing about kids. Why she felt a desperate need to come to a decision, a conclusion, she couldn't explain. But Sully was right, it was one of her "issues."

By nine in the morning, the breakfast rush at the diner was nearly over. Connie stopped by on his way home. He sat at the counter. "Hi, babe. Will you buy me breakfast?"

"I will. What's it gonna be?"

"I want what you want me to want," he said.

She just smiled and shook her head. "I am the luckiest woman alive. Today you should have the breakfast burrito. Then you should go home and sleep."

"Last night wasn't bad. I got some sleep. I'm going to swing by Rafe's and see how the little guy is doing. Then I'm going to check on Sully and see if he needs help today. Then a good nap. Can you decide on dinner? If you bring home the groceries for it, I'll cook."

"You're going to see the baby?" she asked.

"I'm more going to see how Rafe and Lisa are doing. They might be in need of a nap themselves."

When she put his breakfast burrito in front of him, she said, "Just be sure you rest, Connie. You're always thinking about everyone else."

He gave her a flirty grin. "I think about you, that's for sure. And it doesn't make me feel like sleeping."

"I have a feeling you're going to be like a frisky pup when you're ninety," she teased.

"That's my plan," he said, grinning.

"Well, it's my plan, too, so you better take care of yourself. Nap, Connie. And I can make dinner."

When he'd finished his burrito, he put enough tip on the counter to cover its cost and make her smile. Then he kissed her goodbye and left, smiles all around the diner.

Sierra knew she could have talked this situation over with Cal. In fact, she could have talked it over with Cal and Maggie—if she remembered correctly, Maggie was off today. There was always Lola, who would be working in the diner this afternoon, and Lola was so wise. She could call Moody, her AA sponsor, or just go to a meeting and bare her soul. But she did none of these things. Instead, when she was off work at about two, she went to the Vadas house. She was relieved that Connie's truck was nowhere in sight. But there was a chance they were resting so she gave the door a couple of light raps.

Rafe opened the door. "Sierra! We weren't expecting you."

"I know. Connie told me about the baby and I thought I'd come by and see how you're doing." She lifted a take-out bag. "I brought you a cheesecake and some cookies for the kids."

"Oh, you shouldn't do that," Lisa said from behind her husband. She had a chubby baby wearing a onesie against her shoulder. "I've been trying to lose the same fifteen pounds for the last five years at least."

"You always look wonderful," Sierra said.

"That's what I tell her," Rafe said. "But I'm a husband, which means she thinks I'm a liar. Or an idiot."

"You're so sweet," Lisa said. "How thoughtful."

"I'm neither," Sierra said. "I'm nosy! I want to meet this little angel."

Lisa turned him around. He rubbed his little hands in his eyes, then he looked at Sierra and gave her a large toothless grin. "Aww," Sierra said. Then he promptly threw up on his powder blue onesie.

"Oh, no!" Lisa said. "Well, I guess we filled him up. I'm sorry, I—"

"Here," Sierra said, taking the baby and turning him so Lisa could mop his face and pajamas. "Oh, now you feel better, don't you? Elizabeth usually makes sure she gets it on me, but only if I'm wearing something clean and fresh. I think I've smelled like cheese since she came into my life."

"I'll get a new outfit," Rafe said, turning away from them.

"He has a little issue. He doesn't exactly burp," Lisa said.

"But he's okay, isn't he?" Sierra asked.

"He's amazing," Lisa said. "We're watching him very closely, and even though he's four months, he's sleeping on a SIDS monitor. In our room. There are no apparent injuries, thank God for that fantastic car seat. He's going back for another workup tomorrow."

"What in the world happened?"

"I think she was texting," Rafe said, coming back into the room with a clean outfit. "Based on what the other involved drivers said."

Sierra backed up to the couch, put the baby down and began unfastening his pajamas, peeling them off like an old pro. And the baby giggled. There is no sound more invigorating than the helpless giggle of a baby, so Sierra started talking to him—in his language. He giggled all the harder. He laughed all the way through the changing of his clothes, then she picked him up and cuddled him. She looked up at Rafe and Lisa. "Texting?"

"She was awfully young," Lisa said. "Not that texting while driving is limited to the young. She was barely twenty."

"Oh my God, just a child herself. Do you know any more about her? Was she married? Is there family?"

"The highway patrol is investigating and they know where this baby is—I'm sure we'll hear something when there's something to hear."

"Is there a chance he'll be traumatized from the accident? From what he saw and heard?" Sierra asked.

Lisa shook her head. "I don't think so. He might be startled by loud noises or something, but any child would be."

"There's no evidence to suggest he'll remember or understand," Rafe said. "He's just a few months."

"He feels so cuddly and sweet," Sierra said. "I think Connie so wanted to bring this little guy home. I didn't know until last night that Connie is part of the foster care program."

"A lot of us are," Rafe said. "Fortunately, we don't get that much business. This is the second time we've had a baby stay with us."

"Connie asked if I'd think about going through their program so we could be involved if there's a need. But I don't know…" She jiggled the baby and absently kissed his head. "I'd be afraid to get attached."

"Well, we do," Lisa said. "But kids don't get into foster care because they're looking for a vacation. They're in need of affection and stability. Sometimes they're in need of boundaries, a little discipline. Love and patience and direction. There have been a couple we kept track of for a while. They weren't with us long enough to miss us too badly but I felt pretty sure we gave them love and security while they were here."

"She doesn't like to admit it but she cries when they leave us," Rafe said.

"Well, if you're invested enough to help them, then you're invested enough to hurt a little when it's time to give them up, but I always felt they were going to a good place, a safe and loving home," Lisa said.

"Doesn't it get a little crowded?" Sierra asked. Their house was very comfortable, but small. They both laughed.

"Oh, yes," Lisa said. Then she sat down on the sofa beside Sierra and they visited for a while. Even though Rafe was Connie's closest friend and they'd socialized as couples, Sierra was learning things about Lisa for the first time. They'd married young and had their first child right away but the second pregnancy was very slow to come, no logical reason why. Then two in a row—bam! It was between the first and second that Lisa and Rafe got interested in foster care. Once in the program, they just couldn't say no to a child in need of a home.

Lisa was a nurse who went to a part-time schedule when their family grew. She worked in a doctor's office, which really came in handy with three kids and the occasional extra. With Rafe's schedule and time off, she was able to work about twenty hours a week. Their dream was a large plot of land, something like what Connie had built his house on. "The kids need a dog and maybe a couple of horses, and I need a vegetable garden."

"Have you ever seen Sully's garden?" Sierra asked. "It's like a small farm and he's passionate about it. Lately he's needed a little help, but he resists. If you ever want to see it, just let me know."

"I'd love to," she said.

"Babe, I'm going to start dinner," Rafe said from the kitchen.

"Oh my God, is it dinnertime? I have to get groceries and get home!" Sierra said.

"Don't panic," Lisa said with a laugh. "Our dinners get earlier and earlier. Pretty soon they'll be late lunches. But with three kids to get ready for bed—oops, make that four—we're so anxious for bedtime to finally come it's just ridiculous. Plus Sarah, our eight-year-old, has homework every night, if you can believe it." Lisa put out her hands. "You're going to have to give him up if you plan to go shopping."

"He feels like an appendage," she said. "He's sound asleep. Should I put him down?"

"Nah, he could do with extra holding. He might not realize it, but he's been through a lot."

Sierra left the Vadas home feeling refreshed. New. She loved their life in their too-small house with too many kids. Of course, Sierra wasn't completely convinced—she didn't think she'd have a brood. A couple might be nice. A garden—she'd have started one if it wasn't for Sully's. She liked seeing the elk in the yard some mornings or blocking the road.

It was such a nice day, no rain for a change, that she bought hamburger and buns. Too early for corn, she got some zucchini, an onion, mushrooms and new potatoes to put on the grill. And when she walked in, she found Connie with his cell phone in his hand, watching the door. The house was tidy, there were vacuum cleaner tracks on the carpet and the kitchen was spotless.

"I was just going to text you," he said.

She put her grocery sacks on the counter and then put her arms around Connie. "We've been lazy," she said. "We have to decide on details about a wedding and get married. This is silly. We want to and our families are getting edgy. Do you think they're afraid we're going to split if we're not official?"

His big hands circled her waist. "It's already official for me, but I'm off tomorrow if you feel like getting a license." He gave her a look. "What happened to get you in a hurry?"

"I'm ready," she said. "I want us to be a family. I'm not sure what kind of family—I'll look into that foster care program, but I'm not sure that's where we're going. Let's start with me and you. I'm very sure of that."

I have learned that to be with those I like

is enough.

—WALT WHITMAN

7

Sid had a real soft spot for rich chocolate cake and vanilla ice cream. And maybe a little extra whipped cream. And it appeared she was growing a soft spot for Dakota. He'd logged on four weeks at the soup kitchen, including one Saturday night that Sid didn't go. That meant three Saturday nights of cake, ice cream and conversation with Sid. On her Saturday night off she had taken the boys to a concert, some band they were into, but she had to stay away from them and their friends so it didn't really appear they were chaperoned.

"But was it fun?" he asked.

"Sorry, what?" She put her hand behind her ear as if she were deaf.

"Never mind." He laughed. "Listen, Sid, I've invested four Saturday nights, many huge slices of chocolate cake, a dozen beers and burgers, and that's just in the last month. And you haven't given me any indication I'm making progress."

"What kind of progress?" she asked, licking her fork.

"There's no agenda, Sid. I like you and you like me. Most people would be wrestling like crazy lovers do."

"And you think that's what I'm looking for because…?"

He leaned toward her. "You're an adult woman in her thirties."

"I told you, I don't date."

"Yes, you do. You dragged me to a soup kitchen—it was a lure. To earn you I had to display my charitable side, but I screwed up your plan. I like the place. And *this* is a date. Not much of one, but a date. Last week after cleanup, while you were going deaf, I had coffee and cake with Sister Mary Jacob. In fact, I'm thinking I might be more successful if I put the moves on her."

Sid laughed.

"Something has come up," he said. "My sister has decided it's time to get married. Sierra and Connie. They've been together about a year, lived together almost as long and they're finally doing it. It's going to be small. Very small. Family and close friends. No big event but a nice small party. Be my date."

"Really? You need a date?"

"Sid, you know Sierra. You're friends. You know Connie and Sully and a couple of the firefighters who will be there. I hear Connie's mom and brother will come. Be my date."

"What's the price of admission?" she asked with a half smile.

"There's no price," he said. "I might lose my mind and beg sometimes but you will always be completely safe with me. Always. I won't even hold your hand without permission."

"I don't know whether to be flattered by your restraint

or disappointed that I haven't made you lose your mind yet."

He looked at her for a long moment. "Mary Jacob was a more accommodating date."

"What did you two talk about?" she asked.

"Well, the homeless situation. And then she asked me for money or to find people who had money. Then she talked about some of the volunteers she knows. I asked her what she did for fun and she said she was doing it. She's not a martyr, you know—she's doing exactly what she'd be doing if she weren't a nun. In fact, she's only a nun because at this point she can't come up with a reason to give it up. There were some priests, cardinals and popes who she prayed on a long time, apparently to no effect—her words. She's basically a tough old broad."

"I know," Sid said. "I love her. Not Mother Teresa, for sure. She's more like Ma Kettle."

He smiled around a forkful of cake. "You're not old enough to remember Ma and Pa Kettle."

"Neither are you. You know who would play Mary Jacob in the movie? Shirley MacLaine. Except for the red hair. Mary Jacob is a big woman. Would you have taken her to the wedding?"

"I would, except she'd be working the crowd for donations."

"Well, you didn't give her money, did you?" she asked.

"Of course I gave her money," he said. "She was staring at me over that coffee cup, those bushy brows moving around, expressing her innermost thoughts…"

"You should think it through," Sid said. "It's a very worthy cause but you can't fund it. You work hard for your money."

"I know. I'm not going to. But I'm going to hit up some people I know. And I bet there are other ways to get her what she needs. Sid, it's been a long time since I was forced to do something I didn't want to do. And I learned a lesson."

"When was the last time?" she asked. "Just out of curiosity."

"Ah...well, hell, what can it hurt. In the Army I refused a direct order and got in a ton of trouble."

"What's a ton of trouble in the Army?"

"Jail," he said. "Or, as we so affectionately called it, the brig. But I was determined in the moment that I had to do it. It didn't look great in my file. But I think I'd do it again."

"That was very brave of you," she said.

"People do it all the time—go to jail for what they believe in. Journalists do it. Protesters do it. I bet you a hundred dollars Mary Jacob has been arrested." Then he grinned. "Tell me about the boys. Tell me about your brother. Tell me again why you don't have a boyfriend."

So she told him about her nephews and her brother, just brief sketches, but he was very interested. He reciprocated by telling her things she didn't already know about Cal and Sierra. But then she asked the question he knew would come eventually. "Will your parents be at the wedding?"

"I don't think Sierra will invite them. My father suffers from dementia of sorts. Not Alzheimer's, but he's easily confused and travel with him would be a nightmare. It's supposed to be a happy occasion, after all."

"Why are they having the wedding now?" she asked.

"I think it's a time thing—as in they don't have that much of it. And gathering what there is of our family isn't easy. Maggie has her practice in Denver, Cal has a practice here, when the Crossing is full of campers it's hard for Sully to close up shop and in summer Connie has both the fire department and search and rescue duty. And they've decided to become foster parents."

Sid's eyes popped up from her plate. They were round and startled. "Huh?"

"Yeah, some of their couple friends do that and I guess Connie has been through the certification program. Friends they sometimes hang out with have had foster kids and Sierra thinks it's a good idea. I've seen her with Cal's little girl—they're both great with kids."

"Wow," she said. "You make it seem like the whole family is virtuous."

"It's a trick, Sid," he said. "You'll fall in love with me because I gave Sister Mary Jacob a hundred bucks."

She made a *pffftt* sound with her lips. "Not for a hundred bucks I won't."

When he walked her to her car, he grabbed her hand and she allowed it. When they were beside her car he swung her around and pulled her against him. Closely against him. She looked up at him.

"You said I would always be safe with you," Sid said quietly.

"Try to get away," he said.

She pulled back and was instantly free.

"I'm not taking hostages, Sid."

Without warning she flung herself against him, into his arms, dug her fingers into the thick hair at the back of his head and smothered him in a kiss so sweet he was breathless. For a second, shock kept him from reacting. Then he circled her waist with his arms and held her, moving over her mouth with passion and urgency. The taste of her, more chocolate than anything, turned him on and blew his mind. If there had been a private room nearby, maybe she wouldn't have been all that safe. And neither would he.

"Whoa," he said, tightening his arms. "You are definitely worth waiting for."

"I think you're manipulating me," she whispered against his lips.

"I wouldn't even know how," he said, kissing her again. And again, that kiss was hot and crazy. He really wanted her. And yet this was not the time or place. "We're in a parking lot," he said. "We have three choices. We can climb in my truck and make out, we can go somewhere and be alone or we can table this for a while."

She relaxed in his arms. "I'm taking door number three. Under the circumstances."

"I have my own place."

"My brother is probably expecting me."

"I still have my own place," he said.

"It'll keep." She gave his cheek a pat. "I'll go to the wedding with you, but only so you don't have to be embarrassed by having a nun for a date."

"Okay," he said hoarsely. "Can I at least have your phone number now?"

Sid was a little dreamy while driving home. She was having a conversation with herself. Aloud. She'd been doing this since grade school. Eventually she was overheard, especially in the computer lab, and learned she wasn't the only person who did that. She'd ask and answer the questions as they came. Usually mathematical or theoretical, but ultimately questions in every category. It was how she worked things out.

What do you think you're doing, Sidney?

She was hooking up.

But she wasn't good at hookups. She hadn't had very many. And the one she did have turned into a husband! A very bad husband. She wasn't about to let that happen again. She wasn't crazy.

That looked a little crazy out there in the parking lot,

spread on him like butter on bread. But she couldn't help herself. She liked him.

Did she ever like David in that way? She couldn't remember. She'd asked herself a hundred times—was her heart broken because she loved him so much or because he'd betrayed her in so many ways?

In the beginning, before they married, she was very taken with him. He was sweet and attentive. There was her father's death, and David really hung in there.

Uh, he went to the funeral and then didn't he have finals? Or midterms? Or whatever it was, it was so critical.

Everything was so critical…

But she had signed on for it.

She thought that's what people did for each other.

He kept saying, "I'm not doing this for me, Sidney. I'm doing this for us."

There was never any "us."

She gave him seven years!

She supported him for seven years but she was doing exactly what she wanted to be doing.

Was that the problem? The weak link? That she was so involved in her work?

I hate to break it to you but he could have started being unfaithful before you were married and how would you know? her inner voice asked. *Did you ever once check?*

Oh God, I can never be in a relationship again because I can't be one of those women who reads his texts in the dark of night or follows him to see if he's really going back to work!

Then the idea of a garbage collector makes perfect sense…

But he's not really a garbage collector. Well, he really is, but that doesn't mean anything at all—it's his job, not his identity.

Was that where she'd gone wrong with David? Putting too much importance on the importance he put on himself? Didn't her degrees take as much dedication and time and intelligence? She was a scholar! A scientist!

He said she was dull. Boring.

That was name-calling.

It was true.

Sid took a deep, calming breath. There were three things that decimated her about her failed marriage. That David had lied to her for so long and she'd been clueless, that she suddenly realized that not only was she completely alone, she'd been completely alone all along, and third, there wasn't much about her to be attracted to—she was boring. A completely boring computer nerd. That she was a computer nerd on the cutting edge of cyberscience, information technology and artificial intelligence didn't make her a more interesting person. If she and David went out with his friends, doctors who could accomplish complex surgeries and save lives, doctors who would cure diseases, they would invariably ask her, "Listen, I'm having this problem with my operating system…" or, "I don't think I have a good cloud coverage setup…"

Yes, it had all been quite painful, to never feel a part of his life or even of her own life.

But things weren't exactly like that now. Right now she *was* connected. It had been like training for a race— she came out of her quiet, preoccupied, serious place and learned to be more outgoing. She liked people, after all. Anyone who had engaged in a long and complex course of study could tell you about how easy it is to become hyperfocused. She'd had to learn the first way in order to excel in math and then computers, so she had to likewise learn the more extroverted way, getting out of her head a little and appreciating her enhanced social skills.

A few months with Rob and she hadn't been lonely anymore. A few months behind the bar as a bartender and server and it brought such a relief to feel that people actually liked her. Of course, she felt they didn't know the real her—the boring, fixated, dorky person she had left resting inside.

But there was no denying she still grieved the loss of her science. When she was making great strides in the lab, experiencing breakthroughs and making discoveries that could change the world, she felt huge. Inside, of course. But huge and important and confident. With her meltdown, she lost that. She wished she had not let it happen, but she wouldn't know how to stop all the side effects of her personal crisis. Yes, even the most pragmatic scientist is vulnerable to emotional calamity.

She fled to Rob to rebuild herself from the ground up. Then Dakota came along and she felt an instant zing of energy. Well, she must have been ready. She was a woman, after all. She hadn't stopped producing hormones. There was a certain biological science to it, wasn't there? There were lots of theories about why a certain man appealed to a certain woman. About what made all manner of creatures desire the opposite sex. With whales, the males wanted the strongest, fittest females because reproduction was difficult and many cows died giving birth, which made perfect sense to Sid, considering the calf weighed about six hundred pounds. But the whales didn't just mate with the most available female.

And so it was with men and women, she assumed. The right one at the right time with all the right biological configurations from looks to scent to prowess. Whatever the magic was, Sidney went to bed thinking she'd grow old in her brother's house playing Auntie Sid and woke up one morning finding herself wickedly attracted to Dakota Jones.

It was going to be complicated.

Ever since the night his tire had been slashed, Dakota had been parking in a more public place on the street when he went to the bar for dinner. He risked running into Alyssa but he wasn't about to sacrifice any more of his Jeep SUV to the manic charms of Miss Neely. And sure enough, Alyssa was sweeping the sidewalk in front of the beauty shop as he walked up. She stopped and leaned on her broom. He thought briefly of crossing the street, but that would be just plain cruel. He walked right up to her, smiling.

"Hi there, Alyssa," he said. "Getting ready to close?"

"I have one more client. You can come to the shop for a trim if you like. I think I've gotten the message."

"Hmm? What's that?"

"You're all trimmed up but I haven't seen you. I get it—you found another place to get your hair cut. So I tried letting you know that I'm available to date if you're interested, but you ran for your life. It wasn't really necessary to hide your car to keep me from bumping into you at the bar."

"I think you have the wrong impression," he said. "I don't believe I ran for my life—I got a job. And I don't think I hid my car. I'm not parking behind the businesses anymore, that's for sure. I had some damage one night. I'm sticking to streetlights."

"Damage? In Timberlake?" she asked, surprised.

"It's all right, I took care of it. Are there lights where you park?"

"Just over the back door, but we've never had a problem. So...you weren't avoiding me?"

"Not at all. Just going about my business."

"Ha, that's a relief," she said, smiling. "I thought you'd made up your mind about me before even getting to know me! In that case—"

"Alyssa, I'm not available," he said. "I'm seeing someone. If you're looking for a guy who's available, it's just not me. I hope I didn't mislead you."

"But you just got to town!"

"A couple of months ago," he said. "Plenty of time to meet someone."

"Well, for God's sake, who? In *Timberlake*!"

He couldn't help but laugh. "I guess the possibilities are pretty slim, aren't they."

"So, who?"

"Come on," he said with a laugh. "It's just friendly, but I'm trying to turn the heat up. The point is, my interest is somewhere else and it wouldn't be nice of me not to tell you that."

"I thought you heard something…" Her voice dwindled off and she looked at him nervously.

"What did you think I'd heard?" he asked.

"Nothing," she said. "A couple of years ago there was some nasty gossip about me. That's hard in a small town."

Dakota frowned. He assumed it was the usual sexual innuendo. Maybe some of those Vegas trips with the girls got caught on an iPhone when they were compromised. Women really took a hit for all the same things that tended to make men look like studs. He was instantly sympathetic. "I'm sorry, Alyssa. No, I didn't hear anything. But gossip isn't likely to affect me, anyway. You seem like a real nice girl but I have something going on."

"But with who?" she tried again.

"Give a guy a break, would you?" he said, laughing. "I need a little room to work my charm."

"Is that so," she said, not particularly amused.

"Hey, I'm sorry you're upset with me. We're neighbors now. No reason to be pissy."

"I'm not," she said, but definitely was.

"I'm going to grab dinner," he said. "I'm hungry. I'll see you around. Take care." He started to walk away, then he turned back to her. "Oh. I've been getting my trims at the barbershop. The only reason I came into your shop the first time is they were closed. I'm really not avoiding you."

He walked another half block and just before he could cross the street he was stopped by a woman's voice calling his name from the darkness. "Dakota."

He stopped and Neely stepped out onto the sidewalk from the storefront where she had been caught in the shadows. It was not yet dark but the sun was setting and the shadows were long. *Is there a full moon or something?* he wondered. First Alyssa and then Neely? He put his hands in his pockets and looked at her, frowning.

"I guess you're still upset with me," she said. "I know, I know, I was aggressive. It's not typical, I promise. But you're not typical, either, Dakota. You didn't give me any encouragement at all."

"And I suppose that made you angry?" he said, scowling a little.

"Nah, just disappointed. I want to apologize."

"And maybe offer up seventy dollars for the tow and two hundred dollars for the new tire? One was slashed, the rest were just deflated."

She frowned and shook her head. "What are you talking about?"

"My tire was slashed, Neely."

She gasped. "You can't imagine I would do something like that!"

"It was a pretty strange encounter we had. When I got

back to my car, that's what I found. No other cars back there were damaged. And I had rejected you."

"You think I'd damage your car because you didn't take me up on my very slutty offer? Listen, I'm embarrassed, but I'm not a vandal. I wouldn't do that."

"But you would lure a guy into a dark alley—"

"Stop!" she said, holding up a hand. "It was impulsive and stupid and regrettable but I backed right off when you made yourself clear. I was humiliated and couldn't even think of showing my face around here for about a month."

"Why should I believe you?" he asked.

"You can check and see if I have any kind of record, I suppose, which I don't. But I swear to you, I'm not that kind of person. I'd never hurt a fly."

He just continued to stare at her.

"Well, I've certainly learned my lesson, Dakota. And I'm sorry about the tires but I can't imagine who would do that. You have someone pissed off at you?"

"Besides you? No one I can think of. And I did call the police."

"They never contacted me. I suppose you told them…"

"Of course."

She ran a hand straight up her forehead, combing her hair with her fingers. "Oh dear God. It's been such a long time since I was this stupid."

"Let's call it done," Dakota said. "I don't have proof. But it was a reasonable assumption."

"Can we start over?" she asked.

"No," he said, shaking his head. "I'm not going to just forget the experience that quickly. But what we can do is move on."

"We'll be friends?" she asked.

"I don't think so. But we'll behave ourselves."

"Certainly," she said. And then suddenly her face fell.

"Oh God. Oh, no. Oh, Dakota…" Her eyes were large and childlike. "What if…? Oh God, there's this guy. A man I was seeing for a very short period of time. He was intense and a little off and I stopped seeing him almost immediately. I think we went out a few times in a couple of weeks and he was ready to take ownership. I had to block his calls, block his emails, and I did see him hanging suspiciously close to my usual haunts."

"Stalking you?" Dakota asked.

"Almost but not quite. I talked to a friend who's a police officer and the guy hadn't done anything scary or threatening and I couldn't get a restraining order. My friend said I was doing the right thing—staying alert and staying away. He never crossed the line, never damaged my car, broke into my house or tried to corner me or anything. But what if he—"

Dakota just waited, frowning.

She took a deep breath. "What if he was following me and saw us together and retaliated against *you*?"

"I think you better talk to the police in Timberlake," he said. "Tell them about the possibility."

"I don't want to make trouble for him if he's innocent. That might come back on me, stir him up, you know."

"Well, someone isn't innocent, Neely. I had some significant damage to my car. So will you do that for me? Tell the police of this possibility? Before it happens again or gets worse?"

"Sure," she said. "Oh God, I'm so sorry, Dakota. Please say you'll accept my apology."

He gave her a single nod. "No more tricks, Neely," he added sternly.

She put up her hands. "Of course not. Um, I was just going to grab a chicken Caesar…"

He gave her a forced smile. "Then I have an appointment," he said, not even bothering to conceal his irritation.

"Oh, for God's sake! I'll sit at a table or booth, as far away as I can get!"

"I'm going to have dinner at the diner tonight," he said. "Take care." He turned and walked down the street. Though it was tempting, he did not look over his shoulder. He went to the diner and found Lola was behind the counter.

"Hey," he said. "I don't see much of you here."

"Two afternoons a week. It's not for the money, I assure you. On my diner nights, I can feed the boys here." She indicated two young men in a booth by the window. "On nights Trace works at the bar and grill, he usually gets a burger, but the only time he gets vegetables is when I give him dinner. Cole is a little harder to feed—he's nineteen."

"I guess I didn't know Trace was your son," Dakota said. "I eat at the bar a couple of times a week. I see him all the time. Good-looking kids, Lola."

"Yeah, they're gorgeous," she said. "But they're also good. I think. So what can I get you?"

"Just coffee. And I'll look at a menu, but it would break Sid's heart if I let someone else feed me."

"Sid?" she asked, lifting eyebrows. "You and Sid?"

"Well, maybe you shouldn't say anything like that since she hasn't agreed to go out with me yet. But that hasn't stopped me from asking a lot."

"I love Sid," she said, grabbing a cup and pouring coffee. "She's a sharpie, that one. She's helping Trace with physics."

Dakota was taken aback. "Wow. Bartenders are better educated than I thought," he said.

Lola laughed. "She said she took a lot of math courses

in college and she kind of wanted to see if she remembered any of it."

"Huh," he said, impressed.

"She remembers apparently," Lola said. "Excuse me." She turned and went to check on the boys.

Dakota took out his cell phone and made use of that phone number he'd recently scored. I know Neely went in the bar. Will you text me when she leaves and the coast is clear?

He sipped his coffee. A minute later he had a return text. Yes. You're pathetic.

Family connexions were always worth preserving, good company always worth seeking.

—JANE AUSTEN

8

Dakota took his usual seat at the bar.

Sidney gave the space in front of him a wipe and she was grinning. "Have you been hiding in your car? Slinked down in the seat so no one would see you?"

"No, I went to the diner and had coffee with Lola. I thought about having my dinner there but I know how much you like watching me eat."

"It is a particular thrill," she said. "Aren't you being a little ridiculous? Can't you keep the women at bay?"

"I had a doubleheader tonight. First Alyssa caught me on the sidewalk and she wanted a little showdown. Apparently she's been worried that I was avoiding her because of some gossip I might've heard. I didn't hear any. I told her I'm seeing someone."

"Who?" Sid asked, putting his beer in front of him.

"You wouldn't know her," he said, lifting his mug and taking a big sip. "Ahh," he said. "Then, after I got away from Alyssa, I ran into Neely a little down the block. Call me crazy but I think she was lurking. Hiding in the darkness. I didn't see her, then she popped out of thin air. She said she wanted to apologize for her aggressiveness and she wanted to start over. I can't think of a scarier thought. There's something about her… She came up with this story that some guy she barely dated was practically stalking her and he might've been the one to—" Dakota cleared his throat.

"You're hiding something," Sid said.

"Can I have a Juicy Lucy, please?" he asked nicely.

"Yes, when you tell me what you're hiding."

"Why do you care?"

"I might have to rethink this wedding date if you're sketchy."

"I'm not the sketchy one!" he insisted.

He looked at her. She had one hand on her hip and a stern expression that said she wasn't buying any of his bullshit and suddenly he wanted to look at that face every day for the rest of his life. How that happened, right then, right there, he had no idea. He could not lie to her. He sighed. "That night that Neely tricked me with her non-existent flat tire, when I went back to get my car after dinner, one of my tires was slashed. The other three were deflated. Four flats."

"But you didn't come back here," she said, perplexed.

"No. I called my brother and a tow truck. We talked to Stan, the chief. I didn't want to mention it."

"Why, for Pete's sake?"

"I didn't want to seem complicated…"

She laughed a little. Then she turned and put in the order for his hamburger. She checked around the bar to see if anyone needed anything, then returned to Dakota. "You are such a *girl*," she said.

"I am not a girl!"

"We're all complicated, just in different ways. I admit, I have never grappled with the problem of having many handsome men want me," she said.

"And there is no explanation for that," he said, grumbling. "Can I walk you home tonight?"

"Or drive me home," she said. "But don't you have an early start tomorrow?"

"Don't worry about me," he said, though he was experiencing a little surprise. *I must have finally suffered enough*, Dakota thought. *God is throwing me a bone.* "So," he said, changing the subject, "I learned you're helping Lola's kid with physics…"

"I am. Trace. Good kid. Very smart. He works hard in here. He mostly busses and does dishes but every now and then Rob lets him take orders."

"You're good at physics?" he asked, making a face.

"High school physics, Dakota. I'm surprised I can even remember any of it. I think he's teaching me more than I'm teaching him. But that's the key—finding a way to figure it out. If we all went into a subject already knowing everything, there would be nothing to learn. Of course he doesn't already know it—that's why he's studying it."

"You would make a good teacher," he said.

"I'm not patient enough," she said. "About tonight—I don't get off work till nine. And I have to go right home. I want to make sure the boys are in, chores and homework done, that sort of thing."

"You could go inside, check on them, then come back outside to kiss your new boyfriend," he said with a grin.

"I could probably do that, if I had a boyfriend. But not for too long. We get up early, too." Then she turned away and went to serve the bar.

Dakota sat at the bar for two and a half hours while Sid finished her shift, then Rob came from the back wearing a short apron and relieved her of her duty. Dakota nearly leaped to his feet. Then, with a hand on her elbow, he walked with her down the street to where his SUV was parked.

"I can't believe you're letting me take you home," he said.

"It's four blocks. You're going to have to work your charms fast."

"When you check the kids, what does that mean?" he asked her.

"They might need something or have some crisis, like an assignment due tomorrow that they haven't started or something they were supposed to buy but didn't or need a signed permission slip. But Rob usually takes care of those things over dinner. He takes a break from about five till six, maybe more, maybe less. He brings dinner home, goes over the day with them. Sometimes he has to run to the store for them. Sometimes he has to pick them up from practice—baseball or track. We really need another car—Finn is ready to take on some of this stuff. Then it's back to the bar till closing. One of us is usually available to be with the boys with just a few gaps here and there."

"A working family," he said. "I suppose this is how it will be with Elizabeth."

"It's good for kids to grow up with working parents— children emulate their parents. They may not listen to them but they'll copy them, whether they want to or not. That can have a downside if they see their parents doing awful things. Or sometimes there's an upside to seeing their parents doing awful things—they're determined to break out of the dysfunction."

Dakota wondered what she'd think of the way he grew up. He wasn't sure he wanted to know. But his dad was crazy and his mother was a "stay-at-home mom," and that hadn't given him any advantages.

She gave him directions and within a couple of minutes he was parked in front of her house.

"Let me get the lay of the land and then I'll come back and let you know what's going on. If everything is cool, we can talk awhile," Sid said. She jogged up the walk and let herself in.

We talked all night. I don't want to talk anymore, Dakota thought.

Within five minutes she was back. She jumped into the front seat, leaned over the console and kissed him. Not exactly a deep and passionate kiss but not just a starter kiss, either. She pulled away and just smiled at him.

"Cheater," he said. "You brushed your teeth."

"I thought you might appreciate the effort."

"Tell me something, Sid. When did you decide you were going to give me a chance?"

"I'm not exactly sure. You've grown on me. I think maybe you're nice. You worked at the soup kitchen without me. You're consistent—that's a good thing. You make me laugh."

"I've been working that angle," he said.

"I like that," she said.

"It sure felt like that wasn't going to be enough," he said.

"Maybe the rest of it has nothing to do with you," she said. She turned to look at him. "I'm not a little girl, Dakota. I want to have a normal life, too."

His eyes grew large. "What's a normal life to you?"

"Oh, nothing extraordinary. Just friends, family, work I like, a little social life, maybe a guy. You should get a medal. You're the first guy I've even considered."

"I'm honored."

She grew serious. "I'd like to tell you something about

my divorce. It might help you to understand why I'm like I am when it comes to relationships. I don't know who knows—I don't talk about it. Rob might've said things, I don't know."

"I don't gossip," he said.

"I met my husband when we were both in school. He was a medical student, poor, so I worked while he studied. That was our arrangement and I was happy to do it. The moment he finished his residency, he left me. He said he hadn't been happy and he'd been with someone else. I had no idea. I fell apart. I'm sorry that you have to be on the receiving end of this, but the fact is, I might never trust a man again. But over a year later, I'm not sure I want to live my whole life without one, either. There it is—if you have expectations, you could be very disappointed. You might do better with Alyssa or Neely."

He put an arm around her and pulled her a little closer. "That's not gonna happen. I'm sorry about the husband, Sid. I get it. Someone left me suddenly—I had no warning, either. It was hell."

"You weren't married, though," she said.

"No," he confirmed. "It was still terrible. But I don't have any expectations for us. A few hopes, maybe…"

"What is it you hope for, Dakota?"

"Lots of laughs," he said. "Fun. Honesty." He paused. "Nudity."

A spurt of laughter escaped her and she turned her head to look up at him. "A man of simple needs," she said.

"Sid, you're pretty and I like talking to you. I now realize I like kissing you. I'm not looking for a woman to have my babies. Actually, I'm not planning on babies, so that's a problem you don't have to consider. I think the best-case scenario is we have some fun together and I have someone besides my brother or sister to knock around with. And, of course, the nudity." He lifted her chin with a finger and put a soft kiss on her lips. "And you sound like a woman of simple needs, too. I will be trustworthy even though you aren't planning to trust me."

"I never lie," she said. "Actually, it's a problem sometimes. People don't really always want the truth."

"It beats the alternative," he said. "Let's get in the back seat."

"Okay," she said. "But just for a little while. I have an early morning and so do you."

They got out of the SUV and reentered in the back seat. He immediately filled his arms with her. "What do you have to do in the morning?" he asked.

"Get the boys off to school. Some days I drive them. Rob works late so I let him sleep. Then there are chores, maybe errands, work at—"

He'd had enough of her schedule and swept down on her mouth, hushing her and enjoying the minty fresh taste of her, pulling her tight against him. She wriggled herself closer still and no doubt was aware of his excitement. He thought it was promising that without even the benefit of groping he was hard as a bat. But of course he was thinking about the groping to come. And he was a little uncomfortable, bent in his jeans, sucking the hell out of her mouth.

Dakota knew if he suggested anything more she would say no so he just made the most of the closeness, the kissing, the squirming. Then she broke away from his mouth, a little breathless. "I've never kissed a man with a beard before."

"How do you like it so far?" he asked.

"I think I like it."

"You're going to love it later," he said. He slid a hand over her breast.

"I think you're getting a little ahead of me," she whispered, but she dropped her head back and sighed.

"You're so controlling," he said.

"I know. You're going to love it later," she said. "Sunday is the wedding."

"Yes, I think it's going to be a total of nine or ten people," Dakota said. "Immediate family, some flowers, dinner. How late are you allowed to stay out?"

"I'm thirty-six, Dakota," she answered with a laugh.

"Okay, how late are you willing to stay out?"

"I'll cross that bridge when I get to it," she said.

"Oh, boy," he said, nuzzling her neck. "Possible nudity!"

Tom Canaday felt as though he had a significant part of his life returned to him when he found Lola Anderson. She felt like part of him, like the other half of him. She was gentle and good, and whether they were in bed together or sitting out on her porch like now, being with her was the way to intimacy.

"I've never had anything like this before," he told her, holding her hand.

"Well, I certainly haven't," she said with a short laugh.

"We were both married," he said. "We both loved our spouses. And yet..." He brought her fingers to his lips and kissed them. "We need to be married. Is that even possible?"

"It depends on the kids," Lola said. "Trace and Cole are on to us—they know we're serious. Cole asked me straight out if I'd found my forever man and I told him I believe I have."

"He did? He asked you that?"

"Haven't your kids asked you?"

"No, they skipped that part and went straight to teasing me."

She laughed, that low, earthy sound of hers. "That's an even better sign," she said.

"I have to tell you some things. Before I ask you if you can see a life with me, even if we have to wait awhile on account of all these kids between us. Private stuff."

She gave him a look. "You aren't really going to ask me if I can keep a secret, are you, Tom?"

"Even if we're mad at each other?"

"Even if I hate you and want you dead! Of course, I'm going to suffer the worse fate. I tried to stop you but now I'm going to love you till I die."

"Oh, Lola, you are so good to me. I don't feel like I even had a life before you."

"You had one, Tom—it was full of jobs and kids. You want to get the families together to save money?"

"Nah, that's the least of it. Not that I have any money," he added. "It's always been paycheck to paycheck for me. But I'm really good at that, by the way. Nah, this is about my marriage."

"It's not required, you know," she told him. "We both had lives before. We're both beyond them now..."

"I might need a little advice, too. See, I married real, real young. Becky was just my undoing. And I was a boy, thinking with my dick, like boys do. But I loved her and I kept loving her. It's taken me a long time to understand. Becky didn't have a happy childhood. Her family struggled and it just brought out the worst in 'em. My family wasn't well-off, either, but my folks never let it get 'em down and they were good parents. They *are* good parents. But Becky was always looking for more. First it was to get married and have a baby." He laughed without humor. "I should'a looked out for that one.

"Then she wanted a house, so we started fixing up that Victorian we shared with our landlady. Then she got pregnant, then she got pregnant again… Oh, jeez, why am I telling you all this like you don't already know it? I think I might be a little nervous."

She smiled and ran her soft hand over the back of his neck. "Not anymore, Tom. Not with me."

"You're not ready for this, Lola. Becky left when Zach was only two. He's fourteen now. We were just separated a couple of years but then got our divorce. Even after the divorce, I still let her spend nights. Weekends. It was easier if she just came home. We were in that big house and she didn't have much space of her own, not enough room to take four kids back to her apartment for a weekend. They'd have been miserable. And I—" He shook his head. Then he looked at her. "I welcomed her into the bed even though we weren't married and I was pretty sure she was dating around. I'm not an idiot, I know what dating means when you're a grown-up. I knew there were men, though I didn't ask her and she didn't tell me. But I didn't care…"

"Tom, please go easy on yourself. You're human. You had a bond with her and you were lonely. Not to mention overworked and raising four kids. So you got shagged by your ex-wife? Is that the worst thing you could—"

"It's not the worst thing," he said. "Becky eventually seemed to have a good life, a nice place in Aurora, a decent job and girlfriends. I never even questioned how she could afford a nice car and a great town house on her salary working for a plastic surgeon. She was just an office worker. Then she got in trouble and called me for help. She got arrested for soliciting. She said it was all a misunderstanding. Then I found out it was the third time she'd been arrested—all misunderstandings, she said. I hooked her up with Cal Jones. He's a criminal lawyer. He got her case thrown out so she didn't even pay a fine. But, Lola, my ex-wife was a *hooker*. She probably still is."

"Holy smokes, you weren't kidding! If you'd dared me to guess what personal stuff you were going to tell me, that would be way down on the list below 'my ex-wife is a space alien.'"

"I know," he said. "She has a lot of excuses. She was an escort, she said. There are a lot of men, particularly older, very rich men, who want a woman to spend an evening with them when they're in the area. There were several 'regulars' and they didn't necessarily have sex. They had relationships, she said. Conversation. Someone to take to the restaurant rather than eat alone.

"Then I took in her lifestyle and realized these men she escorted paid her a fortune and I may be just a country bumpkin but you don't give a woman a lot of money to watch her cut her meat. So, she said she stopped doing that. But her lifestyle didn't suffer at all so I don't believe her. It changed everything. She can only see the kids here in Timberlake, she isn't allowed to stay over at the house and the kids aren't allowed to go to her house. And she wasn't crawling in my bed again, that's for sure."

"Oh, Tom, you must have been so upset."

"Yeah, I was," he said. "I can still get all pissed off about it if I chew on it awhile. What kind of example is that for your kids? Huh? But you know Becky—she's so pretty and so sweet, she really can manipulate things and get her way. Once I thought about it, I had no trouble picturing her as an escort. Or whatever that was."

"Did the kids notice that you weren't letting her spend as much time with them?" Lola asked.

"Nah. They're fourteen, sixteen, nineteen and twenty-one. They're busy. They're trying to hatch their own plans. Jackson said something about a year ago. He said he noticed I wasn't inviting Mom to stay over. And I said, 'We've been divorced eight years now, maybe it's time I accepted the fact that we're divorced.' And good old Jackson said, "'Bout time, man. You're not that old. Maybe you'll get lucky like me and get a nice girlfriend.' At the time he said that, having a girlfriend was the last thing on my mind." He squeezed her hand.

She frowned slightly. "Are you sure you're really ready to move on?"

"Come on," he said. "We already have. There are a couple of things I worry about. The kids. I've been holding Becky in place by threatening her that I'd tell the kids if she didn't do things my way. I wasn't being mean. I don't want them exposed to her lifestyle. I don't want them in the house she used to entertain men. I wasn't going to have her in my bed. In fact, I drove all the way to Denver for a checkup to make sure she hadn't passed any of her little escort business on to me. I didn't want her staying overnight at all. Luckily the kids barely noticed because she doesn't come that often and we're all like ships passing in the night. But, Lola, what about the kids? I have to tell them, don't I?"

Lola visibly withdrew. "Oh… I don't know…"

He was shaking his head. "I hate pretending. I hate covering up things. You know, my great-great-grandfather was a bootlegger and people still whisper it. I have an uncle who had two families, but no one knows the other family and everyone snickers. They have a million little rat holes they can't talk about. I'm so torn. I don't want my kids not to know the truth but I don't want to screw them up with it, either. When I knocked up Becky in high school, my dad went real hard on me. He told me to get jobs, work, save my money, take care of my family. He didn't exactly reach out. Then when Becky was pregnant the second time my mom took me aside and said, 'Do your best and we'll help where we can. Your dad should be more understanding—

when we got married you were a bun in the oven.' So you know what? I told Jackson—I told him I didn't regret a thing, that my life with my family was precious to me, but he should use his head and plan his children better. Then he might not have to work so hard to take care of them."

"Every family has those things," Lola said.

"They don't have to tell the neighbors, but shouldn't they know the truth? That's how we've gotten along so far—being honest. Telling the truth."

"I don't know," she said again. "This one might be too much for kids. Even adult kids."

"And the other thing—can you be with a man like me? I made some awful mistakes…"

She smiled gently. "I don't see many mistakes in there, Tom. You loved your wife, you didn't want a divorce. Bless her little heart, she lost a good man. I bet she's sorry about that now."

"I don't think so," he said. "Although I do believe she wanted it all—independence and freedom as well as a family, a variety of men who could take her to fancy places and the one at home she practically grew up with."

She leaned toward him and gave him a small kiss on the cheek. "You are my everything," she said. "I can't imagine one more thing I would need."

"You can live with a man who slept with his ex-wife, the hooker, for years?"

She gave him an amused smile. "I don't think you should do it anymore."

He growled and pulled her against him. "God, I love you. You're the best thing that ever happened to me."

"When we figure out a way to shuffle all these kids around and find a place where we can be together, I'm not sure I can share space with your ex-wife."

"We'll figure that out. The kids are real close to moving

on. I don't want them to go far—we'll always have room for them, but… Brenda graduates from high school next year. I'm going to buy her luggage…"

Lola giggled.

"I'm going to talk to my kids…"

"Easy does it, Tom. Let's concentrate on one thing at a time. I'm going to tell my boys that after a year of dating, we're talking about making a commitment, but we're not rushing our families. I just want them to know. I owe it to them that there be no surprises."

"Like any of them would be surprised…"

"Take it slow, Tom. I worry about your girls and how they might take the news about their mom. No matter how she lives her life, she loves them and they love her. Guard that. It's precious."

"Why don't you tell them for me," he suggested.

"Nice try."

Sedona Jones Packard couldn't bring her family to Colorado on such short notice, but she would not be kept away from Sierra's wedding, small and simple though it might be. She arrived on Saturday for the Sunday afternoon ceremony.

"I'm very happy you made it," Sierra said, embracing her. "And if you try to improve or help in any way, you will be banished."

"Just tell me what you'd like me to do," she said.

"Did you bring a dress?" Sierra asked.

"Of course!"

"Then tomorrow at three thirty you can put it on and at four o'clock you can be our witness. Connie's brother is standing up for him and you, my sister, will be my matron of honor."

"Oh, Sierra! You do like me!"

"I love you, but you do get on my nerves. You're so bossy!"

"Not anymore," Sedona said. "I've cured much of that. I don't have to have my way all the time anymore."

"Wonderful. Then get comfortable, play with the baby, visit with your brother, relax and enjoy yourself."

"I'll help with dinner," Sedona said.

"Cal's making dinner tonight. Family only."

"I've got it," Cal yelled from the kitchen.

So Sedona had a glass of wine, visited with Maggie and Sierra, was caught up on all the family gossip—like how Sierra met and fell in love with Connie—and then when she could stand it no longer, she migrated to the breakfast bar, where she could watch Cal at work.

"Will you be turning the flame down on those potatoes pretty soon?" she asked. "You aren't going to boil those beans, are you? Because if you steam them…" Cal glared at her. "Point me to the good dishes and I'll set the table." Then, less than three minutes later, she asked, "Are you sure these are the good dishes?"

Thus, Sedona was banished from the kitchen. But by a unanimous vote, she was elected to clean up.

Sedona was indefatigable. When Dakota arrived, they hugged and greeted each other; he asked about her husband, Bob, and the kids, then she said, "So, what's this about you being a garbage collector?"

"It's an excellent job with great benefits and pay," he said.

"And when will you put your education and experience to use?" she asked.

Sierra called Sully. "The sooner you can get over here and occupy Sedona, the less likely one of us will kill her."

Sully arrived at Cal and Maggie's a little earlier than he had planned, but it became obvious right off that it was not so much to be helpful as to figure out what was going on. He had met Sedona briefly when Cal and Maggie got married but he'd never seen the Jones siblings gathered like this, without a lot of other people around. He asked for a tall iced tea, then sat back and observed. Sedona was telling Cal how to make the dinner, quizzing Dakota about his future plans, insisting that Sierra go over her plans for the wedding day. After a little of this, he took Sedona's elbow in his grip and escorted her to Cal's patio.

"Sit down here and tell me about yourself," Sully said. "I've had a lot of time with your brothers and sister but I hardly know you at all."

Sedona sat in a lawn chair and proceeded to tell him about her husband, Bob, her son, Travis, and daughter, Rayna, about Little League and swim club and her husband's business, which was a successful architecture firm that designed everything from skyscrapers to luxury homes. She elaborated on the kids: one had glasses like his father, the other scared her to death with her love of diving from the high board. She didn't stop talking for twenty minutes.

"You must have a lot of experience in a lot of things," Sully said.

"I suppose," she said. "Why do you say that?"

"You're full of advice," he said. "I know a little about your folks. They sound like pretty interesting people. Why do you suppose each one of you four kids is so accomplished? I think someone should know the formula and write a book about it," Sully said.

"Well, there's no good explanation. We weren't exactly raised to be independent as much as we never had much parenting. Your story is probably more interesting. How do you explain raising a neurosurgeon?"

Sully laughed. "Girl, I take no credit for that whatsoever. Maggie's mother and stepfather saw to her schooling and her discipline. I counted myself lucky if they let her come for a visit. My ex-wife left me when Maggie was only six and kept us separated for years. She said I was a terrible father and she was probably right. I think Maggie is who she is in spite of me, but thank God I didn't hold her back too much."

And just like that, tears gathered like storms in Sedona's eyes and she started crying. Rivers flowed down her cheeks and she used her napkin as a tissue to mop up the tears and blow her nose.

"Here, now," Sully said, reaching out and patting her knee.

Sedona babbled something unintelligible.

Sully opened the back door and called to Maggie. Maggie came to the door with a perplexed look on her face but then took in the sight of Sedona sobbing.

"Oh dear God," Maggie said in aggravation. "What did you say to her?"

"I just asked her about herself. She was telling me about her husband and kids, who, by the way, are perfect and exceptional."

Maggie crouched beside Sedona, pulling her into her arms. "What is it?" she asked gently. "Tell me what's wrong."

With a hiccup of emotion, Sedona looked at Maggie. "We're separated!" she said in a stressed whisper. "Bob moved out, left me and took the kids. He said my perfectionism was going to be the end of us all. I don't know what in the world I'm supposed to do."

"Oh, my," Maggie said, hugging her and patting her back.

Sully stood by the back door. "Well, I guess it wouldn't be a proper wedding if someone weren't bawling."

A man must first govern himself ere he be fit to govern a family.

—SIR WALTER RALEIGH

9

"I shouldn't have come," Sedona said. "It's Sierra's special weekend and I'm just going to ruin it."

"No, that's not going to happen," Maggie said. "You stay right here with Sully. I'm going to make you a cup of tea. We just won't talk about this right now. We'll talk about it after dinner, when the house quiets down."

"I look a mess," Sedona said.

"You're entitled to be emotional when your baby sister is getting married. Just go with it for now," Maggie said, then looked at Sully sternly. "I'm trusting you not to get things riled up while I'm making tea."

"Me?" he protested. "I swear by God I get blamed for everything!"

"I'm warning you," Maggie said. Then she fled.

After a long quiet moment, Sedona spoke. "I'm sorry. I didn't mean to do that."

"Old men and younger women are always getting in

trouble one way or another," he said. "I'm sorry to hear about your situation."

"I'll work it out somehow," she said.

"I think it's a good idea to talk with your big brother later," Sully said. "After I'm gone."

A tremulous smile broke over Sedona's lips. "I've scared you half to death, haven't I?"

"I'm gonna tell you the truth here, in spite of Maggie. I feel a real sadness that you have something to work out, and you will, I'm sure of it. I don't want to minimize that. I been through separation and even divorce and at the time it was the darkest of days. But I got through it and I bet you'll get through it even better than I did—you being so much smarter than I am. But here's the thing. That little girl in there, Sierra, she's like a daughter to me. She's had a very hard time of it and she's come a long way and she's happy. I'd like it if tomorrow is one of her happiest days. Believe me when I say she's earned it.

"One thing you're going to learn when you're older— life has plenty of troubles to fill the days. Sometimes it feels like there's no hope, but just when it seems hopeless, some light will shine through. Now, you get a grip on yourself. We'll get your little sister married and on her way, and once that's done, we'll focus on you. And you can trust me, we won't go down without a fight. You believe me?"

She sat up straighter. "I'm a PhD in psychology and you know what? I think you just did as good a job as any therapist." She sniffed back her tears.

"I didn't say you can't fall apart," he said. "I just said you can't fall apart right now."

Maggie reappeared with tea. "Hmm," she said, handing the tea to Sedona. "You look better."

"I apologize," Sedona said. "That really took me by

surprise. I guess I'm a little emotional. We're working through a couple of issues, like you find in any marriage. Bob is a wonderful, devoted husband. We just need a little time, that's all. Everything will get back on track. Really, our family is known for ticking along perfectly. We don't generally have these kind of issues."

Maggie sat down. "Perfectly, huh?"

"I meant, smoothly."

"We'll talk later," Maggie said.

The Jones siblings, Maggie, Sully and Connie had a great dinner together. Stories were told, laughter was loud, the food was outstanding. Connie and Sierra and Sully were all excused after dinner while the remaining group worked together to clean up.

But when it was time for Maggie and Cal to have a chat with Sedona about her problems at home, Sedona slipped away and went to bed.

"That was a little too obvious," Maggie said.

So it was Maggie and Cal who had the talk. "Your sister is in trouble," Maggie began.

Sierra woke up at dawn and jostled Connie. "When we go to bed tonight, you will be my husband," she told him, the grin on her face as bright as the sun.

"You're not going to change your mind, are you?"

"You can't escape me now," she said. "It's only a matter of hours."

Connie's expression was serious. "Sierra, I'm going to be so good to you, you won't know how you made it this long without me."

She kissed him. "I already don't know."

They had a big breakfast and cleaned up the house, and while Connie went to Cal's to see if there was anything he could do to help out there, Sierra took her time with her bath and prettifying herself. At about one o'clock Connie returned and his mother, Janie, and his younger brother, Beaner, arrived. After a brief visit everyone changed clothes and Sierra put on her dress.

She had driven to Colorado Springs to find the right dress and she was very proud of it. It was an off-white sateen that had a bit of a golden cast to it. It had an off-the-shoulder cowl neckline and was knee-length, and while it wasn't tight, it fit snugly enough to show off her curvaceous figure. She wore her hair down, with a little baby's breath in it.

"Oh my God," Connie said in a whisper. "You're so beautiful. I just want to undress you!"

"Don't you dare touch this dress until we're married! And then you'd better be so careful!" She turned in front of the mirror. "I love this dress," she said.

"You hardly ever wear a dress," he said. "You should. But then again, you in a pair of tight jeans kills me. In a T-shirt makes me weak, too."

She smiled at him. "Connie, I'm a lucky girl," she said.

They went to Cal's in two cars. Janie and Beaner had been invited to stay over, but they declined, opting to leave the bridal couple alone. Cal and Maggie had extended the invitation to them to stay at their place but they declined that, as well. "We're going to drive back tonight," Janie said. "When this celebration is behind us, we'll come back and stay awhile."

At Maggie's insistence, there had been help from a catering service. Hors d'oeuvres, champagne and sparkling cider were ready when the wedding party assembled and their reception dinner was being kept warm. Cal and Maggie's table was extended and appointed with the caterer's china and crystal. The patio had a trellis covered with flowers. Lined up on the patio table were all the flowers for the wedding party—the bride's and matron of honor's bouquets, a corsage for Connie's mother and boutonnieres for the men.

When Sierra saw the flowers, the dining table, the decorations, she began to cry.

"Oh, honey, is it okay?" Connie asked.

"It's so beautiful!" she said. "It's just so perfect. It's exactly what I wanted for us."

When the minister, Rafe, Lisa, Dakota and Sid arrived, they were ready to begin. With Sedona beside Sierra, and Beaner beside Connie, they stood in front of the decorated trellis with the beautiful Rockies in the distance and recited traditional vows, with the exception of a few old-fashioned words like *obey*. It took a total of twelve minutes and then rings were exchanged and Connie took Sierra into his strong arms and kissed her long and lovingly.

"Are you sure it's legal?" Sierra whispered against his lips. "That was so fast!"

"It better be because I'm never letting you go."

"I love you, Connie," she whispered.

"Sierra, thank you. Thank you for loving me."

And with that Sedona let a sob escape and dabbed at her eyes.

A glorious dinner of Caesar salad, lobster, filet mignon, potatoes au gratin, baby green beans and a small wedding cake decorated with orchids was served. Both Elizabeth and Sully were perfectly behaved. And afterward, the remnants of dinner was quickly and silently whisked away by the mother-daughter team that had served them. None of the guests lifted a finger.

By nine o'clock the guests were saying good-night. Sierra and Connie were headed back to their home and dog, exactly what they wanted most.

* * *

Dakota helped Sid climb into his SUV. He started the engine and looked at her. "Did you have fun?" he asked.

"I did," she said, smiling. "Your family and friends are a riot. I already knew I liked most of them, but this was as close as I've been. Lisa Vadas is lovely. Maggie is someone I'd love to get to know better. What a great family."

"You look wonderful, Sid. I didn't know you could get sexier."

"I don't dress up very often."

"I was worried," he started. Then he shut it down.

"What were you worried about?"

"You had a terrible divorce," he said. "I was afraid the wedding, even a simple wedding, was going to make you nostalgic and maybe…unhappy."

Sid laughed. "I loved the wedding. I loved the simplicity of it. It was amazingly simple and beautiful. Intimate. And fun. My wedding was actually kind of awful—maybe I should have taken that as a sign."

"What was awful?" he asked.

"Well, it was far too important to David. He fussed over the details and needed it to be perfect. There were bridesmaid issues, he had family issues, there was arguing, bickering. You've heard of grooms saying, 'Whatever she wants'? Our situation was just the opposite. I really wasn't that into the whole thing but I wanted him to be happy and he had to have some kind of big party even though it put us in debt. I didn't have family to pay for that and he certainly didn't. It was exhausting and unsatisfying. It was pretty, though. I don't know Sierra and Connie that well, but didn't it look like a wedding that fit them both perfectly? And didn't they seem so happy and ready to take on the world when they left tonight? I had a moment of envy. But I wasn't melancholy."

He reached for her hand. "Are you tired?" he asked.

"A little," she said.

"I can take you home now. Or I can take you to my place. It's just a cabin but it's very comfortable."

"I'd love to see it," she said. "And maybe stay a little while."

"It sounds like you've given this some thought," he said.

"Haven't you?" she asked with a lift of one brow.

He chuckled, putting the SUV in gear. "I haven't thought about much else since I met you, Sid."

Given the size of his home, it wasn't necessary to show Sid around. She could see most of it from just inside the door. Dakota grasped her hands and pulled them around his neck. He kissed her softly, then ran his hands down her arms, her sides, circling her waist. He kissed her again. "Tell me if it's okay," he said.

"It's okay."

Massaging her back while he kissed her, he found a zipper and slowly slid it all the way down. He slid a hand inside. "Come on," he said. "I want to fall into you."

He walked her about ten feet into the bedroom, where he gently slid the dress off her shoulders and down, leaving her standing before him in a strapless bra and very small panties exactly the same color as her navy blue dress and strappy heels. He looked her up and down. She stepped out of the dress, stood straight and let him fill his eyes. He loved that she didn't cower, try to cover herself or push away.

"Damn," he said. "I knew about those legs, even if I hadn't seen them. The jeans. You knock me out with those jeans. But this... You're incredible. Do you know that?" One of the first things he noticed was a long scar on her right thigh, but it took nothing away from her beauty.

She just laughed.

"You are!" He hooked his thumbs into the sides of her sheer panties.

"Not yet," she said. She pulled up his shirt and ran her small hands over his chest. "You're falling behind. I seem to be the only one undressing."

"I'd kind of like you to stay like this all night, but that's impossible. I'd explode." He kicked off his shoes and pulled his shirt over his head. He wriggled out of his pants quickly and she stared at him. With a groan, her lips found his as her hand ran over the erection straining at his underwear. Holding her, kissing her, he pushed against her hand. Then she slid it inside and his breath caught. "Now, Sid?" he asked, sliding his hand down the back of her panties. "Can we lose these now?"

She pulled down his boxers and he leaned into her, pressing against her belly. "Now," she said. "Now the playing field is even."

He pushed her gently onto his bed and knelt beside her. He lifted one leg and began to slide off her shoe, then kissed her from her ankle to her panties. "I'd love to leave these on, but there could be injuries." He kissed the other leg, ankle to panties. Then he slowly slid down the panties and grinned as he gazed into her eyes. "A real blonde," he said. He gently rolled her to the side and unhooked her bra, laying her bare to his gaze.

Of course, that left him naked to her eyes, as well. He leaned over her, kissing her mouth, reaching with the other hand into the bedside table for condoms.

"It's been a long time," she said somewhat shyly.

"Is this the first time since…before?" he asked.

She nodded.

"We'll take our time. You can tell me what you want. Or you can stop me anytime something isn't right."

"I'm sure it'll be right," she said.

He slid a hand over her pubis and gently probed that sensitive place in her very center, pushing into her. "Oh, yeah," he said, thrilled by her softness. "It's going to be right." Then he covered her with kisses from her lips to her neck to her breasts and then back again. Her small hands ran all over his back to his firm butt. Before many minutes had passed, she was straining toward him and he was holding back. The condoms still lay on the table and she said, "Please. Please get ready."

"We could wait a little while, make it crazier," he offered.

"I don't want that, Cody," she said, using his pet nickname for the first time. "I want you right away."

He quickly got on it, opening up a package and stretching on the condom. Dakota knelt between her thighs and gazed into her eyes. "I want to see your eyes. I want you to see mine." He slowly lowered himself, touching her first with his fingers, then sliding into her gently. "God," he said. "God."

Her hips lifted to bring him deeper and she began to move against him instantly, holding him against her, kissing him hungrily and whimpering softly. Dakota let her set the rhythm and then moved with her, evenly at first, then harder, then deeper and harder. She bit his lip as a moan escaped her and she froze, pushing against him. And he felt it, the tightening and throbbing against him. He grabbed her butt in both hands and rode it out with her, and when he sensed that she was nearly complete, he rode her hard, bringing her back to the brink again, making her come again. And he let go until his brain was empty.

She panted beneath him; he panted above her, covering her face with kisses. It took some time to calm.

"Are you going to ask me if it was good?" she said.

He shook his head. "I was there. I know it was good. It was powerful."

"I could have been faking," she said with a sly smile.

He chuckled. "Then you are a woman of many talents."

"Oh, Cody, I worry that you could be habit-forming..."

"There are worse things."

"How am I going to explain this to my nephews?" she said.

"Video games," he said. "Tell them we stayed up late playing video games."

She laughed. "You think they'd buy that?"

"Not a chance. But they'll stop asking questions. Especially when you explain we like to play naked."

"I wouldn't want to give them any ideas. It's obvious testosterone has hit our household. They're becoming men before my eyes."

He ran his hands through her hair, spreading it across the pillow. "Every time we've been together, it's been a ponytail. I know that's necessary—you're always around food. But this is good. You're so pretty, Sid."

"Ordinary," she said. "Plain."

He laughed low in his throat. "Absolutely not. You're beautiful."

"Nah," she said, shaking her head. "Thank you, though. I think you're the beautiful one—you have the young girls chasing you. And now you have me chasing you, too."

He touched the scar on her thigh and looked into her eyes.

"An accident," she said. "I was hit by a car when I was nine."

"A bad accident," he said.

"I was on my bike. She...the driver...didn't see me."

"Looks like it must have been pretty serious," he said, running a finger along the scar.

"Compound femur. Four surgeries. Infection, growth plate issues, a year out of school. But as you can see, both legs are the same length—I'm lucky. I think that's the year that drove me into myself, when I became very shy and turned to books. I had a great tutor. And I also became very self-conscious. I had a lot of pain. I limped a little from pain and weakness. I couldn't really run and play so I became studious."

"It's certainly not holding you back now," he said.

"It's ugly," she said. "One thigh is thinner than the other."

He kissed her. "You are so beautiful. These are the greatest legs I've ever known." He frowned slightly. "Sid, you're not paying attention to the guys in the bar—the cops, the firefighters, the locals. Their eyes light up when they see you. They're all grins. I know you've been asked out…"

"They're just being nice," she said. "And we are all friends."

"You don't go out with customers…"

"I made an exception with you." She raked his beard with her fingernails. "I'm glad I did."

"Because I'm great in bed?" he asked hopefully.

"Because Sister Mary Jacob likes you."

He kissed her forehead. "Excuse me for a second," he said. "I'll be right back."

Dakota visited the bathroom. He suspected Sid's ex-husband had not been a good person. He couldn't believe she didn't think of herself as pretty.

He dimmed the bathroom light so it wasn't shining brightly and went back to the bed. He reached for her hand. "Come with me, sweetheart," he urged. "I want to show you something." He pulled her along with him to the bathroom. He stood her facing the mirror and thought, *Dear God, what a sight*. Her golden hair was crazy from making love, falling over her shoulders to cover her breasts. Her eyes were bright, her cheeks pink.

He stood behind her, a head taller, his big hands on her

upper arms. "Look," he said. "You're one of the most beautiful women I've ever seen. Certainly one of the most ravishing I've ever held in my arms." He pulled her hair over one shoulder, baring her neck. He bent to put his lips here. One of his hands slid down her torso, past her flat belly, covering her pubis gently. His other hand slid around to cup a breast. "You're sexy enough to bring me to my knees. Something tells me you weren't told that often enough."

Her eyes closed.

"I want you to look. Look at us." He kissed her neck again. "Not bad," he said, grinning at her in the mirror. He turned her in his arms so he was holding her close. "Want to go back to bed now?" he asked. "We can talk."

She stood on her toes and kissed his lips. "We can talk later," she said.

It was about 2:00 a.m. when Sid asked Dakota if he'd take her home. "I know you have an early start. It's Monday morning."

"Monday's my day off," he said.

"Oh, that's right! And I don't start until one."

"I have a feeling I'll have plenty of energy. You know where to find me if you get restless." He held her close a moment longer. "Did you have a good time?"

"Hmm, the whole thing. I loved the wedding, the evening with your family, this. But I think we should be discreet."

"Are you ashamed of me?" he asked.

"Oh God, no!" she insisted. "We just wouldn't want people making a lot of assumptions about us, wondering if we have future plans, that kind of thing."

"God forbid," he said. "Don't worry, Sid. I won't embarrass you. You don't have to tell anyone you're knocking boots with a garbage collector."

"Oh, Cody, that's not it! I just mean… I don't know what I mean. Let's take it slow. Except when we're naked. Then we can do what we want. Okay?"

He grinned at her and slapped her ass playfully. "You're okay, Sid. I'm not going to advertise how I know you're a real blonde. But damn, you're hard to let go of. Maybe we should see if we're still great together in bed. Once more? Just to be sure it's as amazing as I thought?"

She shook her head. "All right," she said, playfully nipping at his lip. "Even though I'm sure…" she said.

"It's nice to be with you like this," he said.

Until he showed up in Timberlake she was quite sure she'd never share intimacy like this with anyone again. On the one hand, she was relieved he seemed to know what to do, how to be in a relationship like this. On the other… "Have there been a lot of women?" she asked.

"I guess if you started counting with the first one…" he said. "I guess there were. I wasn't looking for a permanent relationship every time I met a woman I really liked, but I wasn't opposed to the idea."

"Have you been in love?" she asked.

"I have," he said. "Have you?"

"I'm no longer sure," she answered honestly. "I thought I loved my husband. I assumed he loved me. When I re-examined that relationship, I'm a little embarrassed that I couldn't see it for what it was. Obviously I was wrong about many things."

"When you reexamined it, did you realize he didn't treat you like he loved you?"

"Yes," she said.

"I'm sorry. But you won't make that mistake again," he said.

"And you? Did you learn some painful lessons from being in love?" she asked.

He was quiet for a moment. "Yeah," he finally said. "We'll be okay, Sid. We're going to enjoy life and be a little less alone. When it doesn't work for you, tell me."

"And you'll just go away quietly?"

"How about we don't talk about me going away so soon. But anything you want or need from me…"

"It's taking a lot of willpower to get out of this bed," she said.

"Yeah, me, too. But I'll take you home because I don't want you to have regrets, not even about leaving."

"I'm really glad I met you, Cody."

"Don't call me that in front of people at the bar, okay? I don't want anyone to pick it up, use it. I love it when you call me Cody. I don't want anyone else to call me that."

"Your brother and sisters…"

"That's them," he said. "That's a whole other thing. But when you say it, it feels personal and I like it."

"Then do me one more time, Cody. I love the way you touch me."

"Good. Because I can't get enough of you, Sid."

It was 4:09 a.m. when Cal lounged in his favorite chair in the great room, his feet propped up on the ottoman. He had hoped to be wrong, but he heard a soft sound from upstairs and then the creaking of one stair. He had intended to do something about that creak—it was kind of loud. But as he heard Sedona sneaking down the stairs, heard her softly curse at the sound, then continue down, he made a decision. He would never fix that stair because he'd have a teenage daughter one day and the alarm could come in handy.

Sedona was carrying her shoes in one hand and her suitcase in the other. When she got to the bottom, she put down the suitcase, opened the purse that hung by a strap over her shoulder and began digging in it. He cleared his throat and she jumped in surprise. "Oh!" she gasped, dropping her shoes. She clutched her blazer over her heart in stunned surprise. After a few breaths, she said. "You scared me! What are you doing up so early?"

"I've been up," he said. He dangled her car keys on one finger. "Looking for these?"

"I didn't want to wake you."

"What were you going to do? Leave a note?"

"I checked with the airline last night and they had an earlier flight they could put me on. I really need to get home."

"Why?" he asked. He sat up, pushed the ottoman out of the way and put his feet on the floor.

"I have things to do. The kids need me to be home. Work needs me. You know, just… This trip was very short notice…"

"I called Bob," Cal said. "You know—your husband."

"Why would you do that?" she asked. "*When* did you do that?"

"Just a little while ago. I didn't wake him. He gets up before five. He likes to run before six, before it gets hot. But then, you know that, don't you? Sit down, Sedona."

"Look, I have a flight and Denver is a long drive."

"Sit down, please," Cal said. "He told me."

"He doesn't know anything," she said. "He has no training whatsoever and he doesn't know anything. He has opinions, that's all. And it's none of your business."

"How long have you been fighting this, concealing this?"

"I don't know what you're talking about!"

"Your marriage isn't in trouble because you're a perfectionist. You've been fighting mental illness by trying to maintain control of your surroundings and the people in your life, but it's not working so well. Bob blames himself, you know. He's been so busy and he hasn't taken you to see someone—he trusted you to do it. And you like to excuse what's going on as harmless habits, but he's found you in trouble too often, hasn't he? You don't sleep, you talk to yourself—or are you talking to someone? Someone the rest of us can't see?"

"No!" she insisted.

"He said sometimes you're a little out of reality. You have manic episodes. Man, is your house perfect, right? You're confused sometimes. Forgetful? Or is that compensating—just agreeing with someone even though you have no memory of what they're telling you? Jesus, Sedona, after what we went through growing up with Jed, why would you accept denial?"

Her chin dropped. She slid onto the end of the couch. She spoke as if she'd lost her breath. "I can't do this," she said weakly.

"Do you know what's wrong or are you just afraid of what could be wrong?" Cal asked. "Bob said his terms were that you see a doctor or he's divorcing you and finding a way to get custody. That's what he said. Are you afraid it's schizophrenia? Are you just paralyzed?"

"I'm functional," she said in a pleading voice. "I have it under control. I'm not like Jed at all. And I'm not self-medicating! Everyone gets a little absentminded sometimes. Lots of women are perfectionists—it's how we manage to be professionals and mothers and wives and—"

"That's not what it is," Cal said. "Bob doesn't enjoy lining up the towels and alphabetizing the canned goods, but if that's the price of peace, he can live with that. It's the insomnia and paranoia. It's the pacing around the basement and talking to yourself for six hours through the night that's making him gray! It's finding you curled up in a ball, sweating and crying, that he can't take. You need treatment! You need medication! What the fuck is the matter with you? Our lives could have been so different if Jed had been willing to take medication! You have to see a doctor!"

"I did! I did see a doctor a few years ago. He confirmed what I knew, gave me medication that made me feel dead inside, but not better. And I'm convinced my way of coping is better than the drugs. I'm no threat to anyone and I manage just fine!"

"With rituals—walking forward and backward and in circles? Cutting vegetables in precise strips? Slicing meat in perfect pieces? Brushing your hair a certain number of times, doing everything a special way?"

She swallowed. "Don't you remember how medicine broke him?" she cried. "How it reduced him to a completely emotionless—"

"Treatment is better than it was thirty years ago! You don't have to be pumped full of Thorazine and dumped like a blob on someone's couch! You're a psychologist, for God's sake!"

The sound of a door opening and feet on the stairs caused them both to turn their heads. Maggie was coming down the stairs. "In two more minutes, you'll wake Elizabeth, and if you do, she's all yours."

"Sorry," Cal said. "It's an emotional issue."

"Go put on the coffee," Maggie said. She tightened the belt of her robe and sat on the edge of the ottoman facing Sedona. "I know you're upset and terrified, but there's no guarantee of his diagnosis. I always encourage my patients to get a second opinion, if there's time. You have no idea what's going on, and until you do, enough hysteria. Bob is absolutely right—until you see a doctor and get all the facts, you can't call the shots. You could have a brain tumor for all you know."

"I don't have a brain tumor," Sedona said. "I've run all the tests."

"You can't run your own tests," Maggie said. "In this family Cal is in charge of criminal law, you are in charge of personality disorders and I am in charge of brain tumors. You're a PhD in clinical psych, and from what I've been told, you specialized in adolescent testing."

"A smoke screen," she said. "Psychologists and psychiatrists are notorious for studying mental illness because they fear it and want a leg up on their own problems. I did the same thing. I wanted to be sure I wasn't crazy. Like our father. I've studied schizophrenia since I was fourteen."

"Well, you can relax now, Sedona," Maggie said. "You don't need the pressure of knowing everything. I know some of the best psychiatrists in Denver. I want you to stay with us or you can use my house in Denver. Probably not for very long, just until I can arrange an evaluation and possible treatment plan for you. I'll walk you through it. I won't let you fall. Working with the brain is a sensitive journey and requires patience. I will be your patience and your crutch. But in case you're confused about what happened here this morning, we just pulled the rug out from under you. Because we all love you, including Bob and your children. It's time for a diagnosis and treatment recommendation. This was what we know as an intervention. I don't think you'll find anyone to help you propagate your denial. And I'm pretty sure it's not schizophrenia, but I'm no expert."

"Why do you say that?" she asked, sniffing back her tears.

"You're functional. Socially normal. One of the hallmarks of the disease is thinking you're functional when you're not, thinking your delusions are real and the real world is a delusion."

"It's just a mild case…"

"We're going to let a medical doctor tell you that."

"Do Sierra and Dakota have to know about this?" she asked, her voice soft.

"Well, not today," Maggie said. "For today, on a whim, you decided to stay awhile. That's good enough for now. Eventually you people have to talk, for Pete's sake. You're all skipping fearfully around this same gene! At least share your information!" Then she looked at Sedona more calmly. "How bad are your symptoms?"

"Sometimes very frightening," she said. "Sometimes I feel pretty normal."

"Tell me about very frightening," Maggie urged.

Sedona looked down. "When I hear voices, when I can't relax, when I'm paranoid and imagine people know what I'm thinking."

"Anything else remarkable?"

"When the inside of my head is so loud and busy I can't sleep, sometimes for long periods of time. And then, of course, the symptoms get worse and the sleeping aids don't work. Then there are some that work a little too well and I'm afraid of addiction or of not waking up. I don't think we really know how bad Jed's schizophrenia is with all the pot he smokes."

"I suggested that at this point it might be counterproductive," Maggie said. "Sedona, those symptoms, while suspicious and disconcerting, don't necessarily prove schizophrenia. You might've been describing an overworked, stressed-out, exhausted neurosurgery resident. I'll make some phone calls today. What else can we do to give you some peace of mind?"

Sedona wore a hopeless expression. "I'm not sure I want any more information about my condition. I'm comfortable thinking it's a light case that flares up sometimes, like when I'm stressed or tired."

"But that doesn't really sound like schizophrenia."

"Jed had quiet periods," she said. Cal delivered coffee to Sedona and Maggie. "I shouldn't drink this," Sedona said.

"Decaf," Cal replied.

"What am I to tell Sierra and Dakota about why I'm still here?"

Maggie shrugged. "Tell them you and Bob are fighting, talking about separating, you needed some time away and don't care to discuss it. It wouldn't be a lie."

"Right," Sedona said.

Maggie smiled. "Also not typical of a schizophrenic. They usually say what's on their minds, however bizarre it might be." Maggie took Sedona's hand. "I will find you a good doctor and I'll take you there myself."

It is not flesh and blood but the heart

which makes us fathers and sons.

—JOHANN SCHILLER

10

Dakota wasn't aware that Sid might say something to her brother about their new relationship, but in thinking about it, of course she would. Sidney and Rob were very close and Sid spent a great deal of time managing their home and the boys, whenever needed. Fortunately at fourteen and sixteen, with their father just down the street at the bar and checking in all the time, they didn't need her supervision very often. Sid snuck out to Dakota's cabin Tuesday morning, then excused herself from work a couple of evenings that week. She brought them a hamburger to-go box and said she couldn't stay long, but they made the very most of their time together.

Then a week after Sierra's wedding, when Dakota was having dinner at the bar, Rob brought his food from the kitchen. He placed it in front of Dakota and spoke quietly. "Be very good to her. She's more fragile than she seems."

Startled, Dakota frowned. He thought about answering with some kind of challenge. Then he thought of his own protectiveness of Sierra. "Of course!" he whispered.

Rob gave a single nod of his head and turned away.

A few minutes later Sid was standing before him, smiling.

"Your brother warned me to be good to you."

"I hope you didn't tell him exactly how good you are," she said with a sly smile.

"I was a little surprised. Not that he warned me. That you told him."

"I had to tell him. If I go mysteriously missing with no explanation, he might call out the search and rescue team. Trust me, it's safer this way. And I told him you were an absolute gentleman."

He got a lascivious glint in his eyes. "I'm having very ungentlemanly thoughts of what I'd like to do to you right now. When can I see you?" Dakota whispered.

"I'm driving the boys to something tomorrow night— batting cage practice—so it would be late..."

"Anytime," he said, grinning. "Do you want to go out?"

"Maybe on the weekend? Friday night, since I'm committed to Mary Jacob on Saturday night..."

"Perfect. Just decide when and what you'd like to do."

"You're very accommodating, Cody," she said so no one could hear.

"I'd be pretty stupid not to be," he said with a grin.

"I do have to work," she said just as some uniformed troopers came into the bar for their dinner.

"Go," he said. "I get a big kick out of just watching you."

He enjoyed the sight of her zipping around behind the bar, loved the quick smile on her lips and easy laugh for the customers, even the men he was tempted to be jealous of. The troopers got a fair amount of attention and conversation, and this made Dakota happy because he knew if this was a cop bar, Sid was always in good hands should the need ever arise. But in a sweet little town like Timberlake, the need would seldom arise.

It took willpower for him to stay away at all. He knew if he gave in to temptation, he would be here every night from dinnertime until she headed home at nine or ten or even later.

But he didn't want to crowd her, overwhelm her. He had other people to see, even if the urge was not nearly as strong. He usually had dinner with Sully one night a week; sometimes he'd drop in on Cal and sometimes Sierra. Sedona had stayed for a few days past the wedding, and even though she could get on his last nerve, he spent one evening at Cal's, visiting with his sister. He was more than ready for her to leave—she seemed to be getting a little more nervous and controlling as she got older and he was not too surprised to learn that her husband was threatening divorce if she didn't find a way to curb her perfectionist tendencies.

He was watching Sid work when a flash of color distracted him. He turned to see Neely walking into the bar. She looked around briefly and then, spotting him at the bar, she turned left and went the other way, looking for a table. She looked back at him and there was no mistaking it; she gave him an angry, nasty look.

Neely took a seat on the far side of the room. He couldn't help but notice her attire, and women's clothes were not something he paid a great deal of attention to. But every time he'd seen Neely, she'd been wearing very expensive and what he assumed were incredibly fashionable clothes. Tonight it was a black leather skirt with a fringe running down one side to the hem, red leather high-heeled boots and a multicolored leather jacket with a lot of red in it. Her hair was down and full and even from across the room he could see her dark eyes and red lips. She didn't look like she was dressed for a casual night in a bar. He was momentarily glad he'd parked his Jeep under a streetlight. She was starting to give him the creeps, coming on to him one minute, glaring at him the next.

But then Sid was back and Neely ceased to exist for him.

"I think people are starting to talk," she said. "You're in here too much and the way you look at me is way too obvious."

"Good," he said. "I'd really like to put up a sign—Sid's Off the Market."

"I was already off the market," she corrected. "Then you showed up and I had a slip in judgment."

"Then we both did. I really like it like this."

"I thought we agreed we'd keep it, you know, kind of low-key. Bad divorce and all."

"Listen, I don't know where this is going, Sid," he said in a low voice, barely above a whisper. "But it doesn't matter how we end up, I would never do to you what he did to you. Right now we're checking it out. And it checks out pretty damn good. How late are you working tonight?"

"Rob went home to have dinner with the boys earlier so he said I could leave by nine if I want to. I really need some sleep!"

"I'll hang around, get you home."

"But I'm not going out tonight. I'm not going to your place. I really am tired. I must be getting worn out somehow."

That made him smile. "I've never felt so well rested in my life."

"I think there's something seriously wrong with you."

"Not anymore," he said.

On Monday, Dakota's day off, he spent the morning with Sid. After she'd gotten the kids off to school and

Rob had gone to work to occupy himself with accounting and ordering supplies, she went to Dakota's cabin. They had a leisurely morning of breakfast, love, quiet talk, and then Sid went home. Dakota was a little afraid of how this morning delight on his day off might change when the boys got out of school.

Having seen Neely's reaction to him the previous night, Dakota decided he was going to follow up on his slashed tires with Stan, the police chief. He waited until after the lunch hour was over, then sauntered into the office. "Hey, Stan," he said. "Got a minute?"

"For you, I got ten," Stan said cheerfully.

"I'll try to be brief. I wanted to follow up on something. I was wondering if the woman whose tire I was asked to fix came in here to talk to you. Neely. I'm afraid I don't know her last name but she's unforgettable. Very beautiful. Dresses real… Rich."

Stan frowned. "Yes, she was here," he said. "Have a seat, Dakota."

"I don't like that look," Dakota said, sitting in front of Stan's desk. They were not alone, which made him even more uncomfortable—there was a civilian woman and another officer, both working in the office. They seemed to be occupied with their own work, but still.

"Did you know she'd be coming in to talk to me?" Stan asked.

"I asked her to," Dakota said. "I bumped into her and told her how much it pissed me off that my tire was punctured and all the others deflated and that I suspected her and she told me she had nothing to do with it. She claimed there was some ex-boyfriend who'd been stalking her or something like that. She seemed a little worried that he might've done that and I asked her to tell you."

"That isn't exactly what she told me," Stan said. "She

told me she asked you to help her put on a spare and after the tire was on there was a bit of a tussle. She couldn't call it assault and didn't want to press charges, but she said you crossed the line. You told her you assumed she'd return the favor with affection. And that she shoved you away and slapped your face."

Dakota was speechless. His mouth hung open; he could feel it. "You have got to be kidding," he said, shock drawing out each word. "Seriously?"

"I'm afraid so," Stan said.

"Jesus, why didn't you call me? Bring me in for a talking-to?" Dakota asked. "Something!"

"You need a talking-to, Dakota?" Stan asked sagely.

"Aw, hell, it was the other way around. She asked me to fix her tire but there wasn't anything wrong with the tire, and once we were alone in the alley, she attacked me. Well, she plastered herself against me and kissed me and I had to peel her off me. You can ask Sid—I left my beer on the bar and was back in less than ten minutes, almost all of that time spent walking to the alley and back." He shook his head. "Holy shit, there is something seriously wrong with that woman."

"So, you didn't come on a little too strong?" Stan asked.

"She's been coming on to me and I guess she's the one who's pissed off. Just so you know, we're trying to play it cool, be discreet, but I'm seeing Sid. I took her to my sister's wedding. We work together at the soup kitchen in Colorado Springs every week. I don't have any interest in this Neely character. And she's real aggressive."

"Neely Benedict," Stan supplied. Then he smiled. "Sid, huh?"

"Don't smile at that," Dakota said. "Why didn't you tell me I was accused of assault?"

"Well, it's not exactly assault as it was described and

there doesn't seem to be a victim, since she said she wasn't pressing charges. She just wanted me to be aware on the chance you're a little *off* and we have trouble with you."

"On the chance *I'm* a little off?" he asked incredulously.

"And then there's the fact that I wasn't inclined to believe her," Stan said.

Dakota sat back in his chair and let all the breath he didn't realize he was holding escape. He ran a hand through his hair. "Well, thanks for saving that for last."

"You might've told me up front about the disagreement, about being set up for some romantic purpose," Stan said.

"Yeah, Cal suggested that. But I watched her get in her car and I had no desire to make trouble for her. I was very stern, told her never to do that again and thought the matter was taken care of. I suspected her of the damage but I didn't have proof."

"I know you didn't do what she said," Stan said. "I have something to show you. Give me a second." Stan clicked the keyboard on his computer, then turned the screen toward Dakota. It was a dark image. Dakota squinted to make it out; Neely's red wrap made it easier. And that was him, bending to look at the tire, then standing only to have her lunge at him. And he grappled to push her off.

"Jesus," he said. "There it is."

"Oh, there's more."

Indeed, it took Neely quite a while to get out of her car after he'd left the alley and then, looking around cautiously, she bent to the task of letting the air out of his tires.

"What's that in her hand?" he asked.

"A tire deflator," Stan said. "With a light."

When there was only one tire left, she went back to her car, dug around inside, then went after the final tire with a knife. Dakota winced when he saw that.

Stan turned the screen back. "Obviously I'd like you to say nothing about this."

"Where'd you get it?"

"Security camera on the back of the bank. It's not very obvious. Apparently she wasn't aware of it. A lot of people think a little hick town like Timberlake wouldn't have any use for such a thing."

"Are you going to arrest her?"

Stan shook his head. "The image isn't quite clear enough. Besides, it would only be a misdemeanor. She might not even get a fine. I'm going to hold on to this while I look a little deeper. This is going to stay between you and me. That's all I'm prepared to say. Except I don't know that you should turn your back when this woman is around."

"Don't worry!"

"I hadn't even looked at this tape yet when she paid me a visit. Not that I don't take you seriously, but it was air let out of three tires—not exactly high crime. But I found her whole presentation a little...odd. She is real pretty, though. Oh, and about Sid? You don't have to be so secretive. Everyone knows you like her. No one would be surprised you're steadies."

"Great," he said. "She wanted us to go slow, not start up the gossip."

"Then you ought not be on the same bar stool three nights a week unless you can manage to drink a little heavier." Then he laughed, but it was more of a giggle.

Dakota made a face.

"Small town," Stan said. "Just when you think you've got a secret..."

"So...where do we go from here?"

Stan folded his hands on top of his desk. "I'll be collecting information. I don't have much use for people who do things like that. I try to think of ways to request their departure from my beat. As for you? Go about your business and see what you can do to be less irresistible to the ladies. Hmm?"

"It's not funny," Dakota said.

"I'm not exactly laughing," Stan said.

Dakota could admit to himself that he'd been lucky with the ladies over the years but he'd never been in a situation like Neely in the alley. "Will you give me a call if you find out something more?"

"I can do that," Stan said. "Listen, I don't consider myself a wise man. I have a little experience, that's all. But I'm gonna tell you something. Don't think I'm talking down to you or anything, but just in general—I've discovered men are stupid. In a situation like this, for example, you're probably thinking you don't have much to worry about up against a girl, and maybe you don't. You're definitely stronger. Probably smarter, too. But if you smell an ill wind, you'd be smart to pay attention. Men tend to think just because it's a girl…"

"She creeped you out, too," Dakota said.

"I'm just saying, I don't take too much for granted. I know it don't seem like it, Timberlake being a small and uncomplicated town, but we've had us a situation or two I could probably sell to a movie channel."

Dakota smiled. "How long have you been doing this, Stan?" he asked.

"Too damn long. Twenty-five years now and retirement is not in sight. Got four kids and three dogs and a happy wife. At least she was happy last time I checked. If it ain't broke…"

"I'd like to buy you a beer sometime, hear some tales. I'd like to hear that one about Maggie shooting some guys who kidnapped a girl. Cal can't seem to even talk about it."

Again Stan's laugh was almost a giggle. "That sure riled

him up, didn't it? I'll be the first to admit, took about ten years off my life. That woman's so frickin' headstrong! I ever get a blood clot in my brain, I want her in the operating room with me, but the rest of the time?" He shook his head. "It takes a big man, that's all I'm saying."

Starting right after their wedding, Sierra and Connie endured several long interviews. Some of the people listed as their references had been contacted, their home had been inspected and their dog had even been evaluated, and the process wasn't nearly complete. But it was not for their certification to be foster parents. No, it was more intense and permanent than that.

The baby Connie had rescued from the car accident was named Samuel Ryan Jergens and his mother had called him Sammy. His maternal grandmother was his legal guardian but she was not up to the job given her chronic illness; she suffered from rheumatoid arthritis and a spinal injury that left her weak and in pain. She had more difficult days than easy ones, not to mention the fact that she was sixty and widowed. Sammy's mother had not married and on his birth certificate the father was listed as unknown. Mrs. Jergens had no idea who Sammy's father was, and according to her, there had not been a man in her daughter's and grandson's life. Rachel Jergens had planned to give up the baby but instead had moved home to her mother's house in order to take care of them both. Rachel had been only twenty.

There were other family members, cousins, though they hadn't seen each other in years. Rachel had no siblings. While Sam was in foster care with Rafe and Lisa, Mrs. Jergens had sought the counseling help from social services and they had come up with a solution—an open adoption. That way Sam might know his biological grandmother through visitation and some of the information about his family history would be passed on.

After a great deal of talking and soul-searching, Sierra and Connie decided this was the answer for them. They wanted to make that sweet little baby their son.

It was arranged privately through an attorney. The second Lisa Vadas heard of the plan, she told Sierra and Connie. There would be no shortage of couples waiting to adopt who would step up, but there was only one man who had actually pulled the little baby from a decimated car. Connie and Sierra would be allowed to foster Sammy until the adoption could be finalized. It would take six months to become his legal parents.

It was June. School was out for summer vacation and for weeks Sierra had paid almost daily visits to the Vadas household to be with little Sam. While Sierra and Connie were screened, the new family was bonding. Finally they were approved for foster care pending adoption and today was the day they could finally pick Sam up and take him home. They had asked Connie's mom and brother to come to Timberlake for dinner and a surprise. They issued the same invitation to Sully, Cal, Maggie, Elizabeth and Dakota. They encouraged Dakota to bring Sid if he wished.

"I'm going to ask you one more time," Connie said to Sierra. "Any answer is all right as long as it's honest. The only thing is we can't change our minds. No matter what bucket of trouble or difficulty we might face, we're in this forever. There are lots of young couples waiting to be parents if you're not ready, so be sure. Can we do this?"

Sierra smiled sweetly and touched her husband's handsome face. "I'm absolutely sure," she said. "I'm so in love with him."

"Have we covered everything?" Connie asked.

"I think so," she said. "If a father turns up, we can manage some visitation, provided he's of good character. We'll be honest with Sam about his roots. If he has medical issues, we're in for the long haul. Same with any behavioral issues. And if he grows taller and stronger than you, you promise not to be jealous."

"You were afraid to have your own child because of possible genetic schizophrenia. We have only his grandmother's word on the family medical history and I think she's a little wacko if you want the truth. What if Sam has mental illness in his family history?"

"I thought we covered that under medical issues," she said. "We will be his champions. We will get him the best medical help if we need to. Remember, we have Maggie in our corner. Connie, please don't make me beg. Sam should live with us. We love him. We have a bond with him."

"Want to make another run through the inventory?" he asked.

"We're ready," Sierra said.

It had been some very busy weeks since their wedding. First, meetings with Mrs. Jergens and the attorney and the social worker. Then to Denver to trade in Sierra's little orange VW, affectionately known as the Pumpkin. She was now the proud owner of a medium-size Honda SUV. It was not orange, but silver. And then there was furniture for the baby, though the crib was in their bedroom for now. Supplies from diapers and wipes to towels, blankets and bottles were neatly stored. The room that would be Sam's was painted powder blue and yellow. But he would be with Sierra and Connie for a while until everyone was comfortable and sleeping through the night.

Sam had some clothes but Sierra still purchased more. She'd had a field day at Target.

"Okay, the lasagna is in the slow cooker, salad in the fridge, bread hidden from Molly in the cupboard, chocolate cake under the glass dome, also safe from Molly, plates and utensils ready for company." Connie ticked off the items, making Sierra laugh.

"Please, can we go get him now?"

They had a brand-new, approved car seat. There were some things that a firefighter was very handy with—anything to do with safety for children was a particular specialty. They had a baby swing, a high chair, a changing table. There were new toys, a lullaby music box, a play box for the crib and a playpen.

Lisa had been packing up Sam's things all morning—there was little enough to get ready. There were still some things at Mrs. Jergens's house but much of it was second-hand, from thrift shops or hand-me-downs, and Rachel hadn't been well stocked, the baby being so young. One thing for which everyone gave grateful thanks—she had not scrimped on the car seat. It had been high quality and saved his life.

When they walked into the Vadas home, the whole family was there. Sam was in the high chair being fed lunch—cereal, vegetables and strained fruit. It was not only all over his face but when he saw the spoon coming his mouth opened wide and he lunged toward it. When he saw Sierra and Connie, he grinned his most handsome toothless grin.

"Oh, my heart," Sierra said in a breath.

"We're all so relieved Sam isn't going far," Lisa said. "This time we won't have a hard time letting him go."

Sierra pulled a chair out from the table and sat beside Lisa. "We're a little bit scared. What if something goes wrong and we can't adopt him?"

"I understand completely," Lisa said. "But there's nothing to suggest that will happen. After just a few days, you'll relax and enjoy him."

"You'll be exhausted and forget to worry," Rafe yelled from the living room.

"As soon as he's had his lunch, why don't you give him his bottle. He'll probably nap for a while and be fresh and happy for his party. Is there anything I can do to help?"

"We're ready. Molly is home, guarding the slow cooker."

"Do you think your family will be at all surprised?"

"Well, they don't know we've been stocking up on baby things," Sierra said. "But they do know we've been visiting Sam every day. I tried to be secretive but it just wasn't in me. I talk about him all the time."

"How have you kept them away from your house and the blossoming nursery?"

"That was easy. We checked in at the Crossing often, dropped in on Maggie and Cal regularly. Dakota has a girlfriend and Sedona has gone home. No one bothers us."

"Oh, they're going to be so surprised!" Lisa said. "And the diner?"

"We had long talks about it and I'm going to continue to work two days a week. I'll work on Connie's days off. It was his suggestion. He thinks if I give up the diner and all the people I'm used to seeing in town, I might get lonely and bored. I'm going along with this for now and we'll see what happens. I think I'm a little too busy with Sully and the rest of the family to get lonely, but..." She shrugged.

"He has a point," Lisa said. "Anything that gets you out of mommy mode on a regular basis helps keep you in balance, especially if you feel like you're contributing. Everyone should feel they're contributing—the guys, the kids, the moms. That's my philosophy."

"That's her philosophy!" her oldest child said.

"Two days at the diner isn't going to contribute much," Sierra said with a laugh.

"Just be careful that you don't find yourself feeling

lonely and unappreciated because you're trapped at home with the kids and the only thing you do is take care of other people and collect complaints from them."

"Gotcha," she said.

"It's easy to ignore your own confidence and self-esteem when everyone seems to need something. All. The. Time."

"We should probably have this conversation in a few months," Sierra said. "Right now I just want to hold Sam and love him."

Lisa wiped off his face and dropped a kiss onto his head. "He is the sweetest baby we've ever had."

"I don't have any trouble believing that. Would you like to join us for dinner?" Sierra asked.

"We're going to have lots of dinners together," Lisa said. "Today is for you and your family, a little time to get to know Sam. They're going to be so happy. Lucky Elizabeth! A cousin!"

A few hours later, amid tears and laughter, little Sam was passed from person to person, cuddled and petted, tossed up in the air, bounced on knees, and he treated them all to the most handsome toothless grins. Sully had more turns with the baby than Sierra expected. As he held him and jiggled him, he said, "Yeah, I guess you're a keeper. Best-lookin' guy at the party."

That best portion of a good man's life,

his little, nameless, unremembered acts of kindness and of love.

—WILLIAM WORDSWORTH

11

Sedona had not gone home at all, as she requested Dakota and Sierra be told. Instead, she had agreed to an inpatient mental health facility. That took some doing—at first she had resisted the very idea. Checking into a hospital, even if it was as plush as any resort, had not been part of her plan. Her plan had been to continue to cope by controlling her environment and keeping secret her greatest fear—that she would soon be as out of reality as her father had been since before she was born.

She had gone with Maggie to Denver, stayed with Maggie in her house and kept a few appointments with a psychiatrist by the name of Nan Tayama, a gentle woman of Burmese decent. "I've known Nan for years," Maggie said. "She is the smartest woman in the world, I think. And probably the kindest. But if you don't connect with her, I know others we can try."

"How is it you know so many psychiatrists?" Sedona asked.

"We like the same part of the body. The brain. I like the physiology, they like the chemistry."

"It's going to take a lot more than chemistry," Sedona said.

"You don't know anything yet," Maggie said. "First you have to be honest about what's happening with you."

Sedona tried her hardest. She gave Nan the benefit of the doubt. Nan was a tiny woman dressed in a suit that made Sedona wonder where she found professional-looking clothes made in such a small size. She assumed Nan was as smart and intuitive as Maggie said, and tried to open up. She explained that she'd started having manic episodes. Her heart would pound violently and she suffered from insomnia. Then the voices began. Usually it was her mother's voice, telling her what to do. She'd already had two children, and believed she was out of the woods for schizophrenia since she was in her late twenties. She used the excuse of needing to be available for her kids and asked about working from home. Her employers accommodated her. Now, looking back, she wondered if they knew something was wrong with her and preferred to keep her out of the office. She was running analyses of psychological testing. It really wasn't necessary that she be available for meetings or presentations as long as she supplied regular reports. And she did—long, meticulous reports. Being alone was better for her; she muttered to herself constantly, unless Bob or the kids were around, then by sheer dint of will she shut her mouth.

She went to see a psychiatrist with a good reputation and he immediately prescribed therapy and medication, but when she couldn't wake up for the children, she stopped taking it and never went back. She was smart enough to know that meds without therapy or therapy without meds just wouldn't do it. So, to cover what she knew was wrong, she made herself a rigid schedule that would disguise the fact that she didn't want to leave the house, didn't want to be with people. She went to the grocery store on Mondays, ran other errands on Thursdays, saw her parents twice a year. If her schedule went awry for any reason it was torture, but no one knew because it was apparent she used her time very well. Her house was perfect, her cooking delicious, her children excelled in school. Of course Bob wanted a social life, but she declined so often he all but gave up. She'd toss in a labored acceptance sometimes, just to keep the peace. He might be having an affair; she didn't know. Didn't really care. Not as long as her life was routine and no one knew her secret.

But it got worse, which of course was her worst fear. She experienced memory loss and confusion. She began to see things—animals in the refrigerator, the walls were crying, there was someone hiding in the closet in her bedroom and she was terrified to look. She couldn't lie still in the dark; it made her bones itch. So she went to the basement—to read, she told Bob. But really she paced and muttered and tried to will it away.

She admitted to Dr. Tayama that she'd thought about suicide.

After her assessment, Sedona spent ten days in the inpatient facility, talking to the psychiatrist every day, taking medicine, enduring group sessions that for her were impossibly terrible. One thing she did grudgingly admit: the drugs were not as bad as the ones she'd been prescribed several years ago and probably a thousand times better than the ones her father had tried. She was resting better, though she'd wake up confused about where she was until she got her bearings.

She walked into Dr. Tayama's office for her regular appointment.

"I'm so happy to see you, Sedona. You look well. Are you having a good day?"

"I think I would like it better if I could have a normal day," she said.

"Then I have good news," Dr. Tayama said. "You are normal. Not average, perhaps, but normal. Your version of normal."

"It would feel good to be everyone else's version," Sedona said.

"Ah, that would be a problem. It doesn't exist. I know it's hard to be objective when you're so far out of your comfort zone, but do you think the meds you've been taking are helping? Are you getting some sleep? Are the voices and images relaxing?"

"I suppose," she said. "Whatever you're giving me is an improvement over what Dr. Schizak gave me."

"That was a combination of Mellaril and Haldol. I don't know how you even got out of bed. I prescribed something that has less tranquilizing effect and isn't an antipsychotic. I thought there was a fair chance your confusion, memory lapses and voices were induced by anxiety-provoked insomnia. Go long enough without sufficient sleep and your brain will conjure anything."

"Anxiety?" Sedona said.

Dr. Tayama nodded. "It's a smorgasbord of issues. Anxiety that produces isolation and sometimes antisocial behavior, insomnia, depression. Add to that some OCD. I'm still not sure if it's the chicken or the egg—was your OCD severe enough to cause anxiety or did your anxiety lead you to attempt to control your environment as though you had OCD? In any case, to be conservative, I wanted to try a drug for anxiety and one for OCD. They behave as well as an antidepressant with some sedative side effects, just not as severe. It seems to be working. You seem alert and rested."

"But Dr. Schizak said I was schizophrenic!"

Dr. Tayama shook her head. "I don't think so. I think *you* told Dr. Schizak you were schizophrenic, like your father, when in fact you had a few symptoms that masqueraded as that disorder."

Sedona pushed back into her chair. "Anxiety!" she said. She laughed as if in relief. "Of all the—"

"It can be very serious, as you can attest. You're not out of the woods, Sedona. Anxiety and OCD have complicated your life, your relationships, your peace of mind, even some cognition. You have work to do. Drug therapy and counseling."

"But it's just anxiety!" she said emphatically.

"You thought about suicide," Dr. Tayama reminded her. "The anxiety was so alienating and frustrating it caused depression. Not following a treatment plan—"

"I think I'll go home now," Sedona said abruptly as she stood to leave.

"Please take a seat and hear me out," the doctor said. "If you leave now it will be exiting a mental health hospital against medical advice. You don't have the best pharmaceutical protocol in place. I can't just write you a prescription or give you a handful of pills. You need treatment, Sedona. Anxiety isn't a state of mind, it's a brain chemistry issue, just like depression or schizophrenia. You are not in control. Not yet. But your prognosis is good."

"I'll be fine now. Now that I know it's not my father's disease the anxiety will go away."

"Not likely," the doctor said. "You're a psychologist, Sedona. You know severe anxiety isn't nervousness or phobia…"

"I spent years recommending behavior modification for

students with test anxiety and it's been very successful. Thank you, Doctor. You've been a lifesaver!"

"I realize you're feeling much better but leaving treatment now is a very big risk. I think we should talk with your husband or siblings, arrange for aftercare, get you set up with psychiatric coverage for medication and a good counselor."

"I can handle it," she said. "I know exactly what to do!"

The doctor stood but she had to look up to meet Sedona's eyes. "This has happened before, Sedona. Often with disastrous results. I wish you would stay for a while, let us complete an evaluation so when you do go home you have the best possible opportunity for a better quality of life."

"I appreciate your effort," Sedona said. "But I hate it here. *Hate* it. I want my home, my family, my bed."

"So would I," Dr. Tayama confessed. "It won't be too much longer. Please. You're not entirely well."

"I know—my version of normal, you said."

"It's manageable. But we need time. You need time. Patience."

"Thank you. Goodbye, then."

"Sedona, take my card," she said. She scribbled on the back. "My cell number in case of an emergency. Call me if you need me."

Sedona, feeling brand-new, took the card, smiled, turned and left the doctor's office.

Nan Tayama sighed heavily and followed with her chart. She made a notation and handed it off to the nurse. It was not a locked facility. Sedona could pick up her personal items at the nurse's station—items they kept locked up mainly to keep them from being lost, borrowed or stolen— her purse, her cell phone, her laptop, her charging cords. About an hour later Dr. Tayama watched from her office window as Sedona, suitcase in hand, opened the back door to what she assumed was a private car company like Uber.

It was very late on a Saturday night when Dakota held Sid in his arms, in his bed, in his cabin. "When I rented this place, it didn't cross my mind that it might be a perfect hideaway for lovers."

"I like it here," Sid said. She patted his chest. "You're a wonderful pillow."

"I'd like to take you somewhere. Away somewhere. You can tell your brother you're going shopping for a couple of days in Denver and we can—"

She cut him off with laughter. "He would never believe that. Besides, I don't have to make up a story for Rob. He's a grown-up. He's not shocked that I have someone in my life."

"And the nephews?"

"Well, I explained a couple of weeks ago that I was dating someone. They don't know you so I just said you were the brother of a friend. I wanted them to know that if I was extra late or even seemed to be missing, I was not kidnapped—I was with you. And if they're worried, they should call my cell."

"How'd they take it?" Dakota asked, propped up on an elbow.

"Finn said, 'Go, Aunt Sid,' and Sean said, 'Ew.' I think that means they both understand what dating means to a thirty-six-year-old woman."

"So should we go away?" he asked hopefully.

"I suppose we can. Or we can just have breakfast here…"

"You'll stay the night?" he asked.

"Would that be good?"

"That would be so good," he said, leaning over her and

kissing her again. "I'm willing to grab a little time with you whenever we can but I'd love it if we weren't on the clock for twenty-four hours."

"At the moment, I don't have commitments…"

"Do you have any in the morning?" he asked.

"No," she said with a laugh. "I did promise to make Sunday dinner for the family. Would you like to come?"

Unbelievably, he blushed. "Sure. I've gotten used to Rob giving me that look like I might be debauching his baby sister, but Sean and Finn are at that special age. I don't know what to expect from them. Could be demoralizing."

"Debauching," she repeated. "You did get a good education in the Army. Your vocabulary is very good. I think you should expect 'Go, Aunt Sid' and 'Ew.' And they might tease, but they don't scare me."

"They don't?"

"Your family was very well behaved. Welcoming, even. They're cool. I am in love with most of them, especially Sam. Was that a huge surprise to you?"

"Everything around here surprises me," he admitted. "Cal and Maggie surprise me. Cal was married before. His wife died a very sad and painful death while I was in Iraq. She had scleroderma. That's when—"

"I know what it is," she said. "Was that long ago?"

"A couple of years before he met Maggie. And I knew Sierra and Connie talked about fostering kids but I didn't know they were thinking about adopting. I didn't know Connie was actually at the accident when Sam's mother died. I think they did the right thing, getting married right away and pursuing the adoption. I haven't been as close to my brother and sisters as I should have been. It's hard when you're in the military and deployed all the time. Now that I'm around them, they're pretty cool people. I keep asking myself if they've always been and I was missing out."

"What did you plan to do when you got out of the Army? I know you didn't pin all your hopes on being a garbage collector."

"I got out kind of suddenly," he said. "I used to think maybe I'd teach. I don't know what—history, maybe. I'd have to go back to school. I never did get a teaching certificate. I studied history and English and political science."

"English!" she said, surprised.

"I think we all did, all four Jones kids. We didn't have a TV—we read. We didn't have many books and we'd read them over and over and then trade them at a used-book store for a new supply. Cal can recite *To Kill a Mockingbird*, practically the whole book. I noticed that Sierra has a full bookcase now, but there are a few completely worn paperbacks—*Pride and Prejudice*. Another is *Wuthering Heights*."

"And your favorite books?"

"Steinbeck. Hemingway. Jack London."

"Ah. And did testosterone flow from the pages?"

"Well, I thought so…"

"We have so much to learn about each other," she said.

"What do you need to know? Do you need to know that I'm in trouble here? Because I've known you three months, been this close to you for three weeks, but it hasn't been often enough. And I already want to sleep with you every night. And not just sleep."

"Sex really works for you, doesn't it, Cody?"

"It does, but that's not really what I was thinking about. I was thinking about rolling over and feeling your soft skin, hearing you breathe—you snore a little. It's a cute snore. When you fall asleep, you curve against me and put your leg over me. Your hair tickles me. Your hands wander…"

"Do not," she said.

"Do so," he argued.

"We still have so much to find out…"

"Tell me what you need to know," he said. "You know I grew up strange—my parents are beyond crazy. It wasn't an easy childhood and we all left as soon as we could, the second we got out of school. Cal and Sedona found a way to go to college but I wasn't that imaginative. I joined the Army." He brushed back her hair. "Is that what you want to know?"

She looked up at him and smiled. "I want to know who you loved."

He rubbed her hair back a little longer. "Not yet, okay?"

"Is it very private?" she asked.

"It's private, yeah," he said. "That's not about you. I have this feeling I don't want to keep things from you. But just not yet, okay?"

"That means you haven't told your family?"

"That's what it means. But I don't want to talk about it right now because I don't want to be sad. You're in my arms and I am so happy. Can you give me a little time?"

She raked her fingers through his beard. "It must still hurt."

"I guess. I want to feel good right now, when you're here, naked, mine for the night."

"Reasonable," she said. "What do you have for breakfast?"

"Bacon, eggs, toast."

"Do you have fruit and oatmeal?" she asked.

"It never crossed my mind."

She sighed. "If I'm going to get a pass from my brother and nephews, we're going to have to stock up."

"Give me a list, gorgeous, and I'll get anything you want."

"Want to explore your woods after breakfast?" she asked. "I brought some outdoor clothes and shoes. In my car."

"An overnight bag?" he asked with lifted eyebrows.

"Uh-huh," she said. "I didn't think you'd say no. And I'm fussy about having my own toothbrush. But I'm afraid I neglected to bring pajamas."

Maggie drove to Denver early Tuesday morning and went directly to her practice. She had left Elizabeth with Cal. She had several patients to see in the office, then she was spending the afternoon in surgery—two simple cases and one complex surgery that could last well into evening. In fact, she might have two very long days, which was why she left Elizabeth at home, though she started missing her the minute she left.

It was almost nine in the evening by the time she got to her house in Denver. She had grabbed fish and chips to go from the nearest pub. She planned to eat in bed with the TV on. She put the take-out food in the microwave to warm up while she changed into pajamas. She loved her little house but when it was quiet, like now, she wanted her husband and baby. While she was working, she was glad to be working, but to be away from them when she wasn't working time seemed to drag.

She was aware that something was different. She couldn't tell what it was. Back in the kitchen, it was so shining clean. Maggie was tidy but she usually left mail or a book on the counter, maybe a water glass or coffee cup in the sink, but there was not so much as a streak or smudge, not a single fingerprint on the stainless steel.

She opened the pantry and her heart sank. Everything was lined up, neatly, organized by size and color and probably alphabetized. Her house had been scoured. She did not want to see her panties folded into neat little squares. But she was pretty sure Sedona couldn't help herself.

When they came to Denver together, Sedona had returned her rental car to the airport and spent a couple of days at Maggie's house. She had unpacked, hung the dress she'd brought for Sierra's wedding in the guest closet, put her pumps under it on the floor, lined up perfectly, and Maggie had taken her to her doctor's appointments. When Sedona had agreed to an inpatient evaluation, Sedona had left behind her dress and shoes.

Maggie checked and they were gone.

It was not likely a burglar had broken in and taken them. And scoured her house. Sedona could not have called Cal—Cal would have told Maggie if he'd heard from his sister. While her fish and chips grew cold in the microwave, Maggie found Nan Tayama's cell phone number in her phone. She texted her. Sedona's dress and dress shoes are gone from the closet and I suspect something is wrong. My house has been scoured, top to bottom. Do you know anything about this?

She waited a few minutes. The good doctor could have been asleep for all Maggie knew. Finally the answer came. She left our facility last week. She said she was going home.

Maggie knew the rules. Sedona had agreed to hospitalization and had not named anyone to receive information about her medical condition, not even her doctor sister-in-law. But just to be sure she had to ask... Did you discharge her?

I did not, came the reply.

Can you tell me when she left the hospital? Maggie asked.

Thursday. Midday.

And that was all Nan Tayama would be at liberty to say, thanks to HIPAA laws. Maggie thanked her and called Cal.

Maggie then called Bob because Cal was clearly flustered. Bob had not heard from his wife. He knew she had agreed to see a doctor in Denver and he had been so hopeful, knew she had decided to stay in an inpatient treatment program, but she hadn't been in touch. Everyone started dialing her cell number, with no results.

By midnight, it had been established that Sedona was missing and that her mental stability was uncertain. Bob had notified the police on the east coast, since the last anyone had heard she was bound for home, and Maggie contacted the Denver and Colorado police, municipal and state.

It was quite early in the afternoon when Dakota walked into the bar. He usually couldn't make it before five on one of his workdays. "Cody!" Sid said. He sat up at the bar in front of her and she looked over each shoulder to see who could be watching, then leaned toward him for a kiss.

"That's nice," he said, giving her a half smile. "Right out in public."

"What are you doing here? Did you get fired?"

"Something came up, Sid. I don't know where to start to explain. There was something going on with my sister Sedona, when she was here for Sierra's wedding. Something I didn't know about. I understand she didn't want her siblings to know but somehow Cal and Maggie figured her out. She's been battling some kind of mental illness and I don't know how serious it is. That's yet to be determined, I guess. Our father is schizophrenic but he's never been treated or medicated, at least not since he was very young. Well," he said, chuckling without humor, "he's been smoking pot almost his whole adult life. Keeps the special friends quiet. According to Cal and Maggie, Sedona is not schizophrenic but she has some disorder that could be very serious if she doesn't get some help and—"

"Oh my God, what's happened? Spit it out!"

"Maggie got her checked into a psychiatric hospital, where she stayed for ten days, but then she decided she didn't need to be there, so she checked herself out. She told her doctor she was going home. Bob and the kids are in Connecticut and haven't heard from her. We can't find her. The police have been notified. They've traced her movements a little bit but then all activity stopped."

"What activity?" Sid asked.

"Well, she hired an Uber from the hospital to Maggie's house. She stopped at an ATM, got some cash, stayed at Maggie's house for a few days, made a plane reservation to go home, hired an Uber to take her to a nice, quiet restaurant, where she had a meal, and that's where we think we lost her."

"You think?"

"There was some activity on her credit card but it was all over the place. Someone could have taken her purse or just lifted the card number from the car service or the restaurant. But she isn't answering her cell, and because she didn't communicate with anyone, we don't know if she's okay or—"

He exhaled. "I'm hoping she's taking a breather. Apparently there were troubles in the marriage that she didn't want to talk about, didn't want to tell me about. I don't blame her. We're not close. Maybe she just ran away for a little while."

Sid shook her head. "From what I saw, Sedona seemed too invested in her family. Even in this Colorado family. Do you know what the doctors said her disorder was?"

"The police are looking into that and we'll know soon.

The thing is, she was last seen in Denver. Cal has a baby, Sierra has a baby, so…" He stopped and just shook his head.

"So?" she asked.

He straightened. "I'm going to find her. I'm going to find my sister. And I'm about the last person she'd want to be found by. I haven't been a good brother."

"I don't believe you," Sid said. "You want something to eat? Drink? A beer?"

"I'd like a sandwich, if you can. And a cup of coffee. I'm leaving from here."

"Of course. BLT? Grilled cheese? Club?"

"Yeah, club. With oatmeal and fruit."

She smiled at him. "I want to hold you," she said. She felt tears come to her eyes. She had never said that to a man before. Her husband, David, seemed to have a million problems. No, he had irritants. She had never wanted to or offered to hold him.

For a split second, she let herself ponder if she hadn't done enough. Then she remembered how selfish he had been and let it go. "Let me get your food. Then we can talk a little while."

She went to her computer and keyed in the order, then anxiously turned back to Dakota.

But who was suddenly sitting on the bar stool next to him? The fancy woman. Neely. She was all smiles. Sid heard her say, "Well, what a surprise! I never would have thought I'd run into a friend at this time of day!"

Dakota gave her a look that said he was disgusted with her. And then he did something Sid would never have expected or predicted. He was completely rude to her.

"Not playing your games today, Neely. I have things to work out." He stood from his bar stool and walked down to the end of the bar near the kitchen door. The look on Neely's face was priceless. She was stunned.

Neely snapped her fingers at Sid. "Hey! Can I get a chicken Caesar?"

"Absolutely!" Sid said. "Coming right up!" And she went back to her computer. Then she brought Dakota a fresh cup of coffee. "I assume you were kidding about the oatmeal and fruit."

"Kind of," he said. "Waking up with you is heaven, even if it means eating oatmeal. Listen, I don't know what this is going to take. I don't know how long. I talked to Tom Canaday and he's not that busy right now so he's going to take my shift on the truck for a while. He said the money will come in handy."

"Will you call me?" she asked.

He grinned and she knew why. "We don't talk on the phone," he said. "We meet in the bar or at the food bank but we don't whisper into the phone like lovers do."

"This seems to be a good time to start. What do you think?"

"What I think is, I could pathetically need you."

"That would be okay. I'd like to be with you on this journey, in spirit if not in person. I think this is a good thing you're doing. I hope she's okay."

"I don't know what to expect, Sid. I always thought Sedona was the most stable kid in our family. I had no idea she was a little fucked up in the head. I mean, I did, but I didn't. You know?"

"You have no idea how well I know," she said. "Tell me what you're planning."

"I have a recent picture from Sierra's wedding. I emailed it to a print shop and they're making flyers for me. I'll go to the restaurant where she had dinner. I have an appointment with the doctor—hopefully she'll give me information I can use to help find her. Cal contacted a private detective to help us and the police have been very supportive. I asked them not to publicly mention her fragile mental state—I'm afraid if she hears that it will drive her away. She's so secretive and proud. I didn't know she was struggling." He looked down into his coffee. "Sedona drove me crazy. Not as a kid and big sister, she was okay then. But once she got married and had kids, man. She drove us all crazy."

"How?"

"I don't know. She ran a tight ship. Her husband was too quiet and preoccupied, her kids too polite and disciplined, her house too perfect, her schedule too rigid—the polar opposite of the way we grew up."

"But isn't that reasonable? If she didn't want the mirror image of the way you grew up?" Sid asked.

"Sometime, later, after we get Sedona back, I'm going to have to tell you more about my childhood and adolescence. It affected each one of us differently. The funny thing is, I thought Sedona was completely unaffected. She glided right off that farm, got scholarships and earned herself a degree in psychology, then a master's and PhD, then a nice husband and a house out of the city. She went back to the farm twice a year to check on our parents. She took her kids a couple of times but I never heard of her taking her husband. I thought she was the most normal one of us. Now I find out…"

"She might have hit a snag," Sid said. "Sometimes you think everything is okay. Not fabulous but perfectly satisfactory. As good as it's going to get. Then something happens and you find out you were barely holding it together."

"Is that what happened to you?" he asked.

"I was keeping a lot of balls in the air," she said. "I dropped the most fragile one. Then the rest of them just went down." There was the sound of a bell. "Excuse me a second."

She turned away from Dakota and went to the counter

to get the salad and Dakota's sandwich. She looked around the bar. Neely was gone.

She took the sandwich to Dakota. "Did you see her leave?"

"I wasn't paying attention. Bathroom, maybe?"

"I wasn't paying attention, either," Sid said. She put the salad at the place Neely had occupied, giving her a chance to come back. Then she picked up the coffee urn and refilled Dakota's cup.

"She's another thing I should talk to you about. Neely. I'll give you some details when there's more time, but don't trust her. She's not all right. She's not what she seems."

Sid frowned. "I think I could've guessed that the first time she snapped her fingers at me for service. Not all right how?"

"I gotta take care of Sedona first, then I'll tell you a story. I was never involved with her in any way. Since I've been here, there's only been you."

"I'm still surprised by that," she said with a smile that felt sentimental. "I hope you'll be okay, Cody. I hope you can find her right away."

He took a big bite of his sandwich. She casually watched the bar to see if there were customers in need and took note that Neely had not returned. He washed down about half the sandwich with water.

"Can I pack up anything for your drive?" she asked. "Drinks? Food?"

"I'm covered. I really hate to leave you. Now that I have to go, I realize how many things I want to tell you. Want to ask you."

"There are some things I want to tell you, too. Like, I didn't exactly work in computers."

He smiled at her. "Sid, I'm picking up garbage. You really think I'm going to have a negative opinion if this is the best job you've ever had?"

"In many ways, it is," she said.

"I need to go," he said. He took a last slug of water to wash down his sandwich, a couple of swallows of coffee. He stood. "I'll call tonight if I can. I won't call if it's late."

"Cody, you can call me at any hour. We're in a crisis mode here. I'm capable of turning off the phone if I can't take a call but I want to hear from you. If you can... No, if you feel like talking to me, please call. I understand you have to be in touch with Cal and Sierra, but I'll be anxious to hear, too. If only to know your progress."

"I am going to miss the hell out of you," he said.

"I'll walk you out," she said.

Just before exiting the bar, she tugged on his shirt, stopping him. She stood on her toes and threaded her hands into his overlong hair, her lips finding his.

His hands went to her hips, pulling her close, giving his lips to her. For a second his eyes were open wide, surprised by this public display. The bar wasn't at all full, but her brother wasn't far away and there were people there. He released her lips reluctantly. He smiled, his teeth so white against that black, trimmed beard. "Wow. PDA."

"I'll miss you, too. Please be safe."

"I'll look forward to coming back to you," he said. And he kissed her again.

The greatest happiness of life is the conviction

that we are loved; loved for ourselves, or rather, loved in

spite of ourselves.

—Victor Hugo

12

Dakota wanted to think about Sedona, focus on her, try to imagine what she might be feeling or fearing. But he was clueless and could not conjure an image of what his older sister, always so much in control, might be going through.

So his thoughts naturally drifted to Sid. He found he faced some serious surprises. Not in her but in himself. He saw her, he found her appealing, he wanted to get to know her better. He wanted to touch her. That was all so predictable, so familiar. He'd actually breathed a sigh of relief. There was an attractive woman who would distract him from darker thoughts, take his mind off the Army, his sense of failure, his disappointment and his loss.

But then something grew in him and he began to really care about Sid. He kept wondering what she'd say next, how she'd make him laugh with her lightning-quick wit, what unexpected activity she'd come up with. The soup kitchen shocked him, but he greatly appreciated her kindness and insight. Hasnaa had said to him, "It's not what you get in life that will make you whole, but what you give." She had given it all. Dakota hoped that Sid was a little more cynical than Hasnaa had been, that she'd wear some cynicism around her like a Kevlar vest, judging the world a bit more harshly and keeping herself safe.

He wanted to be with her because he took great comfort in her. It was not a feeling he was well acquainted with. Oh, he'd been filled with passion for Hasnaa, thinking of her all the time and dreaming about her, wanting her irrepressibly. There was such tension trying to navigate the differences in their lifestyles, customs. He remembered his love feeling like a brittle twig that could snap if the wrong pressure was applied, a love so fragile and volatile it had to be handled with great care. His love had felt explosive!

There was something different about what he felt for Sid. There was definite passion and excitement. It filled him up and gave him a buoyant feeling. He wanted to be in her space, hear her voice, talk with her, listen to her. He wanted to come home to her, kiss her goodbye when he left her, and he wanted to take care of her and be taken care of by her. He wanted to sit at her table, sleep in her bed, learn about her deepest fears and happiest moments. He longed for tender moments of touching and dreaming just as he wanted that white-hot passion that lit them both up till they burst into flame. It was like that infatuation he'd had for Hasnaa but all grown up. There was so much he didn't know about Sid and yet he felt he knew her completely. If she would have him, he would be her companion, her partner.

He was falling in love with her and it didn't leave him at all uneasy. He welcomed the feeling. He hoped it would never end.

He thought about her the whole way to Denver. When this crisis with Sedona was under control, he would tell her. Maybe he would even tell her how he had loved Hasnaa madly and yet somehow he loved Sid more confidently, more intensely, with utterly no doubt.

He'd known her for three months and he was sure he wanted to marry her. Dakota didn't fall in love often, but when he did, he went off the deep end.

He went first to the office supply store to pick up his flyers. Only a hundred for now. He hoped it wouldn't be necessary to get more but the salesclerk assured him they could have them ready in a matter of hours. He went then to the police department—a detective, Santana, was on missing-persons cases and though it was after six, he was still at the office. They had a long chat about the many possibilities and the length of time that had passed since Sedona was last seen.

"She could have been kidnapped. She could have been depressed or upset and checked herself into the Ritz for the week, pampering herself. She could have run off with a friend or lover, covering her tracks. She could have had some kind of mental or emotional breakdown that rendered her incapable of reaching out or left her confused or disoriented. She could be lost."

"She could be dead," Dakota said.

"According to the doctor, your sister has had suicidal thoughts and feelings," Santana said. "But she never attempted suicide, and while the doctor thinks she could have benefited from more therapy, she seemed functional. When she left the restaurant, the sun was still shining. In that neighborhood it's hard to imagine that she'd be snatched off the street. We haven't had so much as a purse snatching there in a very long time."

"And what did the doctor say about her issues?" Dakota asked. "Whatever mental disorder she's struggling with?"

"It's something to be taken very seriously—the doctor believes she may be dealing with anxiety and OCD, both of which can have their mild forms and their very serious forms. I'm afraid we're not sure which. Your sister was responding to medication and feeling better, but she left the hospital before her evaluation was complete. Buddy, there's anxiety and then there's anxiety—and it's not to be confused with nervousness. It's not what you feel when you have to sit in front of a promotion board and they all look like they want to eat you. It's a chemical disorder and it floods the patient's body with fear and paranoia even though there's no apparent cause. It can be a mild case, controlled with breathing exercises and some behavior modification. It can be severe, leaving the patient in a panic attack, curled up in a corner, shaking, crying and disoriented."

"Does anyone know if Sedona has it that bad?"

"Her husband said he found her in a state of panic a few times, but it was so irregular he wasn't sure what was up. She refused to go to the hospital and it passed. She was driving the family crazy with her rituals and sleeplessness, and if she's not sleeping, she could be disoriented, confused, even hallucinating. And then there's OCD…"

"I get it," Dakota said. "A little on the neat and tidy side or obsessed…"

"And not able to walk down the sidewalk because of the cracks or leave a room without flicking the light switch a certain number of times. In both cases, the anxiety and OCD, your sister wasn't sleeping much. She might've been awake for days, in a manic state. She was afraid she was schizophrenic, like her father."

"*Our* father," Dakota said. "I didn't know."

"As I understand it, you've been away. Army?"

"Yeah," he said. "Yes, sir," he amended. "The Army

kept me busy and moving, but the truth is, after I left home I didn't keep in touch very much. I saw my parents a few times and they were just as batshit crazy as when I was a kid. I saw Sedona about as many times and she was wound up and bossy and a rigid pain in the ass. I had no idea it could have been a medical issue." He took a breath and looked down. "I spent a lot of years wondering why I couldn't have been born into another family."

Detective Santana laughed. "Join the club, pal. I could tell you stories, but let's focus on your sister. Maybe when we get her home safe, we can have a beer and I can tell you about an old-world Mexican father who will never forgive me for not living at home and helping start a family business with my brothers. But for now…"

"Where should I start?"

"I have a list of places her credit card appeared before the company shut it off but it's impossible for it to have been her using it. This is her charge in Denver, then Florida, then California, then Texas. Her last use was the restaurant. We've interviewed those people. They were as helpful as we'd expect. We had patrol officers search the surrounding area—nothing to report. The hotels within walking distance have been checked…"

"Hey, if she had a plane reservation, wouldn't she have had a suitcase?" Dakota asked.

"She might have, but we were looking in alleys and Dumpsters for anything that might have been hers. If her purse was lost or stolen, usually the IDs, credit cards and cash are taken out and the purse discarded. There was nothing. But I think you should start there. You might uncover something by talking to the people who last saw her—waitstaff, cashier, busser. Then walk around with your flyers. In the meantime, we're putting her picture up on social media and in the patrol reports so officers can be watching. Do you have any help in the search?"

"For now it's just me but I'm meeting the private detective after I leave here. We're meeting at the restaurant where she had her last meal." That statement made him wince.

Dakota talked to Bob Packard at least twice during the day and every evening. He gave him a full report on what he was learning and urged him to stay in Connecticut on the chance Sedona found her way home. Bob agreed, with great difficulty as he was growing impatient and ever more worried.

"My mother and sister are staying at the house, propping us up and feeding us during this crisis," he said. "I'll stay a few more days but then I'm coming to Colorado to help look for her. That's where she disappeared, that's where she's going to be found."

"I agree that's likely," Dakota said. "Stay where you are a little longer while I keep canvassing the area she was last seen. And tell me more about Sedona."

"I didn't notice anything was wrong for a long time. She was a quirky perfectionist but I worked with a guy who lines up his pens and polishes the glass top of his desk every morning. She was not very social—she didn't like to be around people she didn't know well and crowds made her crazy. Is that weird? I run an architecture firm, and talk about antisocial perfectionists... She was always busy, she worked hard and for a long time was an amazing wife. Amazing. A spotless house, smart and clean children, good food on the table every night. I took her completely for granted, but she said she liked it that way. It wasn't until two, three, maybe four years ago that I started to notice patterns—like a routine for how she worked in her kitchen, a routine to include things like wiping the counter a certain way, then going back and doing it all again…and again… She folded things like napkins a certain way, making a little V at the end of the toilet tissue. And she wasn't sleeping much. She was jumpy and edgy, and when she thought I wasn't paying attention, she was talking to herself. Not a little bit. A lot. That's when I started to get worried. But I didn't think it was anything that couldn't be fixed."

"Did you suggest counseling?"

"Oh, hell, no," Bob said. "I told her to go to a doctor! I told her I bet she should be on some tranquilizer or anti-depressant, like Prozac. I wanted her to do what she usually does—just go take care of it."

"But she said… There was talk of divorce?"

"She was folding clothes that had already been folded, cleaning bathroom tiles with a toothbrush she had to then throw away, washing clothes three times before they were clean… And maybe she wasn't talking to herself. Maybe she was talking to people the rest of us couldn't see."

"We called them Jed's 'special friends,'" Dakota said.

"I started to suspect she was crazy. Like her father."

"The good news is, she is nothing like our father, who is schizophrenic and has an entirely imagined life that isn't based in reality. But Sedona could have similar problems if she's sleep-deprived," Dakota said.

"I'm really surprised she's not manic depressive. I thought that's what I was witnessing. Wide awake for days… What if something terrible has happened to her? I waited too long. I should have taken her to the doctor myself. But I wouldn't have known who to call."

"I'm planning on everything working out okay," Dakota said. "She's going to be okay."

"Man, I thought she *was* okay," Bob said. "I'll never trust myself again."

* * *

During the first several days that Dakota was in Denver, he talked to a lot of people, then began knocking on doors in the neighborhood, particularly those between the restaurant and Maggie's house, to ask if anyone had seen her. The restaurant, small and upscale, was one of several and was located in a neighborhood of shops and salons, a seniors' extended-care apartment complex, a nursing home, a school, a couple of markets, two churches and a group of medical offices. The private detective, Ben Cousins, visited most of the shop owners and was looking for security video, but since Sedona had been missing for more than twenty-four hours before they started canvassing, there was no relevant surveillance video available. Most of the shop owners agreed to put flyers in their windows.

Then they had their first real break—her purse was found. It was emptied of credit cards, money and ID, looked like it had been run over by a truck that left some tread marks on the leather, but inside was Dr. Tayama's business card with her cell phone number written on the back. The doctor said she didn't make a habit of doing that and none of her friends or acquaintances had mentioned losing a purse. Of course, it could have been given to a charity like Goodwill or a homeless shelter and the card overlooked and left inside, but they were operating under the assumption that it was Sedona's purse.

On the downside, it was found fifteen miles away, on the other side of the city, and only served to broaden the search.

Maggie, Cal and Elizabeth drove up from Timberlake to go door-to-door with Dakota. Maggie was able to confirm that the purse looked like the one Sedona carried.

The next day Sierra, Connie and little Sam were there for several hours.

Over the week a couple of people said she looked somewhat familiar but they couldn't say where they might have seen her or even whether it was Sedona or someone who looked like her.

All that week while Dakota and others were canvassing, Ben Cousins and his assistants were making dozens if not hundreds of phone calls, sharing information with the police. They checked bus, plane and train passengers, outlying hotels and motels, called businesses, texted pictures and stayed in close touch with Bob, who continually checked bank balances and ATM withdrawals.

On Saturday, Sid came to Denver. She arrived early in the morning and brought an overnight bag. Just the sight of her at the door to Maggie's house took Dakota by such sweet surprise he grabbed her in his arms and held her so tightly she squeaked. He put her down and kissed her passionately, the kind of kiss he usually reserved for when they were alone.

She pushed him away with a small laugh. "Cody," she said.

"Why are you here?" he asked her.

"I'm here to work. I'll help you today and tomorrow. I'll stay over, if you're okay with that."

"I wish it wasn't this kind of work," he said, pulling her close again. "It's really discouraging."

"Then we'll get through it together, okay?"

They started with coffee and a phone update from Ben Cousins. Dakota put it on speaker so Sid could listen. Today they would visit service stations and convenience stores in the area where Sedona's purse was found. They covered a lot of ground even though there were many stops for phone calls from Bob, Cal, Sierra and others. They ate lunch on the run and got back on their route. Dinner was a quick stop for pizza, and after that, they hit a couple of crowded pubs and talked to the people there, both the wait-staff and customers.

Finally, too late to knock on doors or pester businesses, they went back to Maggie's house, where Dakota had been staying. Exhausted, Sid begged for a shower. Afterward, snug in an extralong T-shirt and soft shorts, hair combed through and wet, she looked for Dakota and found him in the kitchen. He was leaning against the kitchen counter, swirling an amber liquid covering ice.

"I'm having a whiskey," he said. "Maggie has a good se-lection of wine and there's this. No soft drinks, I'm afraid."

"I'd love a glass of wine," she said. "Is there a white wine?"

He opened the refrigerator and pulled out a chardon-nay, showing it to her.

"Perfect," she said. "Maybe we can relax a little bit. To-morrow's another day."

He opened the bottle, poured her a glass and touched her glass with his. "Thank you for coming," he said. "Sid, this isn't how I'd have planned a night away with you to be. I would have taken you to a nice restaurant, put on some soothing music, gotten in that shower with you, rolled around in the bed with you for hours... And I'm—"

"Exhausted, I know. Of course you are."

"And distracted, when I'd like to give you all my at-tention."

She leaned against him and he slid an arm around her waist. "I'm sorry for what you must be going through but I'm so proud of you," she said. "I don't spend a lot of time thinking about men and I sure haven't been wondering what kind of man is right for me. I honestly didn't think there was room in my life for a man after having chosen so badly once and paid such a high price. But, Dakota, you're the right kind of man. A man who will do the right thing, the good thing, even at a personal sacrifice."

"Don't give me too much credit. I haven't done much for my family in the past and I'm feeling a debt because of that. I'm not that good. I'm late, that's what I am. I spent a lot of years waiting for my family to make it up to me because I had a rough adolescence and it never dawned on me that maybe I could grow up and get over it now and do something for them. Then I found out that poor Sedona is about as fucked up as I am."

"You seem like the most normal man I know," she said.

"There are things I should tell you," he said. "Full disclosure—I hated my parents. I was ashamed of them. My father is sick, but I was angry because it embarrassed me. Because people laughed at us, made fun of us. It felt to me like Cal and Sedona were unaffected, though clearly they weren't. I worried a lot about how hard I had it and didn't pay any attention to what anyone else was going through."

"You were just a boy," she said.

"I haven't been a boy in a long time, Sid." He stroked her hair. "The truth is, I didn't have much compassion for my own family until Sedona went off the rails. God, I hope she's all right."

"I hope so, too," Sid said. "It's very scary but just a little less so when families stick together. Friends and family. I'm in this with you. I want to be."

"It's okay. Cal and Maggie are coming back up. So are Sierra and Connie when he has a couple of days. Police have started looking in isolated places, Sid. I think they're looking for any indication a body—"

"Shh," she said. "We're not there yet."

"I'm so goddamn selfish. I want to be alone with you without something like this weighing us down. I want us to spend some serious time learning about each other. I already know where to touch you, how to touch you, how to make you want more, but I don't know what kind of kid you were in high school. I want to know what you did on vacation, what you dreamed of your life turning into. I know your parents are gone now but I'd like to know what they were like. I want to know everything. And I want to tell you everything."

She stopped him with a soft laugh. "That's good, we'll do that. But for tonight, let's just go to bed and practice that touching thing. That should get us through the tough parts. Okay?" She took him by the hand and pulled him to the guest bedroom where he'd camped out. "That will get us through the night."

"Sid, I want to never let you go," he said.

"I can live with that," she said.

There was no point in getting up at dawn. Homes and businesses were barely astir before at least eight and it was Sunday. Dakota had the best night's sleep he'd had in over a week and he was in heaven with the soft and sweet-smelling woman next to him, curling against him. He kissed her forehead. "I love that little snore," he said.

"I bet you'll get over that…"

"I found it adorable," he said. Then he frowned. "That noise is disturbing me." There seemed to be a lot of traffic on Maggie's usually quiet street, more than he'd ever heard before. "Is there a church around here?"

"I don't remember seeing one," she said. "Maybe someone's having a yard sale. When someone has a yard sale in Timberlake, people show up at the crack of dawn to get the first look."

"I don't care if they're going to church or a yard sale, I hate them," Dakota said.

"That's the patient, tolerant Dakota I love so much," she said, laughter in her voice.

The doorbell rang.

Dakota jumped naked out of bed. "Think whoever that is will mind if I don't take time to dress?" he said, giving his hips a crude little shake.

"If you open that door without pants on, I'm finished with you!"

"You're not really fun all the time," he said. He grabbed his jeans off the floor, pulled them on and went out of the bedroom. "It's probably someone with the wrong address for the yard sale…" Not even bothering to zip and button, he flung open the front door.

He was met with the no-nonsense brown eyes and furry brows of Sister Mary Jacob.

"Sister!" he said, turning away, grabbing for the zipper and button of his jeans.

"Sorry to take you away from your photo shoot, Dakota, but a few of us decided our time was better spent here than at Mass."

"Sidney!" he shouted. "It's Sister Mary Jacob!"

Sidney came to the front door completely dressed in sweats and sweatshirt, a smile on her face.

"Oh, Sister, what are you doing here?" she asked, reaching out to hug her friend.

"We came to help look for Dakota's sister," she said.

Sid looked over the nun's shoulder to see a large group gathered on the sidewalk in front of the house. Many of the people they usually served dinner with on Saturday evenings were there, plus a few others.

"You are so awesome," Sid said.

"Then maybe coffee wouldn't be too great a burden?"

"Absolutely not," she said. "Come in, everyone!"

There were fifteen of them in all—the crew from the soup kitchen and some of them brought along friends or family members. Sister Mary Jacob had rounded them up.

Maggie didn't have enough cups but she did have a decent supply of paper to-go cups, probably so she could caff-up on her way to work for those early, early mornings. It took two full pots just to get them all started.

Dakota, now fully dressed, explained that their routes and routine usually started with an 8:00 a.m. phone call from the private detective on the job and it was almost time for him to call.

"Even on Sunday?" someone asked.

"Even on Sunday," Dakota said. "I have to find her." And then he went on to explain what he understood about Sedona's condition, that she could be in a state of panic or confusion, but he had no way of knowing. But no one, certainly not her family, could imagine her leaving them voluntarily. "We hope and pray she hasn't been hurt," he said.

Sedona had made a plane reservation and left Maggie's house in Denver because she knew Maggie would be coming back soon. Maggie was scheduled to work on Tuesday morning and might even be coming to Denver the evening before. She could even bring Cal and the baby if the psychiatrist leaked the news that Sedona left the hospital, though that seemed unlikely since no one had come, the phone never rang and all was quiet. But Sedona had known her period of adjusting was over. She had to leave. She had to go home. She left on Monday afternoon. She had been out of the hospital for four days.

Since her flight wasn't due to leave for hours, she went to a restaurant for an early dinner. She wanted to prove to herself that she could seem perfectly normal and entirely confident. But it was awful. She was aware of every watermark on a glass, wrinkle in the tablecloth, smear or mark on the flatware, grime on the cashier's station. And this was a particularly clean establishment.

When she was finished and had paid, she took a walk down the block. Summer was full upon them and the June sun was reluctant to set. She sat down on a bench in a small park surrounded by little houses and in no time at all she realized her mistake—she would have to try to retrace her path back to the restaurant in order to call her taxi or car service because she wasn't going to be able to give her location.

But she sat.

She knew her medication had worn off—she was feeling all those uncomfortable feelings again. She was edgy, frightened, exhausted, tense. She knew all she would need was a prescription and then all these issues would be over—she would sleep, she would feel blessed calm, unless there was some major stressor invading her life.

But when Bob found out that she left the hospital and hid out at Maggie's, he was going to flip. He'd lock her up again. And the next place might not be as nice!

It was dusk when an elderly woman walked by. She noted the suitcase sitting beside Sedona and said, "Oh, my. This looks ominous."

"I'm going to call a cab for the airport," Sedona told her.

"I see," the lady said. "Going on a trip, are you?"

"I'm going home. I've been…visiting." Then Sedona looked around and discovered she didn't have her purse. "Where's my purse?" she asked. "I don't seem to have my purse!"

"I'm forgetting things all the time," the woman said with a laugh. "Let's walk back to where you were visiting and see if you left it there."

"I was at the restaurant. Loman's. Do you know the place? I paid my check with a credit card so I know I had it. But now…" She looked around frantically, looked up and down the walk.

"That's almost a mile from here," the woman said. "You must have left it there. My house is right there—the one with three boulders near the front door. Would you like to use my phone to call the restaurant and ask them to take care of it for you until you can walk back and pick it up?"

Sedona said that would help. And the woman introduced herself as Alice.

Alice's little house had a very musty smell and was furnished with aging furniture, though the structure wasn't that old.

"My husband and I bought this house a dozen years ago and then he passed away and I live alone now," Alice said. "It's a good house in a good neighborhood. With the park across the street and all the children, I'm happy here. Just old. Forgetful and a bother, but it's only age. So what, I say. There's the phone, dear. I've never had one of those cell things and I'm not going to."

"Then do you have a directory?" Sedona asked.

"A what? What's that?"

"I don't know the phone number of the restaurant," Sedona said.

"Perhaps you should call the people you were visiting," Alice suggested.

Of course Sedona didn't remember Cal's number. Having those things handy on your cell phone was not good for the memory. Alice had a serviceable computer and they managed to come up with a phone number for Loman's restaurant, but they claimed no purse had been left behind. Sedona was getting ready to walk back to the restaurant to see if she'd lost it along the way, but it was now almost dark.

She felt so helpless and she started to cry.

Alice, as it turned out, felt equally helpless. She said her son was planning to lock her up also! He lived in Arizona but claimed his mother couldn't take care of herself and he couldn't visit her every day so he wanted to sell the house she lived in and use the money to place her in a home of some kind. But her house was paid off. Alice didn't want to live in a home! He said she was irresponsible. That he didn't approve of her spending. He sent her an allowance and paid her bills and wouldn't allow her to buy anything without permission. He set up an account at the pharmacy and grocery, but otherwise controlled her money. "He just wants me dead so he can sell this house!"

Sedona spilled some of her story—her husband was threatening divorce if she didn't get mental help! And she'd spent ten days in a mental hospital, and while the medication did make her feel better, it had not been a great experience. She'd been frightened and isolated. She missed her children desperately but was terrified to go home.

Alice made tea and Sedona began to clean the kitchen and the refrigerator. And she found there was laundry to do. The bathroom needed attention, serious attention. All the while they talked. They talked almost through the night while Sedona cleaned and Alice nodded off in the chair, but it was all right, she said. She hadn't really gone to bed at bedtime since her husband died. She'd slept in her chair, about two hours here, two hours there, bored and lonely and always tired.

This is how I will be, but no one will set up accounts or watch over me, Sedona thought.

Sedona had grown to fear the bed—it meant only anxiety and restlessness for her. She saw herself in Alice, a lonely old woman who was seen as a burden, a problem.

That was almost a week ago. The locks on the doors were strong, but Alice didn't get frazzled when Sedona checked them several times a day. The park at dawn or dusk was refreshing and Sedona told Alice more than she'd told her therapist and Alice had told her life story over and over again. The same story actually—she repeated herself. Sedona didn't mind. Sedona cleaned and cooked and taught Alice how to order her groceries by the phone and made her a small chart to check off her meals when she ate them. Sedona kept track of every nickel and promised to send Alice a check when they parted ways. She promised to pay her half and, in the meantime, made lovely little meals for them to share.

Sedona had been missing for ten days. She left the hospital on a Thursday, stayed over the weekend in Maggie's house, left there on a Monday with the intention of flying home to Connecticut but lost her purse, her phone, her money and hooked up with Alice out of necessity. And she was actually quite happy despite her obvious issues. Alice didn't question Sedona's behavior or fuss that she was disturbed by her quirky rituals, like folding and refolding the towels, taking three steps into a room, then three backward steps out and then back in.

But on their sixth day together, Alice's son called as he did every Sunday morning. And Alice said, "I've never been so happy. I have the loveliest roommate! Her name is Sedona!"

A loving heart is the truest wisdom.

—CHARLES DICKENS

13

Dakota and his band of volunteers were not getting off to a prompt start. Up till now it had only been a few people to manage but fifteen was a bit daunting. Sister Mary Jacob stepped up to the plate, fetched clipboards out of her car, while Dakota rummaged around for paper in Maggie's study. Everyone in the group hunted for pens and the nun, a born organizer, begin to assign areas. While they were doing that Cal, Maggie and Sully arrived, Elizabeth with them. Introductions were made and instructions repeated.

Even though they had canvassed much of the area between the restaurant where Sedona was last seen and Maggie's house, they had not gone to the neighborhood in the other direction, away from the restaurant, so that was the mission of the volunteers for this particular Sunday. They went down the sidewalk in pairs, headed for the neighborhood just past the small park, when two police cruisers rushed past them, lights flashing but no sirens.

"This used to be such a quiet neighborhood," Maggie said. "Nothing but excitement the last couple of weeks."

Dakota's cell phone was ringing in his pocket and he pulled it out. It was Detective Santana. "Where are you?" he asked Dakota.

"Just outside my sister's house. Less than a block away with a group of volunteers. What's going on?"

"I think we might have found her but we'll need your ID. The son of an elderly woman called the police and said a woman named Sedona was holding his mother hostage…"

"Hostage! She wouldn't do that! Where is she?"

"The police are en route to Felder Avenue, just three blocks from Dr. Sullivan's house."

"I see them!" Dakota shouted into the phone. He began to jog down the street where the two police cruisers were parked diagonally in front of a little house and the officers were crouched behind the cars, weapons drawn. "Holy shit, what are you doing?" he yelled.

"Stay back, sir! Get down the street and take cover until this is resolved!"

"Is my sister in there? Sedona Packard? She wouldn't hold anyone hostage! Sedona!" he yelled, walking right into the police officers' line of fire. "Sedona! Come out!"

He was suddenly tackled. He went down hard with a very heavy police officer on top of him, a knee in his back. He realized a little late that it was lucky he didn't get shot. "Don't move," the officer said. Dakota felt his hands roughly pulled behind him and handcuffs slapped on his wrists.

"The detective just called, he's on the phone! Let me see if my sister is in there! Take my phone," Dakota pleaded. "Talk to Santana. Come on, man, have you lost your mind?"

"The house is not secure!"

The front door squeaked open and an elderly woman with wiry white hair wearing a purple pantsuit and bedroom slippers stood in the doorway. She just stood there, looking at the scene on her front lawn with a confused look on her face.

"What in the world are you people doing?" she asked.

Sedona stepped up behind the old woman, her hands on the woman's shoulders. Immediately, the police started shouting at her to show her hands and come out of the house slowly.

Sedona had a stricken look on her face, but she did as she was told and the crowd of volunteers was converging rapidly on the two officers and Dakota. Cal ran toward them, waving one of his flyers with her picture on it, trying to rapidly explain that they'd been looking for Sedona for a week.

Ignoring the police, Cal pulled her into his embrace. "What are you doing here?" he asked.

"I just wanted a little time," she said. "I'm afraid the bunch of you and Bob will have me committed."

Maggie ran up to them. "Sedona, no one can have you committed unless you're a danger to yourself or others. You're panicked, that's all. We'll find the right kind of help for you."

"Bob will be furious," she said. "He'll—"

"Bob is worried sick," Dakota said from his place on the grass. He'd wrangled himself into a sitting position, hands cuffed behind his back. "Will you get these goddamn things off me?" he shouted.

"Hey, Bud," the second officer said, holding his cell phone away from his ear. "This is our missing person. Santana is on his way into the station. We're going to meet him there with Mrs. Packard."

"And me," Cal said. "I'm her brother and attorney."

"And I'm her sister-in-law and doctor," Maggie said.

"And I'm her brother and the guy who's going to sue your asses!" Dakota said.

"He's a little cranky," Cal said. "Let him go, huh? Otherwise, he's going to make this worse than it already is."

"Maybe we should wait awhile," the first cop said. "See if he can behave. We already know he can't listen or follow orders."

"You don't know the half of it," Cal said.

"What about Alice?" Sedona asked.

"Alice?" three people said in unison.

Sedona turned and looked at the elderly woman in the doorway. She just stood there, waiting. But a couple of tears made paths down her cheeks. "Oh, Alice," Sedona said, walking back to her and enfolding her in her arms. "Oh, dear Alice, you took such good care of me."

"I didn't," she said, her voice weak and trembling. "I didn't do anything for you. And you were my friend."

"Well, we knew it was going to have to end. I have a family." She looked over her shoulder. "A lot of family. And you have to talk to your son."

"Hmph," she said, wiping her eyes. "Is it too late to cut him out of my will?"

Sedona laughed and wiped her own eyes. "He only wants you to be safe," she said.

"I'm not so sure about that," Alice said. Then she gave a tremulous smile. "My house has never been so clean. Even before I was old."

"One of my gifts," Sedona said. "It comes at a dear price, trust me."

Alice got a shocked look. "Do I owe you something?"

"No, no, of course not. I just meant… Oh, never mind what I meant." She kissed the old woman's cheek. "Thank you for taking care of me."

"A lot of people seem to want you," Alice said.

Sedona looked at the crowd. She didn't know most of them.

"This is going to take some sorting out," one of the officers said, approaching Sedona.

Maggie came to her side. "I'll go with you, Sedona. Your brothers will come. We'll call Bob right away—he's very worried. Everything is going to be okay now."

Sedona had only been three short blocks from Maggie's house, but since it was in the opposite direction of the restaurant the search hadn't covered that area and Alice and Sedona had never noticed the flyers posted everywhere. It was unclear if Sedona had lost her purse or left it at the restaurant or if it had been stolen but her credit cards had been used until they were shut off by companies. It was possible Sedona left it and someone took advantage.

Sedona told her story, an emotional ordeal for sure. To her, it was all very logical. She signed herself out of the hospital and went to Maggie's house, where she used her time alone to prepare herself for how she'd work things out with her family. But her medication wore off and panic set in. As she had done for many years, she forced herself to leave the house, get dinner, make a reservation, behave in a socially acceptable manner. It was very likely the panic that caused her to leave her purse behind. By the time she got to the park without her purse, her phone, her money, she was exhausted and frightened. That's where Alice found her and took her in.

"I'm kind of embarrassed I didn't think of that scenario myself," Maggie said. Sedona was released to the custody of her brothers and sister-in-law. Maggie called Dr. Tayama to report that Sedona was safe and asked her to prescribe the best mild sedative for her condition.

Bob was on his way. Dakota and Sidney were told they could head back to Timberlake, but they decided to stay until they could see Sedona and Bob reunited. Sedona was tense despite a sedative, but Bob was so relieved to see her he just put his arms around her and said, "Let's get this fixed, honey."

Dakota and Sidney finally did escape. They were in two cars. Dakota leaned into her window. "Let's go somewhere for the night," he said. "There's a lodge on our way—the Pinewood Lodge. Give me just a second to call them and make sure they have a room, then will you follow me there?"

"Sounds perfect," she said.

A moment later, he put his phone back in his pocket. He smiled. "Twenty-four-hour room service," he said.

In forty minutes they were pulling into a little hideaway in the mountains. Ten minutes later they were entering a room with a view of the Rockies and a lush valley below them. They had a small deck, a king-size bed, a spa tub and each other.

"It's been a long, stressful week for you," Sid said. "Good outcome, but a long one."

"Thank God she's okay and safe." He laughed. "Thank God I didn't go to jail!"

"Yeah, you're going to want to avoid making a habit of that."

"I know," he said, running a hand through his hair. "How fast can you be naked?"

She laughed in spite of herself. "You're impossibly romantic, you know that?"

He grabbed her around the waist. "I must knock you off your feet, huh?"

She ran her fingers through his short beard. "As a matter of fact…"

They enjoyed a delicious dinner of trout, rice, grilled asparagus with a cream sauce and beet salad. "It's like eating a rainbow," Sid said.

"We have to remember this place," Dakota said.

After dinner they showered and got into bed. Dakota pulled her into his arms and began to slowly and thoroughly worship her body. He kissed every inch of her, from her eyelids to her toes, pausing here and there to deliver some special attention with his tongue and fingers. When he found her lips at last, she was breathless.

"You're right about the beard," she whispered. "There are times it really is magnificent."

"Works for me, too," he whispered back. "Have I mentioned how much I love your body? Your body is so good to my body."

"Quit playing around and come inside," she said.

"Ah, the lady is ready..."

"I've been ready," she said. "I love the way you love me. I didn't know it could be like this."

"Say no more, sweetheart," he said, covering her with his body and bringing it home, taking extreme pleasure in the sighs of pleasure she made. He rocked with her, and when her legs circled his waist, he rode her. He kissed her deeply as she gripped his shoulders, her nails digging into his shoulders. He loved the feel of that passion in her fingertips and then, with a small cry, she came, throbbing around him. It filled him with the urgency he loved and he joined her, letting go, pulsing until there was nothing left in him.

"Oh God," she muttered. "I'm completely hooked on you. You do that so well."

"I thought it was you," he said. "Shit! That condom's still sitting on the bedside table—"

She giggled. "We're okay. I started the pill. I was saving it as a surprise."

"Well, that explains why it was just slightly better this time," he said, burrowing deeper. "We have a nice little routine."

"There's nothing routine about it," she said, holding him closer.

He rolled onto his side, bringing her with him. "When I came to Colorado, I had no idea what I'd find." He gently tucked her hair behind her ear. "I never imagined I would find you. I wasn't looking for this, but God... I think finding you is the best thing that could have happened to me."

"And here I thought you just wanted to get laid," she said, humor in her voice.

"Oh, don't get me wrong, I'm usually open to getting laid. But with you I have so much more. I think you're my best friend."

Her eyes widened. She looked shocked.

"Why are you surprised? I love all the time we spend together." A low rumble of laughter tumbled out of him. "I admit, I like this part a lot. But on top of everything else, you're a true friend. Sid, I know you want us to be cool, but you're going to have to adjust to a reality. I'm in love with you."

"Cody..." she said in a breath.

"Shh, you don't have to say anything. I know you're trying to find yourself, that you were a little lost after your divorce. That's okay. I've been there. And I'll be right here when you're ready. I'm hoping for a good outcome."

"Oh, Cody, I think you're magic."

"I'm glad you think so. I'm planning to pull something out of my sleeve that will last forever. I think we both deserve it. Now kiss me and I'll take care of you again."

"You are a magician..."

Deep in the night, Dakota woke to the sensation of small, soft, urgent hands boldly caressing him. Soft, sleepy laughter rumbled out of him. "Someone woke up frisky," he said. "And wanted me to wake up, too."

"You were already awake," she said, turning toward him. "At least some of you!"

"Do you need me to take care of you? Again?"

"Could you just put me back to sleep," she said. "If it's not too much trouble." Then she wiggled closer and put her leg over his. He responded by turning her onto her back and taking his place between her thighs. "I thought you might do this in your sleep."

"I can," he said. "With you, it's the most natural thing in the world."

He made love to her in her favorite way. It was so amazing to him—they hadn't been lovers for very long and yet they had such a satisfying routine. He knew exactly how to touch her, rub her, stroke her, kiss her and bring her to a shattering climax while he held her in his arms. When she was complete and her eyes gently closed, he kissed her eyelids. "Better, honey?"

"Better," she said. Then she rolled onto her side and he curled around her.

"You're so good for me, Sid," he said in a hoarse whisper. "I hope I'm good for you."

"Mmm," she said, nestling closer.

"You're so good for me," he whispered. "I know you're too good for me. I just might become a better man if I put an effort into deserving you."

She didn't move.

"Sid?" he asked softly. She didn't move. He softly kissed her neck. "Good night. I love you."

Tom Canaday had a good-size backyard, large enough for a vegetable garden, patio and a fire pit surrounded by a few chairs. His oldest son, Jackson, was twenty-one and making great progress in college, studying architecture. Jackson was going to the University of Colorado in the fall to complete his degree, and for this, he would have to live away from home. Tom was grieving; Jackson was ecstatic.

Tom was dealing with a lot more than Jackson going off to finish college, so when his son walked into the kitchen at about nine on a Saturday night, it all came to mind. "Hey, you're home!" Tom said. "No date tonight?"

"Shelly is having girls' night," he said. "I just dropped her at Brooke's, where several girls have gathered to do secret things."

"When you're a little older, maybe she'll tell you what they do," Tom suggested with a grin.

"I don't think I want to know," Jackson said. "I only care about secret things she feels like doing with me."

"Feel like a beer with your old man? Out by the fire?"

"You're not going to lecture me about sex again, are you?"

"I'll try not to," he said, grabbing a beer for his son. "Actually, I've been meaning to talk to you. About Lola."

"Everything is all right with Lola, isn't it?" Jackson asked.

"Yeah, Lola is great. Isn't she great?" Tom asked as they walked outside. He stooped to light the fire. Pinecones, which were plentiful, made great starters.

Jackson laughed at him. "Yeah, she is. What's up?"

"Well, Jackson, we've been talking about getting married. But between us we seem to have a lot of kids…"

"Mostly grown," Jackson said. "We're not going to stop you from getting married."

"We'd like to live in the same house."

"Dad, I'm not going to be here much longer. Nikki's looking to move to a dorm with a couple of girls as soon as they can afford it. We can stack in here when we're all home. Can't we? Cole and Trace cool with that?"

"Lola's talking to them."

"This is easy. Double up Nikki and Brenda—it won't be for that long. Nikki's mostly gone all the time, anyway. I'll share a room with Zach, as soon as I can find a footlocker with a combination lock so he doesn't just help himself to everything… Cole and Trace should be able to share a room—isn't Trace heading out into the world pretty soon, anyway? And Cole's at the community college. Isn't he looking at universities for a degree? Most of us just need a place to flop sometimes…"

"It's nice to know you don't have any issues with me and Lola living together. But there's something else I wanted to talk to you about."

"Okay."

"About your mom," he said. Then he ran a hand over the back of his sweaty neck and muttered, "Damn." Tom took a breath. "Listen, this could go down hard. Your mom didn't have what we'd call a conventional lifestyle."

Jackson just lifted his eyebrows, beer in hand, waiting.

"It was a long time after we were divorced, of course. I don't know why I said *of course*. I honestly don't know how long. She has a job but she also has a second job. She calls herself an escort. She entertains men."

"Oh?" Jackson said.

"She's a good person," Tom said. "I found out a couple of years ago because she got in a little trouble. She might call herself an escort but the police called her something else. Cal was her lawyer—that's what his experience is, criminal defense. I don't think of your mom as a bad person and I don't want you to, either. But I also don't want you to find out like I did and—"

"Dad, I know."

"Know what?" Tom said.

"I know what she does. I don't like it. I don't think it's safe and I can't let myself think about it, but I already know and she's always going to be my mother."

"How do you know?" Tom asked.

"She told us, me and Nikki. She was afraid you were going to tell us and she said your version would make her sound dirty, like some cheap hooker. And she's not."

"Apparently she's not in any way cheap," Tom muttered.

"They could make a movie out of her," Jackson said. "She's like the happy housewife with this sideline. She said she was dating a few men, just a few, and they weren't local. Businessmen, she said. Then, when she kept explaining, she described it as 'seeing' a few men. Nikki was a little nuts at first."

"I never noticed anything," Tom said.

"I know. Mom is single and beautiful and she's really like the nicest person I know. One of these days she's going to settle on one rich old bastard with a big bank account and a bad cough because if there's one thing my mother likes it's to live like she's got money. And that's what she's doing. If she wasn't getting paid for it, she'd be just your regular independent woman, doing as she pleases."

Tom stared at Jackson in amazement. "So you're okay with it?"

"Oh, hell, no, I hate it," Jackson said. "But Nikki was ready to go nuts so I had to think fast before the whole town knew. So I asked a lot of questions to calm Nikki down—I asked her if she was safe, if she was hanging out with bad people, if she was out on the street, if there was any chance of her going to jail or getting hurt. That kind of stuff. Mom tried saying she's given up that activity but I called bullshit on that. I just wanted to know what kind of people she's hanging out with. I think she's got clients she calls friends and she's known them all a long time." Jackson shook his head. "She's grown up, not hurting anyone, and she's gonna live like she wants. But Nikki and Mom aren't close now. Nikki can't help it—it makes her angry and embarrassed. But I convinced her she doesn't have to broadcast it, especially because of the younger kids. Face it—nothing we can do about it."

"Is she okay? Nikki?" Tom asked.

"She's okay," Jackson said. "We're not traumatized. It's pretty obvious why she left us, isn't it? This kind of life wasn't going to be enough. And you know what? That makes me feel really sorry for her."

"Are you sure you're only twenty-one?" Tom said.

Jackson didn't answer. "That's why I'm taking things slow with Shelly," he said. "I love her like mad, but I want both of us sure, going forward, what kind of life we can commit to. I don't want to end up alone with four little kids."

"Jackson, regardless of your mom changing her mind and going her own way, you four kids are the best thing that ever happened to me. I don't regret one thing. I wouldn't give one of you up." He took a slug of his beer. "Except maybe Zach," he said. "He's kind of a pain in the ass."

Jackson laughed. "Yeah, you could've done better on that one."

Dakota and Sid drove to Colorado Springs together on the Saturday nights they worked at the soup kitchen and it had quickly become one of his favorite parts of the week. He was indebted to the group of volunteers who had come to Denver to help him look for Sedona and he was a great admirer of Sister Mary Jacob.

But the ride alone with Sid was a pleasure. That was where they did much of their talking, learning about each other. He told her all about Hasnaa, how they met, how fast they fell in love, how they ignored the differences in their cultures, how she died. "How ironic that a Muslim woman whose life's work was about peace should die at the hands of terrorists," he said. "I was a long time getting beyond that."

"Are you beyond it?" she asked.

"It was a process. I did a little acting out."

"Ah," she said. "Acting out?"

"That's how I got in some trouble in the Army. I was pretty angry. But I had some time to think about things, then I went to Australia, where I had even more time to think, and then I came here. By the time I got here I realized Hasnaa had changed me in a very short time. I'd always been determined to have no real ties, and after Hasnaa, I wanted real ties. I came to my family. For the first time. I met you. I have a niece and, I think, a nephew. Domestic matters like family struggles used to bore me, used to seem so pointless to me. Now I look at my brother and sister and admire them. Sedona used to irritate me. Now that I know how fallible and vulnerable she is, I'd like to see her get whatever help she needs." He paused. "I used to want to be alone. Now I want to be connected."

"All that came out of tragedy?" Sid asked.

"Only sort of. Remember, for as much as Hasnaa meant to me and as hard as it was to lose her, we were together barely a few months. For just a little while I had a view of what life could be like. And it can be so good."

Sid laughed uncomfortably. "I'm not here to fulfill your fantasies."

"But you do, just the same. I've been wanting to ask you about your husband."

"Ex," she clarified. "What about him?"

"Tell me about him. Whatever you think is important. Like, how'd you end up with him?"

"I'm not entirely sure," she said. "I suspect he handpicked me as someone who would work hard for him. On my part? Probably lack of experience. I never dated much. I was dorky and clumsy and introverted, very comfortable with nerds and computers. He was handsome and funny and all the girls wanted him. I didn't even bother taking him seriously when he hit on me. He was a student—a medical student—and I had a good job at UCLA. But I didn't have much social confidence. I was awkward."

"You're sure not awkward anymore," he said, squeezing her hand.

"A lot has changed since nine or ten years ago. But when I was a kid that car accident drove me inside and I turned to books and science. I didn't have a lot of self-confidence."

"You're certainly at full function now," he said.

"That scar does nothing for my bathing suit look."

He chuckled. "Remember, I've seen you naked. Believe me, that scar does not detract. You're beautiful."

"You have to say that," she said.

"No, I don't have to say anything," he said. "I have a few scars of my own, and don't pretend you haven't noticed. The Army hands 'em out."

"Scars on a handsome guy don't—"

"Tell me about the accident," he said.

That took her mind temporarily off scars and feeling awkward. "It was entirely my fault and I'm lucky to be alive at all. I was on my bike, shot out into the street from between two parked cars without looking and bam! Got hit by a nice lady who was driving the carpool. If I hadn't been wearing that ugly God-awful helmet…"

"Aw, man. That must be a parent's worst nightmare."

"It changed my life. I don't know what I'd be like if that hadn't happened, you know? It made me self-conscious and kind of shy. So I was not exactly savvy when this good-looking guy came around. I dated him, married him in less than a year and worked while he went through med school and surgical residency. He was tied up so much— if he had time off, he was studying, so I worked a lot of overtime. It wasn't long before we didn't have much of a relationship. Then he left me."

"I bet there was a lot more to it than that," Dakota said. "You must have been so lonely."

"I enjoyed my work. It might've been boring to most people but to me… Well, it was very important. I wasn't just some techie. I was writing code."

"Programming?" he asked.

"Sometimes. Analyzing. My work was with software."

"Do you miss it?" he asked, giving her hand a squeeze.

"Sometimes," she said. "But it was consuming and isolating and then when David… I suddenly realized I was much too alone. And I collapsed from within." She shook her head. "I don't know if my work ruined my marriage or my marriage ruined my work. I had such a terrible identity crisis. I'm never going to let myself get in that place again. From a shy and awkward girl to an abandoned wife with no one, with nothing. I had to start over."

"You run that bar like a drill sergeant. And you're animated. Outgoing. You have lots of family and friends now."

"That was a really smart move for me, staying with my brother, helping with the bar and the boys. The bar is a social place—if I'm happy, the customers are happy, they look forward to coming in, they leave tips, they bring friends. And I'm getting that empty bubble inside filled with good people. My life has changed so many times—with the accident, with a marriage I couldn't have been prepared for, to coming here. Thanks to Rob needing my help and pushing me, I became a much more confident person. But I'm not confident about making another marriage, Dakota. You're going to have to understand." She bit her bottom lip. "I'm sorry if I misled you into thinking I was some techie. It was more than that."

"I have no trouble believing you're smart, Sid. I knew that from the beginning. And I understand why you're a commitmentphobe right now, after what you went through," he said. "But I bet I'm not anything like him."

She laughed. "There's no question about it."

"I do have secret ambitions, however," he said.

"Oh? Do tell?"

"I'm having a good experience here, too. I don't hate the garbage truck. I've had worse duty, believe me, and I love working with Lawrence. But I'm weighing some other options. Maybe the fire department. And I'm still interested in that teaching certificate." He laughed. "Two important fields guaranteed to keep me from getting rich. Lucky for me, getting rich was never one of my major goals." He pulled into the parking space at the soup kitchen. "We have lots of time, Sid. Would you like coffee and cake tonight when we're done here?"

"I think so, yes," she said. "You never asked me about my husband before."

"We did a lot of our best talking while naked," he reminded her. "I didn't want to know anything about him then."

"Wise," she agreed.

Summer was full on the land as the Fourth of July weekend arrived. Dakota worked hard by day and had perfect evenings. He had dinner at the bar at least a couple of times a week, dinner with Cal, Maggie and Sully at least once a week, dropped in on Sierra a couple of times a week if he didn't have dinner with her, and most nights Sid drove out to the cabin for the night. More and more of her personal items took up residence in his cabin: her shower gel, toothbrush, hairbrush, lotion, a few extra clothing items. He even drove back to Denver to briefly visit with Sedona in the hospital. She had wisely chosen to go back to the hospital where she had originally been diagnosed and was making progress.

His family was settled and he had a fantastic woman in his life. Things had not been this stable and hopeful in his memory. He'd even been kicking around the idea of a brief visit to Iowa to check on the folks, not so much because he thought they wanted him to visit, but it seemed like a good time to try to make peace with his childhood.

Then a very strange thing happened to remind him life was never uncomplicated. While he was in the bar having dinner, his car parked across the street right in front of the beauty shop, someone emptied a pile of hair clippings in the front seat. At first he couldn't make out what it was but soon recognized it to be many colors of finely cut hair. By the time he discovered it, the salon was closed, lights off.

"Crazy," he muttered. He suspected Alyssa, but he hadn't seen her in weeks. Well, he saw her at a distance. He had no reason to think she was malicious, but who else had hair clippings to toss in a car?

He walked down the block and across the street to the police department. He found Officer Paul Castor holding down the fort. "How you doing, Paul?" he asked.

"Not bad," he said.

"Let me ask you something—you have an issue with vandalism on the main street here?" Dakota said.

"Nah. It's well lit, lots of business owners around, stores open. Why? You have a problem?"

He shook his head and laughed. "Someone dumped a pile of hair clippings on the driver's seat of my car."

Castor lifted his eyebrows.

"I know—pretty strange, isn't it?"

"You have a fight with a barber?"

Dakota shook his head. "I guess you never heard that one before, huh?"

"Any damage?"

"No, just a slight mess. I'm going to have to take the car somewhere to get it vacuumed out."

"You're in luck. I have a rechargeable minivac I can loan you."

"That would be great!"

Dakota took the minivac to his car, vacuumed the hair, then drove down to the police department to return it.

He didn't say anything to Sid, though he weighed that decision heavily. It was that old nagging insecurity. He didn't want to seem like he had a lot of trouble following him to a woman who was already trying to keep life simple. But he did go to the beauty shop immediately after work the next day.

"Alyssa?" Maria said. "She's not here but we can fit you in for a trim."

"Actually, I wanted to talk to her."

Maria's smile was instant and wide. "She'll be so disappointed to have missed you! She's on a little trip with a couple of girlfriends. She'll be back on Monday morning."

"But she was here last night?"

"She's been gone since Tuesday night—a long weekend in Vegas. Girls' trip." She clicked her teeth, but smiled. "Nothing but trouble."

"Then never mind—it's nothing. I, ah, parked in front of the shop last night while I went to the bar across the street and someone got in there and went through my stuff. Glove box and console. Nothing was stolen. I just thought I'd ask her if she noticed anything. Anyone."

"Well, I was here and I didn't see a thing," Maria said. "It was light until after closing. That's a nervy thing to do in broad daylight."

"Kids, probably," he said.

"Kids around here aren't perfect, but they're not dumb. If they go through a car, they usually find something to take. Did you have CDs or anything in there?"

He just smiled. "That's the point—there wasn't anything to take. Unless they were interested in my AAA packet and an owner's manual. No worries. But thanks. I appreciate it."

The whole family spent the Fourth of July at the Crossing with Sully and a full park of campers. Elizabeth and Sam were content in their swings in the shade by the lake, Cal and Dakota grilled the food, Connie threw the ball for Molly and Sully's dog, Beau. The only person missing for dinner was Sid. She was with her brother and nephews because the bar was open. She worked until six and then left the bar in the hands of one of the other managers to go home for a backyard picnic with Rob and the boys. At nine she brought the boys to the Crossing to watch the fireworks at the lake. The dogs were a hit with Sid's nephews and Dakota thought a couple of dogs in the family might help him reel in the boys.

Later that week, Dakota walked Sid out to her car first thing in the morning. She'd spent the night even though he had an early shift on the garbage truck. When she opened her car door they both jumped back in shock. The entire front seat—driver's seat and passenger seat—was heaped with garbage. Smelly garbage. Not recyclable paper or plastic but degrading, rotting, wet food.

"Oh my God!" Sid exclaimed. "Who would do such a thing?"

"I never heard a car," he said. "I never heard a sound. I'm pretty sensitive to out of place sounds after a few war zones. Little things, like a click, can be a matter of life and death. Whoever did this didn't drive up to the car. I'm calling Stan. I'll call work and explain that I can't start until later. You can take my car and I'll see that yours is cleaned up."

"How will you manage that?"

"I have lots of resources. Cal, Sierra, Sully. I can do it."

My son, may you be happier than your father.

—SOPHOCLES

14

Sierra was already home from the diner on Tuesday afternoon when Dakota finished his shift and dropped in. Connie had the day off and had been home with Sam. The door was open and through the screen door Dakota could see Connie was cooking dinner, Sam was propped up in his walker, though still so small he couldn't make any headway, and Sierra sat at the breakfast bar folding little clothes. He tapped at the door, announced himself and walked in. Molly barked at him, then jumped on him for good measure, and Sam squealed and raised his little arms; Sierra yelled at the dog to get down. All in all a lovely domestic scene.

"Look what the cat dragged in," Sierra said. "Can you stay for dinner?"

"Probably not, I have errands," he said. "But I have to talk to you about something very weird."

"I specialize in weirdness," she said. "How's Sid?"

"Oh, she's great, considering."

"Considering what?" Sierra demanded. "Did you do something stupid?"

"I'm completely blameless," he said, squatting in front of Sam. He made a couple of playful sounds and asinine faces and the baby giggled like mad. Helpless, Dakota kept it up for a while, then kissed the baby on his head before rising. "This is the happiest baby I have ever seen. He has no idea all he's been through."

"He's amazing, isn't he? I bet if we had one of our own, he or she would be a holy terror."

"I doubt it," Dakota said. "You're both so frickin' sweet. Hey, any chance you have a cold beer?"

"A very limited supply that I'm willing to share with you," Connie said.

"Thanks. Whatcha building over there?"

"I'm marinating flank steak that will go on the grill, corn on the cob and potatoes. There's plenty."

"Thanks but I'm going to head to town. Sid's working. But I have to talk to you guys about something. When I first got to town I met two women right away and both of them hit on me. Alyssa at the beauty shop and some fancy woman named Neely, who happened into the bar."

Connie and Sierra looked at each other with shocked expressions on their faces. "Oh, brother," Connie said. And Sierra followed with, "Boy, can you pick 'em."

"You don't know the half of it," Dakota said. He proceeded to tell them the story from the beginning—Alyssa's rather pitiful and hopeless pursuit, Neely's crazy and almost scary pursuit, the flat tires, hair clippings, the garbage. Neely's convoluted double message to the police chief, accusing Dakota of an assault.

"Garbage in your girlfriend's car," Sierra said. "A little obvious, isn't it?"

"Is it?" Dakota asked.

"Oh, yeah," Sierra said with a laugh. "You sure you want to hook up with a garbage man, sister?"

"No kidding," he said. "That never crossed my mind!"

"Because you don't know how to think crazy. Did you have a thing with one or both of them? Like a little fling?"

"Not even a little hand-holding. I didn't encourage either one of them for one second."

"Listen, Cody, we know both of those characters a little too well," Sierra said.

"What do you mean?"

"I was engaged to Alyssa a few years ago," Connie said. "A couple of years before I even knew Sierra. We lived together in this house. I came home from work in the middle of the day to find her in bed with one of my friends, ex-friends, having some afternoon delight."

Dakota was speechless for a moment. "Tacky," he finally said. "I've been known to use poor judgment from time to time, but even I never did anything like that. Your ex-friend still around?"

"A firefighter," Connie said. "Married, couple of kids, still prowling around. We don't talk. We don't work together. As for Alyssa…" He shrugged. "Apparently she hasn't found the right man yet. You made a narrow escape, that's my opinion. Though maybe she's changed her ways. It doesn't matter to me anymore." He wiped off his hands and picked up Sam, holding him on his hip. "I'm glad you settled on Sid. She's cool."

"I can't wait to hear about Neely," Dakota said.

"She's a lot harder to explain," Sierra said. "She made me a little bit uncomfortable with a rush to friendship. I'd known her for an hour when she suggested we take a trip together. A road trip. I'll admit, she makes such a good first impression I wanted to be her friend. I was new in town—I didn't have any friends yet. Then I caught her in a couple of lies. Not little ones, either. She made up a story about a big, fatal accident. It didn't sound credible and I told Connie."

"So I checked," Connie said. "It's a matter of public record. I just checked the computer for the highway patrol stats—not only wasn't there a fatal accident, there wasn't any accident in the vicinity she claimed. And I guess if you had a run-in with her, she's not done with the lying."

"Was that it? She invented an accident?" Dakota asked.

"Not quite," Sierra said. "This dramatic story came up in the beauty shop and it was Alyssa who said she'd never heard of such a thing, a really bad accident happening without everyone in town talking about it. Then Neely also casually told Alyssa that *I* had wanted to take her on a trip. I didn't say anything but that's when I decided I'd be giving Neely a lot of space. That kind of thing creeps me out."

"She need attention or something?" Dakota asked.

"I don't have the first idea. Some people just lie all the time for the drama of it, I guess. We've all exaggerated. But after that accident story, saying a kid was killed? Saying she was sorry she hadn't been in touch but she was at this dying boy's bedside for days? I felt terrible for her. Is that the payoff? Pity? Now I'd never know what to believe from her."

"You met her at the beauty shop?"

"Not exactly. I met her…" Sierra hesitated. "I met her through friends."

"I thought you didn't have any friends?" Dakota said.

"I didn't have many and none I was close to. I was brand-new in town."

"You met her at AA?" Dakota guessed.

"I didn't say that," she said.

"I know you take your promises seriously so I won't push you to tell me, but just in case you think she's sober, she's not. At least, I know she drinks. I've never seen her drink alcohol, but she does. She kissed me, remember. I had to peel her off me. She'd definitely been drinking."

The surprise on Sierra's face said it all.

"You don't have to say anything, Sierra," Dakota said. Then he looked at Sam, who was busy chewing his fist and drooling all over his bib. He frowned slightly, then reached for the baby.

"Uncle Cody is coming around," Sierra said.

Dakota rested the baby on his hip. "This brilliant baby gave me an idea," he said. "I feel the need to install a nanny cam."

When Dakota left, Sierra was a little overwhelmed by what she'd learned. Connie went back to puttering in the kitchen while she gave Sam his bottle. "This business with Neely sounds almost scary."

"I think Dakota can take care of himself," Connie said.

"Making up tall tales is one thing, but this woman sounds like a stalker."

"It's been known to happen," he said.

"Has it ever happened to you?" she asked.

"Not like that, no. I mean, Alyssa was kind of a pest. I had to tell her to give up way too often, but she never did anything to hurt me or my property." He grinned at Sierra. "I'm making you a treat. Your favorite. Stuffed mushrooms."

"I love stuffed mushrooms. Sam wants to hold his own bottle," she said. "He's taking my job."

"He's feeling independent," Connie said. "That's good."

Sierra started to cry softly. "I want to hold him longer."

"You're crying?"

"Sometimes I think about the fact that he'll never know his mother and it breaks my heart a little. I mean, I so want him to be with us, but his birth mother, gone from his life at such a young age. He won't remember her."

"Sierra?" Connie asked.

"It's been such a troubling day," she said with a hiccup of emotion. "Am I supposed to tell someone Neely is drinking?"

Connie frowned at his wife. "I don't know. I don't know all the AA rules. Besides, what does it have to do with anything? Do you think it's making her act the way she's apparently acting? Dakota doesn't even know for sure it was her, he just thinks— Sierra, *why* are you crying?"

"I don't know. I find it so emotional. A lot of it, you know? Neely's a nutcase, I think. And my brother—he's been alone so long and he has a good woman in his life now, that makes me so happy." She wiped her eyes. "But poor little Sam will never know his real mommy. That's sad, don't you think."

"Honey, are you about to get your—?" She glared at him and he put his hands up as if he was being arrested. "I didn't say it! I almost said it but I caught myself. Do you need a nap?"

"Maybe," she relented. "Having a baby is a lot of work. He sleeps pretty well but he still wakes up sometimes…"

"Why don't you take a little nap with Sam before dinner," Connie said.

"Maybe we should. I've been a little off today. I might be coming down with a cold." She sniffed. "Cody's going to be all right, isn't he?"

"He's a big boy," Connie said. "And we're going to be all right, too. We'll get pictures from Sam's grandma so we can show him some of the family he missed knowing, but don't cry over it—that kid hit the lotto when he got us because he's gonna have a great childhood. He'll have a good mom and dad. He could've been bounced all over the state, but we lucked out and found each other."

"Oh, Connie," she said, sniffing.

"Go take a nap," he said.

She cuddled Sam against her and headed for the bedroom.

"Sheesh," Connie said. But he said it very quietly.

Dakota stopped by the police department on his way to the bar and grill. With the damage to Sid's car, he and Stan were becoming much closer than he would have liked—in a professional capacity. When he walked in, Stan smiled from behind his desk. "Get the smell out?"

"Pretty much, but I had to take it to Colorado Springs to get a good detail job and the ride over was grueling. My buddy from the county, the guy I ride the garbage haul with, came by after you took pictures and wrote up your report. He helped me empty that mess into the truck. It was easier to do that wearing our hazmat suits. Nastiest mess I've ever seen. Then I filled my sister in on some of the details—she already knew Neely was a nutjob. She caught her in some lies, I guess. Not in vandalism, but very colorful lies. So I took a side trip to Walmart and bought myself a surveillance camera."

Stan just lifted a brow. "I guess the next time something happens around your place, you'll have yourself a little movie. I hope there isn't any more bullshit. Even if you had some proof, she'd probably just get a fine. Oh, and lying ain't against the law, unless you're under oath."

"Just so you know, I have guns," Dakota said. "A couple of rifles and a .45. I'm going to take the rifles to my brother's house to lock up and keep the .45. Because... I don't know... When someone trashes your car while you're in the house… If I was burglarized, I'd hate there to be guns stolen. Even by some girl."

"It's just peculiar enough to get my attention. I'm doing a little of my own checking around. We'll talk about that another time. For now, I don't want you to get the idea that just because it's a woman you suspect of giving you grief that means it's not a real threat. And I like the idea that you're storing the rifles at Cal's for the time being, but lock your doors, anyway. And pay attention. That's about all I can advise you. I'd hate for you to shoot her. That'd make a mess of paperwork."

"I didn't do anything to make her think we had a relationship," Dakota said. "I didn't encourage her. And I didn't do anything to purposely offend her. I was polite. Just not interested."

"You don't have anything to defend, Dakota. It's just one of those weird things. We might never get to the bottom of it."

"I'm sure you're far too busy for this kind of BS."

Stan laughed. "This is Timberlake, Dakota. We don't have that much going on. But let me be straight with you here—I don't like the thought of someone doing nasty things to one of my people. Lying about assaults, stabbing tires, fouling someone's car with garbage, and I frankly don't care if it's a man or a woman. So I'm checking out this Neely character. I'll let you know what I find. You let me know what's on your camera."

Dakota smiled. "Thanks, Stan."

Sid was serving in the bar in the afternoon. The happy hour and dinner crowd would be descending on them soon and she'd heard from Dakota that he was on his way over. She was completely unprepared to see Neely come into the bar, dressed to the nines as usual, and jump up on a bar stool, all smiles.

"Hi," she said brightly. "Sid, isn't it?"

Sid frowned. This was a leap from her finger-snapping order for a chicken Caesar. "Have we met?" Sid asked.

"Well, I guess not officially," Neely said, putting out her hand. "I've heard other people in here call you Sid. I'm Neely."

"I know who you are," Sid said. She took the offered hand reluctantly. "What can I get you?"

"Let's see… I almost always have a salad, but I missed lunch. How about a BLT, fries and… Let's see… I don't drink… I just don't like the taste… How about a tonic with a sliver of lime. Two slivers of lime."

"You got it," she said, turning away. She keyed in the food order, then prepared and delivered the drink.

As she was turning away, Neely spoke. "Excuse me, but you seem a bit aloof. Was it something I said?"

"You ordered your meal," Sid said. "And I said, 'You got it.' I think we've covered everything."

"Then why are you so unhappy with me?" Neely asked.

Sid was stunned for a moment. Then she smiled. "You're reading me wrong. I have things to do before the happy hour crowd arrives. Will there be anything else?"

"I was just wondering, when do you get off work?"

Sid tilted her head. "And you're asking because…?"

"Maybe we could get together sometime, get to know each other. Maybe for coffee or dessert. Or if you have days off, I'd love to have dinner. I don't know that many people and we're about the same age. I bet we'd find we have things in common."

"Thank you, that's very nice, but I'm very busy with my job and family and I don't think we'd have much in common."

Neely smiled chillingly. "We have Dakota in common. Dakota and Sierra. Sierra is a good friend of mine."

"Is she?" Sid asked, as if surprised. "I didn't know that. Then you're pretty well fixed up. Excuse me."

Sid went to the kitchen. Rob wasn't there. She went to the small office he kept in the back, behind the kitchen. He appeared to be on the phone with a vendor. She couldn't tell if he was arguing about the price of something or complaining about the cost of a delivery, but she lingered in the doorway until he hung up. "Problem?" he asked.

"A very unique problem," she said. "I'm sure I didn't tell you about this before but there's this woman who's been hitting on and aggravating Dakota and she's in the bar, waiting for her sandwich. She wants to know if we can be friends. Will you please take the bar for ten or fifteen minutes? I'll do anything you ask in return."

He raised his eyebrows in curiosity. "Now I can't miss it."

"She'll hit on you," Sid said. "Don't hook up with this one. She's pure poison."

"I'm a big boy."

"No, you're not all that big. This has fatal attraction written all over it."

"Yeah, and now I *have* to see her," he said.

Because it was irresistible, Sid peeked through the cook's glass to watch as Rob fastened a white apron around his narrow hips and picked up a cloth to wipe off the bar. He completely ignored Neely, but Sid knew he checked her out. Rob never missed a thing. And she'd loaded the bait—Rob was hot. She knew that, even though he was her brother—he was just plain hot. Six-two, strong shoulders from lifting crates of drinks, narrow hips, long legs, big hands and a face that would cause Hugh Jackman to file charges for theft.

She watched as Neely signaled and Rob went to her, cloth in hand. She said something humorous, he said something back, they laughed together for a moment, then he fetched her sandwich and fries and took it to her. There were only three customers in the place so he went through the swinging door to the kitchen.

Sid was waiting. "What did she say to you?"

"She asked where the waitress was and I said, 'What waitress? I just have the bartender until four o'clock.' She asked for you by name and I said you were working in the kitchen for a little while but you'd be back in the bar soon. Then she asked if I was married and I said that I was, to a very jealous woman. She thought that was very funny. But she accused me of making it up."

"Because I bet she knows exactly who you are. She's creepy. And there doesn't seem to be any proof, but we're pretty sure she's been stalking Dakota. And she's tried to alternately pick up Dakota and then accuse him of assaulting her. She's making a mess for us."

"What the hell does she want?" he asked.

"I don't know. Dakota, probably."

"Aw, Sid. What have you gotten yourself into? Are you sure he's telling you the truth?"

"Yes, of course I'm sure!" she insisted. "There are many inconsistencies surrounding that woman and not once have I been confused by Dakota!"

"Were you confused by David?" he asked.

"Not at all. I thought I was stuck with David!"

There. She'd said it. Her brother just looked at her in shock.

"I had a terrible marriage, all right? It wasn't like your marriage with Julienne, young lovers so devoted to each other. Within a year I knew I'd made a terrible mistake but I'd made the promises. I did my best knowing all the time he didn't love me, either. But I didn't realize he was loving someone else—I thought he was loving his career. His plans. We didn't fight, we got along all right. I thought maybe what we had was typical, and besides, I had things to do! It was my fault, don't you see? Because I really didn't care. So failing in that, I— Ach! We can't do this now!"

The kitchen had gone kind of quiet. Rob looked like he was in shock. "If it was lousy…if you didn't love him and he didn't love you…why…?"

"Why would I have a nervous breakdown over it? Because he used me. Because he made a mockery of work that was important. Because I was hanging in there for him, and when he was done with me, he threw me away."

Sid's phone chimed and, thinking it might be a text from Dakota, she pulled it out of her pocket and looked at the screen. "What super timing," she said sourly. "Dr. Faraday, my old boss. Please find time to call me, he says. I really need your help, he says."

"I'll take care of the bar if you want to go call him."

"Not now. He probably has some code problem and I'll need my computer and some quiet. Besides, I should deal with psycho Neely. I'm telling you, she's a little crazy and she's making trouble everywhere. I have no idea what her goal is. If we knew her endgame, we'd know what to solve, wouldn't we?"

"I'll take the bar…" he said.

"No, I've got it." She went through the swinging door just as Dakota was walking into the bar.

Sid watched as he stopped short, recognizing the back of Neely's head. He frowned and she thought, *See! He's not hiding anything! He hates her and might even be a little frightened of her.* He walked all the way around the bar to the far corner, as far away from Neely as he could get.

Sid slapped a napkin down in front of him. "What can I get you?"

"I'd better have a cup of coffee. Looks like I'll have to be alert."

"Sure, let me get that for you." She turned around to pour from the pot, and when she turned back toward him with the coffee, all of a few short steps, Neely had moved to the chair beside Dakota's. And he was wearing a black scowl.

"Now see, I think we all need a do-over," Neely said brightly, seeming to include Sid in her conversation. "I don't know what happened but—"

"What happened is that you told the police chief I assaulted you," Dakota said, his voice gravelly and dark.

"Is that what he said? That's not exactly accurate. It was wrong of me to say anything at all that could be misinterpreted like that, but I didn't say you assaulted me. I just said you kissed me. I admit, that was not the truth. I shouldn't have done that. But I was just embarrassed. And I did apologize to you."

"And the boyfriend who was stalking you?" Dakota asked.

"Apparently my imagination. I haven't seen him around. So," she said, grinning. "We can all be friends now."

"We can be polite," Dakota said. "I think friendship between us is not in the cards."

"Well, that's pretty rude," she said indignantly. "I humble myself in front of you, take blame I shouldn't really have to take, and that's your response?"

"I'm not going to be manipulated, Neely. That's my response. I'd like to order an early dinner, if you'll excuse me."

Neely sat there for a moment, shock etched on her beautiful face. Then she turned in a huff and walked out of the bar.

Sid put the coffee down in front of Dakota. "And that's at least the second dinner she hasn't paid for. Maybe third. That's quite a racket—get your feelings hurt and storm out. Without paying."

"Glad I parked under the light out front," he said. "Your car. Where is it?"

She chewed her lip. "I left it at Rob's and walked to work. The boys are home. The sun will be up for another hour. All the neighbors are out on their porches and in their gardens. Surely everything will be all right?"

"Her confidence is chilling," he said. "She's got a story for everything and then a story for every story. What the hell does she really want?"

"You, I think."

"Nah, that's too simple. With her looks and apparent money, she could find a guy who has a lot more to show for his life than I do."

"Oh, Dakota," she said with a headshake and a smile, wondering when was the last time he looked in the mirror. "I'm not going to flatter you."

"Good, then could I have a club sandwich with chips and a cold beer?"

"Yes, you can. And I told Rob a little about her. I told him it appeared she was stalking you but there didn't seem to be proof."

"Any chance he's going home to have dinner with his boys?"

"I could ask," she said.

"You might want to tell him that I just pissed her off and to check on your car."

As July passed, Tom and Lola planned a family gathering—Lola's sons and parents and her sister's family; Tom, his kids, his parents, brother and brother's family. It was a very large group and there was a purpose. So they put out two grills and Lola made extralarge salads and a big pot of beans and got the families together. And made their announcement. They planned to combine their households in the fall.

"Why the fall?" Tom's mother asked.

"Once all the kids are in school and we have a good fix on where everyone is headed for the year, we're going to reconfigure bedrooms. Jackson is going to be living in an apartment in Denver, Cole is taking a dorm room at the university, Nikki is saving for a dorm suite with her girlfriends, Trace is starting at the community college and Brenda is entering her senior year of high school. We think we can combine households here without crowding too much," Tom said.

"Except it won't be our house," Trace muttered under his breath.

Tom seemed to be the only one who heard him, but Tom was an expert and well practiced in hearing the mutterings of kids even in a noisy house. He heard Trace say he didn't want to live in a big house with a ton of people and at some point maybe he'd go live with his dad.

Other than that, there seemed to be a real air of celebration. The families had known each other for years. They hadn't been close exactly, but when you grow up in a small town, you tend to know at least a little bit about a lot of people. Tom's parents and brother were delighted that at long last he was settling down with a woman he could actually share his life with. Lola's parents were thrilled that after so many years of raising her sons on her own, working two jobs and managing her home, she would have a partner she could hopefully grow old with. Tom's family liked and admired Lola; Lola's family liked and admired Tom.

Everyone seemed to have a wonderful time; there was a great deal of laughter and a few stories were told about Tom and Lola growing up. When the guests had all departed, when the kids finished their chores and Cole and Trace had gone back home to Lola's house, Lola and Tom finished the dishes that were left.

"We have a small problem, I think," Tom said.

"Trace," she replied.

"So you know?" Tom asked.

"There's been a little grumbling. I can't really explain it because I know he likes you. He doesn't disapprove of us."

"Then let me handle this. Just let me try, and if I run into trouble I'll back off."

"What are you going to do?"

"I'm not sure. I think he has some anxiety about a lot of things. Starting college. His brother leaving home. You giving up your house, which has always been his home base. Not just his home, but his security. He might be asking himself, what will happen if you give up your house, move in here and it doesn't work out? Then what?"

"I told him we've talked about that—that I'm not going to be without a home. That I'll never be without a home. That we hope to buy and sell more homes, maybe keep my house as a rental. That when we combine households we combine everything and you would never leave me broke and homeless. And he asked me how I knew that and I said that I knew you. And sadly, I didn't really know his father that well. I thought Trace was adjusting to the idea."

"Well, the kids come first," Tom said. "Let me talk with Trace. Maybe I can put his mind at ease."

"I'm sorry, Tom," she said.

He put his arms around her and she rested her head on his shoulder. "Shh. You don't have anything to be sorry about. Six kids, Lola." He laughed. "If you think they'll stop throwing us a curve now and then after we get married, you're naive." He kissed her cheek. "I'm surprised it wasn't Brenda."

"Why Brenda?"

"Oh, she's the most like her mother and a little spoiled. Fortunately for us, Brenda's dying to share space with Nikki. Nikki has great clothes. And Trace is a handsome kid. Great selling point."

"Oh God, what if—"

"Don't borrow trouble."

"I just had a shudder run through me," she said, leaning against him again.

"They're fourteen to twenty-one. We're going to shudder a lot for about ten more years. Then we get to start shuddering over the grandkids."

Make yourself necessary to somebody.

—RALPH WALDO EMERSON

15

For a week or two, Neely seemed to have disappeared.
She didn't come in the bar, didn't bother either Sid or Dakota, wasn't seen around town. Dakota wondered if all that
had been required was for him to be very stern, very unapproachable. He did check around his cabin for signs of
footprints, tire tracks or other disturbances, and he looked
through his surveillance video. He looked quickly, but he
looked.

"She doesn't live in Timberlake," he said to Sid. "Maybe
she's wandered off to greener pastures."

"Didn't she say she was invested in businesses around
here?" Sid asked.

"Yeah, she said that," he answered, smiling. "So what?
She said a lot of things."

"I'm going to look up business licenses in Timberlake,"
Sid said.

"Would that necessarily show you investment partners?"

"I'm very good," she said. "If there's a record, I can find it."

"Let's not obsess about this. I just want her to go away without leaving a trail of destruction."

"And I want to be ready, if she happens to come back. She hasn't bothered your sister, has she?"

"I've only seen Sierra twice since the Fourth. She was fighting off some stomach thing and said not to come near her in case she was contagious, but she's fine now. You ask me? I think she's exhausted. Sam is awesome but he's a handful. He's crawling. And waking up very early in the morning and not wanting to go to bed at night."

"We all need to get together," she said. "Maybe on the weekend?"

"Sure. But I have to tell you, I really like being in a routine with you. We can both work, see each other regularly, there haven't been any surprises..."

"It's only been a little while."

"But it's been good," he said. "What would you say if I told you I don't need much more than this to be completely happy for the rest of my life?"

"I'd say, I'm not ready to talk like that," she said.

"All right. But can I talk like that?"

"You said you weren't ready to put down roots."

"I'm pretty surprised by how much I enjoy being around Cal and Maggie and Elizabeth as well as Sierra's sudden family. I kind of feel like this place is peaceful enough to calm the inner beast. I could live and work here. I'd like to see this place in winter. Do you ski?"

"Me?" She laughed. "You saw the leg, Dakota. I missed that stage."

"I could teach you. I bet Rob and the boys ski."

"You want to haul trash for the rest of your life?" she asked. "Because I don't want to be a bartender forever."

"What do you want to be?" he asked.

"I have a few other skills. In fact, my old boss called me. I've been trying to help him with a programming issue long-distance but I think I should go back to my old lab, work with him for a few days. It would be good in a number of ways. It would tell me some things about myself—like how over it am I? Do I really want to move on to something new? Am I fully healed from my bad experience and my awful divorce?"

"Tell me the truth, Sid—do you need to find out if you should run away from me?"

"Oh, Cody, no," she said. "You're the best guy I've ever had in my life! Not that there were many. I'm so crazy about you. It's just that… Well, there's just this one thing. I don't want you to rescue me." She put her palms on his cheeks. "I want to rescue myself."

He was quiet for a moment. "I'm not sure I get it."

"I know," she said. "I can't really be with you until I'm sure of who I am. And who I am is more complicated than you realize."

"Try me," he said. "I come from a wacko family, my sister is in the hospital on drugs to calm her frazzled head, I've been in military jail—you have no idea how much I can understand."

"Kind of a dramatic résumé, now that you mention it," she said.

"Sid, that has nothing to do with you and me…"

"All right, take it easy," she said, smiling. "I think it's a good idea for me to go back to California and work with Dr. Faraday for a few days. Maybe a week. I should take a look at my old job, my past friends. I've talked with Rob. He's trying to work it out with the other night manager. It won't be for long and I will talk to you every day."

"When are you leaving?"

"In a week or two. When Rob has the schedule worked out. This is a good time—the kids aren't in school and they're helping out in the kitchen almost every day."

"The best piece of news in this is that I don't think Rob can manage without you," Dakota said. "That's good for me."

It took a while for Tom and Lola to work out a time when Tom might catch Trace alone. July was already in its fourth week and it was hot, even in the higher elevations. It was steamy but the forest was brittle.

Tom sat outside on Lola's porch. Trace was due home from his job at Rob's bar and had told his mother he was going to get together with a few friends that night to play baseball. It was his typical routine. If Trace worked days, he played ball at night, and if he worked nights, he played ball during the day. Whatever the schedule, he played ball. It made Tom smile.

Trace came up the walk, shirttails hanging out and shoes unlaced. He'd generally graze from the fridge, drink some water, make a quick change, grab his glove and bat and head for the park. Tom stood.

"You looking for my mom?" Trace asked.

"No, she's working at Home Depot tonight. I was waiting for you. I was hoping we could talk for a few minutes."

"Why?" Trace asked.

"I got the idea we have one or two things to work out," Tom said. "Come on, give a guy a break. Sit down here." He lifted one of two bottled waters on the small outdoor table that separated two chairs. "Here. You look a little dry. Take a load off."

Trace, reluctantly, it seemed, sat down. Tom reclaimed his seat. "Let me start out by saying, I love your mom a lot but we're not going to rush you. I can tell you're pretty worried about us combining households. You're probably wondering where you fit in if we turn into one big family. We don't have to do that right away. We have lots of time. We want you to be ready."

"You said fall," Trace said. "When school starts…"

"That's not carved in stone, Trace. If you're not ready, we can wait."

"But you want to live together."

"Oh, yeah," Tom said with a self-conscious laugh. "It's amazing to love a woman like your mom and have her love me back. I never thought I could be this happy."

"And everyone else is okay with this idea of all of us living in one house?"

"Some more than others," Tom said. "Nikki wants to move to a dorm in Denver at the big campus and she is definitely not excited about sharing a room with her younger sister. Zach, on the other hand, is aching to get closer to Jackson's stuff, but Jackson is looking for a footlocker with a lock on it. I don't think Jackson or Cole care what we do—they're not planning on living with their parents much longer, anyway, but they still need a place to stay when they're not at school."

Trace was quiet for a long moment. "I've lived in this house almost my whole life. Since I was five, anyway. I don't remember the house we lived in before."

"You boys and your mom have been here a long time. Is that what bothers you? Not having this house as an anchor?" Tom asked.

"Sort of," he said with a shrug. "Or maybe it's that we'll live in *your* house."

"Ah. That makes sense. Can you think of it as your mom's house?"

"Listen, man, I like you. You're a good guy and I know you like my mom. I don't have any problems with that. It's just that this is where we live. Where we've always lived. And I don't want to move. That's all. It's not personal."

"Gotcha," Tom said. "You planning to live with your mother the rest of your life?" he asked.

"No!" Trace said. "Until I get my own place, that's all!"

"When you're...like...twenty-six?" Tom asked.

"I just turned eighteen! Hopefully I'll be living in my own place by the time I'm twenty-one."

"So if we could wait three more years to get married and move in together...?"

"But then I figure me and Cole will come here for holidays and stuff," Trace said.

"Oh, I get it. So you want this house and your mother to stay the same until you decide you're done. With it and with her?"

"That's not what I mean!"

"Can you be a little more clear about what you mean?" Tom asked. "Because Lola and I decided from the start, our kids come first. We don't want to rock your world too much, so if you're going to get sideways about us getting married and living in the same house, we'll just wait until the idea is more acceptable. But it would help to know what it is you need. So we can try to make it happen."

"I should be talking about this with my mom," Trace said.

"Then why haven't you done that? Because I think your mom is worried. She's ready for a positive change. Both of us are. I got divorced a long time ago, too. We're both ready to have a steady shoulder to lean on. Someone to talk about the checkbook with, someone to divvy up chores with. Oh, and your mom has been dying to buy a fixer-upper, remodel and sell at a profit—use all the skills she's learned working at Home Depot. And I've done that twice. We thought if we plan right, we can turn our partnership into a business, too. We'd love to do that. We're a lot alike—we both have worked as many jobs as it takes to keep our families afloat and we'll continue to do that."

"So what's the big deal, then?" Trace asked.

Tom took a drink of his water. "Well, the big deal is, it's hard to love someone and not get to see them. When you live in separate houses and you work a bunch of jobs, just finding the time to talk is a challenge. Naturally we'd like to lie down together at night, wake up together in the morning. We'd like to be able to share our days while we do the dishes or spend a couple of hours in front of the TV just not talking. That's all. We don't want to inconvenience anyone. We just want to spend time together. Quality time. But…" He stood up. "We took an oath. Our kids come first. We'll be patient. Would you do us a favor, though?"

"What?"

"Would you talk with your mom about this? Tell her your honest feelings? She really needs to know how you feel."

"Why don't you just tell her?" Trace asked.

Tom shrugged. "I might not see her for a couple of days. She's working and I'm working and we have two houses and six kids to take care of. I'll try to remember to, but she'd probably appreciate it more if it came straight from you."

"Okay," he said weakly. "Sure."

"Thanks for being honest with me, Trace," Tom said. "See you later."

"Yeah," Trace said.

Tom started down the walk and then he turned. "There is one more thing. I'd consider it a privilege if you could accept me as your stepfather. We couldn't do this if we didn't care about each other's kids. Your mom is really looking forward to having daughters. It would make me proud to add you and Cole to my family. Just so you know."

Trace didn't say anything.

Tom didn't really expect him to.

"Do I thank Sid for this born-again Dakota Jones?" Cal asked.

"Born-again?"

"You've gone from the AWOL Dakota Jones to Dakota the family man."

"No, it's not Sid's doing," he said with a laugh. "It could be, if she'd give in a little."

They were in Dakota's Jeep, headed for Denver. It was Monday, Dakota's usual day off. Maggie wasn't due back in Denver until Wednesday, so she stayed home with Elizabeth; they were going to Sully's, where Maggie would help in the garden and Elizabeth would probably eat dirt.

Sedona had been released from the hospital and was staying at Maggie's for a couple of days. Bob had come to Denver to check her out and fly home with her, but her brothers asked if she could stay long enough for them to see her.

"Sid is definitely one of the things holding me in Colorado," Dakota said. "It hasn't been very long for us but I like it. Don't get too excited. She's going to string me along for a while."

"And why is that?"

"I guess she wouldn't mind me telling you. She went through an ugly divorce and is coming up a little short in the trust department. She's not inclined to bet on a man."

"Especially one she hasn't known very long?" Cal asked.

"I'm starting to think the longer we're together and the better she gets to know me, the more it terrifies her. She's going back to LA sometime soon to give her old boss a hand. But I think it's more than that. As far as I know she hasn't been back since Rob brought her out here. I bet she wants to know if there's anything about that old life she misses."

"Any worries that she'll move back?"

"I have no idea."

"And if she does?"

Dakota sighed and concentrated on the road. "I'm not likely to give up easily."

"You seem altogether different than the man I thought I knew," Cal said.

Oh, really? Dakota thought. *I ran away from home, spent a lifetime in the Army, went to war a bunch, lost the love of my life to a terrorist, went to jail for a while... Why would I change?*

"There are things you don't know about me," Dakota said. "I've been too private. There was a woman who changed my life."

He told Cal about Hasnaa. They talked all the way to Denver.

Cal looked at Dakota's profile.

"You can start over and enjoy a happy life. Look at how things have turned out for me. I lost Lynne but then I found Maggie. I guess you thought that only happened to you, huh?"

"If you tell me it happens to everyone, I'm going to be very disappointed. I think I'm special."

Cal laughed. "I hope Sid takes pity on you, because I like having you around. Never thought it would happen," Cal said.

Sedona greeted them at the door. Though it was July, she wore slacks, a sweater set and fashionable leather flats.

From the time she discovered life after the farm, she opted for country club casual clothing, never jeans. While Sierra still wore jeans with tears in all the right places, Sedona always looked like a schoolteacher.

Cal and Dakota took their turns hugging her. She touched her hair and said, "I haven't had a proper hair color in quite a while and I'm getting gray."

"You look great," Dakota said. "Let's get some coffee or something. Then you can tell us how you're feeling."

Bob came from the kitchen to shake hands with the men. He thanked them again for all their help, especially in finding Sedona.

"Sierra couldn't come with us," Dakota said.

"She called. She said the demands of the new addition to their household has her running low on energy. I'll catch up with her when we're both doing better," Sedona said.

They all sat at the kitchen table with coffee and some bakery coffee cake that no one touched. Dakota tried not to look too hard at Sedona but his dark, heavy brows betrayed his emotions. She seemed fine, but every action and movement was as if she'd just awakened from a nap.

"It's going to take a little time for Sedona to get used to the medication. It may even have to be adjusted. But as Sedona tells it, she doesn't feel any inner turmoil," Bob said.

"What do you feel?" Cal asked.

"I feel a little too calm. I guess that's the medication. The one thing I fear the most," she said, "is that everyone thinks I'm crazy."

"Anxiety isn't crazy," Cal said. "As Maggie explains it, it's a chemistry thing—some people's serotonin levels are wacky and that can cause depression or anxiety or any number of things. So there are medications to manage that."

"I don't have much anxiety, but I now have depression," she said.

"There's a process," Bob said. "Sedona is going to come home, see a psychiatrist for her medication and a therapist for her counseling. It's not going to be a quick cure—she has spent way too long fighting her fears. She needs a rest."

"You look a lot better than you did the last time I saw you," Dakota said. "But different. I don't know what's different."

"This is how you look when you realize you aren't losing your mind. And I haven't had a panic attack in quite a while. They're terrible."

"I'm sure they're terrible to have," Bob said. "They're also terrible to see. More than once, I found her curled up in a corner, sweating, crying, talking to herself."

"I went to a doctor several years ago, and after telling him about Jed and answering some questions, he said I was obviously schizophrenic. He put me on a heavy medication and I got worse. I could hardly get out of bed and then I was hallucinating."

"That set us back about five years," Bob said. "And everyone jokes about OCD but the real thing is no joking matter. Half the time Sedona couldn't sleep because of anxiety and the rest of the time it was because canned goods that weren't alphabetized were dancing in her head."

"Everything had to be my routine or I couldn't function. I've never been good with change…"

They talked for a while about her plans. Sedona and Bob were going to fly home the next day. The talk of separation was off the table for the time being, but Sedona said she understood that if she stopped taking her meds or attending therapy sessions, Bob wasn't making any promises.

"But we're going to communicate better," Sedona said. "I can't risk staying with a bad practitioner just to keep the peace when the outcome could be worse."

After an hour or so, Bob left to get some sandwiches.

"Cal, I owe you for putting your foot down and confronting me. At the time I hated you, but I'm glad you called Bob. And, Dakota, I still can't believe you left your job and devoted yourself to searching for me. I don't know what might've become of me if you hadn't done that."

"You must have been so scared," Dakota said. "I couldn't sleep at night, thinking of you living in a box under a bridge."

She laughed. "With all my scraps alphabetized? It's more likely you'd have found me hiding in some store or warehouse, curled up in a sweaty ball, after I'd organized everything."

"It's good you're doing better," Dakota said.

"We'll see how much better I am when I've been home awhile. I'm afraid I've hurt my family."

"Listen, you did your best. You had issues, but you tried. Sometimes you have to accept nobody's perfect," Dakota said.

"Even me?" she asked with a sly smile.

"Sedona, the problem isn't that perfectionists are hard on themselves," Cal said. "They're hard on the people around them. When I talked to Bob he said he'd be happy to hang all the towels with a level and alphabetize the canned goods, but whatever was happening to you was much more serious than that. He was terrified. He loves you."

"I know," she said softly. "I hope he can forgive me."

Dakota was quiet a moment. "For better or worse," he finally said. "Most couples have plenty of both."

Connie took some personal time from his shift to go home. With any luck Sam would be napping and he could have a serious talk with Sierra. But he found them on the floor together, playing.

"Aw, you hoped to hit naptime," she said with a sly smile.

"I did, but not for boom boom. I want to talk to you."

"Is something wrong?" she asked, pulling Sam closer, into the little hollow made when she sat cross-legged.

"Yes, Sierra, something is wrong. You've been a little off for about a month. You might be anemic. Or maybe you have some infection or something that just isn't taking hold. Or maybe it's something scary, like fatigue syndrome. I don't have a clue. I started looking on the internet—there are about a hundred possibilities. But we're done screwing around with this. I made you an appointment with Dr. Culver. She's at the urgent care clinic down the road from the firehouse. She's new around here and really nice—you'll like her. She's going to draw some blood, get some lab work, see if she can figure out what's going on. Hell, you could have some heart infection or kidney disease making you weak and tired."

"Oh," she said. "I'm sorry. I didn't know you were so worried."

"I'm not exactly frantic, but I suggested a checkup about fifty times and you didn't do anything. So I made you an appointment. Tomorrow, when I'm off. I'll take care of Sam."

"Okay. I guess that's completely reasonable. But I bet there's nothing wrong. Just, you know, the occasional bug I don't quite get over before it hits me again."

"Right. That was one of the things the internet didn't turn up. That kind of occasional, uncertain bug. So you'll see the doctor tomorrow morning at ten. But first," he said, reaching into his back pocket and pulling out a long, slim box. "This."

She took the box from him. "A pregnancy test? But I haven't even been late!"

"It's the first thing the doctor is going to check."

"I'm on the pill! I've been completely regular!"

"Just go pee on it and remove the question from my mind," he said.

"But we've decided to adopt and foster on account of—"

"That's fine, if it works out that way. For right now you act like a woman with a little touch of pregnancy. So pee!"

"But, Connie, I've had all my periods, right on time, everything is—"

"I want you to do this," he said. "Do not make me squeeze you over that stick!"

"Jeez," she said. "Don't get all testy, okay?"

He reached for Sam. "Now," he emphasized.

"Fine. But you're going to feel silly."

"I'm very good at that," he said.

With a surly huff, she got off the floor and disappeared with the pregnancy stick. Connie held Sam on his lap. "Here's the deal, bud. When you sign on with us, that means I'm your dad. That means you'll have to count on me as the one who teaches you about women—how to understand them, how to talk with them, how to negotiate with them, how to make things work with them. And as you can see, I'm a little dense about that. Your mom is teaching me the rules. I'm slow to catch on but I'm getting there. By the time you really need to know, I'll be a damn genius."

Sam gurgled and flashed his big toothless grin.

A bloodcurdling scream came from the bathroom, causing Sam to jump, his eyes as big as hubcaps. His lower lip quivered. Molly jolted in her sleep and sat up, one ear flopped inside out.

"That could be a bad sign or a good sign, depending on your perspective. Let's go see."

Sierra was sitting on the closed toilet lid, her arms

crossed over her knees, the test stick dangling from one hand. Her head was down and she was crying. She lifted her head when she heard Connie open the door. "Oh, Connie, what will we do?"

"I'd like to start by talking about it," he said.

"How did this happen?" she asked.

He shook his head. "It's not like we screwed up, Sierra. You were on the pill."

"Maybe I got befuddled with all that was going on. I missed a couple, so I took them when I remembered and not at the same time every day. But I thought we were good."

"It's okay. This is a good thing."

"Sam is only six months old yet and here I am—"

"We're going to be busy," he said.

"We're going to do this?" she asked. "Are you saying we should do this?"

"Come here, Sierra," he said. "Come on, honey."

She went to him and he enfolded her with Sam into those big fireman's arms, kissing her cheeks and eyes. He drew her backward until he was sitting on the edge of the bed, Sierra on his lap and Sam on hers. "I'm saying we should do this. I'm saying it's ours, it came out of us, came out of our lovemaking, came out of our love for each other. It wasn't planned, it's going to be inconvenient, but we can manage. Lucky for us, we can manage."

"But you agreed, the risk of schizophrenia..."

"I agreed that if you found having children a little too frightening given your father's disease, I can live with that. But see this little guy right here? Our little guy? He came out of a smashed car. There are a lot of risks, honey. Parents have to be brave, strong and smart. I think we're up to it."

"Oh, Connie, I'll worry all the time. Not only is there mental illness in the family, but addiction!"

"I think the last statistics I read, addiction touches every family. Thank goodness you're an expert on it. So, don't be afraid. We're going to raise Sam and he's going to have a little brother or sister."

"I told you," she said. "You're taking a big chance on me."

"I don't regret it one bit," he said. "You feel like shit sometimes because you're pregnant. You've had morning sickness and you're fatigued. You're going to have a few more complaints along the way, too. But all in all, it's going to be awesome. I love you."

"You are too good," she said, stroking his cheek.

"Apparently I really am too good," he said, grinning. "I blew right through birth control pills and nailed an egg."

"Please don't get all cocky," she said.

"Too late. I'm feeling very invincible right now."

"Now what?" she asked.

"Now I think we convince Sam to take a little nap and get busy."

"But I'm pregnant!"

"I hear it's even better that way."

"Well, me getting accidentally pregnant sure hasn't diminished your sex drive!"

"It has not."

"I don't think he's ready for a nap," she said.

Sam yawned so big his open mouth almost swallowed up his face. He put his fist in his mouth and his head on Connie's shoulder. "That's my son," Connie said. "He'll be asleep by the time I get my boots off."

Sierra took the baby to his room. "I'm not sure I'm in the mood," she said as she was leaving.

"That's my favorite part," Connie said. "Getting you in the mood."

Love...is an able master; he teaches us to be

what we never were before.

—Molière

16

Dakota was experiencing an existence of calm and peace that he'd never really had before, at least not for days and weeks on end. Nothing about the Army had been peaceful, even though there was much about it he had loved. Even his most blissful days with Hasnaa were overshadowed by the challenges of their cultural differences; they had not come even close to figuring out how they were going to manage to be together long-term. She would never give up her work and he wasn't sure what he'd do without the Army.

But as August arrived, life had never seemed more settled. Sedona was back home in Connecticut, in the hands of a good doctor, sleeping at night. "Sometimes during the day, as well," she said with a touch of laughter in her voice. "And counseling up the nose—Bob and me, individual, group. I'm so overloaded with counseling I couldn't even begin to tell you if it's working."

But she felt all right. There was no panic in her voice.

Sierra was looking forward to the court appearance at the

end of the month that would settle their adoption of Sam. Elizabeth was pulling herself up on the furniture and had four teeth in the front of her mouth. They looked huge when she smiled. Sully had come to think of Sierra as another daughter. It wasn't so long ago, when Maggie was single, that he'd thought he'd never experience the joy of grandparenthood. Now here he was with a little one on each knee.

The happiness Dakota found when he was able to spend time with Sid soothed his soul. When he made love to her, it rocked his world.

He picked Sid up at her house early on Saturday evening. They went together to the soup kitchen, something he particularly looked forward to. The other volunteers had become friends, even though there was no socializing outside of their volunteer night. And he'd grown a fierce admiration for Sister Mary Jacob, who put so much energy into caring for others.

"Why couldn't you be my mother, Mary Jacob?"

"The pope forbade it," she slung back easily.

Dakota and Sid were sharing a laugh over Sierra's recent shock and Connie's puffed-up excitement as they walked into the food hall. Before they even got to their aprons, they spotted a familiar face. Neely. Smiling beautifully. Positioned behind the pan of potatoes with a spoon in her hand.

"Oh. My. God," Sid said.

"That's it," Dakota said. "That's no accident!"

"It can't be. I'll talk to Sister," Sid said, heading for the kitchen.

Dakota just stood there inside the door for a moment and then he followed Sid. By the time he found them having a private talk in the corner, he picked up the words *stalking* and *vandalism*.

"You think this woman is bad news, Dakota?" Sister Mary Jacob asked.

"Definitely. She accused me of assaulting her when nothing could be a bigger lie. According to people who have known her, she lies quite a bit. If her lips are moving, you should suspect something. I'm afraid we're not going to stay. Sid has Friday, Saturday and Sunday off—put us on another night."

"The Saturday night crowd are your friends. I'll move her. We'll get by without you tonight. We have enough people to serve and clean up. I'll see you both next weekend."

"I don't know if she's crazy or just determined and obsessed. You better be careful," Dakota warned.

"Don't worry about me," Mary Jacob said. "I have friends in high places."

"That almost makes me want to stay, hearing you say that. You can't just rely on prayer."

"You naive boy," she said. "I know karate. And I know the police chief. She's not going to give me any trouble. I'm a nun, for God's sake."

Not that anyone would know it by looking at her.

"If anything goes strange with her, call us," Dakota said.

"Absolutely. We'll see what happens when I schedule her on another night. You two, go on. I'll tell the others you had something come up. Suddenly."

"I might not be available next week," Sid said. "I have a few things to do out of town."

Dakota shot her a look. She'd been saying she hoped to spend a few days at her old job, helping out her former boss with something, but they hadn't talked specific dates. He was secretly hoping it just wouldn't happen.

"Don't worry about it, we'll get by. Go now. Before we draw a crowd."

Dakota said hello to a couple of people in the kitchen, shook a couple of hands, made some excuses and promised to see them later. "Let's go," he said, taking Sid's elbow to steer her out. He made it a point not to look back at Neely. He wondered how the hell she found out about the soup kitchen.

He drove away. "Let's get closer to home and get a drink. How about that?"

"I'll have a glass of wine," she said. "Maybe two, since you're driving. Jesus, that's so disturbing."

"I just don't get it," he said.

"Me, either. Look, I think you're a hunk. But seriously? What's she going to do with you when she gets you?" Sid pondered aloud. "You're mad as hell! This doesn't have happily-ever-after for her stamped on it!"

"This is a first for me," he said. "So—you've made travel plans?"

"I've been talking to Rob about it but hadn't nailed anything down. But, seeing Neely at the soup kitchen, I think now is an excellent time for me to take that trip. And it would give me peace of mind if you'd agree to stay with Cal while I'm gone. I don't want to think of you alone at the cabin."

"I'm armed."

"Even more reason. Cody, I don't want to even imagine you shooting someone!"

"I hate to break it to you, but in wars—"

"I know, but this isn't that. Yes," she said. "We're at an interesting juncture. A crossroads. This is the time for me to look at my past and see if I can reconcile it. And maybe decide where to go from here. You should do the same. Then we should talk about what will happen next with us."

"Together?" he asked hopefully. "Are we going to talk about where we go together? Because I'm not ready to give you up."

"We'll work this out. And we should figure out what to do about Neely! This has to stop."

"I'll call Stan tomorrow."

"Tomorrow is Sunday," she reminded him.

"I know where to get his cell number. And I'll ask Cal to help me with this—he knows everything about the law."

She sighed heavily. "I'm not running away, Cody. Dr. Faraday asked me specifically if I could come in and consult. I'll be paid. He genuinely wants my input. He trusts me."

"Just a few days?"

"Let me see what I'm dealing with. I promise to keep you informed. We'll talk every day."

"Why does it have to be you?" he asked, his voice demanding.

"I was very invested in his project. I know what I'm doing. At least, I did before a year of slinging drinks."

"You're saying you're the only one qualified to do this? Now, when we're just getting around to talking about *us*?"

She was very quiet. "Yes," she said quietly. "This is a good time for me to go back there, see what I really want. Need." After a moment, she said, "Maybe you should just take me home."

He grabbed her hand. "Please, Sid. No. Come home with me tonight."

"If you're sure. I can't say no to you."

"That's what I'm counting on," he said. "Sorry I barked. I'll keep my head."

"Please. I think right now we need to be supportive of each other. We need to not go crazy. God, we've dealt with enough craziness."

They were quiet for a long spell.

"I have some of your favorite wine at home. Let's skip the bar and go to the cabin. Let's get our heads on straight. We're a little shook up, I think," Dakota said.

"I think so," she agreed.

There was no reason to get up early. It was Sunday morning. The bar would open later. Rob and the boys would probably sleep in. Dakota made himself bacon and eggs while Sid had her fruit and oatmeal. It was ten before they cracked the cabin door.

The first thing they saw was the paint on the Jeep's hood was burned off and full of bubbles.

"Stay here," Dakota said. He took a couple of steps toward the Jeep, then stepped back to the doorway. He pushed Sid inside and locked the door. "Acid," he said. He pulled out his phone and dialed 911. Then he opened his laptop, signed on and looked at the video from the security camera. He scrolled through hours before she came into view. It had been nearly dawn. The image was perfectly clear thanks to the camera's night vision, infrared LEDs.

"It's going to be a busy day," Stan said to the small gathering inside Dakota's cabin.

Dakota sat at his desk, laptop open. Stan, Cal, Officer Glenda Tippin and Sid all looked over his shoulder at the screen.

"Dakota, can you download this and email it to me?" Stan asked.

"Sure," he said. "Now what? Do we get to arrest her?"

"Sure, but that's not going to be very satisfying. It's malicious destruction of private property and, at the end of the day, it'll probably be a fine. You can take her to court for damages, but what we really want is to make her go away. See, I've been doing a little checking—Ms. Benedict has a record. Sort of."

"Sort of?"

"Well, there have been two restraining orders that I can find. She's broken into a house and created some havoc, destroyed some property, followed people. She gets in trouble, blows it off. She's a poser. She slides into communities and groups, invents a new Neely, attaches herself, makes a nuisance of herself. She gets fined, gets sued, throws money at her problems. Yeah, madam comes from a rich family and apparently she can buy off her victims."

"Good," Dakota said. "I'll take some of her money. The damage to the Jeep is considerable."

"Agreed, but what troubles me the most is her playing around with dangerous items like knives and acid." Stan shook his head and ran a hand through his sparse hair. "Jesus. I'm no genius, but I think she's escalating. And I want her the hell out of my town."

"Do we even know what she's done?" Sid asked.

"Yeah, I know some things," Stan said. "She claimed a man led her on. I don't know what he did or if he did anything at all, but he was married. Neely put the family through quite a bit for a long time, until they moved. Then there was someone she met in a yoga class. A woman. A single woman. Neely wanted to be her best friend, stalked and pestered and created mischief until the woman got a restraining order. Apparently she did things like break into the woman's house, did her laundry, set her table, prepared food left in the refrigerator. My wife asked, 'What do I have to do to get her interested in me? I wouldn't press charges!' Four kids. My wife doesn't have much of a conscience if housework and cooking are involved—she'd sleep with the devil.

"I've talked to Neely's older brother. When I asked him if he knew a woman named Neely Benedict, he asked, 'What did she do now?' Our short conversation suggested she's been like this since she was about five—no empathy or conscience whatsoever, very spoiled, very entitled. I suggested it would help mightily if they'd cut off her bottomless pit of money and he said he's not feeding her family money. She's getting paid out of a trust. Oh, and her brother doesn't want her back."

"Great," Dakota said.

"She said she was invested in small businesses around Timberlake, but I sure can't find anything about that," Sid said.

"Oh, she's made herself well-known around town, stopping in this business and that, acting like an heiress looking for a home for her money. But these are pretty simple folks around here and they're not looking for a partner or investor. I guess we just don't think like that." Stan laughed. "Can you imagine this fancy woman driving out to Sully's to try to entice him into letting her buy in?"

"Do we even know where she lives?" Cal asked.

"I'm not just some hick cop," Stan said. "Of course I know, though I admit, work is harder when the suspect tells about half the truth. She lives in Aurora. Nice house on the country club golf course. I'm friendly with the Aurora chief. And the state trooper captain. We like to help each other out when we can." Officer Tippin cleared her throat. "All right, no need to try to keep me honest, Tippin. I get most of my computer help from Castor. So what?"

"Do you have a plan, Stan?" Dakota asked.

"I do, indeed. I plan to appeal to her sense of fair play. When she comes to me to discuss the situation, I'll offer to allow her to make restitution. She'll want to do that. Then I'm going to suggest Timberlake isn't right for her."

"Swell," Dakota said, not very encouraged.

"Meantime, until we get our differences straight, I'd like you to stay somewhere else. This cabin is awful isolated to be at the hands of some loony woman with acid. Jesus, I can't even let myself think about the possibilities."

"He'll stay with us," Cal said. Then he looked at Sid. "Plenty of room for you, too, Sid."

"Thanks," she said. Then she exchanged glances with Dakota. He knew immediately. She wasn't hanging around for this.

* * *

A tow truck was called and eventually everyone had dispersed. Dakota and Sid rode back to Cal's house with him, then Dakota borrowed Cal's truck to take Sid home.

"Can we just talk a bit?" she asked. "Can we park somewhere and talk?"

"You know I'd always say yes to parking with you," he said. She could tell it was all fake cheerfulness. He knew what was coming.

"Cody, none of this is your fault, but I don't want to be in the middle of it," she said. "With any luck Stan will have this sorted out and you'll be done dealing with the crazy one. This is a perfect time for me to get this trip out of the way. I'm very loyal to Dr. Faraday. I've been trying to help him sort out a problem via computer but going there, to my old lab and my old colleagues, will serve more than one purpose. I should know if I want to go back to that career field. I did train for it for a long time. And I should know if I can make peace with the past. That's the only way a person can move on."

"And what else, Sid?" he asked. "Do you need to know if you'll miss me?"

She smiled gently. "I know I'll miss you. This will be good for us. We should see how we feel about things after a brief separation."

"Didn't we do that while I was in Denver looking for Sedona?"

"Kind of, but you were challenged with an important mission. I need to do the same thing. It's been sneaking up on me, needing that important mission. I have to see how that feels."

"It was so perfect for a while, wasn't it?" he said, running a knuckle along her peachy cheek. "Like a time out from the real world. I know you have more important things to do than tend bar. I should probably stop pretending I'm a garbage collector. I should—"

"You don't have to be in a hurry," she said. "I hear snowplowing is fun."

"What really happened, Sid? Was it just your lousy husband?"

"It was mostly him," she insisted. "I think I'd been working way too hard, playing and relaxing way too little. I was too alone. It happens to people like me, you know? I was working in a university. I watched brilliant professors go off the rails. When the work is meaningful, it can get intense. When it gets too intense…"

"How do you keep that from happening?" he asked.

"I have some ideas. Coming to Colorado to be with family gave me balance. Working in Rob's bar gave me people. Then there's you." She leaned over and kissed him. "Now that I've been with you, I have a new perspective. A jackass like David could never catch me now."

"Good to know," he said.

"Cody, if I'm going to go to LA, I want to go now. I feel bad about abandoning you before Neely is rounded up and stopped, but you have your family to shore you up. And I'd only get in the way. Now that she knows we're together, she's getting more destructive. I'm going to fade out for a week or two…"

He laughed sarcastically. "It was a few days. Now it's a week or two."

"I'll talk to you. Let's see how long it takes Stan to do something about Neely."

"I don't want you to go," he said. "I also don't want you to be anywhere near her."

"You went to Australia and walked for a month," she said. "That was your way of letting go of the past. What

I'm doing shouldn't panic you. For me, this is like a good workout."

He shook his head. "You are such a beautiful nerd."

"It'll go by fast."

"When do you think you'll leave?" he asked.

"I'm going home to look up flights," she said. "The sooner I go, the sooner I'm back."

"I just want to be sure you're safe," he said.

She laughed. "There's so much security in and around that computer lab, it's almost ridiculous."

"Where will you stay?" he asked.

"I'm not sure," she said. "I'll email Dr. Faraday's assistant and ask her to set up something. Could be anything from a hotel to guest housing. It'll be perfectly safe and comfortable."

"If you want me to go with you—"

"God, you'd be bored out of your mind! You couldn't get clearance into the lab and I'm sure I'll be putting in long hours. No. Let me do this. It's not as scary as you think. I'll be back."

"Convince me," he said, reaching for her. "Kiss me like I have nothing to worry about."

"My pleasure," she said.

Sid was able to arrange a flight out on Monday and Dakota drove her the two hours to Denver to catch her flight. Then she generously loaned him the use of her car since his was going to be in the shop for quite a while. He had barely arrived back in Timberlake when his phone rang and he saw it was Stan.

"What's up, Chief?" he asked.

"I wondered if you had time to stop by the office before close of business. I just want to give you a heads-up."

"Can't you just tell me on the phone?" Dakota asked.

"I can't, sorry. You need to see something."

"I'll be right there," he said. "The sooner we get this over with, the better."

Dakota walked into the small, storefront police station to find Stan and Officer Cantor grinning as they looked at the computer screen. "Just so you're ready, Dakota, tomorrow at midnight, this goes out on social media."

There was the surveillance video of Neely pouring acid on his car, coupled with a sliver of the video from the alley. Her face was much more recognizable in the dark alley video when it was put together with the better, more clear camera video from Dakota's cabin. "So?"

"We've formed a nice little collective of small towns in the area, including Vail and Aurora, who will launch this public service announcement, looking for this woman."

Dakota was not impressed. "What good is that going to do?"

"You on Facebook or Twitter, Dakota?"

"I have a Facebook page but I never look at it. I keep up with people, though. Just not that way."

"You are behind the times," Stan said.

"Like over twelve years," Paul Cantor said. "I thought military men used it all the time."

"I guess most of them do," he said. "So, what do you expect to happen?"

"Honestly? We expect to bring her in, that's what. Her friends and neighbors are going to recognize her, share it. She might see it herself. Most police departments have active social media connections helping them alert the public about important issues, encourage people to call in suspicious criminal activity, keep the dialogue open. All the TV stations have social media—they want their audience to talk to them. A lot of them will pick up this request to identify this woman. It will probably make the news."

"But we *know* who she is!" Dakota said.

Stan and Paul both chuckled. "We do, don't we," Stan said. "And pretty soon everyone will. We might be this little out of the way town but I expect at least seventy-five percent of the population has Facebook and Twitter. Hell, that's our president's favorite form of communication. Though you gotta ask yourself…" He cleared his throat. "Your stalker is going to be exposed."

Dakota was silenced for a moment. "Aw, shit, she's going to burn my house down," he said.

"It's on the Timberlake Police page, buddy. Just camp at Cal's awhile longer till we hear from the lady. And I'd bet my retirement we'll be hearing from her quick," Stan said.

Dakota sighed. He wasn't encouraged. "You guys are just a bunch of candy asses," he said. "Wouldn't it be a lot more effective to go cuff her and charge her?"

"I might do that eventually," Stan said. "Right now I'm thinking long-term."

"Oh, man," Dakota said. "I'm truly fucked."

When Dakota got back to his brother's house, he helped himself to a cold beer. Cal emerged from his office, took note of Dakota's beer and got one for himself.

"What's the latest?" Cal asked.

"Stan's planning to catch her with Facebook."

Cal whistled. "Crafty," he said, a facetious tone in his voice. "You think maybe Stan's been police chief too long?"

Sierra sat on the exam table in a paper gown. She swung her feet, midway between hysteria and euphoria. There was a light tap and the door opened. A lovely woman around her age walked in, reading the folder. She smiled. Dr. Culver's name was embroidered on her white lab coat. "It appears you've explained the mysterious fatigue?" she said by way of a question.

"So the pregnancy stick says," Sierra answered.

"Congratulations. How do you feel?"

"Nauseous in the morning, tired in the afternoon. And a bit worried."

"About?"

"I was taking birth control pills," Sierra said. "I looked it up on the internet—it says that's nothing to worry about."

"For once, the internet is correct. The worry comes a bit later, when you're aware that at least that particular pill isn't going to keep you from getting pregnant. You'll have to try something stronger. Or different. Or maybe double up. But you can cross that bridge when you get to it. Right now I'd like to do a checkup."

"To be sure I'm pregnant?" she asked.

"To be sure you don't have anything else going on. I don't have an ultrasound and I'm not set up for a pelvic, but I can get that ready fast. If you want me to have a look."

"Would you know for sure? If you looked?"

"I trust those darn pregnancy tests, to tell the truth. But I can get some other bases covered—like rule out ovarian cysts, uterine tumors, et cetera. I just can't tell you how far along without an ultrasound. I'll get some routine bloodwork done, a urine test, and we can find you an obstetrician."

"I'm very worried about hereditary disease," Sierra said.

Dr. Culver put a blood pressure cuff around Sierra's arm and it automatically pumped itself tight. "Anything in particular?" she asked.

"My father is mentally ill. He isn't under the care of a doctor, but he has so many special friends it's certainly schizophrenia."

"Onset of that particular mental disorder isn't usually until the early twenties. You have years before something ke that might show up. Any other relatives with mental illness?"

"My sister has OCD and anxiety…"

"Not related to schizophrenia," she said. "Your blood pressure is fine. Let me go get my bucket—I'll draw your blood."

"Bucket?"

"My supplies," she said. "Be just a minute." She exited and was back almost instantly. The doctor fixed the rubber band around Sierra's upper arm, and while she looked for a vein, she chatted. "If you're having a lot of worry about mental illness, we can certainly fix you up with a counselor. But the bottom line is there is a ninety-five percent chance your child is going to be in excellent health and live to a ripe old age, provided you take care of yourself. There is a three to five percent chance he or she could develop a medical problem or have an accident. He could get meningitis or Lyme disease from a tick or fall in a backyard pool. You'll have to be on your toes, but you know that already. With you and Connie obsessing over the baby, I predict he or she will be strong and healthy and outlive you by many years. Of course, you could encounter something rare, something frightening." She popped another tube on the needle. "A counselor could help you not be scared until you have some reason to be. And a counselor would also help you resist dreaming up shit. Oops, I apologize. Yes, the doctor has been known to swear. So sorry."

Sierra was grinning. "I like when you swear."

"I'm trying to quit. So, I'm going to make sure you're not anemic—pregnant women suffer from that sometimes. And that you don't have diabetes or blood in your urine. And if you'd like me to, I'll measure your uterus and see if I can guess the sex of the baby."

"Really?" she asked.

"Yes, I really do guess. But of course I have absolutel
no way of knowing. Do you want me to peek and see i
your cervix is blue and your uterus just slightly swollen?

"Yes, please."

"I'll get a Pap done while I'm at it," she said. "Let m
grab a nurse or someone. Would you be upset if I had th
janitor… Never mind," she said, laughing. "Of course
will be a nurse."

And then she was gone again. Sierra was in love wit
her.

Twenty minutes later, Dr. Culver said, "I'm guessin
four to six weeks. Everything else in the pelvis is fine
And you can go ahead and stop taking those birth contro
pills." She laughed happily at her joke.

"Did Connie tell you we're in the adoption process?"

"No, he didn't mention that," she said. "On a waitin
list?"

"No," Sierra said. "We're fostering a little boy, si:
months old. His mother was killed in a car accident an
we're adopting him with his maternal grandmother's ap
proval."

"Six months?" Dr. Culver said. "Wow. You think yo
were tired before…"

"I know. Can you wave your magic wand and make thi
little surprise a girl?"

"I charge extra for that," she said. Then the docto
leaned close, squeezed Sierra's shoulder and said, "You'r
going to have a wonderful family. Try not to worry. Try t
enjoy all the enjoyable parts—there are many. And whe
you're at the end of your rope, you can come in and com
plain to me for a dollar a minute."

Sierra laughed.

"I can't count the number of patients I've had who ge
pregnant just a few months into the adoption process. It'

mazing. I think holding a baby must make some women ire off eggs like rockets."

"Is it really only three to five percent that things go erribly wrong?"

"Oh, sweetheart, I have no idea. I made that up. But I et I'm close if not right on!"

Sierra went home feeling especially blessed. It looked ike they had a healthy and beautiful baby boy and a perectly blossoming pregnancy.

Two days later, the doorbell rang and her world crashed nd burned.

Mrs. Jergens stood there with another woman, introduced as the social worker from the county. Mrs. Jergens vas a little hunched from her arthritis, the knuckles on er hands swollen and some of her fingers bent. "I can't lo it," she said. "I can't give away my flesh and blood grandchild."

Family not only need to consist of merely those whom we share blood, but also for those whom we'd give blood.

—CHARLES DICKENS

17

Sierra grabbed her chest. She tried to keep her head even though her heart was hammering. "Come in," Sierra said. "Let's talk about this."

"I'm not going to change my mind," the older woman said.

The social worker introduced herself. "I'm Jeanne Blasette," she said. And then she looked down.

"I didn't say come in and change your mind. Just please come in. Sam's having a nap but he won't be asleep long. Please," Sierra said, holding the door open. She thanked God the house was perfect. She'd thought about leaving the clean laundry on the sofa to fold, all the shoes scattered, dishes in the sink. But she'd had a spurt of energy and knew she'd better make use of it. There were even vacuum cleaner tracks on the carpet.

Molly sauntered into the room, and when she saw they had company, her back end began to wag and wiggle ferociously. "Molly, sit," Sierra commanded. Molly must have heard the panic in her voice because she instantly sat with no argument.

"Can I get you something to drink? At least a water?"

"I'll have a water," Mrs. Jergens said, leaning on that cane with two hands.

"Please, sit down. I'll get you both water."

When she got to the kitchen, she grabbed her phone off the counter and texted Connie. Can you come home? They're taking Sam from us! I'll text Cal. And to Cal she texted, Help! Sam's grandmother is here to take him away from us! Can you come?

Then she grabbed two bottled waters from the fridge and two glasses, taking them back to the living room. "I texted my husband, Mrs. Jergens. I'm sure if he's not out on a call, he'll be here soon. Can you tell me what happened?"

"I just couldn't sleep over it," she said, tears coming to her eyes. "I should at least try to take care of Sam. He's mine, after all."

"I know it must have been a very difficult decision, but we won't take him away from you. You'll be a part of our family." When she said the word *family*, she hiccuped a little.

"My cousin's girl, Sandy—she said she'd stay with me and help with the baby. That should make it easier."

"But what if you get sick?" Sierra asked. "Or have a particularly bad day and just can't lift him? Or hold him? He's already a hefty little guy."

"I know you're disappointed but I can't take a chance that I'd have terrible regrets! I had to make a decision before the adoption is final. Once it's final… You wouldn't want me to wait until then. Then we'd have to go to court and I don't know that I'd do so well, with the arthritis and all."

"Mrs. Jergens, you did a very brave thing, letting us

apply to adopt him. I know you wouldn't have done that if you weren't suffering from medical issues. You wouldn't have had to, I know that. But where will you be in five years? I don't know too much about rheumatoid arthritis—is it likely you can get stronger? Or weaker? Will Sam have to be given up then because of health reasons?"

"Well, there's the thing. If Sandy works out, maybe Sam will stay in the family!"

"Do you have a lot of confidence of that?" Sierra asked nervously. "How old is Sandy?"

"She's nineteen," Mrs. Jergens said. "My daughter was twenty!"

"Tell me about Sandy," Sierra asked. "Please?"

"My cousin's daughter," Mrs. Jergens said. "I've known her since she was born."

"But I thought you didn't have much contact with your extended family," Sierra said. "You said there were cousins, but they lived far away and you hadn't had much contact."

"Sandy's people live in Nashville. She's looking for a chance to get away, make something of herself, get out of Tennessee. She'll like it here."

"But what will happen in a year or two years when Sandy doesn't want to be a babysitter and caregiver? What will you do? At two, Sam is still going to need so much tending." Sierra turned her watering eyes toward the social worker. "Ms. Blasette? Have you talked with Mrs. Jergens about all the possibilities?"

Jeanne Blasette sat forward on the sofa. "We've talked at length. She wants to try to raise Sam. She wants to honor the memory of her daughter. I've suggested she leave Sam in foster care in that case. You both could agree not to finalize the adoption, her cousin's daughter could come and help around the house, you could bring Sam to her for visits and if all is well and it looks like it could work out with her cousin's daughter, then she could claim her grandson permanently."

"Yes," Sierra said. "Leave things as they are awhile longer, let's see how—"

"But that's not what I want," Mrs. Jergens said. "I spent about five hours on the phone with Sandy and her mother. We're all straight on what we'll need. If I have a baby to tend, my grandson, there will be added disability to help with the cost of having another member of the household. We've been working this out for a week. She's getting to my house today. She just called from Colorado Springs and said she's almost here."

"Please think this over," Sierra begged. "I'm afraid that even with help, Sam could be too much for you. He's a lot of baby. He's the best baby in the world, really, but even the best baby—"

"I've made plans," the woman said.

"Do you have furniture and supplies for him?" Sierra asked.

"I'd like to have back what I gave you," she said. "My neighbor loaned a crib. Jeanne brought a car seat for him. We'll need formula and—"

Sierra shot a glance at Jeanne Blasette. "Why didn't you call me and warn me this was going to happen?"

"We were talking about it, trying to work out the details, and then Mrs. Jergens decided she wanted to pick him up today. She didn't ask me to come along but I didn't want you to have questions and not be here to answer them. I had to move around some appointments but I wanted to be here for this. I know the shock is difficult. I wish I could say this sort of thing never happens, but..."

"It happens all the time," Mrs. Jergens said. "My own kid was in foster care for a couple of years way back when… I had some money problems. I got it straightened out and got her back…"

"Oh dear God," Sierra said.

"You'll need a little time to put together a bag for him," Ms. Blasette said. "I brought a gym duffel for you to use if you don't have one."

"We're going to wait until my husband and brother get here," Sierra said.

"Why?" Mrs. Jergens said.

"My husband loves his son, ma'am. I'm not letting him leave this house without Connie here. And my brother is my lawyer. Hopefully he's on his way. Let me check my phone." Sierra went to the kitchen and picked up her phone. "Yes, they're both coming."

"Go get him right now," Mrs. Jergens demanded. "Grab some diapers and clothes. My neighbor can help me with the rest. They have a teenager who drives—he can come back here and pick up things. I'm not waiting around. I know the law, I know my rights."

"He's asleep," Sierra said. The woman was so dispassionate that Sierra became afraid of what she or this cousin might be like if Sam wasn't easy, wasn't perfect, if they were tired or inconvenienced. "Please, I beg of you, let's not end our relationship like this, in one afternoon. Let's go more slowly. Let me care for Sam, bring him to you for visits, have some trial time to see if you really want to take on a full-time baby."

"No," Mrs. Jergens said. "Would you like to pack his things or should I just go get him out of his crib right now?"

"Don't do that," she begged. "He'll be cross if you wake him. Connie will be shattered if you just take him without—"

"Then get him," she said, giving her cane a stamp on the floor for emphasis.

Sierra jumped. "I'll get some of his things ready," she said weakly.

"I'll help," Jeanne said, standing to follow Sierra.

When they got to the baby's room, Sierra turned on the social worker. "My God, you have to know how terrifying this looks! Mrs. Jergens isn't capable of taking care of a heavy, rambunctious little boy! And this cousin? We don't know anything about this cousin!"

"I'm going to try to keep an eye on things, but remember, she's not under the scrutiny of child welfare. She hasn't done anything wrong and she's his closest living relative."

"She hasn't done anything yet," Sierra said. "She's mean! And careless!"

"I'm afraid I'm without options, Mrs. Boyle. She can refuse to complete the adoption process at any time. But I will check on her. On them."

"This can't be happening," Sierra said. "We love him so much. He's so happy with us."

"I'm sorry. Let's put a few things in the duffel for him. Let's at least make sure he has what he needs."

Tears rolled down Sierra's cheeks. "I can't," she squeaked.

"Yes, come on. Here we go," Jeanne said. She opened the duffel on the changing table and filled it with disposable diapers, wipes, onesies, pajamas. She went to the bureau and opened a drawer to reveal a full complement of little outfits. "Can you tell me which ones came from his grandmother? So we can give them back?"

Sierra felt as though she was wading through quicksand as she took the few steps to the bureau. She picked through the stacks and pulled out a few small items. "He's grown since he came to us. I don't think these will even fit him anymore."

"Can you please part with some clothes that will fit? Shoes? Not for her—for him."

Some fussing and squirming sounds came from the crib. "This can't be happening," Sierra said, lifting Sam into her arms and snuggling him close. "Oh God."

Sam protested being hugged so tightly and he started to cry.

"Let's get his things together," Jeanne said. "How about some formula and baby food? Just enough to get them through a couple of days?"

"I need to change him," she said, her heart ripped to shreds. "He's going to be hungry. Please, can I change and feed him? Please?"

The sound of the front door opening and closing could be heard.

"What's going on here? Sierra! Sierra!" Connie burst into the baby's room and enfolded Sierra and Sam in his big arms. "What the hell?"

"The adoption isn't final," Sierra said, choking on the words. "They're taking him away!"

"Maybe not," Connie said. "Cal is on his way. He's calling Mrs. Jergens's lawyer."

"Connie, please," she sobbed. "Please don't let her take him. Go talk to her, please. Please. She hates me."

"Did he just wake up?" Connie asked. Sierra nodded against his broad chest. "He's soaked," Connie said. "Go ahead and change him. I'll talk to Mrs. Jergens."

By the time Connie was back in the living room, Sierra heard her brother's voice, as well, both of them pleading rational arguments, trying to change her mind, dissuade her from taking the little boy.

"Sierra, do I have to take the baby?" Jeanne asked. "Shall I change him and make him a bottle? Are you too upset to—"

"I'll do it," Sierra said. She carried on, changing him, finding some outfits that would fit him and dressing him in one, putting his bitty shoes on his feet, crying the whole time. Her emotions had Sam fretting, whimpering and wiggling around, making it all the harder.

She carried him to the kitchen to find a bottle. Jeanne had followed her, raiding the baby supplies in the kitchen and adding some to her duffel.

"Can we have the rest of this formula?" Jeanne asked. "Cereal and jars of fruit? You don't seem to have much…"

"Sam eats food I make," Sierra said. "I just have these jars for those days I don't have time to make his food for him. He likes mashed bananas and oatmeal. He likes to pick Cheerios off his tray. I cook his vegetables and smash them with a fork. He loves potatoes, loves smashed sweet potatoes. I make applesauce," she said, ending with a sob.

A short distance away Connie and Cal continued to argue with Mrs. Jergens, pleading with her to give the Boyles a few days to prepare, asking Mrs. Jergens why she hadn't contacted her lawyer to tell him she was backing out of the adoption. Sierra gave Sam his bottle while they argued. And then Mrs. Jergens had had enough.

"Do I have to call the police to get my grandson turned over to me?"

The room went suddenly still. Quiet.

"Don't get crazy," Cal said. "Is there nothing we can do to make you reconsider? This young family is heartbroken, as you can see."

"As heartbroken as I was to learn my daughter was dead? I have to do this. I can't give up my grandson."

"Will you at least call your lawyer?" Cal asked.

"I'll call him," she said. "Not in front of all of you."

"Okay," Cal said. "Let's not make things harder. I want you to hear me on this, Mrs. Jergens. The Boyles are very bonded with your grandson. They want nothing so much as to give him a strong, loving family and to watch him thrive. If you get him home and have a moment of doubt, please don't hesitate to call on any of us. We'd all be happy to step in and help. We've all grown to love the boy."

Connie went to Sierra. She sat on a kitchen chair in the corner of the room, as far away from them as she could get. "Come on, baby," he said gently. "Let me have Sam."

She held him against her shoulder. She shook her head. "No," she said. "No, Connie, no."

"Baby, we don't have a choice," he said, gently pulling the little boy into his arms.

"No," Sierra cried. "Oh God."

Connie carried the baby to Mrs. Jergens, kissed him on the head and handed him over.

Mrs. Jergens struggled to hold him in one arm and hang on to her cane with the other. For a tense moment it looked like she might drop him, but she managed to get out the door. Jeanne Blasette scrambled along behind, opening the back door of the car for her and helping her get the baby situated. They could hear Sam crying as they took him away, Mrs. Jergens driving her car. When the sound of the car engine could no longer be heard, the house was silent but for the sobbing of Sierra.

Connie went to her and pulled her into his arms.

"Thanks for trying, Cal," he said.

"I'm not giving up," Cal said. "I've left messages with her lawyer. Maybe he can talk some sense into her."

"Thanks. We'll take any help we can get." He dropped back onto the couch, holding Sierra on his lap. "I'll stay home the rest of the shift. I just have to call my captain and tell him. He'll understand."

"What can I do for you right now?" Cal asked. "Can I

get some food together? I can call Maggie and ask her for a tranquilizer or something."

Connie was stroking Sierra's hair, rocking her. "Nah, Sierra's pregnant. She won't take anything now. I'll take care of her."

"Pregnant?" Cal said in a whisper.

"An accident, but we're happy about it," Connie said. "Okay, we're not happy about anything right now. It's safe for you to leave. I can take care of my wife."

"I'll keep at it, Connie."

"Great. Just don't tell us anything that will get our hopes up only to have him torn away from us again." He kissed Sierra's head. "We love him. We want him to be okay."

"Me, too," Cal said.

Sierra cried for hours. In early evening at the urging of Connie she agreed to eat a little canned chicken soup and drink some water for the baby's sake. "You can't get dehydrated, it could hurt the baby."

"I can't stop crying," she said.

"That's okay," he said. "I'm here. Let's take care of you and the baby. We don't need any more heartache." He spooned the soup into her as if she were the baby.

"I've gotten a bunch of texts," he said. "No one wants to get in our space and bother us, they don't want to call and wake anyone if they might be sleeping, but there are offers of food, company, prayers, anything. Cal told the family—Maggie, Dakota and Sully. My captain told some of the guys. Lisa and Rafe want to offer comfort when you're up to it. They're waiting to be told the coast is clear."

"Do you want company?" she asked. "Because I don't."

"I don't need company," he said. "I need to take care of what's left of my family."

After a few hours and a little food and water, Sierra fell

into an exhausted, troubled sleep. She woke in the dark of night and the clock by the bed said it was 2:00 a.m. She heard some fussing and for a split second she thought the baby was back, fussing in his crib. She sat up with a start.

A dim light from the living room illuminated the crack in the bedroom door. She pulled herself out of bed and went toward the sound. She found Connie sitting bent over on the living room chair, his head pushed into a soft toy, muffling his cries. He sat, alone, sobbing his heart out.

She went to him, kneeling at his feet, rubbing a small hand over his back.

Connie raised his head. "We didn't give him any of his toys."

"We'll take some to him," she said. "Come to bed and let me hold you."

"I'm okay," he said, sniffing back his tears, wiping his cheeks with the back of his hand.

"Neither one of us is okay," she said. "Come to bed with me. I need to take care of what's left of my family."

He stroked her cheek. "You okay?"

"God, not at all," she said. "But we're going to hang on to each other and get through this. There isn't anything they can throw at us that will break us. Because we're a really powerful team."

"Lotta tears on this one," he said.

"Yeah. It might take us a while to get through it."

"I can't imagine what I was thinking, saying I liked being around family, after all," Dakota said. "My family is falling apart."

"Some rough times have been had," Sully said. "How's my little Sierra getting by?"

"Connie says she cries way too much, but in deference to her pregnancy, she's eating and resting. And she took some toys to Mrs. Jergens in Fairplay. She said everything looked okay and the cousin was a nice enough girl. Sam was as excited as a puppy to see her and then didn't want to let her go. The cousin said, 'Y'all visit any old time.' Connie said Sierra cried for hours afterward." Dakota shook his head. "Those poor kids."

"This Jones family has had some high drama," Sully said. "What about you?"

"What about me?"

"There's a rumor going around that you've had some drama, too. Your girlfriend is out of town and you had yourself a stalker?" Sully chuckled. "That's pretty interesting stuff."

"Yeah, there was this woman vandalizing my property," Dakota said. "She must've thought that would make me desire her. It did not. Sid thought that was a perfect time to go to California and do some work for her old boss. She's been gone a week. I don't love it, but Sierra is my main concern now."

"I wish she'd come out here," Sully said. "You know, Maggie's mother divorced me and took Maggie away when she was about six. I didn't see her at all for years and I grieved something terrible. I think that was the right thing for her mother to do—that girl needed better schooling and parenting than she was getting here. But that didn't make it any easier. I don't know that I can entirely relate to what she's going through, but I'd sure like to see her."

"I'll tell her that, Sully," Dakota said. "And for what it's worth, even with all the drama, I like the connections I've made here."

"Don't fret too much, son. That girl will come back to you."

"I hope so."

"And Sierra is strong. She'll get through this, but I wish she'd come and see me."

"I'll tell her."

Despite Dakota's worry and concern over Sierra, Sid was constantly on his mind, as well. He talked to her every evening. She sounded tired but happy. She was putting in long days but she said it was so wonderful to work beside Dr. Faraday again. "He reminds me that I have abilities I shouldn't take for granted."

"Is he almost done reminding you of that?" Dakota asked. "Because I miss the hell out of you. And everyone is falling apart back here."

"And no sign of Neely?"

"Did you expect there to be?" he asked. "She's a ghost."

Neely had been invisible for nine days and she was ready to reemerge. It had been her experience that, given a little time, people didn't remember things. If they did remember, they doubted themselves if a question was thrown at them. They would begin to think, *Oh, maybe that wasn't exactly what happened. I could be mistaken.* She sauntered into the bar and grill, hopped up on her favorite stool and looked around. Not many people present. It was Dakota's day off and from diligently watching she had learned that he liked to visit the bar early in the afternoon, sometime between lunch and dinner, so he could be mostly alone with the bartender.

She'd gone to a lot of trouble with her appearance today. She always did.

She tapped her finger on the bar, waiting. The last nine days had been dull and she was ready for a little fun. She hadn't been having much fun. She shopped. She'd done a little shoplifting, simply for the thrill. She'd picked up a couple of guys, but they were so eager and willing it just hadn't been much of a challenge. She'd had a lot to drink and amused herself with the idea that she'd played this AA crowd with her hard youth and difficult sobriety, so she went to a couple of meetings in Denver, picked up one of her guys there. It took him five minutes to fall in love with her. She was bored out of her skull.

Finally someone came out of the kitchen. He slapped the napkin on the counter. Then he looked at her. They connected eyes.

"Where's the usual bartender?" Neely asked. "Sid?"

"My sister? She's away."

"She's your sister?"

He lifted a brow. "Something you didn't know."

"Well, of course I didn't know. I don't spend very much time here!"

"And I'm afraid you won't be," Rob said. "We won't be extending service to you. I'd like you to leave."

"You can't do that!" she said.

"Well, look at that. You are completely flabbergasted. The police are looking for you. Maybe you should check in with them to get the full story."

"What the hell are you talking about?" she demanded.

He chuckled. "Oh, man, you are not nearly as smart as everyone thinks, are you? The police department put a video on Facebook and Twitter, looking for this woman who likes to slash tires and pour acid on vehicles. That would be you, correct?"

"I have no idea what you're talking about!"

"The local news picked it up. You're wanted, it seems. I knew exactly who it was but didn't know your name, just that you'd been in the bar. Looking into it a bit further, turns out you like to vandalize the property of *my* patrons and *my* sister. That makes it personal."

"You're out of your mind," she said, pulling her phone

out of her purse. "You're going to be pretty embarrassed…" She started clicking away on her phone. "Why are you just standing there?" she asked hotly.

"I'm so interested to see your expression when you find it. The Facebook post from the police has gone viral."

"You better be kidding," she grumbled.

"Just search for 'Woman pouring acid on Jeep's hood,'" he suggested with a bland smile.

It took a couple of moments, then she gasped. Her eyes narrowed. Her features suddenly relaxed. "This is contrived. Photoshopped."

"I doubt it," he said. "You might want to check in with the police."

"What for?" she asked. "It's some kind of hoax. Give me a club soda with a twist of lime. Now."

He stood there for a second, then he called a kid from the kitchen. "Trace, you know who this is?"

"The woman from the news? Looks like her."

"Thanks," Rob said. He turned back to Neely. "No club soda. No lime. No service. You're not welcome here."

"And if I don't leave?" she asked.

"I'll call the police. They'd be happy for the call."

She grunted and left.

Neely stomped down the street to the police department. This was outrageous. She would get this straightened out. She walked in. "Where's the chief?" she demanded of the two people behind the counter.

Stan came out of the back, stirring a cup of coffee. "Well, hello there," he said. "And how can I help you?"

"You can start by putting up a retraction of this bogus video you have on your Facebook page!"

"Come in, Ms. Benedict," he said pleasantly. "Have a seat here at my desk. I can see you're upset."

"I'm not at all upset," she said. But when a female police

officer opened the little half door at the end of the counter, she entered and went to the chief's desk. "I'm going to sue you, that's all. And you'll not only run a retraction, you'll pay through the nose."

"I doubt that," he said. "Both videos have been verified as authentic. I guess you didn't notice the camera at the back of the bank building. That one's a little fuzzy, since you had your head down a lot. But with a little help we got a couple of good close-ups."

"You're full of shit," Neely said.

"And that little cabin that Dakota Jones rents? Well, some strange things have been happening to Dakota's car and on his property so he worried about something happening to the place while he was away. He has some nice furnishings in there. He had a surveillance camera sitting right up in the corner, right behind a bird's nest. Convenient."

"You're just lying," she said. "It's all Photoshopped!"

"From what?" he asked, lifting his eyebrows. "Nah, it's the real deal. And our sister cities in the valley were kind enough to run the videos, too. Including Aurora. A few of them ran it on their local news. It's made the rounds. I'm surprised you didn't notice it sooner."

She relaxed into her chair. She smirked at him. "If you think you have a case, why aren't you arresting me?"

The female police officer stood from behind a desk. "Boss?"

"You can go. I know you have things to do, Tippin. Thanks." He looked back at Neely. "I'm sorry. What was that question? Oh—I got it. Arrest, right. Well, to tell the truth, that took some thought. See, I can charge you with malicious mischief and malicious destruction of property. I think it's a terrible thing you did. Our judge will think so, too. But the penalty that goes with it," he said with a shrug.

"Just not satisfying enough. So I thought about it and decided I wasn't going to charge you this time. Instead, I'm going to save these videos in case there are more. I hate the thought there could be more, but I wouldn't be surprised. It seems to be your pattern. You know—those restraining orders, vandalism, breaking into houses, stalking…" He scratched his head. "I wasn't too surprised to learn this wasn't your first brush with the law. Disappointed but not surprised."

She smiled at him. "I wasn't even on probation," she said. "So, pffftt."

"You were, too," he said. "So, we're just watching. Everyone is going to be watching now that they all know what you're capable of. I did talk to your brother. He said he sympathized with us but there was nothing he could do."

She growled low in her throat before she could stop herself. She bared her teeth. But she regained control quickly. "If you knew who I was, why ask the public to identify me? That's going to get you into big trouble."

"It won't get me in any trouble. But now that you mention it, I should probably run your picture and say you were found and that no arrest has been made at this time."

"You. Wouldn't. Dare," she ground out. "I have a very good lawyer!"

"I bet he cherishes the day he ran into you," Stan said. He cackled. "You must be making him rich."

"You'll be sorry you tried to ruin my reputation with all these false accusations," she said.

"Good. Sue me. I need the publicity. And you sure do. People are already looking at you sideways, so if you bring a big fancy lawyer in here to try to do hurt to the people in this town, you'll get more unpopular real fast." He got a harsh look on his face. "I don't want this shit in my town."

"It wasn't me," she said.

"It *was*. There's so much evidence it makes me tired. But I don't feel like putting you through the boring effort of writing a check to make it all go away. I'd just as soon you go away. But in case you're fool enough to think you can test me on this, bear in mind, we'll be watching you. Closely. All of us. The Timberlake police, other police, citizens who don't like that sort of thing, everyone will be watching."

She got to her feet, her expression serene. "You better make this go away before you're sued."

She strode toward the door.

"I'm going to keep track of you," he said to her back. She stopped suddenly. "But I'll give you a tip. If you were to leave, I wouldn't be bothered to track you out of state." She took two more steps. "You might want to check and see where Officer Tippin put that GPS tracker on your car."

She stiffened before she could stop herself. She turned around. "He came on to me," she said angrily.

The chief stood. "No, he didn't," he said. "It's all on the video. Dakota Jones is a decorated war hero. In my town that just fucking trumps lying trust fund babies. You're done here."

Neely stormed out of there before she said one more thing. She drove down the main street a little too fast, leaving that shithole town in her dust. She took a slight detour to a rather isolated lookout with some parking. No one was there. She parked and turned off her engine. She got her mirror out of her purse—it was a sterling silver compact mirror. She held it under the wheel wells, front and back bumpers, under the car doors. She groaned in equal parts anger and frustration. Then she eased down on her back and slid under the car with her compact mirror and her phone flashlight, looking for the GPS tracker.

While she was under there, she saw the tires of a car pull up behind her car.

Neely wiggled out from under her car and stood face-to-face with Officer Tippin. Officer Tippin, Neely thought, was homely and mannish, so she sneered at her. Tippin was a cow, Neely thought meanly.

"Car trouble, ma'am?" the officer asked.

"No, thank you very much," she said, brushing off her short satin skirt. "Can you move your car so I can be on my way?"

"Absolutely, ma'am," she said. And she smiled.

Neely thought she'd sue her also. After she traded in this car.

Stan sat behind his desk, staring at the computer screen, tired. The door opened and a grinning Officer Tippin stepped in.

"Boss, it was classic. She actually rolled under her car looking for a tracking device."

Stan grinned but it wasn't a big grin. "I'd have loved seeing that."

"You don't need a tracking device—she's easy to follow. She's kind of a ninny."

"No," Stan said. "She's pretty smart. She just has no empathy and very little fear. She's arrogant and malicious. And she has some tools—looks and brains being primary." He took a breath. "She's a psychopath."

A dog reflects the family life. Whoever saw a frisky dog in a gloomy family, or a sad dog in a happy one?

—ARTHUR CONAN DOYLE

18

Ten days and counting, Dakota thought. The August heat had become oppressive, unusual for this part of the country. Or maybe it was his mood. He missed Sid. He talked to her every evening, texted her when he could dream up something to say, sent her a picture of his newly repaired Jeep. He tried to stay upbeat and positive. But she'd said she'd be gone a few days, then a week or two. It took her hours to answer his texts and, more often than not, he had to leave a voice mail and she'd call him back late.

He was afraid he was losing her, afraid she wasn't coming back.

That was tremendously difficult with all that was going on. Sunday dinner with the family had become dark and sad. Sierra and Connie were nursing broken hearts and would be for a long time to come.

On Monday he got a text from Stan asking him to stop by the police department when he had time. He braced himself for more bad news. That seemed to be the trend in his family right now.

"She's gone, Dakota," Stan said. "Apparently Neely decided this wasn't her ideal place, after all."

"How do you know?"

"We've been keeping an eye on her. Not surveillance exactly. But it seemed in everyone's best interest to at least have her license number and home address. Seems like she skipped out on her lease a few days ago. She registered her new car in Dallas."

"New car?" Dakota asked dumbly.

Stan just shook his head. "She had some cockamamy idea there was a GPS tracker on her car. Can't imagine where she got such an idea."

Dakota smiled in spite of himself. "Remind me not to doubt you again."

"Why, thank you," Stan said. "I'm not going to spend a lot of time following her movements. Angry as it makes me at the stuff she was capable of doing, and much as the good people of this town think I'm just on paid vacation, I do have real police work to do. I might have Tippin or Castor see if they can locate her in a few months. Just because."

"Thanks," Dakota said.

"If you see her around here, even at a safe distance, you best tell me. I think the woman has an evil streak."

"Obviously," Dakota said. "Trust me, if I see her coming, I'm running in the other direction. Now, you think you ran her off just by embarrassing her on some social media network?"

"Not exactly," Stan said. "In fact, I doubt she has the capacity to be embarrassed. She's really cold as ice, isn't she? But the woman likes an audience for her stories and just about everyone around here is all done believing anything she says. Poor thing can't even get a club soda at the bar down the street. She needed a fresh field to plow."

"What the hell do you suppose she wants?"

"I bet she doesn't even know what she wants. I suspect she enjoys keeping people off balance and the attention she gets from stirring things up. I suspect a personality disorder."

"You ever run into anything like this before?" Dakota asked.

Stan laughed. "In law enforcement?" he asked. "Hell, boy, liars and troublemakers is just about all we got!"

When Dakota left the police department, he walked down the street to the bar. It was almost lunchtime and Rob was watching the bar. "How's it going?" Dakota asked.

"Not bad. How about you?"

"Up and down. I just got some good news from Stan. It seems Neely has blown Dodge. Looking for new friends and playmates."

"That is good news," Rob said. "Something to drink? Eat?"

"How about a Coke," he said. "Have you talked to Sid lately?"

"A couple of days ago. She sounded kind of tired."

"But happy?" Dakota asked. "She sound happy to you?"

"I don't know that I'd characterize it as happy. She did sound kind of, I don't know, satisfied? I'm just guessing here, but I think that work makes her feel more self-confident than slinging drinks and packing lunches for the boys. Haven't you talked to her?"

"Not as much as I'd like," Dakota said. "I'm surprised. Busy as she was while she was here, she seemed to have plenty of time. Are they working her to death?"

"While they have her," Rob said.

"And she likes that?" Dakota asked.

"Oh, yeah," Rob said with a laugh.

"She said that kind of work overwhelmed her," Dakota said. "She said she ran into big trouble not having balance. It takes her longer and longer to answer a text or call me back. I'm wondering if she's coming back. Did she tell you she's coming back?"

Rob leaned on the bar. "Dakota, I didn't ask her."

"Okay, I need a little enlightenment," Dakota said. "I want her to be happy. I want her to have whatever she needs to be happy. But I'd sure like to know if I fit into that plan."

"Ask her," Rob said.

"Ask her to choose between computer programming or us?"

"Yeah, that was romantic," Rob said. "It's not computer programming exactly."

"Then what is it? Exactly."

Rob just stared at him for a long moment. "What do you know about Sid?" he finally asked.

"That she worked in computers. That she was overworked in computers. Writing code, she said. Software not hardware. That it could be intense and lonely. I guess I just don't get why it had to be her for this project. Don't they have plenty of programmers in California? This Faraday—he have a special interest in her?"

Rob looked at him in shock. Then he stuck his head in the kitchen. "Trace," he yelled. When the boy came from the kitchen, Rob said, "Man the bar. Do not serve alcohol. I'll only be ten minutes."

"Okay," Trace said.

"Dakota, my office. Come on through."

Dakota followed. Rob's office was very small. He had to move a chair out of the way to close the door. "Sit," Rob told Dakota.

"Why do I get a bad feeling?"

Rob didn't answer. "Listen, I don't know why the two of you haven't talked about this but Sid is special. She's a genius."

"I don't have a problem believing that," Dakota said. "She must be the best programmer in the west."

"She's a physicist. A PhD. A Rhodes scholar. She might be writing some code but it's far more complicated and exceptional. They're working on quantum computing, the sort of high-speed, complex, intuitive computing that can lead to artificial intelligence. The computer they're working on is processing and analyzing DNA. It can process millions of pieces of information in seconds. Less than seconds. She can explain this much better, not that you'll understand it any better than I do. Molecular genetic research will change the world, save lives, wipe out disease, and they're creating and constantly refining the quantum computer that's doing it. She's working with a Nobel laureate. Do they have a lot of people with her qualifications? I don't think so. She is so important in this field it's mind-boggling."

Dakota gulped. "Hang on," he said. "Let me scrape my chin off the floor." He shook his head as if to settle the pieces in place. "Man, look at what can happen when a kid is in an accident and can't go out and play."

"Nah, she was born that way. She has an IQ that puts a lot of geniuses to shame."

"Now I really have no idea where this leaves me. Us."

"I hate to break it to you but she was this smart way before she met you. She didn't explain all that to you?" Rob asked.

"Not the way you did," he said.

"Let me tell you what else she is," Rob said. "A flesh and blood woman with a huge heart and a very soft center. Even geniuses can get their hearts broken. She has a very intimidating brain but around here people just think of her as Sid the bartender and they don't treat her like she can't be a friend, can't be loved. She's fun and funny and loyal. I didn't kill the last man who used her and dumped her but I might kill the next one."

"Don't be ridiculous," Dakota said. "I'd never hurt her." Dakota stood. "Is there anything else I should know?"

"That should do it, I guess."

Dakota grinned. "Damn, who knew I had such magnificent taste in women."

"Yeah, who knew," Rob said. But he wasn't smiling.

Trace had been eavesdropping. Not exactly on purpose. Only for a minute. He had gone to fetch Rob because someone wanted a glass of wine with their lunch and he heard that little speech. He didn't know all that about Sid. She'd helped him with physics but he just thought she was good at math. He hadn't even suspected...

It had a pretty strange effect on him. Not the part about her being over-the-moon brilliant. About her being made of flesh and blood and feelings. He was pretty quiet the rest of the day. When he was done with work, he didn't go straight home. He went to the diner. His mom was working.

"Well, hey there, Trace," she said, smiling. "Do you want some dinner?"

"Nah, I ate something at the bar."

"Going to play ball tonight?" she asked.

"Yeah, I might hit a few with some of the guys, if I can find anyone. So, I broke a promise."

"Oh?"

"Yeah, I promised Tom I was going to talk to you about my worries about us all moving in together and I didn't."

"That's okay, honey. He told me you two had talked. I

thought you might get around to it eventually. We don't want to rush you out of your comfort zone."

"Yeah, that's nice. I'm, like, the only one who still has a comfort zone. Sid's off working in California, Dakota misses her, Rob *really* misses her—he's working some long hours and so am I. Sierra... I don't even want to think about Sierra..."

"She's in a lot of pain," Lola said. "They love that baby."

"So I was thinking about stuff. I think it's nice of Tom to make sure I feel okay about things. And to offer me space in his house. And I think it would make you really happy."

"Only if you're there, Trace. If you decide to try to live with your dad, I'm worried it would be a strain on you. And I'd just miss you too much."

"No, I'm not going to live with him. Why would I go live with a guy who can't even make it to one of my baseball games? You or Tom or both of you made it to almost every one this year. Look, Mom... I think I was being a little selfish. I guess we'll all have some adjustments but you found yourself a good guy. I think he'll take good care of you."

"What are you saying, Trace?" she asked with a slight frown.

"I want you to be happy, Mom. Let's do it. Let's move in together."

"It's important that you be happy, too," she said.

"Yeah, I know, Mom. I appreciate it. Pretty soon I'm going to have to stop expecting my mother to take care of me being happy all the time."

She got that look on her face, like she was very touched and might cry. "I'll always do everything I can to make you happy."

"I'm going to miss our house," he said.

"Maybe for a little while," she said. "But I bet we have some good times at Tom's house. Last time we all got together, you and Cole and Jackson hung out around the fire pit and it sure sounded like you were having a good time."

"Yeah," he said. "Mom? Did you know Sid is, like, a genius?"

Lola lifted her eyebrows. "In my mind she was if she could help you with physics. I stopped being able to help you with math years ago."

"The things you don't know about people, huh?"

"Who told you that?" she asked.

"Oh, I kind of overheard it, so maybe we shouldn't spread it around." And his cheeks took on a pink stain.

Lola looked at him slyly, smirked and said, "Gotcha."

Sam had been gone for a week and Sierra had cried her heart out every day. The day after he left she went to Mrs. Jergens's house with a box of toys he liked to play with and it looked like everything was working out for them. The cousin, Sandy, seemed pleasant and thoughtful. And Sam waved his arms like propellers he was so excited to see Sierra, so she held him for a while.

She wasn't sure if seeing him and holding him made her feel better or worse. She went back two days later, bringing an offering of brownies for the women and a bag full of baby food for Sam. Again he was excited to see her and she snuggled him so close he squeaked. The house was a little messy; perhaps Sandy was having a hard time keeping up. And Sierra cried all the way home.

She went again two days later. No one answered the door and she left disappointed, so she went back the very next day. She knocked and she could hear Sam crying so she stayed at the door. She had cookies this time and a couple of new teething rings for Sam. She knocked again and again; Sam continued to cry.

She'd played this scenario in her mind but she thought she was just kidding herself, that it was never going to happen, but what was she to do if she found him hurt or neglected? She wasn't the child welfare department. But she would call the social worker or the police, if she had to, and that would guarantee that Mrs. Jergens would never let her in the door again.

She knocked again and the door swung open. "Mrs. Jergens!" she gasped. The woman looked bloody awful and was leaning on a walker. "What's the matter?"

"I'm having a hard day."

"Let me help with Sam," Sierra said, pushing her way gently past the older woman and walking into an extremely messy house. "Where's Sandy?" Sierra asked on her way to the bedroom where Sam's crib was kept.

"Who knows," Mrs. Jergens said.

Sierra thought about that walker. *How do you carry a baby with a walker? And if you need a walker, does that mean that without the use of it you could fall? Hurting yourself and the baby?*

Sam was sitting up in his crib, crying pitifully, his face wet with tears and snot. "Oh, sweet boy, what's wrong, huh? Come here, it's okay, come here…" She lifted him into her arms and held him close. She kissed his neck. He didn't smell very good. And he was wet. "Let's get you fixed up. Are you hungry? We can fix that, too, yes, we sure can." She cooed to Sam as she put him on the changing table—a rickety changing table—and took off his sagging, soggy diaper. "Oh, honey, that's better. Let's clean that up and get you comfortable."

Sierra cleaned his bottom and put some diaper rash ointment on him. She cleaned his face with a fresh wipe, put a new dry diaper on him and a shirt, though she couldn't find a clean one. Or maybe it was just an old, stained shirt, but she didn't think so. With Sam on her hip, she went back to the living room. Sierra looked around—the kitchen was a mess of dirty dishes and glasses, shoes and clothing and other debris such as magazines, food wrappers, disposable diapers rolled up and taped closed, empty soda cans and all the rudiments of living scattered everywhere. Mrs. Jergens's medication sat on the table beside the couch. Not exactly babyproof. Thank goodness Sam wasn't walking yet.

"Mrs. Jergens, he has a diaper rash. It looks kind of bad. What's going on? Where's Sandy?"

"She said she needed a break, asked me for forty dollars and left."

"Good Lord!"

"Two days ago," Mrs. Jergens added.

"My gosh, how did you manage?"

"It wasn't exactly easy," she said. "And now I'm in so much pain from lifting and carrying the baby yesterday I can hardly move today."

"Why didn't you call me?" she asked.

"I was fine. I thought she'd come back. Just take him. Take him," she said with a wave of her hand. "He won't stop crying, anyway."

Sierra was stunned for a second. Then her heart began to pound. Then she felt genuine terror. "And so in a couple of weeks you'll change your mind again? And come without warning to snatch him away again?"

"I doubt it," she said drily.

"Or you'll find another cousin…"

"Definitely not that," she said.

Sierra thought about it for a second. She wondered if she just snatched Sam with the clothes on his back, if she could get away and never be found. And have a baby without Connie?

She prayed. *God, I have never in my life needed You this much. God, I am powerless. This is in Your hands.*

She pulled out her cell phone and dialed her brother Cal. He didn't pick up. She texted him 911 and he called her back directly.

"Sierra?" he asked, worry in his voice.

"Cal, I came to Fairplay to visit Sam and found Mrs. Jergens in a terrible fix. Her caregiver and helper has run out on her, her house is upside down, she's in too much pain to pick up the baby and she told me to just take him."

"Do not," Cal said emphatically. "Can you call the social worker?"

"I didn't think to take her number." She lowered her phone. "Mrs. Jergens, do you have Jeanne Blasette's phone number?" Mrs. Jergens poked around in her purse and produced the card. "I have the number," Sierra said.

"Give it to me," Cal said. "I'll call. Don't take the baby home. Wait there for me. I just don't want anyone to ever imply that you took him."

"Can you hurry?" she asked with tears in her voice. "I don't know if he's okay. He's just lying on my shoulder…"

"Do you need an ambulance?" Cal asked in a breathless voice. She could tell he was on the move. She heard his car door slam and the engine of his car start.

"Let me find out from Mrs. Jergens what he's eaten. I'll call an ambulance if I need one."

Cal got the address from Sierra, said he was on his way and disconnected.

"The only person that needs an ambulance is me," Mrs. Jergens said.

"When did Sam eat last?"

"He had a bottle a couple hours ago," she said.

"How long ago since he was changed?" Sierra asked.

"He hasn't been starved or neglected but after yesterday I was in too much pain to pick him up, so I changed him in the crib, gave him a bottle in the crib and that's the best I could do today. That damn Sandy! I should've known! Those people were always irresponsible!"

"So he hasn't been held? Since yesterday?"

"But he was taken care of!" she said. "Just go and leave me alone."

Sierra stepped outside the house and took a deep breath of fresh air. Sam wrapped himself around her like a little monkey. She walked up and down the sidewalk between her car and the front door and just hummed to him. And cried.

She called Connie. "Oh, Connie, I'm in Fairplay at the Jergens house. I have Sam. She told me to just take him!" Then she explained what she had found and that Cal was on his way. "I'll call you when I'm on my way home and you can meet us."

It was almost thirty minutes before Cal pulled up but right behind him was Jeanne Blasette. Cal went to Sierra immediately, pulling her and Sam into his arms. "I talked to her lawyer," Cal said. "The adoption process hasn't been stopped but he recommended she sign a short statement saying she turned the baby over to you. Jeanne and I will witness it."

"Are you all right, Sierra?" Jeanne asked.

"Not really," Sierra said. "Can I take him home?"

"Give me one second," Jeanne said. She nearly ran up the walk to the front door and opened it. She didn't even go inside but just talked to Mrs. Jergens. Then she was back. "I'd like you to take Sam to the doctor. I'm sure he's fine, but just to take precautions, have him looked over.

Your brother and I will finish this business together. It will be all right."

"But she still has every right to call it all off," Sierra said.

"We're just going to take this one day at a time," Jeanne said. "I think I can honestly say that everyone involved wants Sam to be in your safe and loving home." Then she leaned close and said, "Mrs. Jergens can't do it. She wants to and can't. Treat her with mercy. But take Sam and go now."

Cal nodded in agreement.

Connie was waiting for her when she arrived at the urgent care office with Sam. Dr. Culver, all calm and beautiful, took them all right back to an exam room, but Sierra was not letting go of the baby, her son.

"Tell me what happened," Dr. Culver asked, while slowly and gently pulling Sam to her. He whimpered at being parted from Sierra, but she stayed close while she described what she had found. While Sierra talked, Dr. Culver took off Sam's shirt, listened to his heart, his chest, looked in his mouth and his ears.

"He's all right, Sierra," she said. "He's a little upset. Let me get you a dry diaper." She opened the exam room door and spoke to someone and a disposable diaper appeared. "Is that two wet diapers in the last hour?" she asked.

"He was soaked when I got there."

"He's certainly not dehydrated," she said with a small laugh. "Keep putting this cream on him until the rash is gone." Dr. Culver flipped that wet diaper off and the clean one on like an old pro. "You're going to be fine, aren't you, Sam. You want your mommy."

Sierra reached for him, but the second he was secure in her arms, he reached for Connie.

"He's kind of stinky," Sierra said.

"He needs a bath," Connie said.

"And clean clothes."

"Did you bring anything out of there?" Connie asked.

"It was so messy and dirty I didn't want anything."

"Good," Connie said. "We start fresh."

"He's got a sad look in his eyes," Sierra said. "I think he was left to cry."

"Take him home," Dr. Culver said. "Clean him up and hold him. When he smells your house and his sheets and is back in familiar territory, he'll be his old self."

Sierra told Connie she wanted a quiet day, just the three of them. Texts kept coming in, asking if everyone was all right. They tried to hold off on visitors but it was impossible. First it was Maggie and Elizabeth, then Cal came over to check on them, then Rafe and Lisa, then Sully. In no time at all Sam was laughing and playing and being licked by Molly over and over, like she was checking to make sure he was all right.

The only one not present was Dakota, who Cal reported had left town suddenly. On a mission.

Dakota was able to get on the campus, no problem. He even located a campus map; it just wouldn't tell him where Sid was. He texted her. What building are you working in?

Why?

I'm here, but I don't know where you are.

You're here?

I'm stalking you. Can you give me ten minutes?

She gave him the building number and name of the building and told him he should just park in front—she'd come down to meet him. Once he got there, he could see why. There was limited parking and entry required an ID badge. Upon closer inspection of the large glass-and-steel front doors, there was a keypad and key slide for entry there, as well.

The students around this group of buildings looked a little different. They were older, for one thing. Instead of shorts and flip-flops, they were wearing slacks and shirts. He pushed his sleeves up and leaned back against his rented car.

"You can't park here, sir," a security officer on a bike told him.

"I'm not parking," he said. "I'm waiting for my girl-friend."

"Then you can't wait here," he said.

Just then, Sid came out. She was dressed like one of the older students—pressed tan pants, white shirt, leather flats, hair in a bun. Her ID badge hung on a lanyard around her neck. In fact, there were several ID badges. He stood from his leaning position.

"Cody?" she asked, totally perplexed. And to the se-curity guard, she said, "It's okay, Gary. He's with me."

"Okay, Dr. Shandon," the young man said, riding off on his bike.

"What are you doing here?" she asked.

He opened his arms. "Is that any way to greet an old lover?"

She stepped into his arms. "You're not that old."

He burrowed his lips into her neck. "I had to see you. Had to. Kiss me."

"In front of all these people?" she asked, looking

around. There were only a few people, all walking with a purpose to their next destination or to the parking lot.

"You can give me a more meaningful kiss later, but for now…" He kissed her lips and tried to keep it brief and discreet. "Sid, I'm proud of you," he said. "I love you and I'm proud of you."

"What's this all about, Cody?"

"You didn't really explain what you were doing here," he said. "Your brother did. This isn't just some computer programming, as you led me to believe. This is mind-blowing, futuristic, world-changing, quantum computing. And here you're Dr. Shandon."

She smiled at him, her eyes twinkling. "Do you know what quantum computing is?"

"It's not bartending, for one thing. There was a part of me that thought you were running away from me, but you weren't. You were running to your field of study, at which, I'm led to believe, you are one of the rare experts. I thought you were having a fling with Dr. Faraday."

She chuckled. "He's seventy-four and has a lovely wife and many smart grandchildren."

"And this stint—this consulting job. You've been working so hard. How does it feel?"

"Important," she said. "Vital. Valued. They needed me and I was useful. Taking a break and going to Colorado to get my footing in life was a good idea. Doing this work is also a good idea."

Dakota shook his head. "How did that idiot you were married to ever let you get away?"

"He said I was dull. Antisocial, boring, incredibly flat in the personality department and arrogant."

"God," Dakota said with an incredulous laugh. "You are none of those things! You're social, exciting, interesting and, if anything, self-effacing. When did you get your PhD?"

"Six or seven years ago. Or eight," she added.

His hands were on her hips. Her hands on his arms, looking up into his eyes. "You're the most exciting woman I know. I never once heard you mutter the words *doctor* or *scientist* or *Nobel*."

"Well, I certainly was never considered for that!" she said.

"If you're so boring and unappealing, why do I just want to get you naked right this minute?"

"Shh," she said, but she laughed. "You are a very strange man, Mr. Jones. Who ever heard of wanting to make love to a geek?"

"I bet Mrs. Gates does it all the time."

"Is this why you're here? To tell me I'm not boring to you?"

"Yes. No. To tell you I'm proud of you, proud of the sacrifices you've made to do something this important. And to tell you I'll support you. If you'll have me. If you need to be here in LA, I'll come to LA. If you need to live here to do your work, I can live here. The important thing is that you know I respect your dedication and I'm behind you."

"Our families are in Colorado..."

"I know—quick flight. But I checked, Sid. There's no world-famous quantum computing lab in Timberlake. If this fulfills you, you should do it. It's about time the seas parted for you. I can be happy anywhere if I'm with you."

She didn't say anything for a moment that stretched out.

"And if you don't want a man in your life, you have to say so. Or if you just don't want a specific man following you around, say, for example, me, you tell me. Just say you don't want me and I'll go. I'll probably be terrible about it... It could kill me, now that I think about it... But..."

"Cody, I've never wanted anyone in my life the way I want you," she said. "And I don't want to be in LA. I may come back here to this lab if I'm needed, if it's convenient, but two weeks away from you is way too long. My heart has been aching for you. If you're happy in Colorado, that would be perfect for me."

"What about this, Sid? This is important work and you love it."

"It is and I do. But there are research and development labs in Colorado that would be happy to have me. We could be close to Timberlake. We could talk about us."

"You ready for that?"

"Yes. I'm in love with you, too. Couldn't you tell?"

"I wanted to believe that's what I felt. Will you let me spend the night tonight? Then tomorrow I'll get out of your hair…"

"You can spend the night, and then tomorrow let's both get back home. Together."

"Just to be clear, I want to marry you, Dr. Shandon. I want to spend the rest of my life with you. I've never wanted anything so much. Will you say yes?"

"I'll absolutely marry you. I'll have to. It's the only way I can keep all the women back." She got on her toes and gave him a quick kiss. "I want you all to myself."

"I think we're definitely on the same page." He hugged her close.

"Am I going to have you all to myself or are we still being harassed by Neely?"

"Nah, Neely has found greener pastures. Oh, so much has happened in the two weeks you've been gone, it's mind-boggling. I have a lot to tell you. Then we can go home and help celebrate all the happy endings."

"Mine will be the happiest of all," she said.

Kindness in words creates confidence.

Kindness in thinking creates profoundness.

Kindness in giving creates love.

—LAO TZU

epilogue

On the last day of August, right before the Labor Day weekend filled up the town of Timberlake and Sullivan's Crossing campground, Sierra and Connie appeared at the courthouse with Sam in their arms. A friendly-looking judge was on the bench. When it was their turn to go into the courtroom they were followed by lawyers and a witness or two.

Cal, Maggie and Elizabeth were there, dressed in their finery. Dakota and Sid filed in. Sully was there. Connie's mom and brother were there. Rafe and Lisa followed. Three more firefighters entered.

The judge watched this entourage and smiled. He waited patiently until everyone in the gallery was settled and quiet. "Well," he said. "Now I see why we couldn't do this in chambers. Lovely family you have here, Mr. and Mrs. Boyle."

"Thank you," Sierra said happily.

"I see some things in my court that are sad, that are

tragic, that make me angry, that frustrate and baffle me. But this beautiful story makes my heart glad. I personally think everyone should know about it. I think it should 'go viral.' Isn't that what you young social media people say? Here we have a firefighter and paramedic called out on a terrible accident and thank God he was able to rescue a little guy, unhurt. And he and his wife wanted to keep that little guy and become his new family. What a beautiful story. What an excellent, selfless sentiment. And apparently not just the firefighter and his wife welcome this little guy, Sam, but the whole family and half the neighborhood. Sam," he said, leaning over the bench and looking at Sam. "It looks like you have chosen a very good family for yourself." The judge sat back and smiled. "By the power vested in me—"

With one rap of his gavel Sam legally became part of the family.

* * * * *

Keep reading for a special preview of
The Best of Us, *book four in Robyn Carr's*
New York Times *bestselling*
Sullivan's Crossing series.

On the first really warm, dry day in early March, Dr. Leigh Culver left her clinic at lunchtime and drove out to Sullivan's Crossing. As she walked into the store at the campground, the owner, Sully, peeked around the corner from the kitchen. "Hi," Leigh said. "Have you had lunch yet?"

"Just about to," Sully replied.

"Let me take you to lunch," she said. "What's your pleasure?"

"My usual—turkey on whole wheat. In fact, I just made it."

"Aw, I'd like to treat you."

"Appreciate the sentiment, Doc, but it's my store. I can't let you buy me a sandwich that's already bought and paid for. In fact, I'll make another one real quick if that sounds good to you." He started pulling out his supplies. "What are you doing out here, middle of the day?"

"I wanted to sit outside for a little while," she said. "It's gorgeous. There are no sidewalk cafés in town and I don't have any patio furniture yet. Can we sit on the porch?"

"I hosed it down this morning," he said. "It's probably dried off by now. Got a little spring fever, do you?"

"It seemed like a long winter, didn't it? And I haven't seen this place in spring. People around here talk about spring a lot."

Sully handed her a plate and picked up his own. "Grab yourself a drink, girl. Yeah, this place livens up in spring. The wildflowers come out and the wildlife shows off their young'uns. Winter was probably long for you because everyone had the flu."

"Including me," she said. "I'm looking forward to the spring babies. I got here last summer in plenty of time for the fall foliage and rutting season. There was a lot of noise." She took a bite of her sandwich. "Yum, this is outstanding, thank you."

"Hmph. *Outstanding* would be a hamburger," he groused. "I'm almost up to burger day. I get one a month."

She laughed. "Is that what your doctor recommends?"

"Let me put it this way—it's not on the diet the nutritionist gave me but the doctor said one a month probably wouldn't kill me. He said *probably*. I think it's a lot of bullshit. I mean, I get that it ain't heart healthy to slather butter on my steak every day, but if this diet's so goddamn healthy, why ain't I lost a pound in two years?"

"Maybe you're the right weight. You've lost a couple of pounds since the heart attack," she said. She had, after all, seen his chart. When Leigh was considering moving to the small-town clinic, she visited Timberlake to check out the surroundings. It was small, pleasant, clean and quiet. The clinic was a good urgent care facility and she had credentials in both family medicine and emergency medicine—she was made to order. It was owned and operated by a hospital chain out of Denver so they could afford her. And she was ready for a slower life in a scenic place.

When she first arrived, someone—she couldn't remember who—suggested she go out to Sully's to look around. People from town liked to go out there to swim; firefighters and paramedics as well as Rangers and search and rescue teams liked to hike and rock climb around there, then grab a cold beer at the general store. Sully, she learned, always had people around. Long-distance hikers came off the Continental Divide Trail right at the Crossing. It was a good place to camp, collect mail, restock supplies from socks to water purification kits. That's when she first got to know Sully.

She had looked around in June and moved to Timberlake the next month. She might have missed the spring explosion of wildflowers, but she was in awe of the changing leaves in fall and heard the elk bugle, grunt and squeak in the woods. It took her about five minutes to fall in love.

"What have you done?" her aunt Helen had said when she visited the town and saw the clinic.

She and her aunt lived in a suburb of Chicago and Leigh's move was a very big step. She was looking for a change. She'd been working very long hours in a busy urban emergency room and saw patients in a small family practice, as well. She needed a slower pace. Aunt Helen wasn't a small-town kind of woman, though she was getting sick of Midwestern winters.

They were the only family either of them had. Leaving Helen had been so hard. Leigh had grown up, gone to college and medical school and had done her residency in Chicago. Although Helen traveled quite a bit, leaving Leigh on her own for weeks or more at a time, Leigh was married to the hospital and had still lived in the house she grew up in. But Leigh was thirty-four years old and still living with her aunt, the aunt who had been like a mother to her. She thought it was, in a way, disgraceful. She was a bit embarrassed by what must appear as her dependence. She'd decided it was time to be an adult and move on.

She shook herself out of her memories. "Such a gorgeous day," she said to Sully. "Nobody camping yet?"

"It'll start up pretty soon," he said. "Spring break brings the first bunch, but until the weather is predictably warm and dry, it ain't so busy. This is when I do my spring-cleaning around the grounds, getting ready for summer. What do you hear from Chicago?"

"They're having a snowstorm. My aunt says she hopes it's the last one."

Sully grunted. "If we'd have a snowstorm, I wouldn't have to clean out the gutters or paint the picnic tables."

"You ever get a snowstorm this late in the year? Because I thought that was a Midwestern trick."

"It's happened a time or two. Not lately. How is your aunt? Why hasn't anyone met her yet?"

"She made a couple of very quick trips last fall. I wasn't very good about introducing her around. Besides patients, I didn't really know a lot of people yet. She's planning to come here this spring, once she finishes her book, and this time she'll stay awhile." Leigh laughed and took another bite of her sandwich. "That won't cause her to leave the laptop at home. She's always working on something."

"She always been a writer?" he asked.

"No. When I was growing up she was a teacher. Then she was a teacher and a writer. Then she was a retired teacher and full-time writer. But after I finished med school, she grew wings. She's been traveling. She's always loved to travel but the last few years it's been more frequent. Sometimes she takes me with her. She's had some wonderful trips and cruises. Seems like she's been almost everywhere by now."

"Egypt?" Sully asked.

"Yep. China, Morocco, Italy, many other places. And the last few winters she's gone someplace warm for at least a couple of months. She always works, though. A lot."

"Hmph. What kind of books?"

Leigh grinned. "Mysteries. Want me to get you one? You have any aspirations to write the tales of Sullivan's Crossing?"

"Girl, I have trouble writing my own name."

"I'll get you one of her books. It's okay if it's not your thing."

"She been married?"

"No, never married. But that could be a matter of family complications. My mother wasn't married when I was born and the only person she had to help her was her big sister, Helen. Then my mother died—I was only four. That left poor Aunt Helen with a child to raise alone. A working woman with a child. Where was she going to find a guy with all that going on?"

Sully was quiet for a moment. "That's a good woman, loses her sister and takes on her niece. A good woman. You must miss her a lot."

"Sure. But…" She stopped there. They had been together for thirty-four years but they ran in different circles. "We never spent all our time together. There were plenty of separations with my education and her travel. We shared a house but we're independent. Aunt Helen has friends all over the world. And writers are always going to some conference or other, where she has a million friends."

But, of course, she missed Helen madly. She asked herself daily if this wasn't the stupidest thing she'd ever done. Was she trying to prove she could take care of herself?

"Well, I suppose the waiting room is filling up with people."

"Is it busy every day?" he asked, picking up their plates.

"Manageable," she said. "Some days you'd think I'm giving away pizza. Thanks for lunch, Sully. It was a nice break."

"You come on out here any time you like. You're good company. You make turkey on whole wheat a lot more interesting."

"I want you to do something for me," she said. "You tell me when you're ready for that hamburger. I want to take you to lunch."

"That's a promise! You don't need to mention it to Maggie."

"We have laws that prevent talking about patients," she informed him, "even if she is your daughter and a doctor."

"That applies to lunch?" she said. "That's good news! Then I'll have a beer with my hamburger, in that case."

"Next time is my treat," Melissa said.

"I'll look forward to it," he answered. Eli's words had
a ring of sincerity that again warmed her far more than it
should.

They walked outside into a lovely April night, rich
with the scent of the ocean, with flowers, with new life.

She could hear the low murmur of the waves along
with the constant coastal wind that rustled the new leaves
of the trees next to the restaurant.

Oh, she had missed it here. She had lived in many
beautiful, exotic places since she'd left Cannon Beach,
but none of them had been the same. She had lived
here longer than anywhere, from the age of thirteen to
eighteen. It was home to her.

"That was lovely," he said when they reached
their respective vehicles in the parking lot. "The most

enjoyable meal I've had in a long time. Thank you for inviting me."

"You're welcome. Thank you for insisting on paying for it."

"Yeah. Thanks," Skye said cheerfully. "It was fun."

Melissa couldn't make a habit of it. She was far too drawn to him.

"Have a good evening, Eli."

Their gazes met, and those shadows prompted her to do something completely uncharacteristic. She stood on tiptoe and kissed his cheek, intending it only as a warm, friendly, welcome-home kind of gesture.

He smelled delicious, of soap and male skin, and it was all she could do not to stand there and inhale.

She forced herself to ease away, regretting the impulse with every passing moment.

"Good night, Melissa. Skye, it was a pleasure. Persuade your mom to take you to my dad's place sometime soon so you can practice your pool game."

"I will! Thanks."

"See you Monday," she said.

"Put some ice on that wrist," he answered, his voice gruff.

She nodded and ushered her daughter to her vehicle. Though her wrist still ached, the injury seemed a lifetime ago.

Don't miss
A Soldier's Return *by RaeAnne Thayne,*
available February 2019 wherever
Harlequin® Special Edition books and ebooks are sold.

www.Harlequin.com

#1 *New York Times* bestselling author

ROBYN CARR

returns to Sullivan's Crossing with a heartwarming story about friendship and family.

Sierra Jones has put her troubled past behind her but the path forward isn't yet clear. A visit with her big brother Cal and his new bride, Maggie, seems to be the best option to help her get back on her feet.

Cal and Maggie welcome her into their busy lives and she quickly finds herself bonding with Sully, the quirky campground owner who is the father figure she's always wanted. But when her past catches up with her, it's a special man and an adorable puppy who give her the strength to fight for a brighter future.

Available now, wherever books are sold!

ROBYN CARR